Praise for
Meet You in the Middle

"Sharp, clever repartee propels this irresistible, very modern, wonderfully warm and optimistic romance that asks the eternal question, Do opposites really attract?"
——*New York Times* bestselling author Jayne Ann Krentz

"Daniels has written one of those romantic comedy masterpieces that makes your stomach flip, your heart explode, even as you can't help but laugh out loud at the sheer cleverness of the writing. Absolute perfection—the best romantic comedy I've had the pleasure of reading, ever."
——*New York Times* bestselling author Lauren Layne

"Smart, sexy, and satisfying! Daniels has penned an engaging enemies-to-lovers contemporary romance set against a Beltway backdrop that gives an insider's look at the people and politics of Washington, DC, while maintaining the heart and humor of two people falling in love against all odds. I loved it!"
——*New York Times* bestselling author Jenn McKinlay

"Sassy, sweet, and deliciously sexy, *Meet You in the Middle* is a wickedly fun read. Loved it!"
——*USA Today* bestselling author Nicola Marsh

Meet You in the Middle

DEVON DANIELS

JOVE ★ New York

A JOVE BOOK
Published by Berkley
An imprint of Penguin Random House LLC
penguinrandomhouse.com

A JOVE BOOK, BERKLEY, and the BERKLEY & B colophon
are registered trademarks of Penguin Random House LLC.

Library of Congress Cataloging-in-Publication Data

Names: Daniels, Devon, author.
Title: Meet you in the middle / Devon Daniels.
Description: First edition. | New York: Jove, 2021.
Identifiers: LCCN 2019059956 (print) | LCCN 2019059957 (ebook) |
ISBN 9780593199213 (trade paperback) | ISBN 9780593199220 (ebook)
Subjects: GSAFD: Love stories.
Classification: LCC PS3604.A5327 M44 2021 (print) |
LCC PS3604.A5327 (ebook) | DDC 813/.6—dc23
LC record available at https://lccn.loc.gov/2019059956
LC ebook record available at https://lccn.loc.gov/2019059957

First Edition: February 2021

Printed in the United States of America
1   3   5   7   9   10   8   6   4   2

Book design by Elke Sigal

For Patrick.
You're the reason I can write a romance novel.

Meet You ★in the M★iddle

Chapter 1

There's a special place in hell for people who waste my time.

Wasting time is at the top of my list of pet peeves, right around being charged for hotel Wi-Fi, people who are rude to servers, and incorrect hashtag use (hint: #ifitlookslikethisyouredoingitwrong).

I have a mountain of work I could and should be doing, but here I am, languishing in this eerily silent office, listening to the ticking of the world's loudest clock as it crawls farther past our appointment time: 4:26 . . . 4:27 . . .

Typically, I'd rather swim with sharks than schedule a late-afternoon meeting—though frankly, many of the politicians I work with are just as dangerous. I prefer to catch people early and fresh, their brains full of bipartisan possibility and artisanal coffee from Cups, the watering hole of choice for Senate staffers.

A day in the life of a congressional aide looks something like this: Show up at nine brimming with optimism that you can change the world. By ten, the morning's inflammatory headlines have brought you down a peg, but you're still in the game. By noon, you've put out a fire that your well-meaning but power-hungry boss started with an errant quote. By two, you've stopped counting the number of ranting phone calls you've fielded from angry constituents demanding your boss's impeachment or resignation (either will do). By three, you're questioning every decision that led you to work in the fiery hell pit that is politics. By four, you're hanging by a thread. A meeting at the end of the day? You're asking for trouble. A meeting at the end of the day with the *opposition*? Sign my death warrant now.

My phone dings with a text. My mom's sent me some Justin Timberlake meme; he's eating from what looks like a plate of pasta but is actually his *NSYNC-era hair. It's ridiculous, but enough to lift me out of my salty mood, for the moment anyway. I text back asking if she's looked into train tickets yet, and when she responds with a GIF of Alfonso Ribeiro doing the Carlton dance, I'm left to wonder just when I became more mature than my mother.

I giggle in spite of myself, earning me a bewildered look from the staff assistant. Of course, *now* she acknowledges me. I smother my laughter and assume the demure expression of the dignified, professional woman I'm supposed to be.

My meeting is with Benjamin Mackenzie, legislative director and gatekeeper for Henry "Hank" Hammond, illustrious seven-term senator from the great state of Ohio. When I'd emailed Mr. Tardy for the Party a few days ago requesting a meeting, I got back a polite but clipped response letting me know it was four o'clock today or three weeks from now. I was simultaneously intrigued and annoyed. Who's so booked they can't meet for a month? He's either the most popular guy in DC or *way* too self-important—and since I've never heard of him, I'm going with the latter.

Maybe his delay is no accident. Maybe he's purposely keeping me waiting in some sort of twisted power play to show me who's in charge. I wouldn't be surprised, since just about everything is a power play in this town. Well, joke's on him. I already know he has the upper hand. And the lower hand. Basically, I'm devoid of hands.

I distract myself by looking around Hammond's lobby. Overstuffed leather couches in a shade of deep cognac—check. Ornate gilt-framed portraits of the senator with former presidents and heads of state—check. I work in this same building—on the same floor, in fact—and all the congressional offices are variations of the same, in both layout and design.

I'm here on behalf of my boss, Senator Carol Warner of New Hampshire: champion of the women's movement, favorite of cable news anchors, and all-around feminist rock star. After bouncing around in a series of staff positions for various DC power brokers over the past few years, I fought my way up to Senator Warner's senior legislative assistant (and have the bruised elbows to prove it). With her name on my résumé I can get a job anywhere I want. Not that I'm looking to leave—working for Carol is my every dream realized.

Several months ago, we introduced the Child Care and Education for Working Families Act, the same bill I'm here today to fight tooth and nail for. It's the first legislation I've drafted almost entirely on my own, and it's as precious to me as a newborn. We developed the bill in the months before the presidential election with the confidence that both the Senate and House would stay under Democratic control—and with the victory of the first female president of the United States all but assured, our legislation was considered a shoo-in for passage.

That was before our candidate lost the election, Republicans won the House *and* Senate, and all hell broke loose.

A few months later and the bill is on life support. Our new goal is to force a floor vote, even if it will more than likely result in defeat. To improve our odds, Senator Warner assigned me the unenviable task of going door to door to convince several of her friendlier, more moderate conservative allies to cross the aisle.

It's been going as well as you might imagine.

I silently recite my standard pep talk: This bill is important, right, and just. It makes child care more affordable for struggling families, expands educational options for preschool-age kids, and improves teacher training. You'd have to be soulless to oppose this bill. You may as well admit to hating puppies and kittens.

Of course, nothing in politics is ever that simple.

I finally hear voices approaching in the hallway, the noise crescendoing as a herd of men troops into the office lobby. Most give me a cursory glance before vanishing into the recesses of the office—all except one, who peels off from the pack and stops in front of me.

"Ms. Adams?"

When I realize this must be Benjamin Mackenzie, my first reaction is to gulp. *Imposing* would be one way to describe him. *Massive* is another.

He's attractive enough: wide across and barrel-chested, with a square-cut jaw, thick dark hair, and strong eyebrows to match. Actually, his hair's a little on the longish side, like he couldn't be bothered to cut it this month. The fact that I even notice such an innocuous detail tells me I've been in DC too long. I'm so used to impeccably groomed, too-slick political operatives that anyone who defies the norm stands out.

But it's his size that has me doing a double take. He's well over six feet, as broad as he is tall. He has that corn-fed, all-American rugged look, like the type of guy you see in those off-roading truck commercials. I picture him doing figure eights against a backdrop of featureless mountain ranges, then heaving himself out of his dusty vehicle looking no worse for the wear, trusty yellow Lab at his heels.

"Uh, yes. Kate Adams," I stammer. *Chill, Kate.* I stand and hold out my hand. "You must be Mr. Mackenzie?"

He pauses, something unidentifiable flickering across his features. "Mr. Mackenzie is my dad. Call me Ben."

"Nice to meet you, Ben."

His eyes hold mine just a second longer than necessary. "Likewise."

I notice the sudden absence of the rapid-fire keyboard soundtrack of the past half hour and peek over his shoulder just in time to catch the staff assistant eyeing his backside. *Indeed.*

Ben motions for me to follow him and leads me out the main entrance, heading down the hallway. The leather crossbody he has slung across his chest is stuffed to bulging and probably weighs more than I do. Just looking at it makes my shoulder ache.

He unlocks the door marked SH 724, holding it open for me as he flicks on the lights and motions to one of the two chairs at his desk, and I make myself comfortable while he settles in. He starts unloading things from his overfilled bag—a laptop, stacks of files, loose papers—arranging them in tidy piles on his desk. When he's done, it looks like an architect's 3-D model of a skyscraper city, with towers of varying heights stacked up like Legos.

He reaches across his desk to grab something, and his wingspan is enormous. I wonder idly where he buys his suits. They must be custom-made, though who could afford such a thing on our paltry salary? It's a mystery.

"Thanks so much for fitting me in," I begin, conveniently ignoring that he kept me waiting. *Ooze that southern charm.* "Your schedule seems a bit intense."

"Sorry about that. There's a lot going on with the tax plan right now."

Senator Hammond is chairman of the Finance Committee, so I suppose it makes sense that Ben would be working on tax reform. Still, the mental image of this muscle-bound behemoth hunched over a calculator is so incongruent, I want to laugh.

"Huh. That makes more sense now."

"What makes more sense now?" He plugs in his laptop and sets it off to the side.

"Why you couldn't meet for three weeks."

His pause lasts just a beat too long. "We're meeting now, aren't we?"

Ooh, we've got a live one here. I sit up a little straighter. "That we are."

"So, Ms. Adams," he says, back to digging in his bag. "You're here about the child care bill?"

"Ms. Adams is my mother. So please, call me Kate."

He glances up at me, casting a boyish grin in my direction. It's transformative, his smile, the kind that takes a face from serious to mischievous in the blink of an eye. I wonder how old he is. I'd pegged him as midthirties, but I mentally revise that downward.

His eyes move over me as if I'm familiar. "Okay, Kate," he says, still smiling like he's amused by me. "Why don't you tell me why you're here."

"I'm here on behalf of Senator Warner to discuss the Child Care and Education for Working Families Act we introduced a couple months back. I wanted to give you a brief synopsis of the bill, answer any questions you have, and see what we can do to get Senator Hammond on board."

"So this is the Democrat proposal for subsidized child care?" He sinks heavily into what must be an industrial-strength chair.

I cringe at his characterization. "Well, kind of, but there's a lot more to it than that. The goal of the bill is to provide families with additional resources for—"

"I've read the bill, I know what it's about. I also know it has no chance of passing."

Record scratch.

I smile tightly through clenched teeth. *So this is how it's going to be.* "If it didn't have a chance, I wouldn't be here."

Something in my voice must get his attention, because he finally quits organizing all the crap on his desk and looks at me properly. His eyes flick over me from head to toe, lingering briefly on my heels. This pair is one of my favorites—turquoise suede with an asymmetrical toe line and a tiny row of pearls dotting the back heel. They're the mullet of footwear: business in the front, party in the back.

He squints at them for a moment as if mystified, then drags his eyes back up to mine, a small frown settling on his mouth. "That bill is going nowhere. You must know that. And Hammond would never vote for it." He speaks slowly, his tone patronizing, like I'm some sort of simpleton who doesn't understand English.

My face heats. "How about you listen to my pitch for thirty seconds before you shut me down?"

"Why, when I know what the answer will be?"

"Do *you* speak for Senator Hammond?" It's a challenge—and the politest way I can think of to neuter Mr. Big Swinging Dick.

His eyes narrow. "As a matter of fact, I do."

I narrow mine in a mirror image. The moment stretches.

"Well, *oh-kay,*" I say, interrupting our impromptu glaring contest. "Thanks for keeping me waiting for thirty minutes, then *not* giving me the opportunity to discuss the legislation. I'll be sure to let Senator Warner know that her *friend* Hank Hammond wouldn't give her the time of day."

I slap my presentation folder shut in preparation for a dramatic exit. I think I'll knock over one of his stupid skyscraper stacks while I'm at it.

"I'm sorry, have I offended you?" He seems genuinely confused.

"How could you tell?"

The corners of his mouth start to curve as if he's going to laugh, but he smothers it quickly. "Am I really the first person who's told you this bill is dead in the water? You think legislation imposing new regulations on businesses is going to pass in a Republican-controlled Congress?" His tone clearly communicates: *You can't be that dumb.*

"It will if we can get enough Republicans on board."

"I see." He nods gravely, steepling his fingers under his chin. "So who have you gotten so far?"

I walked right into that one.

I hesitate, but there's no point in lying. He could find out without much digging. "Callahan and Roscoe."

"They're lying."

"They're *not* lying," I snap. "They're considering it."

His phone starts buzzing on his desk but he ignores it. "Well, it sounds like you'd prefer me to BS you, so Senator Hammond will take this under advisement. We'll let you know," he drawls.

My frustration builds into outright fury. Even in the egotistical cesspool that is the DC swamp, this guy sets a new benchmark for repulsive behavior. I can't believe these are the people I have to grovel to.

His next words make me wonder if he can read my mind.

"Look, maybe I was a little abrupt," he concedes, pinching the bridge of his nose, "but I've had a long day and just thought I'd save us both some time. Would you rather I let you go on and on about a bill I know Hammond will never support?"

Apparently that's his apology.

"*Now* you're so concerned about my time?"

"I am *very* sorry I was late," he says evenly. "Though I suppose I should have told everyone that my appointment about a doomed child care bill was more important than rewriting the tax code?"

My mouth drops open but no sound comes out.

"Too abrupt again?" He smirks.

I can only gawk at him. He's rendered me mute.

Ben leans forward, seemingly more interested now that I'm melting down in front of him. He's like a hunter, sensing my distress and looking to step on my neck.

"Is this your first bill, Ms. Adams? Because you seem to be taking this very personally."

I finally recover my voice. "Is this your first time conversing with another human? Because this has got to be the most condescending conversation I've ever had."

"Sorry, I'm incapable of bullshit. Hazard of the job."

"Is one of the hazards also being completely closed-minded? Or is that just one of the many hazards of being a Republican?" *Good one, Kate.* I do a mental fist pump.

That earns me a scowl. "I notice you didn't answer my question."

"My previous experience is irrelevant to this meeting."

His mouth turns up in that smirk again. I wish I could smack it off. I'd leave an angry red handprint on his big stupid face.

I glare until he throws his hands up in surrender.

"Fine. You're right, I kept you waiting, so it's only fair for me to give you some time. Why don't you tell me why I'm wrong about this bill? Let's see if you can change my mind." He folds his hands on his desk like an angelic schoolboy, though his tone communicates that this is all a big waste of time.

Even so, I seize my opportunity. "You can't make a snap judgment on the bill without knowing the specifics. This is a bipartisan issue. Rising child care costs are a major pain point for families, especially those living under the median income. Lack of access to affordable care is the number one reason women drop out of the workforce."

"I'm well aware that the child care system needs overhauling. There's a GOP-backed bill already introduced that tackles this via tax credits and flexible spending accounts. Now, *there's* a bill Hammond will support."

"That bill doesn't go far enough. Ours ensures universal access to high-quality preschool programs for all three- and four-year-olds, including children with disabilities, as well as earmarking funds for teacher training."

I'm pretty sure he didn't hear the last part because he's started rummaging in his desk drawer. Once he finds what he's looking for—

apparently, a can of nuts—he cracks open the lid and tosses a handful in his mouth, chewing noisily.

The look I shoot him is lethal.

"What?" he says defensively.

"Should I continue, or wait until snack time is over?"

"I'm hungry. I've been in a meeting for three hours." At my frown, he holds out the can. "Sorry, would you like some?"

I stare at him. "What I'd like is just five minutes of your undivided attention."

"Only five more minutes? You got it."

His phone starts vibrating again on his desk. I glance at it, but his eyes stay on me.

"Clock is ticking, Ms. Adams."

He's trying to piss you off, Kate. Don't let him. I take a deep, steadying breath. "Women are hugely supportive of this bill. Our polling indicates eighty-three percent in favor."

"Never mind who's gonna pay for it, right?" He grabs his water bottle and takes a long swallow. "Look, I get it. It's a nice idea in theory."

"In theory?"

"The last thing Hammond would support is *more* regulations. We're pretty busy dismantling the last eight years' worth that completely paralyzed job growth throughout the state. Hammond's entire agenda hinges on that promise."

He eyes me as I process this. Something about my silence seems to soften him a touch, and when he speaks again, he almost sounds sympathetic.

"Look, I'm not trying to be rude. It's just a fact. Subsidizing a program like this is a nonstarter."

I register pain in my hands, and when I look down I realize I'm white-knuckling the arms of the chair. I peel my fingers off one by one.

"So there's nothing I can say to convince you. Nothing Senator Warner can offer in exchange."

"Nope. She has nothing we need." He grins, baring two perfect rows of white teeth. He's a walking advertisement for orthodontia.

"Why don't you run it by your boss?"

"I'll do that." Translation: *Not a chance in hell.*

"Can I ask you something? If you weren't even going to listen to what I had to say, then why'd you bother taking this meeting?"

His face goes a bit deer in the headlights, like he's scrambling for a plausible lie.

"Sometimes things can surprise you," he finally says haltingly. "Look, Ms. Adams—"

"It's *Kate*," I say tersely.

"Kate, then." His eyes flare a little on the syllable. "You caught me on a bad day. I'm eyeball-deep in drafting legislation that's supposed to juggle the competing needs of fifty people who all seem to think *their* provisions should be the priority." He exhales an exasperated breath, as if the weight of the world rests on his oversize shoulders. *Cry me a river, buddy.* "I hope you'll forgive me for being a little short."

I let out a clipped laugh and stand, shouldering my workbag. "A little short. *Right.* Thanks for your time."

He stands too. "You know, there are other ways to go about what you're trying to do that would garner bipartisan support. You could make it a tax play entirely if you got Senator Warner to lobby for a credit—"

My laughter erupts in a staccato burst. *Ha-ha-ha.* "Thanks, but I don't need your help."

He cocks his head to the side. "Really. So tell me again, why are you here?"

I have *got* to stop setting myself up like this. "I have no idea why I'm still here, actually. This meeting has been a gigantic waste of my time. And your *much* more important time as well."

"Right. Well, I tried. You can lead a horse to water . . ." He shrugs like he's gone to the ends of the earth for me and come up empty.

"Are you this rude to everyone, or just me?"

"I think it's just you. You seem to bring it out of me." Even he seems confused by this.

"If I behaved like you, I'd be out of a job," I mutter. "Speaking of which, does Senator Hammond know the type of person he has working for him?"

His eyes sharpen. "And what *type* of person am I?"

"You're a rude, offensive, patronizing . . ." I falter. God, I wish I were better at slinging insults. It goes against my nature. "Oaf." *Oh geez.*

My insult seems to delight him. "*Oaf?* Are you making a reference to my *body*, Ms. Adams? I'm not sure if you've heard, but hashtag time's up on sexual harassment in the workplace."

I have a brief hallucination as we face off. I'm launching myself over the desk and grabbing him by the ear the way my grandmother used to do to me. I'll bring this fool to his knees. I'll tan his hide like cheap leather. I'll slap that smug grin off his face and it will be *so* satisfying.

I drop-kick the fantasy away. I have nothing to gain by continuing this. I spin around and head for the door, grateful to be leaving this chamber of horrors behind.

"I don't think Hammond has any complaints about me." His voice chases my back. "In fact, I'm pretty sure he wishes he had ten more of me."

"I think you might need a bigger office. I'm surprised your head can fit through the door." I yank it open.

"It was *very* nice to meet you, Kate," he calls.

"Wish I could say the same," I toss back.

His laughter echoes over my shoulder as I slam the door behind me.

Chapter 2

I hightail it back to my office, anger and anxiety clashing in my stomach. I let that get *way* out of hand. Grace under pressure is practically one of my job requirements. The fact that I failed so spectacularly in my mission *and* earned an enemy in the process makes me a little sick.

I breathe a little easier once I step through my doors. *Ahh.* Back to my domain.

Senator Warner's suite of offices is located on the seventh floor of the Hart Building, one of three Senate buildings surrounding the US Capitol, or what's known as the Capitol Complex. Hart houses about fifty senators and their staffs, the other fifty split between the Russell and Dirksen Buildings. All three are connected by long hallways and tunnels, which means a ton of walking, but I don't mind. It's a rare day when I don't hit my ten thousand steps.

I actually prefer Russell to Hart—the domed ceiling, crystal chandeliers, and heavy wooden doors evoking the archetypal *Mr. Smith Goes to Washington* version of DC you see in the movies. That marble rotunda in the background of every cable news interview? That's Russell. I'm there every day but I still get goose bumps every time I climb the grand

staircases. Hart is more of a modern office building, with speckled fiber-
board ceilings and carpet that gives me static shocks.

But Hart is the center of everything, a building teeming with life—
and these days, protesters—at all times. The glass-walled offices are laid
out along the building's outer perimeter, with an open atrium in the center where an immense sculpture installation entitled *Mountains and Clouds*
resides. To me, it looks more like random black geometric shapes than
mountains and clouds, but that's art for you. Some people complain
about the lack of privacy (and I get it; the building is basically a giant
fishbowl), but I find it all entertaining—the constant commotion, the
tribal camaraderie, the simmering resentments that boil over into passive-
aggressive window-sign wars the week of a big vote. There's an odd intimacy to it, a sense that we're all in this together despite our differences; a
big, dysfunctional family forced to sit across from each other at the
Thanksgiving table.

When I walk into reception, the TV is blaring CNN, per usual. It's
one of the prerequisites of the job—the constant surveillance of cable
news, like an IV drip that can't be turned off. Sometimes I even dream
in a headline scroll.

The first thing I do once I enter my office is whip off my blazer; I'm
overheated and some days it feels like a straitjacket. I love fashion, but
the stodgy political environment doesn't exactly encourage sartorial expression. It's business formal all the time, especially for meetings I attend with Senator Warner. There's a strict dress code for appearing on
the Senate floor and I follow it to the letter.

My only rebellion is my heels.

When I first moved to DC, it took a week of wearing monotonous,
soul-killing suits before I decided sporting outlandish heels was going to
be my rage against the machine. Now it's my signature. No matter how
conservative my attire, you better believe I'm wearing flamboyant foot-

wear, usually with some type of embellishment: a bow, a buckle, a tassel, a stud. Most of the time they're hidden under a desk—but I know they're there, and that's just enough civil disobedience for me.

As I hang my jacket on the back of my chair, my eyes catch on the double photo frame I keep front and center on my desk. The left side displays a shot from my mom's college graduation: she's holding a pigtailed, chubby-cheeked version of me tight and beaming, her rolled diploma raised in victory. The picture on the right is similar but age-progressed—we're hugging at my graduation, and this time I'm the one celebrating. It's the best possible reminder of why I'm here, why I need to keep fighting—even if it means putting up with brutes like Ben Mackenzie.

I have my mom to thank for my career path. At just eighteen years old, she got pregnant with me at her senior prom. Yep, I'm that cliché. She was a teen mom before doing so meant landing your own MTV show.

She never married my dad—or more accurately, my dad never married *her*—and thankfully her parents offered to help raise me. When I was a toddler, she worked during the day and toiled away at night classes to get her degree in hospitality management while I got spoiled as my grandparents' little angel. She currently works for a chain of luxury hotels in New York, where she moved from our small town outside Nashville as soon as I went off to college at UNC Chapel Hill. My paternal grandparents did their best to help too, not that paying for some dance classes could make up for their son's absence in my life. My childhood wasn't picture-perfect, but I didn't want for anything—except a father, of course.

I open my laptop and sigh. It's after five, but I hate leaving work with the equivalent of a seventy-car pileup in my inbox. I settle in to clear my emails, following up on some committee business, responding to a couple of constituent emails that have been passed my way, and compiling a list of talking points for an upcoming speech Carol will be giving. At six fifteen, I hear Stephen's voice boom out from his desk.

"Candy time!"

Stephen Campbell is Carol's scheduler, and his job is basically what you're thinking. Like a glorified secretary, he keeps her calendar, arranges interviews, organizes travel, and keeps her on schedule, which, because of how sought after she is, is sometimes chopped into five-minute blocks.

Stephen was the first friend I made when I got this job. He's hilarious and loyal, though gossip is his self-admitted weakness. He filled me in on all the office drama before I even had a chance to meet everyone. I don't recommend this—it made for some awkward introductions—but we were inseparable after that. He's also a southern expat, so we just get each other like few others do.

I stand and stretch, ambling out to his desk. He holds up Red Vines and dark chocolate M&M'S, which he knows are my favorite. I grab the Red Vines just to keep him guessing.

This is our evening routine. Before Stephen leaves for the night, we catch up on the day's goings-on—though it's more like Stephen catching me up on gossip since I'm completely clueless. He once confided that the candy stash is his secret weapon. Guilty consciences seek guilty calories.

"You look tired," Stephen announces without preamble. Ah, my least favorite insult in disguise.

"Should I smile more, too?"

"Ooh, someone's cranky. Bad day?"

"Terrible." I kick off my heels and collapse onto the communal couch, propping my legs up on the table. I need a pedicure. "You would not believe this guy I had to meet with over in Hammond's office."

"Do tell." Stephen swivels around in his chair and rips open the bag of M&M'S, spilling them all over his desk and cursing. "Today's been super boring, so spill."

"First of all, he showed up half an hour late for our meeting, then had this chip on his shoulder the whole time, like I was the one wasting *his* time."

Stephen wrinkles his nose. "Ew."

"And then he goes on and on about how busy he is rewriting the tax code. Like I'm supposed to be impressed."

"So he's working on tax reform? That's got to be pretty intense right now."

"Excuse me, Stephen." I snap my fingers at him. "We do not *care* about him. *I* am the injured party here. Please focus."

He covers his heart with his hand. "What was I thinking? Empathy for others is so ten years ago. Carry on."

"You should have seen him. The guy was a human Goliath. Like a linebacker, only bigger. I would have been afraid of him if he wasn't such a douchebag."

"Was he good-looking?" He throws an M&M up in the air and catches it in his mouth.

"Good-*looking*? Have you been listening to a word I've said?"

"I have, and you just referred to him as a football player, which implies muscles, which has piqued my interest. Many jerks are, unfortunately, attractive. So, was he?"

"That, that—doesn't matter!" I sputter. "I wasn't there to get a date. I was there to get my bill passed!"

He raises his hands, placating. "Calm down. I'm asking for a reason. Maybe he was acting out because he was into you. Guys are immature that way, you know. Or maybe he was intimidated by you. Wouldn't be the first time." He leans toward me, resting his chin on his hand. "Important question. Did you use your hair on him?"

"Oh my God, you and my hair," I groan.

"What? If I had your hair, God knows I'd be using it to bring men to their knees."

"Oh, really? In the *workplace*?"

"Why not? You're much too scrupulous. You and your *ethics*," he says with exaggerated air quotes, and I laugh in spite of myself. "Give that glorious head of hair a toss, bat those baby blues, and any man will be putty in your hands." He dramatically flips a pretend mane.

"I'll remember that next time I'm *out of the office* trolling for guys."

Stephen's exaggerating, but like a lot of southern women, I have big hair. It's long and blond and, honestly, I'm more vain about it than I'd like to admit. I baby it with absurdly expensive products and bimonthly cuts at an overpriced salon in Georgetown. I'm not proud.

I blame my mother for this. She's beautiful and I've spent my life chasing her perfection. At forty-five, she still turns men's heads in the street—and rocks long hair like she's Christie Brinkley. It's one of the reasons I can't bring myself to crop it shorter; it's one of the few things that reminds me of home. When I moved north, I dropped my accent but kept my hair.

What I always considered an asset, though, quickly proved a liability in the restrained, austere world of government. In my first week of work alone, I'd fielded so many Elle Woods jokes—and naughty intern jokes—that I considered shaving my head entirely. Instead, I started taming it into submission any way I knew how, which usually means restraining it in a boring bun, like today.

"I'm just saying, God gave you that hair for a reason. You're a fool if you don't use it to your advantage."

"That wouldn't have worked with this guy, trust me. He was all angry snorting bull, insult this, boast that." I massage the back of my neck, drained. "I guess my chances of getting Hammond on board now are slim to none, and Slim just left town, as my gramps would say."

"Well, you knew that going in."

I growl, exasperated. "Whose side are you on?"

"Well, what did you expect from this meeting?"

"I expected to get through two sentences of my pitch! I expected common courtesy! This jerk-off didn't even humor me. He shooed me away like I was some annoying little gnat."

Reliving Ben's contempt is pissing me off all over again. The flip side of venting sessions with Stephen: my blood pressure goes through the roof.

"I'm picturing him like a lumberjack, with a plaid shirt and a hat with earflaps. And a mullet."

I snicker at the visual. "You're not far off. He's probably some inbred *Duck Dynasty* type from the sticks. Backwoods Ben Mackenzie: tax reformer by day, hulking redneck by night."

Stephen hoots.

"And he's the legislative director! He's literally one of Hammond's top guys. How do you even get that job when you're that big a dick?"

"He probably got the job *because* he's a dick. You know how that goes." Stephen rolls his eyes.

"It's so hypocritical. If I were the world's biggest bitch, I'd never get hired. In fact, I'd get fired. Blackballed."

"Sing it, sister. Preach." He holds his hands up like he's in church.

I'm on a roll now. "I mean, no wonder our parties can't get along. This guy is Exhibit A. He personified every stereotype: egotistical, closed-minded, patronizing. And I thought midwesterners were supposed to be these sweet farm boys with impeccable manners? He was even arrogant about Ohio, for crying out loud. Maybe I'd be more inclined to listen to someone who wasn't from a flippin' flyover state."

"Actually, I'm from Texas," a deep voice rumbles from over my shoulder. I swivel my head around just as a massive figure steps through the doorway.

Oh, sweet baby Jesus.

It's him. Benjamin Mackenzie.

Chapter 3

Oh my God.

Heat floods my face. Actually, that's an understatement—it's basically melting off, *Raiders of the Lost Ark* style. Shame-adrenaline floods my system and I'm having an out-of-body experience.

I won't be able to walk this back no matter how hard I try. It's like when you write an email tearing someone to shreds and then instead of sending it to your intended recipient, you mistakenly email it straight to the poor soul you've just annihilated. Except this is worse, because I said it *to his face.*

I rewind my memory, frantically cataloguing the worst of what I just said. Maybe he only just got here. Maybe he didn't hear much. I brave a glance at him. He looks angry, his expression as dark and ominous as a gathering storm.

So, yeah. Unlikely he missed all that.

I glance at Stephen and his mouth's hanging open in a large O. We're like twin Big Mouth Billy Bass fish. You could mount us on a wooden plaque and hang us on the wall and I think we'd be less stunned than we are right now.

I make a choking noise and start scrambling to my feet, but Ben holds up a hand.

"Don't bother getting up. I wouldn't want to interrupt your bashing session. And to think I was coming over here to *apologize* for my mood earlier and wish you luck getting your bill passed. Which, by the way"—he huffs a laugh—"you're gonna need."

He turns and disappears through the door he materialized from. I look back at Stephen with wide eyes and a swinging jaw. His face mirrors mine—frozen in shock.

"I did *not* see that coming," he says, a little dazed. "Scratch what I said about this day being boring."

Before I can reconsider, my legs propel me off the couch and I dash out the door after him. I have no clue what I'm going to say, but I do know I need to apologize, stat. I don't have time to put my shoes back on so I stagger out barefoot and immediately slam into the two flagpoles stationed outside our office, which collapse around me in a tangled heap. I bleat like a dying animal.

At the commotion, Ben glances back. When he sees me flailing on the floor, he takes a deep breath and looks up at the ceiling, as if praying for an intervention. He casts me a piteous look but grudgingly walks back and holds out a hand to help me up.

"I'm so sor—"

"Please don't tell me you're about to say sorry," he cuts me off as I fumble around trying to right the American and New Hampshire State flags. "We both know you meant every word you said. I think we're way past pretending for politeness's sake."

Apparently satisfied that I'm not crippled, he pivots and strides down the hall faster than a racehorse at the Kentucky Derby, his bag banging against his hip like the lash of a jockey's whip.

I limp after him, feeling about as pathetic as a woman who's humiliated herself in front of someone twice in one day can feel. I banged my leg so hard, I'm sure a bruise has already formed. It's throbbing proof of today's epic failure.

I catch up and grab his arm. "Look, I don't know how much you heard, but I was just venting—"

He whips around. "I heard *jerk-off*, *inbred*, *dick*, and *redneck*. Did I miss any other clever nicknames?" He. Is. *Pissed*.

It's so appalling to hear my laundry list of slurs rattled off that I'm momentarily stunned silent. This is the worst I've ever been called out, and that includes when my sorority sister and I got caught whispering during our anthropology final. I'd thought I was going to die of a heart attack under our teacher's accusing stare, but I'd gladly return to that classroom if it meant escaping this fresh hell.

I decide to go on the offensive. I draw myself up to my full height—which, unfortunately, isn't all that impressive, seeing as how the top of my head only comes up to about his shoulders. My AWOL heels would really help right about now.

"You were awful earlier and you felt bad. I just said some awful things and now I feel bad. Let's just agree we both have things to be sorry for." I'm determined to fix this. Southern etiquette runs deep.

"I don't feel bad anymore." He turns and resumes his furious march down the hall, heading toward the elevator, or stairs, or whichever way is away from me. I trail behind him a few paces. I can't let it go.

"You're the one who was a jerk to me for no reason. I was only reacting to *your* bad behavior."

"I just told you like it is. I didn't attack you personally."

"There's telling it like it is, and there's being an asshole."

I mentally cringe at my cursing. My mom would not approve. Oh well. She could hardly judge me for this. I'd like to think if she were here, she'd be cheering me on.

He glances back, steel in his eyes. "If you don't mind, I think I've been insulted enough for one day."

We finally reach the elevator and he stabs the DOWN button so violently, I'm surprised it doesn't pop off. We stand in silence, but after racing to keep up with his long-legged stride, I'm struggling to catch my breath. He notices my bare feet and his entire face wrinkles in distaste.

"I hope I never get to be this way," I say, more to myself than to him.

"And what way is that?"

"Completely jaded. You want to mock me for being idealistic, fine. Better that than cynical and miserable."

"You don't know anything about me." His voice is glacial.

"On the contrary. I only needed two minutes to learn everything there is to know about you."

"Is that so? Don't keep me in suspense." He hits the DOWN button repeatedly, as if jabbing it fifteen times will make the elevator arrive faster.

I bite my lip, hesitating. This is my last chance to take the off-ramp. I should apologize maturely, wish him well, and hope like hell that chatter about our confrontation doesn't get around.

But here's the thing: I'm not hard to get along with. I don't cause drama, and I'm certainly not one for burning bridges. But as I stand here and take in his combative stance and restrained anger, I'm transported back to how I felt in his office earlier today. Degraded. Belittled. Dismissed. I recall his condescending expression when he asked if this was my first bill, and white-hot rage courses through my veins.

So I burn that bridge straight down to the ground and roll in the ashes.

"Well, you're a Republican, so that tells me plenty about how you see the world. You clearly don't care about helping families or children who really need it. Why waste time on that when you can shower your wealthy buddies with huge tax breaks? Pat yourself on the back about your precious tax plan all you want, but we both know you're just helping rich men get richer and businesses shirk their financial and ethical responsibilities. You're also rude, patronizing, and unprofessional. Apologizing for your bad behavior would have at least redeemed your character slightly in my eyes, but so much for that. So overall, I'm gonna say you're the perfect example of everything that's wrong with this town."

I stop, out of breath, and a little stunned I just said all that.

He looks stunned too. He stares at me, his mouth slightly agape. "Well." He seems to be struggling to find words. "My bad behavior has nothing on yours."

He takes a step toward me and I have to fight the urge to step back. I force myself to meet his gaze, but when I do, I'm struck by a lightning bolt.

His eyes are a vivid shade of green I've never seen before. I hardly know how to describe the hue—like a mix of emerald and jade, wax-leaf trees and mossy grass. They're absolutely brilliant, practically glowing in their intensity. I start to step forward to get a closer look before I remember he's the devil and rein myself in at the last second.

"Since you've nailed me exactly, why don't I do you?" He cocks his head to the side, a sinister smile settling on his mouth. I hold my breath.

"You're a ball-busting liberal feminist who's got it *all* figured out. You blindly follow the party line and never stop to question the BS you're fed. Your reaction to every political issue is to scream 'feminine oppression.' You're judgmental and intolerant of anyone who dares hold an opinion different than your own. Just another bleeding heart who has no idea how to come up with effective real-world policy. Free child care, free health care, free college, free everything! Never mind who's going to pay for it. What could go wrong?"

He leans closer, and this time I do step back. "I'm sure you're the type of woman who gets offended if a man deigns to open the door for her. You're also an uptight, entitled princess who's clearly never heard the word *no*. So overall, I'd say you're the perfect example of everything that's wrong with *women*."

Whenever I've seen a movie where a woman hauls off and slaps a man, I've always secretly wondered what it would feel like, just how angry you'd have to be to feel like hitting someone is an appropriate response. I wonder no more. My fingers tingle at my sides.

He watches me as my fury builds, a wisp of a smile on his face. "You're right, all that name-calling *did* help me feel better."

The elevator doors finally open and he steps inside, punching a button.

"How dare you." My words come out in a strangled growl.

"Careful, Kate. You're gonna need my help over the next eight years a lot more than I'll need yours."

"Eight years?" I sputter. "Try four. Three and a half. And the world will end before I ever ask for your help again."

He shrugs, his expression smug. "You better hope that's what happens, because my new mission in life is to piss you off. You want Hammond's support? You'll have to go through me to get it."

He chuckles like this is hilarious as the doors shut in his face.

Chapter 4

Three days have passed since my ill-fated meeting with Ben, and I consider myself #blessed that I haven't had another run-in with the Oaf, as Stephen and I have taken to calling him. Not that I haven't noticed him around the building—frankly, he's impossible to miss. He's tall enough that I can spot him down a hallway and head in the opposite direction, and the handful of times I spy him getting on or off the elevator, I take the stairs. The upside of dodging Ben Mackenzie: My calves have never looked better.

Luckily, winter session is one of our busiest times of year, so I don't have much time to dwell on the situation. I'm still working on drumming up conservative support for our bill as well as juggling other legislative research. By the time Friday rolls around, I could weep in relief. Carol travels back to New Hampshire most Fridays to attend to state business, and in her absence the office is as quiet as a church.

Which makes the morning disruption that much more infuriating.

I've just returned from a coffee run when I spot a manila envelope on my desk marked *Kate Adams, SH 708*. My regular mail stack arrives in the afternoons, so it must have been hand delivered. I open the envelope and extract a heavy paperback book with a note paper-clipped to the front cover. When I see the name on the letterhead, my blood runs ice-cold.

> *Ms. Adams,*
>
> *Saw this and thought you could use a brushup. I've taken the liberty of highlighting a few passages you may find useful.*
>
> *Please don't hesitate to reach out for help. I have a lot of experience drafting successful legislation, and my door is always open for idealistic dreamers like yourself.*
>
> *Yours in displeasure,*
>
> ~~*Inbred Redneck Jackass Oaf*~~
>
> *Ben Mackenzie*

I unclip the note from the cover and let out a gasp.

Legislation for Dummies.

I flip through the book and it's a blur of yellow highlighted passages blanketing nearly every page. He's made "helpful" annotations in the margins like: *Try not to insult the people you need on your side*; *Draft a bill that has a chance in hell*; and this gem: *Bizarre footwear won't distract people into voting yes.*

"Stephen!" My shriek can probably be heard from the White House.

He's in my office in seconds, breathless. "What is it? Did you find another roach in here?"

"Worse." I toss the book on my desk like it's singed my fingers.

He picks it up and starts thumbing through it. When I hand him the note he whistles, low and slow.

"Did you see him come in here? Was he in my office?" I duck under my desk and check for booby traps.

"Calm down. And no, I think it was dropped off by an intern."

"It's probably laced with anthrax."

Stephen glances around nervously. "Be careful how loudly you say *anthrax* in here."

He isn't kidding. Hart was one of the buildings shut down years ago due to anthrax contamination. Hundreds of staffers were displaced from their offices for months. People who worked here at the time speak of it like they survived the apocalypse.

I lower my voice to a whisper. "Do you know any anthrax dealers?"

"Oh, honey, we don't need anthrax."

"What do you mean?"

"You're going to send him back something that's more obnoxious than this." His eyes take on a diabolical glint. I remind myself never to cross Stephen.

"Is that even *possible*?"

He exhales loudly. "Come on, where's your competitive spirit? Are you a fighter or a doormat?"

I gnaw on the end of my pen as I consider it. I suppose I could come up with something that will get under Ben's skin. He exposed some of his pressure points during his elevator rant, and I can use them to my advantage. A smile blooms as my brain swirls with possibilities.

"Am I right?" Stephen's devilish grin matches my own.

"You're so right. Don't get mad; get even. As usual, I bow down to your pettiness."

"I consider that a great compliment." He inclines his head and I'm snickering as he leaves my office.

I spend the next twenty minutes googling around for negative press about the Republican tax plan. I hit pay dirt when I stumble across a recent story highlighting how a schoolteacher earning a sixty-thousand-dollar salary will collect a meager tax savings of a dollar fifty per week.

The writer of the piece helpfully juxtaposed that pitiful statistic with the millions in deductions large corporations are set to receive.

Then I draft my note.

> Ben,
>
> Thank you so much for the reference material—from your personal library, I take it?
>
> Since one good deed deserves another, I thought I'd send some background research on your tax plan. That extra $1.50 should really be life changing for schoolteachers! Think of all the things they can buy (I've included just a few examples). The $1 trillion added to the deficit is a nice bonus. You must be so proud.
>
> Yours in discontent,
> Kate Adams

I fumble around in my desk until I collect a half-empty pack of gum, a small box of staples, a coupon to Subway, and a handful of spare change and toss it all into the envelope. I eye a stray tampon for a minute before deciding to throw it in. He looks like the kind of guy who will squirm at the sight of feminine hygiene products. I cackle like a half-cracked villain as I call for an intern to deliver my retaliatory missile.

It goes on like this for the next week. On Monday I receive a *Wall Street Journal* op-ed: WHY LIBERALS WILL BANKRUPT THE NATION IN THEIR QUEST FOR A SOCIALIST AMERICA. On Tuesday—and coincidentally, National Diversity Day—I send him a roundup of tweets ridiculing the Republican Speaker of the House for a photo he recently posted of the current class of House interns. In a sea of a hundred faces, not one is of color.

On Wednesday I get an article entitled, HOW WEARING HEELS CAN

SERIOUSLY IMPAIR WORKPLACE PERFORMANCE. I figure he must have doctored that headline until I google it and find out it's real. *Damn it.* On Thursday I send him *Gigantism in Twenty-First-Century America: A Report.* I had to do some serious digging to find that one.

I have to admit—the whole thing is pretty entertaining. It's like we're back in high school, passing origami-folded notes during homeroom. There's something deliciously old-school about his handwritten missives, even if their contents do make me question my commitment to nonviolent conflict resolution. I'd never admit it out loud, but I've actually started to look *forward* to his hate mail. Sometimes it's the only fun I have all day.

I must be losing my mind.

Before I know it, word of our feud spreads and the mail war takes on a life of its own. Everyone in the office wants in on our domino rally of hatred. Stephen's so invested in the drama that I have to create a separate folder just to corral all the link-filled emails he sends me for inspiration. A group of us dissect each of Ben's notes, drafting stinging rebuttals that leave us all in stitches. It's become an office bonding ritual, and I pat myself on the back for bringing everyone together for a common cause.

Taking down Benjamin Mackenzie.

★

"You have to join it!"

I'm headed back from lunch with Stephen and Tessa, another staffer on Senator Warner's team. They're currently trying to peer-pressure me into signing up for LeftField, the new Democrats-only dating app that everyone in the office is talking about. Their tagline: "There are plenty of libs in the sea." I wish I were kidding.

"No way." I punch the UP elevator button and turn to face them.

"Come on, I have to live vicariously through you!" Tessa whines, as though that should sway me. She's been in a long-term relationship with her boyfriend, Luke, for as long as I've known her. "When was the last time you even went on a date?"

I cringe inwardly. My social calendar is pretty barren—though in my defense, who has the time? We work all hours with the same people day in and day out, and interoffice dating is frowned upon. Where would I even meet someone? I should probably be Tinder-ing, Match-ing, Hinge-ing, and Bumble-ing like everyone else I know, but going on semiblind computer dates after a long day at work seems like an almost comical form of torture. And frankly? I just don't care enough. I'm a happily independent woman, and the only times I wish things were different, it goes away in five to seven days.

"The last guy was the one who only ordered skinny drinks, remember? I ditched him when he asked me what kind of conditioner I used."

"He was unfortunate," Stephen concedes. "But all the more reason to sign up. You need a palate cleanser."

"Why can't *you* just join?"

"Oh, believe me, I am. But you're doing it with me."

"I'll set up your profile for you!" Tessa pleads, clutching my arm.

The elevator dings behind me. "Guys, stop. I don't need to join Left-Field to find a date."

The words have barely left my mouth when I see Stephen's eyes go wide as he takes in something over my shoulder. I spin around—and come face-to-face with Ben Mackenzie. Only this time, he's not alone. A tall, glossy-haired brunette hovers at his side, pressing her lips together in amusement. Ben doesn't bother with such subtleties, donning a Cheshire Cat grin he aims right at me.

My face flushes hot with embarrassment, but I can't show any weakness. He's like a shark; he'll smell blood in the water.

"Ben, how *lovely* to see you again," I say, my voice dripping with insincerity.

His eyes spark at my brinkmanship. He opens his mouth to respond but then pauses, glancing at our myriad companions, and I watch the internal struggle play out on his face. Mock me and look like a jerk, or play along?

Social propriety wins out. "Kate, how *great* to run into you," he says, his voice equally disingenuous. I step aside so he and his brunette arm candy can exit the elevator.

"Hey, man," Stephen pipes up, like they're BFFs or something. I shoot him a traitorous look—*what a turncoat.*

The brunette eyes Ben and me with confusion, clearly sensing something is rotten in the state of Denmark. Since Ben hasn't bothered to introduce us, I extend a hand.

"Hi, I'm Kate, and this is Stephen and Tessa. We're on Senator Warner's staff."

Her expression of polite indifference shifts on a dime, her upper lip curling ever so slightly.

"I see. Corinne," she says, grabbing and releasing my hand so swiftly you'd think I have an infectious disease.

"For what it's worth, Kate, I agree," Ben drawls, that cocky grin still plastered across his face. "You shouldn't have to join a discriminatory site like that to get a date."

"Good thing it was just a joke," I respond, smiling through gritted teeth. I could claw his eyes out. To prevent it, I ball my hands into fists so tight my nails bite into my palms.

Corinne doesn't look confused anymore—in fact, she's looking at me like something smells bad. She places a hand in the crook of Ben's arm, subtly tugging him away. "We should go. We don't have long before we need to get back."

"Of course. Enjoy your lunch," I tell them, my voice syrupy sweet. *I hope you choke on it.* As I brush by him to enter the elevator, Ben catches my elbow.

"On the other hand, you may want to reconsider the app," he murmurs in a voice low enough that the others won't hear. "Where else will you find a man with a fetish for uptight ballbusters?"

My jaw drops, but by the time I process his insult, he and Corinne are already halfway across the lobby. I gape soundlessly as the elevator doors shut in my face.

Chapter 5

I think Ben's bugged my office.

There was an envelope waiting for me on my desk this morning when I arrived. Nothing too unusual about that, since I'm averaging one piece of hate mail from Ben every other day. But when I opened it to find a snarky editorial about the Capstone Pipeline drilling project, a chill ran through me.

Only yesterday, Tessa and I had a meeting in my office about this very issue. We worked on a statement for Carol that addresses the current drilling controversy but it hasn't been released yet. There's no way he could know about it.

No way—unless he's listening.

And it's not the first time it's happened, either. Some of his recent missives relate to specific initiatives I'm working on. At first I thought he was just guessing well, but I've clearly underestimated his aptitude for skullduggery.

My already hyperactive imagination shifts into overdrive. I consider frisking everyone who enters my office to see if they're wired. I sweep my office for listening devices, though that mostly involves me picking things up and shaking them. I have a sneaking suspicion that isn't how wiretapping works.

When I share my theory with Stephen, he tells me I've gone off the deep end. In fact, he dismisses it so swiftly that I become suspicious of him too. Maybe Ben has something on him and is forcing Stephen to feed him intelligence from the inside. I interrogate him over lunch, but he doesn't crack.

I might be watching too much *Homeland*.

Maybe it's all in my head, but when it comes to Ben I don't believe in coincidences. To cover my bases, I add a postscript when I send out my next poison-tipped spear.

> *PS. Surveillance without a warrant is a federal offense. If you've bugged my office, I will find out.*

He replies with a postscript of his own:

> *PS. Paranoid much? Have you seen a doctor about your delusions?*

★

"Kate, wait up."

I turn when I hear the voice belongs to my colleague John Conrad, chief of staff for Senator Maxwell (D-Maryland). We were just in a meeting together but I booked it out the door as soon as it ended, intending to make it to the Senate gym before it gets too crowded. If I dillydally, all the good machines will be taken.

"Where you headed?" he asks, jogging to catch up with me.

"Just the gym. What's up?" I ask, not breaking my stride.

"I'll walk you. I had an idea for your bill," he says, and my stomach jumps.

John's boss is one of Carol's closest allies in the Senate; they regularly cosponsor each other's legislation and almost always vote together. As a result, John and I are frequent collaborators and close friends. He's funny and attractive in a perfectly polished, presidential candidate type of way; kind of Patrick Dempsey in *Sweet Home Alabama* smooth. He can be a bit intense—I sometimes wonder if he thinks about anything besides politics—but he's incredibly smart, which for me trumps just about everything else.

"Do you know Paul Bradley over in Senator Moreno's office? He mentioned they're looking for bipartisan support on their transportation bill and I thought this could work in your favor. Infrastructure seems like something Warner could get on board with, especially in exchange for Moreno's vote on the child care bill."

"I think she'd be open to it," I say excitedly. *Finally, some good news.* "I'll reach out to Paul ASAP. This is so helpful, John, thank you."

He smiles. "You can thank me by letting me take you out for a celebratory dinner when the bill passes."

We chat about the details until we reach the gym and I say goodbye and head into the women's locker room. As I'm changing out of my work clothes, I hear someone enter. Glancing up, I recognize the ponytailed brunette, sweaty and svelte in her designer activewear. *Corinne.*

When we lock eyes I can tell she *really* wants to ignore me, but we both call upon the social etiquette drilled into us since birth and fake-smile at each other. *Guess all that sorority rush training was good for something.*

I can't help myself—I'm on a high from John's news and feeling rebellious. "Corinne, right?"

She eyes me guardedly as she twirls the combination on her locker. "Right. And you're Kate."

She's already surprised me; I wouldn't have expected her to remember my name. Or admit to it, anyway.

"So you must work with Ben, then? I don't think you said." If she knows about our feud, it would certainly explain her frostiness.

She gives me a thin-lipped smile. "Among other things," she says, prying open the door and burying her head inside.

So they *are* dating. Or hooking up, maybe—hard to tell from that vague statement and her suggestive little smirk, which will undoubtedly require a brain bleaching later.

"Is it crowded out there?" I ask, bypassing those disturbing mental images, determined to kill this ice queen with kindness.

"Not too bad." She slams the locker shut and turns to face me. "So how did that dating app work out for you?" she asks, smiling innocently.

Innocent as a fox. "I didn't actually join it. My friends were just messing around."

"Oh." She flicks her ponytail back and shoulders her bag. "Well, Ben might think apps like that are silly, but I think they make perfect sense. Why not cut through the crap and find someone who thinks like you do? Can't say I wouldn't do the same if I was stuck in the dating pool." She pauses. "No offense."

"Oh, none taken," I reply dryly.

There's a beat of silence as we size each other up. My cheeks ache from holding this phony smile. I'll have to scrape it off later with a putty knife.

"Well, good luck," she says, her tone reassuring, like I'm some charity case to be pitied.

I narrow my eyes at her back as she flounces out, thinking of the old platitude: *The couple that preys together stays together.* Those two deserve each other.

I'm still smarting from her low blows when I head into the gym—

and immediately spot Ben running on one of the treadmills lining the back wall. *I cannot win today.* His back is to me, but I still jerk my gaze away when I realize I'm checking out his ass.

What? I'm a feminist, not blind.

I should avoid him, I know I should, but it's like I have a devil on my shoulder today. I need to regain some ground and the pull to antagonize him is too strong.

I walk right up and take the treadmill next to his, surreptitiously peeking at his machine's display as I climb on—8.0.

I set mine for 8.1.

I know he sees me, but neither of us acknowledges the other as we run in silence for a minute—until I hear a couple of beeps and slide my eyes over.

He's upped his speed to 8.2.

I increase mine to 8.5.

"It's so cute how desperate you are to beat me."

I swivel my head toward him, frowning at his stupid smirk. *Cute?*

"I *know* I can beat you. I'm a sprinter."

I regret the words as soon as they're out. I just broke my own cardinal rule: Do not reveal any personal information he can use against me. I wouldn't be surprised if he excavates my old high school running records just to taunt me.

"A sprinter, huh? You like to finish fast?" He laughs at his double entendre.

"I haven't had any complaints."

"Things must be going well on Donkey Date, then?"

"Donkey Date?"

"You know, the app for people who refuse to date outside their own echo chambers."

My blood pressure spikes. The sudden rush of adrenaline causes my stride to falter, and for the next few seconds my brain is wholly focused on not flying off the treadmill.

Don't let him see you sweat, Kate.

"Forget it. You're not worth it."

"You know, a dry spell is nothing to be ashamed of. It happens to the best of us."

I clench my jaw so hard I nearly crack a crown. To prevent myself from committing murder in a federal building filled with security cameras, I increase my speed again and focus on leaving Ben in the proverbial dust.

He takes the hint, and for the next couple of minutes the only sounds are the pounding of our feet on the whirring belts and our panting breaths. We're silent in our quest to best each other. My lungs are burning and white spots dance in my vision, but I'd rather die on this treadmill than slow down.

Eventually I hear a chuckle, followed by a rapid-fire set of beeps. "Don't hurt yourself, Goldilocks. I was already on my warm-down."

I smother my reaction to this new nickname as he rolls to a stop, guzzling from a water bottle as he steps off the treadmill to leave. I can't resist.

"You should get used to losing to me," I call as he walks away.

He stops. Pivots. Saunters back to my machine, casually draping his arms over the handrail. I glance at them and they're so massive they crowd my field of vision—ropy mounds of skin and sinew, each curve revealing yet another heavy muscle. I wonder idly if I could fit both my hands around one of his biceps. I doubt it.

"Losing, huh? Those are fighting words."

"Someone is *very* touchy about losing to a girl," I pant.

His eyebrows jump. Sweat pours from his brow, and when he grabs the hem of his shirt to mop his forehead, I get a flash of about thirty-eight perfectly defined ab muscles. *What a waste of a man.*

The brief distraction is my literal downfall. Before I can register what he's doing, he's reached over and pushed the EMERGENCY STOP button. In my fight to stay upright, I almost miss his parting words:

"Whatever helps you sleep at night, *Princess.*"

★

On the last Wednesday of February I get a call from my dad, "just checking in," as he always says. It's around the same time every month, so I'm pretty sure he calendarizes it.

My relationship with my dad looks something like this: My grandparents have a nickname for churchgoers who only show up on Christmas and Easter: Chreasters. As in, "We need to get to the service early because all the Chreasters will take up the good seats." Well, for the first half of my life, I had a Chreaster father. When he was in college, I only saw him during holiday and summer breaks. He was a visitor, a guest, a blurry figure occasionally dropped into my memories. For me, dads felt about as real as Santa Claus.

After he graduated, he took a job in sales that required constant travel. While Nashville was technically his home base, I rarely saw him except for the occasional meals or outings my mom would force me to endure. Rinse and repeat. By the time I reached middle school and he decided he was ready to be more involved, the damage was done. Still, our relationship improved some—just in time for him to get transferred to North Carolina for his job.

It used to be that I could count on seeing him over the holidays, but that changed when I was in high school and he met and married Melanie, ten years his junior—and only eight years my senior. I get along with her fine—the fact that we're so close in age makes things both easier and more awkward—and four years ago they had their first daughter, Alexis, and recently, baby girl number two, Annabelle.

It's weird to have toddler half sisters at age twenty-seven, especially when all I'd wished for growing up was a sibling. I haven't met the new baby yet, but Alexis, the four-year-old, is adorable and I love her to pieces. Since I don't get to see them very often, I'm more like the cool aunt than a sister. Still, I do the requisite things to stay connected: gifts on birthdays and Christmas, FaceTime calls where we play virtual Barbies, polite fawning over the photos Melanie texts me. No one can say I abandon my family members.

I love my dad. I do. If anyone saw us together, they'd never guess the truth of our thorny relationship. We rarely discuss it, but it's always there, hovering like a rain cloud, felt like a phantom limb.

Our check-in goes as it usually does—I ask after my sisters and Melanie while he digs for insider details on some of the more scandalous recent headlines. He loves to talk politics, and while he leans conservative, I enjoy our debates because he's such a good sparring partner; he's one of the few who can stump me. When we say goodbye, it feels too quick.

What I don't say: *Until next month, Dad.*

★

"Sounds good. Yep, we'll talk more next week. Thanks so much, Paul."

I hang up and do a little victory dance in the middle of my office. John's tip about Senator Moreno is looking more promising by the day, resulting in a meeting next week to discuss a vote swap. *Maybe the tide is finally turning.*

"Good news?"

"Omigod!" I shriek, jumping a mile. I whirl around and see Ben lurking in my doorway like some sort of cat burglar. "You have *got* to stop just appearing out of nowhere. You could have given me a heart attack!" My heart hammers against my ribs as if to confirm my statement. "How is someone your size so stealthy, anyway?"

"I'm a gentle giant."

I almost laugh but manage to hold it in. "Why are you here? I'm not in the mood for a confrontation." I won't let anyone rain on my parade tonight.

He ducks through the door, instantly displacing all the air in the room and taking up what feels like every inch of available space. I hate that he's intimidating me in my own office.

"I was just leaving and saw your light on. How late do you usually stay?"

"Why? Planning on robbing me?"

He rolls his eyes. "Just answer the question, Katherine."

Katherine. A faint buzzing sound builds in my ear, like feedback from a broken power cable. "Am I in trouble, *Benjamin*?"

He doesn't answer, just stands there with one eyebrow cocked.

I sigh. "It depends on the night. Six, seven o'clock? Probably the same as you."

"How do you get home?"

"With my feet." I give him an *Are you an idiot?* look. "I walk."

"You walk home alone, in the dark, every night?" He sounds incredulous. "Do you at least carry a weapon? Mace? A Swiss Army knife? Anything?"

I blink at him, bewildered. *Is this some kind of joke?*

He holds up a finger. "Wait, let me guess. You'll defend yourself with your sharp tongue and cutting remarks."

"Seems to have worked well enough so far." I give him a big phony grin.

He's not amused. "Unbelievable. We live in a city with one of the highest murder rates in the nation and you walk home every night without protection." He shakes his head. "Did your father ever teach you any self-defense, at least?"

My spine stiffens. "How I get home is *none* of your business," I snap.

"It'll be my business when they're looking for someone to identify you at the morgue."

"Did I win the anti-lottery or something? It's Friday night. Can't we take weekends off from this vendetta?"

He slides his bag off his shoulder, letting it drop to the floor, then folds his arms across his chest. We swap defiant stares.

"Should I take this macho bouncer pose as a *yes*?"

"Grab your stuff. I'll walk you home."

Um, *what*? I want to laugh, but I think he's serious. "So you can off me with no witnesses? That's okay. I'm good."

"You're *not* good." His green eyes flash with frustration. Stupid luminous eyes. "Seriously, just forget everything else. It's not safe to walk home by yourself. I'm not comfortable with it."

"Well, it's a good thing you don't need to be comfortable with *my* life choices."

He sighs and tugs at his tie, loosening it until it slides off, then undoes his top collar button in a quick, practiced motion. It's such a profoundly male gesture that I pause, my outrage momentarily derailed, my vision narrowing in on the small triangle of skin visible at his neck.

I jolt when he speaks. "Don't make reckless decisions just to spite me." He's rolling his tie into a tightly coiled circle.

"I'm not doing anything to *spite* you. Geez, check your ego. And stop shedding clothing all over my office. This isn't your bedroom."

He ceases his rolling. "Do I make you nervous, Princess?"

"You make me *something*."

His mouth twitches. "I promise I won't try to jump you on the way home. Scout's honor."

Of course he's a Boy Scout. "Look, I appreciate your concern. And I'm sure there's no ulterior motive for it, like wanting to toss me down a sewer. But I've been walking home—*by myself*—for years now. And I'm just fine, thank you very much."

"Where do you live?"

"None of your business."

"How far is it?" Good Lord, he will *not* be deterred.

I'm sick of this game. I turn and grab a stack of papers off my desk and cross the room to my filing cabinet.

"Kate. How far?"

The way he says my name, my actual name, stops me. I don't think I've ever heard him use it before. "Like ten minutes. Listen, I don't need a big brother."

"Do you *have* a brother?" His voice bleeds irritation.

"Nooo." I draw it out like he is very slow indeed.

"That's too bad. Maybe if you did, he could knock some sense into you."

He's skated too close to a sore subject, and now I'm pissed. "Well, I *don't* have one, it's just me, but thank you for your *brotherly* concern. You may go now."

I lurch away from the filing cabinet and immediately trip over his deathtrap of a bag, barely catching myself on the edge of my desk before I go sprawling.

"Can you *please* move your murse?" I give it a swift kick.

"My *murse*?"

"Your man purse. God, everything about you is way too big. Your body. Your head. Your stupid bag."

He picks up right where I left off. "My brain. My capacity to prove you wrong."

"Your ego."

He holds my stare and I sigh, squeezing my eyes shut. Maybe when I open them, he'll be gone.

"Don't you have somewhere to be?" I ask, flicking my hand in a shooing motion. *Like with your wicked witch of a girlfriend.* God only knows how much frostier she'd get if she knew he was in my office, coating the place in testosterone.

He squints at me for a moment, like he's making a decision about something. Then he nods once, picking up his bag and slinging it over his shoulder.

"Well, you have a *great* weekend, Goldilocks. Hope you make it home alive. Or not. I don't care if you don't, right?"

He turns and strolls out while I glare daggers at his back. Since he can't see me, it's not very satisfying.

I pack up my things and head out a few minutes later, though I can't shake the strangeness of our encounter on my walk home. I know I shouldn't let him get to me—it's what he wants—but I can't seem to help it. He's just so . . . and he's such a pain in the . . . and he makes me want to . . . *gah.*

But underneath all the annoyance, there's something else. A nagging feeling in the back of my mind that I'm missing something. When I replay our conversation, my memory freeze-frames on the look in his eyes when he offered to walk me home. It was . . . possessive, somehow. Almost proprietary.

Weird.

Even weirder that I liked it.

Chapter 6

Ben's words pinball around in my head all weekend. Is he actually concerned about my safety, or is this just another one of his power moves? It's hard to reconcile the man-beast who's been so desperate to knock me down with the anxious worrywart who looked at me with concern in his eyes. How strange to think that Ben is capable of genuine human emotions.

I'm sure it was an aberration.

My suspicions are confirmed when I arrive at work on Monday and there's already an envelope waiting for me on my desk. I should've known a tiger couldn't change its misogynistic stripes. War: still on.

I rip it open and it's a recent story from the *Post*: SPATE OF MUG-GINGS HITS CAPITOL HILL. So we're still on that, then.

And that's only the beginning. Throughout the week, he bombards me with stories highlighting district crime statistics. Tuesday: DC LANDS ON TOP 10 MOST DANGEROUS CITIES LIST. Wednesday: a crime heat map focused on the Capitol Hill area, complete with a highlighted warning that "residents should exercise caution when out after dark." On Thursday, it's a list of local police stations, gyms, and martial arts studios offering self-defense classes. The guy is straight-up nuts.

And yet . . . am I crazy for thinking it's kind of sweet?

I'm guessing this mail is supposed to "scare me straight," but what Ben doesn't seem to realize is that he rattles me more than any mugger ever could.

★

I'm so exhausted by Friday that I barely notice the package at first.

It's been a long week, full of fire drills and petty dramas that've kept most of the staff chasing our tails. Carol hosted a town hall in New Hampshire last week, and of course some grandstanding heckler used it as his opportunity to bait her into a contentious back-and-forth—and because all the world's a stage, the moment immediately went viral. While such incidents have become commonplace in my job—I've lost count of the number of controversies I've lived through—it made for several headache-inducing days of damage control.

The one bright spot was my meeting with Senator Moreno's team, who seemed more than receptive to working with us on the child care bill in exchange for Carol's show of support on their infrastructure legislation. It's exceedingly difficult to secure allies across the aisle these days, and it's thrilling to have a glimmer of hope that my bill could one day become reality.

Nevertheless, by Friday morning I am ready to call it a week. I'm juggling my purse, workbag, coffee, and a file someone shoved at me as I walked in the door when I spot the bulging envelope sitting ominously atop my desk. This must be how celebrities feel when deranged stalker-fans stake out their house and leave dead roses on their doorstep. I orbit around it warily as I shuck my coat and various personal items, mentally running through the possibilities for its contents. Judging by the theme of this week's correspondence, it could be anything from a stack of milk cartons with children's faces on them to a set of nunchucks.

I open the envelope gingerly and when I shake out its contents, something in hard plastic packaging clatters onto my desk: a combination pepper spray–rape whistle on a key chain. The packaging promises an instant takedown of any number of dangerous predators at an eardrum-shattering volume only bats can hear. As usual, there's a note attached.

Kate,

Although I stand by my thoughts on the subject, I may have come on a bit strong last week. Consider this a peace offering. If you need to pretend it came from someone else, that works too. Either way, I'd appreciate it if you'd put it on your key ring.

If anything ever happened to you, I'm sure there's someone, somewhere, who would miss you.

When six thirty rolls around, I pick up Ben's "gift" and traverse the perimeter of the seventh floor to Senator Hammond's suite of offices. It's been a few weeks, but Ben's office number is branded on my memory like a bad tattoo.

I knock lightly. There's a beat of silence before his voice rings out. "Yes?"

Just hearing his deep baritone makes my arm hairs stand on end. *Prepare for battle.*

"It's Kate." I pause awkwardly. "Adams."

I hear rustlings inside the office. The creak of a chair. A few seconds later the door swings open and Ben's large frame fills the threshold. He looks like he's struggling not to laugh.

"Hi, Kate . . . Adams."

"Shaddap."

He opens the door wider, motioning me inside. "To what do I owe the pleasure?"

The sight of his desk chair triggers a sweat-inducing flashback to our last meeting in this office, but I shove aside my PTSD and sit. His desk is even messier than before—still covered with stacks of papers and files, but they're taller now, and there are more piles on the ground. I make a face at the chaos. How can he work like this?

"I thought I'd come by to acknowledge my receipt of this . . . *unique* gift." I hold it up as proof of his derangement.

His face lights up. "Do you need me to show you how to use it?" He motions to it with grabby hands.

"I don't think it requires a PhD."

He plucks it from my hand and cracks open the packaging. "You should play with it a little so you know how it works. You'd be surprised how you can freeze in the moment." He tosses the clamshell into a trash can underneath his desk and slides the little instructional pamphlet across the desk to me. I've never seen him so animated.

Except for when he told me I was everything wrong with women, of course. Can't forget that.

"You need to hold it while you're walking. It won't be helpful if it's buried at the bottom of your purse. Also, look around and make eye contact with people. Women who are distracted or on their phones are typically the ones targeted for muggings or . . . other things." He demonstrates, holding it in front of his chest while aggressively eyeballing invisible perpetrators.

"Has anyone ever told you you're *cra-zee*?" I whisper the last part like I'm spilling state secrets.

"You can call me whatever names you want as long as you add it to your key ring," he says, handing it back over.

"How could I not, after that *charming* note you included with it?"

He presses his lips together, suppressing a smile.

"And not that it's any of your business, but I *do* know the basics of self-defense. An instructor came to my sorority and did a whole demonstration. Walk with keys in your hand so you can jab an attacker in the eye. Don't wear a ponytail. Don't use headphones on a run. See?"

He arches a brow. "So you think those cute tips will help you fight off a guy my size?"

"I've also seen *Miss Congeniality*. I know how to SING—solar plexus, instep, nose, groin."

He shakes his head, apparently unconvinced that movie trivia can have real-world applications. How dare he thumb his nose at Sandra Bullock.

"The point is, I'm not stupid. It's a short walk, it's busy and well lit, and I've never had a problem. I'm an independent woman, and I depend on me." I'm Beyoncé now, apparently.

He groans. "I was afraid you were going to say something like that. You have a false sense of security."

I sit back and cross my legs, considering him. "Is this a trick?"

"Is *what* a trick?"

"You, pretending to care. I can't figure out what your game is." I twirl the key chain around on my finger. If I whipped it at him, it could take an eye out. It's tempting.

He leans forward, resting his elbows on the desk. "There's no game. I just take safety seriously. Especially when it comes to stubborn women who insist on ignoring the very real risks they're taking."

"You know, the only person I'm tempted to use this on is *you*."

He pauses. "That's probably fair."

That's probably fair?

"See, you're not doing much to convince me this isn't a trick. Did you hire someone to jump out at me on my way home or something? Give me some warning so I don't wet my pants, at least."

He laughs, shifting in his seat. "There's no trick, I promise. But I do owe you an apology."

I nearly fall out of the chair. "Say what? Come again?"

His cocksure smile suddenly looks a little . . . nervous. "I owe you an apology, Kate. You're right, I was an asshole to you at our meeting. Working on this tax plan has been . . . challenging, let's just put it that way. I haven't been myself. It was a bad day, and the stress got to me."

He rakes a hand through his hair, closing his eyes as he massages the back of his neck. When he opens them again, his hair is thoroughly mussed, with sections sticking up at all angles. It looks hilarious and disheveled and . . . kinda hot, actually. Like sexy bedhead. I mentally slap myself for the errant thought.

"I promise, I'm usually a nice person. People like me."

"Are you kind of a big deal?"

"Absolutely. I'm *very* busy and important." He holds my gaze until we both start laughing. "Anyway, it's not an excuse, just an explanation. I'm sorry I took my stress out on you."

His genuine regret takes the wind out of my sails. I didn't think he was capable of self-reflection or remorse, let alone an apology. It's destabilizing—I marched into the lion's den and instead encountered a declawed kitten. In the silence that follows, I find myself growing uncomfortable, unsure how to behave around him without guns blazing.

I eye him guardedly. "What brought on this crisis of conscience?"

"Maybe I just want to make sure you'll put that on your key ring."

"So is that *all* you're sorry for?" I'm not letting him off the hook that easily.

"What do you mean? I think I've been pretty well behaved otherwise." He raises one eyebrow, then the other, alternating back and forth. I wish I could do that. When I try, I look like I'm having a seizure.

"Belittling my work? Calling me names? You sorry for any of that?"

"What? No way. Getting under your skin is the most fun I've had in years."

I blink in surprise as Ben grins at me from across the desk. I can't quite decide if I've just been complimented or insulted, but there's something so contagious about his smile that I find myself grinning back.

I clear my throat. "So does this mean we're *friends* now? Or what?"

"Or what, I think." His wink tells me he's kidding.

I'm overheating again. Something about this office makes me sweaty. It's stuffy and small and way too full of him.

"Well, anyway, thanks for this." I hold up the key chain and move to get up, avoiding his eyes. "I'm feeling safer already."

"Or you could just let me walk you," Ben says casually. "The offer still stands."

My heart jumps. "Oh no, you—I mean, I don't . . ." *Speak words, Kate.* "I actually have plans tonight. Going out with some girls from the office. Well, some girls and Stephen," I amend.

It's not a lie—I actually do have plans tonight. It's one of the girls' birthdays and we're taking her out for drinks. While I'd usually beg off—screaming over loud music is something I was happy to leave behind in college—I've decided it's time to start putting myself out there more. I'm hardly going to meet Mr. Right if I'm home watching last night's Shondathon.

"Ah. Well, have fun." The way he's eyeing me is so strange, but he sounds sincere at least.

I start to stand, then pause again. "Okay, can I just say one thing? You need to deal with this mess," I say, motioning to his desk. "No wonder you're stressed-out—these piles could drive the Dalai Lama to a psychotic break."

"I find other ways to relieve stress." His eyes on mine are so green and intense, I get flustered and have to look away.

"H-how's that?" *Smooth, Kate.* Stammering like a teenager. I may as well be wearing a neon sign that says, I'M THINKING DIRTY THOUGHTS.

He eyes me strangely. "Running."

"Running?"

"I run the Mall on weekends," Ben says, turning back to his computer and tapping a few keys. "If you'd like to take a rematch to the streets."

Wait, is he *inviting* me to run with him now? I'm getting whiplash from all the twists and turns of this conversation. I respond the only way I know how—with snark.

"Oh, you like being embarrassed? I'll see if I can rustle up an audience this time."

"I start at nine at the Capitol. Don't oversleep, Goldilocks."

I narrow my eyes at the nickname and his lips twitch. Now that I know he's just trying to get a rise out of me, though, I won't give him the satisfaction. "I'll think about it."

As I turn to leave, the AC kicks on and his blinds flutter at the window. I glance over, and something about the way his eyes track mine hot-wires my brain and I pause midstep. My intuition coaxes me—*pay attention*—and when he subtly straightens in his chair, I *know.*

Could it be? All this time, I've never stopped to think about what Ben's looking out on. I cross to the window and yank open his blinds.

I'm looking directly into my own office.

My window is less than fifty yards from his, my blinds wide open as if to say, *Come have a look!* I can see everything: my jacket hanging on the back of the chair; my FEMINISTS ARE THE MAJORITY poster propped against the window; the STOP THE DRILLING Capstone Pipeline bumper sticker tacked up on my bulletin board. I can even make out the brand of my water bottle from here. How long has he been watching me?

"You are *kidding* me." It comes out in a strangled gasp.

"Took you long enough to figure it out."

"How would I have figured it out? Your blinds are closed!" I slap my hand so hard against the glass, I'm surprised it doesn't shatter.

"All the better to spy on you."

I whirl around and he's chuckling. "This is how you've known what to send me." It's all falling into place. I'm such an *idiot*. "I thought you'd bugged my office. I accused Stephen of being a mole!"

"You've been watching too much TV. The answer was always right under your nose."

I point at him. "You're a *cheater*."

He raises his hands in the air. "I did *not* cheat. Can I help it that I'm more skilled in psychological warfare? We all must utilize our God-given talents."

"You're worse than a cheater. You're a peeping Tom. A peeping *Ben*!"

If possible, his smile grows wider. "I haven't seen you changing your clothes, but do me a favor and give me a heads-up if you're going to."

I growl and smack his blinds open the rest of the way. They hit the wall with a satisfying *thwack*. "You're a pervert *and* a cheater. These are staying open from now on."

"Thanks, I've been dying to let a little light in."

I shoot him a death glare as I spin on my heel and yank open his door.

"Nine a.m. sharp, Goldilocks!" Ben calls out behind me. "I wait for no man! Or woman!"

I flip him the bird.

Chapter 7

I spend the night tossing and turning, trying to decide if Ben's covert activities provide just cause for standing him up—but when Saturday morning dawns uncharacteristically warm and sunny, I decide the universe must be trying to tell me something. Once I don leggings, a tank, and my Apple watch to track my run, I'm out the door.

The route Ben mentioned, the National Mall loop, spans about four miles of prime DC real estate: the Capitol Building down to the Lincoln Memorial and back up the other side, encompassing such iconic landmarks as the Washington Monument, the World War II Memorial, and a handful of Smithsonian museums. It's a popular route for locals and beautifully scenic, especially in April when the cherry blossoms bloom.

When I arrive at the Capitol just before nine, I spot Ben immediately, stretching by the large, currently bone-dry fountain out front. I'm able to observe him for a moment undetected and the thought that springs to mind is: *different*. I can't pinpoint it exactly, but something about his easy, relaxed demeanor, the alternate environment, or maybe just the shedding of his suit feels intimidating in a new, more personal way.

He waves when he sees me approaching and I relax a little; I'd wondered if he might regret his impulsive invitation in the light of day. I'm still not sure what to think about him—are we friends or frenemies? I'm used to needing body armor in his presence, but last night, he'd been almost . . . nice? I wonder which Ben I'll get today.

"You made it, Goldilocks. Was your sleep just right?"

In one sentence, my question is answered.

"I couldn't resist the idea of beating you twice."

He grins. "Easy, tiger. We're out of the office—how about we drop our weapons for today? Just two people out for a run on a beautiful March day. What do you say?"

I shrug my assent and we set off at an easy pace, both of us quiet and getting our bearings in this unfamiliar territory outside the office. We're not the only ones out enjoying the weather—as we jog we're dodging other runners, bikers, strollers, and leashed dogs, but I don't mind. The rare sun has everyone out to play, pasty legs be damned.

He breaks the silence first. "So how was your big night out last night?"

I make a face. "It was all right."

Truth be told, it was pretty lame. Although I was part of Operation: Score Hot Men (Stephen's working title), I spent the majority of my time talking to . . . Stephen. Not exactly a night that will make it onto my Insta stories. "How about you?"

"Watched the Caps game and fell asleep, so I'd say my night was a winner." He nods at my watch. "What's your pace?"

"Let me check." I glance at my watch. "Well, look at that, it's none of your business."

He rolls his eyes. "If you're so worried about me beating you, let's sync our watches. Then we'll know for sure who's faster. Think about it, we could compete all day long. Who takes more steps. Who climbs more stairs. Who burns more calories."

I eye him suspiciously. "What other information does it share?"

"Not much, just your social security number. Bank account info. All the notes you've written about me in your diary."

"Should be fascinating reading for you."

His eyes spark. "Tell me more."

"I can't. You'd end up sobbing in the corner."

He turns the full spotlight of his smile on me and I can't help but smile back. Am I actually having *fun*? Running with Ben is like a dual workout—one for the body and one for the mind.

"That's all right. If you're too intimidated by me, I totally get why." He lifts his shirtsleeve and flexes his biceps in my face. "Do you know where the weight room is?"

I catch a whiff of his skin, that enticing musk-spice mixture of *sweat* and *male*. My body hums to life like rusty machinery.

"Quoting *Tommy Boy*, huh? How original."

He casts me a rare look of approval. "Look at that, you've surprised me. The Princess knows her comedies."

"I was an only child. I watched a lot of TV," I say dismissively, though I'm reminded of something I've been wondering. "Where did you go to school?"

"University of Virginia. And you, a Chapel Hill grad. Are you as basketball obsessed as everyone who goes there?"

I nearly trip over my own feet. "How do you know where I went to school?"

"There's this little thing called the internet? Social media? Maybe you've heard of it. A rather useful tool when you're trying to gather in- criminating information on your opponent."

How is it possible I didn't think of this? I am the world's worst spy. "So you Facebook-stalked me? Guess my friend request must have got- ten lost in the mail."

"I know, it's so weird how Mark Zuckerberg hasn't incorporated enemy requests yet. Such a missed opportunity."

I shake my head, mildly disturbed that he has this information advantage over me.

"So what made you choose North Carolina?" he inquires as we pass by the golden dome of the Museum of Natural History.

There's a lot of dysfunction wrapped up in that answer, so I give him the sanitized version. "I wanted to get away from Tennessee, try something new."

"Overbearing parents?"

"Not really," I hedge. "I just wanted to start somewhere with a clean slate. I loved all the games, the social scene. My sorority."

He makes a face.

"What, you have something against the Greek system? I would have bet money you were a frat guy. Cocky and obnoxious. Cargo shorts and popped collars. Keg stands." I peek over at him. "You're very fratty."

He looks offended. "Uh, no."

Huh. "That surprises me. UVA is such a big Greek school."

"I'm a nonconformist. Groupthink doesn't interest me."

I bark a laugh. "Says the Republican."

"I think for myself."

"*Sure* you do."

There's a break in conversation as we weave our way through a cluster of backpacked teenagers, and for the first time, it occurs to me how evenly matched Ben and I are. Both athletes, from the South, went to East Coast schools, doing similar jobs. I'm sure if we'd met under any other circumstances, we would have gotten along swimmingly. It's too bad he works for the wrong side.

"Don't you think it's weird we never met before?" I muse aloud once we clear the crowd. "It's not like you're easy to miss."

"I'm sure if we'd met, you never would have given me the time of day. Since I'm the enemy and all." There's something funny in his voice. He must still be bent out of shape about my elevator rant.

"Oh, please. I'm very tolerant and open-minded, especially when it comes to misguided folks like yourself."

"*Right*. So open-minded, you seek out Democrats-only dating sites."

"I did *not* seek out . . ." I heave a sigh. *Forget it.* "Whatever. We all have our deal breakers."

"*You* might have deal breakers, but I have . . . sort of a reverse list. Criteria I'm looking for in a woman."

"Oh, I cannot *wait* to hear this." I wonder how Corinne fares on this "ideal woman" list. "Wait, let me guess. She's tall and thin with double Ds. She stays home and does your laundry. Doesn't talk back."

He ignores me. "She has to be smarter than me."

I can't resist. "Smarter than *I am*, you mean?"

"Looking to throw your hat in the ring?"

His smirk tells me he set me up on that one. Damn it, I have to stop underestimating him. Those muscles are a smoke screen.

I groan inwardly. "All right, what else?"

"Mostly the things you'd expect: she has to want kids, should like to travel, have a good sense of humor, should enjoy active pursuits." He coughs. "You know, like running."

I give him the side-eye. "And I'm sure she'll be a conservative," I add, thinking of Corinne again.

"Empirical data would suggest," he concurs. "Then there are sillier ones like . . ." He thinks for a second, then snaps his fingers. "She has to love queso. That's a big one. Friday night with my girl, a margarita, and some queso. Sounds like a dream, doesn't it?"

"Queso? As in *cheese*? That ranks as most important on your 'ideal woman' list?"

"Nah, not the *most* important. That's only for me to know." He taps his temple, something unidentifiable hooding his eyes. It's gone in a blink. "But queso's right up there."

Before I have a chance to delve further into this absurdity, my watch vibrates with an incoming FaceTime call. I tap Ben's elbow to let him know I'm stopping, then unzip the hidden pocket on my leggings and pull out my phone.

He looks bewildered. "Where on earth did your phone just come from?"

"It would be very unsafe for me to go running without my phone, Ben. I'm surprised you wouldn't know that." He makes a face as I shush him. "This'll just take a second. My mom demands that we FaceTime every weekend, and if I don't answer, she'll assume I'm dead in a ditch."

"Ah, so she must be aware of how you get home at night."

I shoot him a dirty look as I answer. "Hi, Mama!"

"Katie Cat! Where are you? Show me on the screen!"

"Katie Cat!" Ben hoots behind me. *Great.*

"I'm out for a run on the Mall." I flip the camera and rotate slowly to give her a panoramic view.

"It's so beautiful," she says wistfully. "You're so lucky to live in such a gorgeous place. All that history!"

I shake my head, laughing—she says this every time we talk. I flip the camera back toward me, and with no warning, Ben crowds onto the screen, jamming his head on top of my shoulder.

"Mrs. Adams? How *lovely* to meet you. Wait, you're Kate's *mother*? You could be her sister." *If only he knew.*

My mom laughs merrily, thankfully choosing not to enlighten him about the less-than-savory details of my birth. "Well, who is this? And please, call me Beverly. Or Bev!" Then she giggles. Actually *giggles*.

I wrench the phone away. "That's just Ben." I struggle to explain him, my mind cycling through the possibilities: *He's my colleague. My archenemy. The Incredible Hulk. The bane of my existence.*

"He's my running buddy," I finally tell her. I see his features pinch in irritation out of the corner of my eye.

My mom raises an eyebrow. "A *running* buddy? Well, I'm so sorry to interrupt." Her exaggerated wink could induce facial paralysis.

"Mom, *stop*. You're not interrupting." Ben smirks in my peripheral vision, and I swing the other way so I can't see his smug mug. "Can I call you when I get home?"

"Sure, honey. I wanted to confirm some times with you before I book my ticket, but just call me later. Have fun on your run and be safe. It was nice to meet you, Ben!" she calls out, her voice teeming with pathetic hopefulness. She's about as subtle as a freight train.

Ben presses his face back into the nook of my neck. "It was nice to meet you too, Bev. And don't worry about Katie Cat. I'm keeping a *very* close eye on her."

He's cackling as I hang up.

"Boy, am I glad I overheard that. Katie Cat is so much better than Princess. And think of all the iterations: Kitty Cat, Scaredy Cat, Kitten, Purrrrrincess—"

I take off running while he's still midsentence. My watch dings with a text a minute later.

Mom: How have you not mentioned this guy?? He's so cute!

★

We make a pit stop at the Lincoln Memorial water fountains, and while I'm catching my breath Ben launches into a circuit of superhuman calisthenics: running the stairs, lunges and squats, then sit-ups and push-ups—the impressive kind, with clapping in between. If I tried to do it I'd probably fracture my face, but he makes it look easy, setting a break-neck pace. He's clearly in better shape than I am. Yet another reason to hate him.

I do some stretching of my own, but once I'm done there's not much for me to do besides stand there and wait for him to finish. As he completes his jumping jacks with military precision, my gaze zeroes in on the sliver of stomach revealing itself on every up-clap: ripped abs, flat belly, tan skin, the lightest smattering of dark hair at his navel.

Holy smokeshow.

He abruptly stops jumping and I hastily avert my eyes—but not before he catches me.

His smile is a slow build. "See something you like?"

"Just thinking it's amazing what steroids can do."

"No muscles on your Donkey Dates, then?" He tsks. "Damn shame."

"Keep that up and you'll be swimming in the Reflecting Pool."

"If you want me in a wet T-shirt, all you have to do is ask."

"Pass."

He's chuckling as he approaches me. "Aren't you worried you might be missing out on something?"

I arch an eyebrow. "Missing out?"

"By writing off half the male population."

I laugh, dry and caustic. "I *know* I'm not missing anything. Unless intolerance, small-mindedne—"

The words die on my lips as Ben takes another step toward me, so close I have to tip my head back to look up at him. This is an invasion of my personal space. *What is he doing?*

"You're sure about that?"

He's standing way too close—like arms-brushing-against-mine close. I'm reminded of middle school dances: *Leave enough space between you for the Holy Spirit.* Ben is flouting the Almighty.

"You don't think you could *ever* be attracted to someone on the other side?"

Ah. I see what he's up to now.

I should step back. I should slap him, frankly. But a larger part of me wants to see where he's going to take this—or maybe, *how far* he's going to take this.

"I was thinking you might want to . . ." He trails off, his voice dropping in both tone and volume, as he leans in further.

I should definitely take a step back now. Make a joke—*ha-ha, nice try, you've made your point*—but it suddenly feels very important, very *necessary*, to stand my ground. Beat him at his own game.

"Want to what?" I ask brazenly, meeting his gaze head-on. My voice sounds funny now too, hoarse and a little thready.

His eyes flare slightly at my boldness, a flash of approval lighting his features. Like he's proud of me for meeting him halfway. Like it was a test and I passed.

And that knowledge pleases me way more than it should.

"Want to . . ."

He drops his mouth to my ear, and his breath on my neck gives rise to a fine layer of goose bumps entirely out of place in this warm sun. I turn my head and the slight movement brings our faces in line, our mouths mere inches from each other. Seconds tick by as we stare at each other in a charged deadlock. *Who will break first?*

"Want to . . . race me to the Washington Monument. Go!" he yells suddenly and takes off at a sprint, and I nearly reel backward from the sudden loss of him.

Whoa.

Ben takes advantage of his head start, widening his lead as I trail slowly behind, wondering what the hell just happened.

What I don't let myself wonder is why I'm already short of breath when I've barely started running.

Chapter 8

It's been several days since our close encounter on the Mall and I haven't run into Ben once—but that doesn't mean I haven't seen him. *Oh, have I seen him.*

Per my "request," he's left his blinds open and it is absolutely unhealthy how much I've enjoyed watching him. Not that I'll let him catch me stalking—I've perfected the one-eye-on-my-computer, one-eye-on-the-window maneuver—but I think he must know I'm surveilling him because he propped a massive TAX REFORM sign in his window. I'm certain it's for my benefit.

My round-the-clock stakeout has netted me some nifty intel. He paces when he's on the phone, so much so that watching him circuit his office makes me dizzy. His typing posture is so deplorable, I'm surprised he's not a hunchback. He fiddles with his tie constantly. He drinks from one of those refillable water bottles all day long, and each time he takes a swig and wipes his mouth, my throat goes dry. Once when he was on the phone he smiled a lot, which simultaneously pleased and annoyed me. He never looks my way—or at least, I've never caught him.

I know he was just messing with me on our run, trying to prove a point, but that hasn't stopped me from obsessing over his actions and my reactions—or rather, my *lack* of a reaction. Why did I just stand there like a pillar of salt? I should have kneed him in the groin. And the worst part is, he knows he rattled me—when I finally caught up to him, I was monosyllabic for the remainder of our run. I blamed a lack of oxygen, but there's no way he was fooled.

I can't let him gain the upper hand like that again. The only problem is, my body's not getting the memo my brain is sending. Each time I leave my office or approach an elevator, a frisson of anticipation zaps through my body like the current from a lightning strike. I'm sixteen again, an obsessive schoolgirl tracking her crush in the hallways. I've wracked my brain, trying to recall the bits and pieces of his schedule I know, but the thing I can't figure out is if I'm trying to run into him or avoid him. I wonder how he'd react if he knew I was mentally mapping his route like Magellan.

I'm currently hotfooting it over to Union Pub for a happy hour in honor of Tessa and Luke, who—surprise!—got engaged over the weekend. When I walk in, it's wall-to-wall humanity, packed as ever with the postwork Capitol Hill crowd. Suit jackets have been cast off and sleeves rolled up, bottles of beer in hand while classic rock blasts from the speakers. I scan the room and spot Tessa immediately, standing in the center of a group and showing off her ring.

Once I wrestle my way through the crush of bodies and greet her, I glance around. "Where's Luke?"

"Fighting the masses at the bar." She waves a hand in that general direction and I feel a pang of self-pity. How nice to have someone to slay the proverbial dragon for you in pursuit of a cocktail.

Tessa sees my expression and whips out her phone. "What do you want? I'll text him."

"A glass of chardonnay would be great," I say in relief. "Whatever they have."

She types furiously, then slides the phone back into her pocket. "I hope he sees it," she mutters, then taps the girl standing next to her on the shoulder. "Kate, have you met . . ." and I'm lost in a sea of introductions to some of their friends.

I'm in the midst of an animated conversation with one of Luke's coworkers when Tessa jabs an elbow into my side.

"Ow, what?"

"Two o'clock," she murmurs in a low voice, nodding in the direction of the entrance.

When I turn to see what she's talking about, my eyes land on a familiar figure: Ben's just walked in, flanked by a tall guy with sandy blond hair and California surfer-guy good looks. My pulse breaks into a canter and I immediately feel self-conscious, like I'm wearing my underwear outside my clothes or something. Before I can analyze my reaction, Luke appears, juggling two drinks in each hand. We greet him like a hero freshly returned from the front lines.

"Thanks, Luke," I say gratefully, then hold up the glass in a toast. "And congratulations! I'm so happy for you guys."

"Thanks." He turns to Tessa and pecks her on the lips. "Just glad she said yes." They beam at each other and I feel another pang. *Jealousy is unbecoming,* I remind myself.

Tessa's eyes are trained over my shoulder. "He's looking over here," she hisses.

"Who's looking over here?" Luke asks, sipping his beer.

"Oh, this awful guy from work who's been harassing Kate just walked in."

I open my mouth to protest, not wanting to endorse this not-exactly-accurate version of events, especially when we're *kinda-sorta, I don't know, maybe?* friends now. Maybe it wasn't my best idea to bring the whole office into this feud.

"Do you need me to kick his ass for you, Kate?"

"Oh—no." I laugh. *Good luck trying, Luke—you're like half his size.* "It's fine. It's not that big a deal, really. It's pretty much blown over, anyway."

Luke puffs out his chest. "Who is he? Point him out."

"Don't be obvious, but he's over by the door. Big guy with the blond friend."

Luke casually turns to scan the room, and when he turns back, he looks uneasy. "Are you talking about Ben Mackenzie?"

"You know him?"

"Uh, yeah. Also, I invited him."

"What?" Tessa and I say at the same time.

"He's on my kickball team. You know, Ball on the Mall?"

Tessa stares at him. *"That's* the Ben you have a man-crush on?"

"I do not have *man*-crush," Luke says, insulted. "He's just . . . a cool guy." He waves Ben over, ignoring the dark look Tessa's casting his way.

"Do not *wave*—" she says, then sighs and turns to me. "I'm sorry, I had no idea this was the same Ben. Luke has all these random kickball friends, I can't even keep tra—"

"Luke!" Ben's voice booms behind us and I jump, nearly dropping my wineglass. "Congratulations, man."

He slaps Luke on the back as Luke motions to Tessa. "Ben, this is my fiancée, Tessa."

"We've met," she says coolly, and Luke elbows her.

"It's great to see you again, Tessa," Ben says, humor ringing in his tone. He finally turns and acknowledges me, feigning surprise. "Kate! Fancy meeting you here."

"Ben," I say dryly.

His friend reaches a hand out to Tessa, then Luke. "Hi, I'm Marcus, Ben's colleague and party crasher looking for a happy hour. Congratulations on your engagement." He flashes me a wide, easygoing grin. "Hi, I'm Marcus."

"Kate," I respond, shaking his hand.

"Kate?" He squints, tightening his grip on my hand. "Wait, are you *the* Kate? The one who's been giving my friend here such a hard time?"

My jaw drops, and I swivel my head to Ben. "I'm sorry, I've been giving *you* a hard time? What kind of lies are you spreading?"

Marcus's face lights up. "Well, this just got more interesting. Kate, I'd *love* to hear your side."

"Why don't you let me know what he's told you, and I'll figure out what to debunk first?"

Marcus grins while Ben stands there looking unamused. Tessa and Luke are following the exchange with interest, heads bobbing back and forth like Ping-Pong balls.

"He wouldn't have told me anything at all, but I just happened to be one of the people in attendance at a meeting where he opened his mail and a *tampon* fell out."

I've just taken a sip of my wine, and the spit-take that results is one for the ages. I'm laughing-slash-choking, and Marcus makes a big show of thumping me on the back.

"*Please* tell me more," I beg once I can breathe normally again. "Don't leave anything out."

"I'll never forget the look on Mack's face. Fucking priceless."

Ben reaches a big hand out and shoves Marcus into the crowd. "Why don't you get us a couple of drinks, Marcus?"

I step between them. "Why don't you get the drinks, *Mack*? It sounds like Marcus has some interesting stories to share." I scoot closer to Marcus and flash him a megawatt smile. "You were saying?"

"You're famous around our office," he confides, clearly relishing the opportunity to push Ben's buttons. I think I'm enjoying it more.

"Famous? *Moi?*" I parrot, glancing over my shoulder at Ben. He's looking a little green around the gills.

"You got him all worked up, and that's not easy to do. Plus, it's nice to finally meet a woman who's immune to his charms."

"*Charms?* Who is this charming person you speak of?" We both simultaneously turn and look at Ben. He's scowling.

I hold my hand out like Vanna White. "I rest my case."

"The way he described your reign of terror, I expected a real shrew. I see he left just a few details out." He smirks at Ben. "All of a sudden your mood lately is making a lot more sense."

Ben fixes him with a look that's cold enough to freeze ice, which Marcus expressly ignores. Eventually Ben sighs and shrugs off his jacket, tossing it on a nearby table, then grabs and loosens his tie. I flush as I recall how many times I've watched him perform this same routine from my office this week. How strange that I'm starting to recognize his habits.

Marcus turns to me, a glint in his eye. "So, Kate. Are you single?"

Ben groans. "This isn't Tinder, Marcus."

I sense violence afoot, so I break in. "If I may be so bold as to infer the point of your question, I'll just let you know that I don't date Republicans. That's a hard no for me." I'm looking at Marcus, but deep down I know I'm directing it at Ben.

But apparently my statement isn't the deterrent I expected, because Marcus's eyes spark in challenge. "Did you hear that, Ben? She doesn't date Republicans."

"Yes, it's a real loss for us," he says wryly.

Marcus narrows his eyes almost imperceptibly, an unspoken conversation passing between them in the span of about five seconds. Eventually he blinks and turns back to me.

"Well, Kate, *I* think you'd be worth disaffiliating for." He gives me a panty-dropping smile that I'm sure works for him ninety-nine percent of the time.

Unfortunately for him, I'm the one percent. "That's quite a pickup line, especially in this town." I pretend-swoon and punch him lightly on the arm, and I watch Ben's eyes follow my hand. "Does it ever work?"

"You tell me," he says, laughing. Where are all these alpha males coming from? There must be something in the water over at Hammond's office.

"So if this guy doesn't do it for you," Marcus continues, jerking his thumb at Ben, "who is your type, then? Blonds, maybe?"

"I don't know," I hedge, enjoying the opportunity to mess with him *and* Ben simultaneously. "It's always felt a little too Barbie and Ken for my taste."

"But for me you'd make an exception?" He wags his brows.

I giggle. "You're fun."

"Thanks, I try."

Ben clears his throat, and when I glance at him, he's folding his arms across his chest, mouth set in a firm line. I lean toward Marcus conspiratorially.

"I think we're pissing him off. He's doing his angry bouncer pose again."

Marcus hoots, then throws me a wink before turning and clapping Ben on the shoulder. "I think I owe you a beer, buddy. Kate, if you'll excuse me. It has been an absolute delight to finally meet you."

Ben glares at his back as he disappears into the crowd, then turns to me. "Please ignore everything he said. He's just trying to fuck with me."

"And clearly he's quite good at it. So, I'm famous, huh? What exactly have you told people?"

He sighs heavily and shakes his head, scanning the bar over my head and looking everywhere but at me. I let my question hang in the air for a moment, but he looks so agitated I decide to cut him a break. "Relax, you're famous around my office too, so we're even."

"I am?"

"Maybe I'm letting the cat out of the bag here, but just about everything I send you is a team effort."

"Really?" He looks surprised. And pleased.

"Really. Not the tampon," I clarify with a grin. "That was all me. But everything else, yeah. It takes a village to keep up with you."

I'm sure I'll regret feeding his ego like this. I think of a sign at the zoo: DON'T FEED THE ANIMALS.

I nod in the direction of the bar. "So how long have you and Marcus been friends?"

"Who says we're friends? I'm his *boss*."

"Only true friends throw each other under the bus like that."

"*Friend* is such a strong word."

When I laugh, he relaxes a little. "Five years. Minus the last five minutes. I brought him over with me from the Ways and Means Committee when I got the job with Hammond."

As if he can hear us talking about him, Marcus shows up, shoves a beer into Ben's hand with a "Here you go, Mack," then keeps right on walking. *Smart man.*

"Mack," I echo, trying that nickname on for size. *Nah.* Too nice.

With no warning, the crowd at my back surges and I'm shoved violently into Ben's chest. Wine goes flying, soaking my sleeve to the elbow. Ben grabs my arm with one hand and my glass in the other, steadying me with a firm grip. The guy has serious catlike reflexes.

"You okay?" His eyes search my face with concern and I feel it heat.

"I'm okay. My shirt is not." I wince and shake out my arm.

"Let's get out of traffic."

He tugs me toward a back wall, grabbing some napkins from a nearby table along the way and passing them to me. I swipe at my sleeve uselessly and he hands back my glass when I give up.

"You've got a little . . ." he says, pointing, and then his hand is coming toward my neck. My heart does a little flip-flop as he gently disentangles a few strands of hair from my necklace, a cross made of tiny pearls hanging on a gold chain. It's a hand-me-down from my grandmother, and one of my most prized possessions.

For such a huge guy, he sure has a soft touch. Perhaps I was wrong to call him an oaf. "Thanks," I murmur.

He nods and leans a shoulder against the wall, holding his beer in front of him like a shield. "This is different," he says, motioning to my hair.

I twist it around my wrist self-consciously. "After-Hours Kate lets her hair down," I say defensively. I'm not in the mood for any *Legally Blonde* jokes tonight.

He makes a little humming noise in his throat, then waves at someone over my head. I twist around to see who, but it could be any one of a hundred people.

"How do you *know* everyone? I never would have expected to see you here. Luke and Tessa don't seem like your type of crowd." The unspoken insinuation: they're both Democrats.

He rolls his eyes heavenward. "I don't choose my friends based on party affiliation. Unlike some people I know."

"Everyone seems to think you're so nice. You've really got them all fooled."

"I *am* nice."

"I guess that means you're only mean to me, then," I muse. "Everyone else gets Dr. Jekyll and I get Mr. Hyde."

"Maybe you're the only one getting the real me." He winks one eye and then the other, back and forth a few times. I have *got* to figure out how to do that.

"God help me. Well, don't let me hold you back." I motion over my shoulder to his friends. "Feel free to go mingle with your kind."

He looks amused. "Nah, I'm happy right here."

"You live to torture me."

"Maybe." He smiles, a small one, like he's keeping a secret. "But I did realize something the other day."

"What's that?"

His eyes catch and hold mine. "I'd rather argue with you than get along with anyone else."

Chapter 9

I blink at him as a ball of heat forms in my stomach and sweeps up my rib cage, blooms into my chest cavity, and steals my breath. What he said—no, the *way* he said it—feels superior to any compliment I've ever gotten. I want to hug it to my chest. Tattoo it on my skin. Brand it on my memory.

I breathe out, with effort. "You're quite an enigma, Ben Mackenzie."

"How so?"

"I can't decide if you like me or hate me."

He opens his mouth, then closes it. He seems as caught off guard by that bit of honesty as I am.

"Sometimes I can't figure it out either, Princess." He rubs a hand over his mouth like he's trying to wipe away a smile. "I'm hungry. You hungry?"

Changing the subject. Good idea.

"Starving, actually," I admit.

"I'll go order us something. If I'm not back in ten minutes, just wait longer." He squeezes my shoulder before heading over to the bar.

I *cannot* figure this guy out.

But I don't get too long to think about it because as soon as he's gone

Tessa corners me, forcing me into a chair at one of the tables our group has commandeered.

She levels me with a pointed stare. "What are you doing?"

"What do you mean?"

"I thought you hated this guy. What happened to your feud?"

I sip my wine, taking my time answering. "I guess technically it still exists, but we called a truce."

"That didn't look like feuding. It looked like flirting."

I sigh and set my glass down. "We were just talking, that's all."

"Are you into this guy? Tell me the truth." Her brown eyes are sharp on mine.

"Tessa, *no*. No." I add a third one for good measure. "Nope."

She narrows her eyes. Apparently denials in triplicate are unconvincing. "He's been *awful* to you."

I squirm in my seat. I feel like I'm under cross-examination. "He *was* awful, at first. But he apologized, and I accepted it."

She looks unimpressed.

"Look, I don't need to make enemies of the people I'm supposed to be working with. It's unprofessional, and it certainly isn't going to help me get this bill passed. It was time to bury the hatchet."

As I state my case, I track Ben out of the corner of my eye. He's chatting with a couple of women as he waits to order food, and they're hanging on his every word, preening and tossing their hair, laughing too hard at his (likely subpar) jokes. I roll my eyes; the mating call of females is so transparent. When I swing my gaze back to Tessa, she's watching me intently.

"See? He's over there picking up chicks right now. Plus, I think he's dating that girl we saw him with in the elevator." I flash back to Corinne's cryptic *among other things* comment and shudder.

Tessa sits back and folds her arms. "I feel the need to remind you of what happened to Shannon."

I groan. "I don't need to hear about Shannon."

She continues like I haven't spoken. "She started dating that guy in Representative Stark's office even though we all knew it was a bad idea. 'He's different,' she said. 'It'll be fine,' she said. And what happened to her?"

"She got fired," I answer dutifully.

"Fired for leaking him confidential information! And what happened to *him*?"

"Nothing."

She pounds her fist on the table. "Nothing! And after all that, did their relationship even work out?"

"It did not."

"No! He cheated on her with some intern from Stark's reelection campaign. Meanwhile, her career has never recovered." She leans back again, her expression troubled. "You need to be careful."

I laugh, but there's an edge to it. "I can see you're trying to protect me and I appreciate that, but there's no need. Ben is just a work colleague. It is purely a business relationship. In fact, it's not even that, since he's made it crystal clear that his boss will never support our bill."

Her eyes soften as she leans in, placing a hand over mine. "I'm sorry if I'm being harsh. And trust me, I get what you'd see in him, okay? I have eyes. It's just, I know the kind of guy you're looking for. You want something long-term, like what Luke and I have. And I want that *for* you."

"I know you do." I think I know what'll get her off my back. "How about this. To prove I'm *not* into Ben, I will let you set up a profile for me on Donk—on LeftField."

She gasps. "You will?" She clutches my arm, Ben all but forgotten. "Yay! I think it'll be *so* great for you, Kate. I'll help you screen the guys. I'll find you someone *amazing*!"

By the time Ben makes it back ten minutes later, I'm pretty subdued. When he slides me a fresh glass of wine across the table, I can't hide my surprise.

"Thank you," I say, meaning it. Maybe there's hope for him yet.

I listen quietly as Ben and Luke swap stories of life on the field or diamond or whatever the heck Ball on the Mall is referring to—frankly, it sounds less like a sporting event and more like one long argument over who has the best team name: Nasty Pitches versus Fake Boos versus Master Debaters. When our food arrives—wings, nachos, and sliders—a collective cheer goes up from the group, and Ben and I swap nonplussed looks. So much for our dinner.

As we listen to Luke and Tessa perform an elaborate retelling of their engagement story, one of the women Ben was chatting with at the bar sidles up, smiling flirtatiously as she slips him a piece of paper. He smiles back politely as he slides it into his pocket without looking at it.

Seriously?

He catches me watching and smirks. I wrinkle my nose in distaste.

As soon as everyone breaks into side conversations, I nod at him. "Aren't you going to see what it says?"

"I already know what it says." He loads up a nacho and one-bites it.

"So are you gonna call her?" *See, Tessa? I can prove I'm not interested.*

He shrugs.

"What, does she not like queso?"

He smiles faintly. "She has to be my best friend. She wasn't a best-friend type."

"How would you know that from talking to her for five minutes?"

"It only took you two minutes to know everything there was to know about me."

I groan. "Let it go, already. Geez."

He chuckles as he tips his head back to swig his beer.

"You know, you're awfully picky," I point out, selecting an extra-cheesy nacho. "You sure this perfect match exists?"

"Oh, she exists." His smile looks a little forced.

"How can you be so sure?"

"The perfect girl for me is out there, trust me. Compatibility isn't an exact science."

"Is *compatible* code for *submissive*? You want some hood ornament who agrees with everything you say? *Snooze*."

"That's pretty rich coming from someone who refuses to date outside their political party."

That raises my hackles. "I don't see *you* dating across the aisle."

He shrugs. "I wouldn't say no. Opposites attract and all that."

"You don't really want someone who's your opposite," I scoff.

"Says who?"

"Says . . . *life*. You'd spend all your time arguing. That's not a recipe for a healthy relationship."

"Depends on the type of relationship," he mutters. He's concentrating very hard on his plate of chicken wings.

"What does that mean?"

His eyes flick up to mine, then back down to his plate. "Never mind."

"No *never mind*. What did you mean?"

He blows out a breath before looking up at me again. "Sex, Katie Cat. Dating your opposite would make for some amazing sex. Arguing as foreplay. Fighting, then making up. Wanting to kill each other, then rip each other's clothes off." His eyes spark. "Don't you agree?"

This conversation just veered *way* off course. "I guess I've never really thought about it." Although I am now. *Jesus.*

It plays out in my mind like an old Hollywood movie. It's black-and-white and I'm backlit beautifully. Ben and I are yelling at each other and I slap him across the face. He throws me over his shoulder and I beat his back while he carries me into a room and throws me down on a fancy four-poster bed. He pins my arms above my head while I thrash and fight, and then he begins to ravage me.

Ben reads me like a book. He crosses his arms over his chest, a slow, wicked grin stretching across his face. I don't like this smile. It's suggestive and indecent and a bunch of other things it shouldn't be.

"You ever been with someone who's given you a run for your money, Kate?" Something in his tone makes me want to stand up and run.

"Hate sex isn't my style." My voice wobbles a little on the word *sex*. I look longingly at the door. I could make a break for it.

"It's not mine either, but for you I'd make an exception."

Oh God. He went there.

"It'd be like scratching an itch. And in our case, there'd be no friendship to ruin, right? It's a win-win." He takes a long, slow pull from his beer, keeping his eyes trained on me.

"This is inappropriate."

"Let me guess," he says, setting his bottle down. "Most men have no idea how to handle a woman like you." He leans forward, lowering his voice. "But let me assure you: I am *not* most men."

My vision tunnels in as the thumping music fades into the background. The only thing I hear is my heartbeat in my ears. The only things I see are those eyes.

Don't let him do this to you again, Kate.

"Okay, you've had your fun." I try to sound dismissive, but my voice quavers, totally undermining my false bravado.

"Have I?" He arches an eyebrow.

"You're just trying to get under my skin."

"Is it working?"

"Will you cut it out, please? You're making me nervous."

"Why?"

"Because I can't tell if you're joking."

He stares at me for a long moment, then sighs and picks up his half-eaten chicken wing. "Relax, Katie Cat. I'm just kidding." He pats my hand.

I exhale slowly, not wanting him to see how thrown I am.

"But let me know if you change your mind, and maybe I won't be."

"*Ben.*"

He waves me away, like the subject is closed. "So what's the status of your bill these days?"

"Um . . ." I swallow hard and blink a few times. I can't downshift that fast. My brain is still flashing the phrase SEX WITH BEN like neon lights at a circus fair. My clothes feel like sandpaper on my skin. I cough and try to untuck my blouse from my skirt without him noticing. "It's going . . . okay, I guess. There've been some positive developments, so I'm cautiously optimistic. For a while there I thought I'd have to give up."

He looks genuinely surprised. "No way. Not you."

I shrug. "It's a numbers game, and we both know they're not in my favor."

He points to the last slider on the plate, raising his eyebrows, and when I shake my head he grabs it.

"Don't give up. I'm rooting for you," he says, talking around his mouthful.

"Since *when?*"

He swallows, washing it down with another swig of beer. "I never said I thought the bill was a bad idea."

"That's *exactly* what you said!"

"That is *not* what I said. I said you were barking up the wrong tree with Hammond. I never said anything about my personal feelings on it. As a matter of fact, I believe I tried to suggest some alternative strategies, but you shut me down."

"Are you saying you'd vote for it if you could?" The thought strangely warms me.

"Honestly? No. The sentiment behind the bill is good, but there are other ways I'd go about what you're trying to accomplish." When he sees my face fall, he quickly adds, "But I love an underdog story."

"Why couldn't you have just said that when we first met?"

"Would things be different?" His eyes fix on me with interest. This intense stare of his is unnerving.

"I don't know. I guess we could have been friends," I say lamely.

"And here I thought we *were* friends now," he says, not breaking my gaze. "Aren't we?"

There's a loaded silence as we consider each other, but I'm saved from answering by Marcus, who turns to us from the next table.

"What are you kids getting into over here?" he singsongs suggestively, like he's caught us in flagrante delicto. I rip my eyes away from Ben's and smile at Marcus unsteadily, and his eyes narrow a fraction.

"If you'll excuse me, gentlemen, I need to run to the ladies' room."

I escape to the restroom, taking some time to freshen up and plot my exit. Ben's had me off-balance all night, and I need to get out of here before it gets any worse. Besides, I'm tired and beyond ready to whip off this bra. The call of comfy pants is strong.

When I get back to the table, everyone's engrossed in a conversation with Luke about a case he's working on. He's consulting for one of the law firms involved in the civil rights versus religious liberties case that's made it all the way to the Supreme Court.

"No one really knows what's going to happen," Luke is saying. "It could go either way."

"I wonder what kind of repercussions it will have for small businesses," Ben says.

"Well, we all know which side *you're* on." It comes out a little sharper than I intended.

Ben gives me a measured look. "And how would you know that, exactly?"

A bunch of eyes land on me. Maybe that second glass of wine wasn't the best idea.

"Because we all know who the Republicans support in this case."

"That doesn't mean *I* do."

"Sure it does. By the transitive property."

He looks at me like I'm speaking Swahili. "I'm sorry, by the *transitive property*?"

"Yes. Your party supports a certain side, and you're a member of that party; therefore by the transitive property, you also support it."

"That is definitely *not* how the transitive property works."

"Yes, it is. If a equals b and b equals c, then a equals c. You're not the only one who knows math, Einstein."

His face has gone red. "The transitive property of equality applies to number sentences, not complex social issues. This is real life, not ninth-grade algebra."

"Thank you so much for mansplaining that to me, Ben," I fire back.

"Well, that escalated quickly," Marcus says.

I'm warming up to this debate now. "The transitive concept applies to plenty of other things besides numbers. Haven't you ever heard of the transitive property of hooking up?"

"I have," Marcus pipes up helpfully.

"Shut up, Marcus," Ben barks.

"If I hook up with Tessa and Tessa hooks up with Luke, then by extension, I've hooked up with Luke."

Ben slow blinks. "I'm sorry, I didn't hear anything after you hooking up with Tessa."

"Me either," says Luke.

"Me three," says Marcus, not to be outdone.

"*Argh*, forget it. You can't even follow the most basic logic."

"Logic? I'm not sure *what* I just heard, but it definitely wasn't logical." Ben's huffing all over the place.

"Don't try to Jedi mind trick me with your math voodoo. I know what I'm talking about." I have no idea what I'm talking about, actually, but triggering him like this is delightful.

"You are completely wrong about this, but that's not even the point."

"Then what is the point? I hardly even remember what this argument is about now."

"Me either," adds Marcus. "But I am *so* here for it."

"The *point*," Ben says through gritted teeth, "is that I'm actually open-minded while you only pretend to be."

"*What?!*"

"You heard me. I make up my own mind about what I believe while you just spout the party line."

This again? "You're going to sit there and tell me with a straight face that you're more open-minded than I am? Seriously?"

"Yes, *seriously*. If people don't fit into your little box, then they're out. Just a piece of advice, Kate: You shouldn't write people off just because they don't think the same way you do. It's a bad look."

"I don't *write* people off. And I *don't* need your advice." I stand and grab for my purse, but he gets to it first and holds it out of reach.

"Oh, you don't? Because I'm pretty sure you wrote me off the second you met me—maybe even before—and I've watched you do it with plenty of others. Not five minutes ago you told Marcus you'd never date a Republican. How open-minded is *that*?"

Marcus raises his palms and slowly slides his chair away.

"Knowing who I do and do not want to date doesn't make me closed-minded. It makes me *smart*."

I make another grab for my purse, but it's futile. He's like a parent holding his child's favorite toy out of reach. I have about a quarter of his wingspan.

He tilts his head. "You're so sure you're more open-minded than I am, prove it."

"How exactly would I *prove* something like that?"

"With a . . . bet." He's totally making this up as he goes along. I would laugh if I didn't want to punch his face in.

"How will a bet determine which of us is more open-minded? Will there be a *jury* deciding?"

His face sparks with sudden inspiration. "No. We'll decide. I'll come up with something you have to do that's outside your comfort zone, and vice versa. It could be an event or a task or . . . I'm not sure what yet, but you get the idea. I think it'll be pretty obvious who's more open-minded after that."

"So you're going to force me to do something I don't want to do?"

"It's not *forcing* you if you agree. It's a bet. Those are the terms. Take it or leave it. Of course, if you leave it, you're forfeiting. I'm automatically the more open-minded one." His eyes glow with mischief.

I narrow mine in response. I'm no fool. This is clearly a trap, and if I take this bet I'll be walking right into it. But how can I back down now? He's painted me into a corner.

"So do we have a bet?"

Beat this guy at his own game. Whatever it takes.

"Fine. In, I guess."

He reaches out and grabs my hand, giving it a little squeeze-shake. I squeeze back as hard as I can, trying to crush his bones. He smirks at my attempt, his smug grin silently taunting: *Like you could ever hurt me.*

"I look forward to proving you wrong."

"I look forward to proving *you* wrong. Hey, did you order more food?" I point over his shoulder.

"Where?"

When he turns to look, I grab my purse and run.

Chapter 10

On Thursday morning Carol is notified by the subcommittee considering our bill that they're not recommending it for a floor vote, the unspoken reason being that it doesn't stand a chance. And just like that, it's dead. In one brisk email, nine months of my work—of my *life*—goes *poof*.

It's not like you see in the movies. There's no miraculous Hail Mary into the end zone, no David slaying Goliath, no rushing around at the last minute to *get out the vote!* Our bill joins the other ninety-six percent of proposed legislation in the crowded graveyard of squandered time and wasted effort. It's almost comical how little fanfare there is. Or it would be, if I weren't so devastated.

Adding insult to injury? Ben's mocking voice is one of the first things I hear after Senator Warner breaks the news.

You're wasting your time.

That bill is dead in the water.

It's going nowhere. Surely you must know that.

I can't even escape him in my own head. I glare across the atrium, then leap out of my chair and yank the blinds closed. That'll send him a message.

I spend the rest of the day hibernating in my cave-office, practically catatonic with disappointment. Friday is more of the same. I sleepwalk through my tasks in a near trance, and not even Stephen's usual antics can lift me out of my funk.

Late in the day there's a knock at my door, rudely disturbing my past half hour's activity of staring at the wall and frowning. I sigh and swivel my chair around to find Ben in my doorway, a concerned look on his face.

"Hey."

"Hey." I spin back so I'm facing the wall again. "If you're here to say I told you so, please don't bother."

There's a pause. "No, I came to investigate why your blinds have been closed. But I just heard . . ."

"Who even *told* you?"

"Stephen." *Note to self: Stab Stephen to death later.* "But I would've hoped to hear it from you."

"Oh right, I'm so eager to publicize my failure. Especially to *you*."

"Kate, there will be other bills. Plenty of them."

I say nothing.

"You did your best. You can't control the outcome."

I don't know what it is about his presence—that he knows how badly I wanted this, or the gentle, sympathetic tone of his voice—but I'm struggling not to cry. I stare at a crack in the wall, blinking furiously, willing the tight feeling in my chest to dissipate before I break down in front of him.

"It happens to everyone. Pretty soon you'll be wrapped up in something new and this will be a distant memory."

"This pep talk is very helpful. What other clichéd gems do you have for me? Should I keep a stiff upper lip? Dust myself off and try again?" I brace a little at my nastiness, but I can't seem to help it. Being mean to him is my default setting.

"Well . . ." He hesitates. "I do have some ideas about how you could resurrect this, if you come at it—"

I whirl back around, and this time, I'm pissed. "Can we save the postmortem, please? That's not what I need right now." I blow out an angry breath. Better angry than weepy, I guess. I just want him to *leave*. Why won't he take the hint?

"Sure." He shoves his hands in his pockets, but that stupid piteous look is still on his face and it is *killing* me. He thinks I'm pathetic. The balance of power between us is totally lopsided and I hate it. "What *do* you need right now?"

I stare at him dumbly.

"Is there anything I can do for you?" he repeats. "What are you doing tonight?"

I can't handle this fake, nice Ben. I want to be left alone to wallow, not listen to him talk to me like I'm some injured bird. I wish he would just insult me already so our equilibrium could be restored.

"I have *plans*."

I lay it at his feet like a tribal offering; it's a golden opportunity to roast me about Donkey Date. He doesn't bite, though. He shifts his feet—it must be killing him not to make a meal of this—but he says nothing. *Exasperating.* Guess I'll have to try harder.

"My *friends* are taking me out." I say *friends* with extra emphasis, my tone letting him know: *You are not my friend, and I don't need anything from you.*

That works. His eyes shadow for a moment before he dips his head in a brisk nod.

"Have a good time with your *friends*, then." He turns to leave, shutting the door quietly behind him.

I thought I'd be relieved when he left, but as I stare at the closed door, I feel even more bereft than before he showed up.

Here's the funny thing: I actually do have a Donkey Date tonight. I wish I were kidding.

Tessa kept her promise from the bar and set up my LeftField profile, and apparently at warp speed, because by the next day she giddily shared that I'd matched with Ian, an admittedly great-looking lawyer who lives in Adams Morgan. I agreed to meet him for dinner on Friday night, figuring his career outside my immediate political bubble was a point in his favor. Of course, this was before I got news of the bill, and when I told Tessa and Stephen I needed to back out, they flat-out refused to let me. Literally—they changed the app password and locked me out of the account.

As an apology for their "tough love" (their expression, not mine—I used some other choice words), they offered to take me out for a drink before my date to "pump me up." I make sure to order the priciest glass of wine on the menu in retribution.

I've got to hand it to my friends—they're doing their best to be my hype squad and laugh me out of this, but I'm a lost cause tonight. They keep trying to one-up each other with increasingly pathetic toasts:

"To failure!" *Cheers!*

"To losers and haters!" *Clink!*

"To wasting our lives trying to make the world a better place!" *Fizz.*

"To supersize men who come by to rub your nose in your own pain and disappointment!" I add gamely, raising my glass.

They both stare at me. *What, too far?*

"Seriously? Ben kicked you while you're down?" Tessa says, incredulous. "I swear to God, I don't care how big he is, I will take that guy out."

Stephen's eyeing me skeptically. "You know, I spoke to him, and it didn't seem like he was gloating."

Under the table, I kick his shin as hard as I can with my pointy-toed heel.

"Ow!"

"*That's* for telling him about the bill. Stop talking to him about me. In fact, stop talking to him, period," I snap.

"*Reeeeer,*" he hisses, curling his fingers into cat claws. "He seemed concerned about you, is all I'm saying."

I make a face as Tessa breaks in, holding up her phone.

"You guys will have to finish this later. It's seven fifteen and Ian'll be here any minute."

They leave me with a flurry of hugs and kisses and *good lucks*, and I move from the bar to a table, settling in to wait for my date to arrive.

And wait.

And wait.

Three more glasses of wine, one untouched plate of food, and more than an hour later, I'm still waiting. When it becomes obvious the guy isn't going to show, I spend most of that time mentally drafting the hateful review I plan to leave on his profile—but I can't even get the satisfaction of posting it since I'm *still* locked out of the damn account. I delete the app off my phone in a fit of pique.

So much for Donkey Date.

While I'm sure I'll end up laughing about this someday, if I start now I'm pretty sure it'll spiral into hysterical sobbing. I consider texting Tessa and Stephen to commiserate, but frankly I'm pissed at them for getting me into this mess to begin with. Besides, I can't stomach any more of their *rah-rah*, *chin-up* pep talks tonight—or worse, their pity.

I should've expected this—the date deserter, the bill failure, all of it. Hasn't the sum total of my life experiences taught me anything? Each and every time I get my hopes up, they eventually come crashing down in a fiery blaze of wreckage. And since bad things always happen in threes, God only knows what's coming next. With my luck, I'll get into a car accident on my Uber ride home.

To escape the pitying looks of my well-meaning but nosy server, I pay my check and wander out—then wander into the place next door, sidle up to the bar, and order a martini. Why not? Getting drunk alone is a fitting end to my worst week ever.

I take in my surroundings as I wait on my cocktail. Whereas Invisible Ian's restaurant of choice was a trendy hotspot, this place has an old-school boys' club vibe. Deep leather booths with patinaed nailhead trim line the perimeter while dark wood floors stretch across the dimly lit space. Shiny brass and leather stools are bolted to the floor underneath a long, gleaming wooden bar. It's the type of place where I imagine clandestine CIA activity going down in a shadowy corner booth.

My phone buzzes with a text.

Ben: I really am sorry about your bill. I know how much it meant to you.

I snort. I'll just bet he's sorry. *Not.*
I text back:

Me: You win some, you lose some.

Or at least, that's what I meant to text. When I look at the phone after I send it, it reads:

Me: YOur winsssome yuu lonessome

I squint at the screen. That isn't right. Oh well, I'm sure he'll get the point.

Another buzz.

Ben: Are you okay?

I sigh and toss the phone on the bar, picking up my drink and taking a big swig. Or rather, I try to take a swig, but the glass is empty. I peer into it, trying to decipher how it got that way.

"What are you drinking?" A swarthy-looking man who kind of resembles Rhett Butler slides onto the stool next to me and motions to the bartender.

"Dirty martini."

I laugh at how I sound, like I'm straight out of one of those classic black-and-white films I sometimes catch on AMC. *Dirty martini, straight up. Extra dirty.* I giggle, then hiccup.

Swarthy Guy orders one, then smiles at me. "So, what's your name?"

I'm just about to answer when my phone starts chirping. Another text. No, not a text. A call.

Ben is *calling* me.

Up until a moment ago, I've never heard from him via text or call, and now *both*? How did he even get my phone number? Syncing our watches was surely my worst mistake ever.

I slide my finger across the screen. "Hello?"

"Kate? Are you okay?" His deep voice reaches across the line, settling over my skin like a shroud.

"Oh, Benjy, I'm fine. I am super fine." Except it comes out like *shooper fine*.

There's a pause. "Where are you?"

"I am at an establishment for eating and drinking." I'm proud of myself for how clearly I say it. "Although I never did eat any food." I think about that. *Huh*. Now I'm hungry.

"Is someone there with you? Your friends?"

"My friends left, but I stayed. I made a new friend, though." I lean over to not–Rhett Butler, who's making no effort to disguise his eavesdropping. "What's your name?" It comes out like *Wasser name?*

I hear Ben swear under his breath. "Kate, what's the name of the restaurant you're at?"

"You know, I'm not sure. It has tables and booths. The booths are leather. They look like your crossbody bag." I giggle. *Crossbody* is a funny word.

"Is there a bartender nearby?" His voice holds an edge.

"Not near enough, if you ask me." I snicker.

"Can you get their attention, please?"

"Sure." I wave my arms above my head, dropping the phone in the process. "Bartender! Bartender!"

The bartender's in his midfifties and dressed like an old-timey saloon barback with a vest, armband, and string necktie knotted at his throat. All he's missing is a greasy curlicue mustache. His expression is aggrieved as he makes his way over.

"Yes?" he asks, eyeing me warily. I hold the phone out to him wordlessly.

"Hello?" he says, leaning a hip against the bar. He listens for a moment before his face shifts into a hard mask. "Look, buddy, I only served her one drink. I can't help it if she came in here already loaded."

I snort—who says *loaded*? Men who wear saloon costumes, apparently.

He shoots me a dirty look but is quiet as he listens to whatever Ben is waxing on about. He glances at me, his face relaxing a little. Then he says, "Clive's on K Street. Yep, no problem."

He hands me back my phone. "You're cut off, honey."

What? How dare he! "Ben!" I scream into the phone. "You're not the boss of me!"

But nothing's there but dead air. He's already hung up.

★

Ten minutes later and I'm learning a lot about my new friend Damian, who works on the Hill as a pharmaceutical lobbyist. He's also giving me sips of his drink whenever Bartender Buzzkill isn't looking. That's my clever new nickname for him, which I find hilarious. He does not. It might be because I keep trying to order a whiskey sling and sarsaparilla, but whatever. You'd think someone dressed for the Wild West would have a better sense of humor.

Damian is really funny. So funny, in fact, that when I laugh and go to punch him playfully on the arm, I lose my balance and slide off my stool. I feel, rather than see, the large hand that grabs me from behind and steadies me, and then a massive form steps between Damian and me. I watch as Damian shrinks back, eyes wide as he takes in the behemoth before him.

A new buzzkill is here. Buzzkill Ben.

"Benjy!" I shout gleefully, throwing my arms around him from behind. I've always been an energetic drunk.

He doesn't turn to look at me or acknowledge my outburst. He towers over Damian, an intimidating brick wall suddenly erected between us.

"Leave. Now."

His voice is low and menacing and brooks no debate. I wish I could see what his face looks like—though judging by Damian's expression, it's very scary indeed. It's like I'm witnessing a live-action *National Geographic* special: *Observe the alpha male as he picks off the weakest of the pack.*

Somewhere in the deep recesses of my brain it occurs to me that I should be upset that Ben is scaring off a potential suitor, but I'm so riveted by the scene unfolding before me that it barely registers. I watch in fascination as Damian gets up off the stool and mutters an apology—to me or to Ben, I'm not sure whom—then slinks off, disappearing out the door.

I'm so disappointed in Damian. What a wimp. Why are all the guys who like me such wusses?

"Well, well, well. Buzzkill Benjamin Mackenzie is here!" I giggle at my cleverness. "Does everyone always do exactly as you say?"

"Not everyone," he answers curtly.

He sounds mad. I crane my neck to get a better view of him but he's looking past me to find the bartender, his eyes unreadable. A muscle pulses in his neck.

"What are you even *doing* here?"

He finally turns and acknowledges me, but when I see the expression on his face, I almost wish he hadn't. The look he casts me is so full of pity and contempt that I physically recoil. And I thought his *injured bird* look was bad.

What, am I not allowed to go out drinking? I'm a grown woman. I hardly think that qualifies me for a public shaming by Mr. Rogers over here. I shoot him a glare and stew in righteous indignation.

Meanwhile, Ben's finally gotten the bartender's attention and motioned him over. He approaches Ben slowly, trepidation written all over his face. Jesus, is *every* male scared of Ben? How disappointing.

"Is she paid out?" Ben asks. He is all brisk efficiency.

Bartender Buzzkill nods and hands him my credit card and receipt, flicking his eyes toward me apologetically. What is the collective noun for a group of buzzkills? A brood of buzzkills? A band of buzzkills? I snort at my own hilarity.

"Thanks." Ben pockets my card and receipt, then turns toward me, hooking his arm around my waist and effortlessly lifting me off the stool with his superhuman strength.

"Hey, hey. I can walk by *myself*," I say crossly, swatting at him. Before the words are even out of my mouth, I stumble in my four-inch stilettos and nearly face-plant onto the shiny mahogany floor. It's in a herringbone pattern. How chic.

But before I can, Ben catches me—it's becoming a habit—steadying me with strong hands on my arms. When I'm upright again, we're standing so close our chests are touching.

Chapter 11

I've never really looked at him so close up, and from this distance I register a slew of things I never noticed before: the faint five-o'clock shadow dusting his jawline; his hair, curlier than I thought, falling over his ear a little; a tiny silvery scar cutting through his right eyebrow; the kaleidoscope of colors in his eyes conspiring to make them glow so obscenely. These eyes should be illegal.

"How'd you get that scar?" I reach up and touch it.

He eyes me warily. "Fell off my bike when I was twelve. Flew over the handlebars. Are you ready to go?"

I remember something and snake my hand around to his back pocket. He tenses, catching my forearm. "What are you doing?"

"Taking back what's mine, of course." I pinch out my credit card and wave it in his face like a golden ticket. He blinks slowly, his expression darkening. *Touchy.*

He wraps an arm around my waist and half walks, half drags me toward the front entrance. I can't even argue, since I can't seem to walk more than a few steps without toppling like a Confederate statue. When we make it outside, the cool air hits my face like a slap.

"Fresh air feels good."

"I bet it does, Drunky Drunkerson."

Something about his flippant response breaks through my drunken fog, triggering the realization that Ben is really, truly here. I study him, taking a mental inventory. He's wearing dark jeans—I've never seen him in jeans before—and a thin, long-sleeved green shirt. No, a sweater. I squint. Well, I can't tell if it's a shirt or a sweater, so henceforth it shall be known as a shirt-sweater.

One thing I do clearly notice is how good he looks in it. Damn good.

The color suits him, the green bringing out his extraordinary eyes. The fabric hugs every muscle and curve of his massive frame like it's been poured over him, molding to his ridges and planes like liquid gold.

My drunk thoughts are weird.

"Yes, you needed some air." He's still propping me up, one arm curled around my waist while the other taps on his phone. "So look, I don't know what's going on, but it's going to take twelve minutes for an Uber to get here. We're near enough to your apartment to walk in that time, so that's what we're going to do." He eyes me skeptically. "You think you can walk?"

"Of course I can," I say, indignant. I hold my arms out and heel-to-toe along the curb like a balance beam. "I walk the line," I croon, doing my best Johnny Cash.

Ben yanks me away from the curb, drawing me tight to his side, and sets off walking. I'm propelled forward through no effort of my own.

"You know I had a Donkey Date tonight."

He flicks his eyes to mine but doesn't comment.

"I got stood up."

"His loss."

I start laughing, causing my stride to falter, and his arm tightens around me. "Oh, come on, don't go soft on me now. Say I told you so. I know you're dying to."

He shakes his head.

"I sat there like a loser for an hour. My server thought I was pathetic." I peer up at him. "Seriously? Nothing?"

"I'm not gonna give you a hard time tonight no matter how much you want me to, so you can quit trying. It's not a fair fight."

"You mean now that I'm so tragic?" I scoff. "I don't need your pity-niceness." My heel hits a crack in the sidewalk and I wobble, pitching sideways.

"Okay, this isn't gonna work."

Before I can ask what he means, he sweeps me off my feet. Literally, he bends down, hooks an arm underneath my knees, and scoops me up like I'm lighter than air, a feather on a gust of wind.

"What are you *doing*?" I cry, fighting him.

"Carrying you. I really don't need you breaking an ankle on top of everything else."

"This is so antifeminist," I fume. "And I'm wearing a skirt."

"That's why I'm not piggybacking you."

I grumble but eventually stop struggling and clasp my arms around his neck. What choice do I have? Besides, walking home in these heels would be a level of torture on par with waterboarding.

I know I shouldn't poke the bear—especially when said bear is carrying me—but I can't help myself. "This must be your dream come true. The knight in shining armor swooping in to save the damsel in distress."

He doesn't react—*Where is this newfound restraint coming from?*—so of course, I poke again.

"Only I don't need saving. I could have gotten home on my own, thank you very much."

His look is one of thinly veiled disdain. "Sure, Kate. You probably would have gotten home, to that douchebag's apartment."

"Maybe I *wanted* to go to his apartment."

I feel him stiffen beneath me.

"Besides, I'm not an idiot. I know how to call an Uber, Benjy." Something occurs to me. "Hey, how do you know where I live?"

He doesn't respond right away, the muscle in his jaw ticking. "I just do." His voice is so quiet I have to strain to hear him.

"Benjy, have you been stalking me?"

"Quit calling me Benjy. It sounds like a dog," he snaps. *Oooh, cranky Benjy.*

I mock gasp. "Wait, you *don't* like being called degrading nicknames?"

He's setting a brisk pace, my weight clearly no match for his Herculean stamina. It's a chilly night and I should be cold, but the heat seeping from his body into my skin is relaxing me on a cellular level. It's like being wrapped in a cozy Ben blanket. I could get used to traveling this way.

"You know, I'm not even that drunk. I didn't need you to cut me off."

"Not that drunk. *Right.* You're what, a hundred and twenty pounds dripping wet? You'd be wasted after two drinks. And by the looks of you, you've had a lot more than that."

"What are you, the booze police?" I explode. "You're so freakin' uptight. *You* could use a drink."

"*I'm* uptight? You're the one who can't even swear properly. Who says *freaking* instead of *fucking*? You should try a real curse, you might feel better."

I wave my hand. "Cursing is unbecoming."

"'Cursing is unbecoming,' says the feminist." He shakes his head in disbelief.

"My mom doesn't like cursing. When I do it, I feel like I'm disrespecting her."

"As opposed to how respectful you're being by going out and getting wasted at a bar alone? I'm sure she'd be *thrilled* to see you like this."

I turn my face away. "You don't know anything about my mom."

"Why don't you tell me, then?"

I'm not too drunk to recognize his diversionary tactic for what it is. I'd call him out on it, but I'm in that chatty drunk stage where I actually *do* want to talk about my mom.

"Oh, she's a lot of fun. We're very close. She's hardworking and focused and smarter than she lets on. Also, she's kind of nuts. Like she just discovered GIFs and now she'll barely communicate any other way. She's sort of going through a secondary adolescence. It's like a midlife crisis but without all the bad decisions. What else? She's optimistic. A hopeless romantic." I make a face.

He smiles lightly. "Yeah?"

"Yeah. Even though she has no reason to be."

"What does that mean?"

I wave his question away as if to say, *Story for another time.*

"Well, what's wrong with being a hopeless romantic?" he tries instead.

"Oh, I don't know, how about *everything*? Let me count the ways. Putting up with crappy behavior you'd never accept from anyone else. Constantly putting your dreams last. Unrealistic expectations about how your life is going to turn out." I tick them off on my fingers. "Besides, the term *hopeless romantic* doesn't even make sense. It's so depressing. I don't know why I'm the only one who sees that."

"What do you mean?"

"Think about it. By its very definition, it's saying romance is hopeless. So why do people act like it's some swoon-worthy character trait?"

"I don't think it's a bad thing to be optimistic. Glass half-full."

"You *would* think that, with your 'perfect woman' list. That's hopeless if I've ever heard it." He frowns. "Whatever. I've seen too much. In my sorority, I had a front-row seat to every worst-case romantic scenario. You wouldn't believe how many women act like every problem can be solved with a bouquet of flowers. I mean, how dumb." I make a retching noise.

"Now you have something against *flowers*?" He looks like he's struggling not to laugh.

"There's nothing *wrong* with flowers, per se. They're just such a waste. If a man gives me flowers, I'm what, supposed to swoon? They require a bunch of work to keep them alive, only to die within a week regardless? How about getting me a *real* gift that lasts, that I can savor for longer than a few days?"

He blinks. "Wow. You really *aren't* a romantic."

"When you think about it, flowers are really the perfect metaphor for relationships," I muse. "They're beautiful for a time, then they start to die and they stink and you work desperately to save them and bam! They're dead. It's over."

"You should write greeting cards."

A laugh bubbles out of me. "You're funny tonight."

He nudges my shoulder. "I'm always funny. You just don't want to admit it."

"And humble too." I fight a smile. "Anyway, I suppose what really gets to me is the expectation that some guy is just going to swoop in and carry you off and all your problems will be solved. The end."

He quirks an eyebrow. When I realize why, I flush. "Present situation excluded, of course."

He smirks, repositioning my body to gain a better grip, and I watch his considerable muscles flex and stretch as he resettles me in his arms.

It is sexy as hell.

In a flash of memory, I recall something I've been dying to know and span my hands around his biceps, stretching my fingers to see if I can get them to touch. It isn't even close.

"I knew it!" I yell in jubilation. "I need a third hand!"

He looks at me like I'm certifiable. "What are you talking about?"

"Your muscles, of course." I sigh, petting his sweater-clad arm like a pony.

A surge of exhaustion suddenly hits me like a tidal wave. The last couple of days have been so draining and I'm tired to my bones. I close my eyes and let my head fall to his shoulder, reveling in the feeling of being taken care of for once. I can hear him breathing in little huffs, feel the rise and fall of his chest beneath me. It's hypnotic.

Being so close to Ben is a peculiar thing. It's doing strange things to my brain. For the first time, I can smell him. He smells like . . . like . . .

I press my nose into his neck, inhaling deeply. His stride momentarily falters.

"What are you doing?"

"Smelling you." I inhale again. There's a faint, intoxicating cologne scent and . . . something else. "You smell like a forest mixed with cinnamon and . . ." I sniff again. "Soap."

The ghost of a smile curves his lips as he resumes his previous pace. "Oh yeah? Well, you smell like vanilla and coconut."

"I do?" I try to sniff my chest.

"Not right now. Right now, you smell like a distillery."

"Oh." I pause. "My shampoo is coconut." I toss my hair in proof and his entire expression changes, his face going slack. He drags in a heavy breath but says nothing.

"So I guess this means you've smelled me before?"

His eyes dart to mine for a split second, then focus back on the sidewalk ahead. "Maybe."

"Huh." I wonder idly if he likes my scent, because one thing's for sure: I like his. I like his *a lot*.

I ponder what intriguing blend of products would produce an aroma of pine and cinnamon—if I stalk the men's grooming aisle at the store, I'm sure I could figure it out—but I'm interrupted from my musings when he shifts me in his arms again and I start to feel self-conscious.

"Am I too heavy? I can walk." It's a halfhearted offer that fools no one.

His look is pure scorn. "Please."

"I know I'm not exactly the daintiest gal around, even if you do make everyone else seem tiny by comparison."

"You're dainty enough. Though *dainty* probably isn't the word I'd use to describe you."

"Ooh, how *would* you describe me then? This should be good."

A devilish grin climbs his face. "The words that come to mind aren't appropriate to say in front of a lady."

I smack him upside the head and he laughs.

"Fine, I'll do you first." I squint at him as if I'm thinking hard. "Let's see, you are big. Manly. Annoyingly smart. Hilarious."

He looks at me sharply, but when I take notice and stop speaking, he faces forward again. *Interesting.* I monitor his expression closely as I continue.

"You're maddening. Overprotective. Disciplined. Misguided. Incorrigible. Entertaining." I purse my lips. "Secretive."

His eyes flare a bit on that one. *Curiouser and curiouser.*

"And one more I just learned tonight. Kind."

This time when his arms tighten around me, it almost feels possessive.

The silence is deafening. "What do you think? How'd I do?" I bounce in his arms, an eager little perfectionist craving validation.

He swallows and I watch the movement of his throat up close. "I think . . . that was a lot of big words for someone who's inebriated." His voice has dropped an octave and it comes out sounding husky and rough, like he's just woken up.

"Ooh, inebriated. Look at you with the SAT words! And here I thought you were only good at math."

He rolls his eyes.

"All right, do me now." He clears his throat and I wonder if he also noticed my unintentional double entendre.

He goes quiet, and all I can hear are the night sounds around us: the occasional car whipping by, a dog barking, the blare of a faraway car horn. *Hurry up, hurry up,* I prod in a mental gallop. We're approaching my block and I don't want to run out of time. My liquid courage has given us a fleeting window of opportunity for candor, and now I'm desperate to hear what he *really* thinks of me.

"Kate, you are headstrong. Clever. Competitive. Determined. Distracting." His voice does something funny on this one, catches, and he shakes his head slightly as if to clear it. "You're tough. Humorous. Reckless."

He glances at me, his gaze lingering on mine for the briefest of moments, and the look in his eyes makes my breath hitch. It's as if he's considering something, and whatever he sees in my eyes gives him his answer.

"Striking." He says it with finality, the word echoing around us like a sonic boom.

What does *striking* mean? Attractive? Beautiful, even? Or just memorable? That I stand out, but in a bad way? I stare at him as I attempt to puzzle this out, but I'm distracted from further analysis when my apartment building comes into view.

"That's where I live!" I shout, pointing. I have the attention span of a gnat right now. I'm like a dog that's spotted a squirrel.

"I know." Ben is amused.

"How do you know?" I realize now he never answered my question. *Sneaky Benjy.*

"Because I live across the street. I've seen you walking home."

I look at him like I'm seeing him for the first time. Ben lives this close to me and I didn't know? He really is so mysterious.

I'm oddly disappointed to be home; I wish we could keep walking. He's so . . . not his usual self tonight. It's unexpected. Pleasant. I can almost pretend he's a normal guy I've met out somewhere, some strong, dashing, and witty fellow with big, sexy muscles that—who knows—I may get to feel up when I get home.

I really must be drunk. Sexy? *Pah.* Ben is not sexy. Ben is my adversary, a dangerous opponent I'd do well not to underestimate. The man who's currently carrying me like a newlywed groom is the same one who promised to make my life a misery just a few weeks ago. Ben is not a nice guy.

Though he seems to be doing a very good impression of a nice guy tonight.

He continues to hold me as we walk into my building and onto the elevator and all the way up to my floor, which seems a bit like overkill, but who's complaining? When we reach my door he sets me down gingerly, keeping one arm anchored around my waist. I fish through my purse for my keys, then hand them to him to unlock the door.

I look up at him dreamily. "This was very nice of you." I'm clinging to his arm like a toddler with separation anxiety. As he fumbles with the lock, I place my hand over his, halting his progress.

I graze my fingers from his wrist slowly up his arm, stroking the muscles visible through the thin fabric of his lovely shirt-sweater. He's so warm, and touching this man has become my sole desire, my only focus, our feud be damned. I let my hand blaze a trail up his arm—biceps, triceps, deltoid—feeling every curve of his incredible physique. When I reach his shoulder, I pause. There is really something to be said for these huge muscles.

His whole body has stilled. "Kate. What are you doing?"

It's the same low, suggestive voice he used earlier, and I'm quivering at the sound all over again. There's a dull ache in my stomach that's getting sharper and heavier by the second.

"I'm not doing *annnything*," I say, my own voice slurred with desire and intoxication. I'm afraid he's going to stop me, so I slide my palm over his collarbone to his chest before he can, appreciating his well-defined pectorals, the heat radiating from his rib cage. My hand winds a slow, meandering path downward, exploring the miles of firm torso beneath my fingertips. I brave a glance up at him, and he's staring at me intensely, his eyes alert and blazing green.

I hum in contentment. "Your eyes are so very green. Like a green light. Green means go."

I step forward unsteadily, finally allowing myself to do something I've desperately been wanting to: I stare up into his eyes, examining them with unabashed curiosity and concentration. They're deep and fiery and so arresting I wonder how anyone can look at him without being reduced to ashes. It's like staring into the sun.

"Did you know they glow? Especially when you wear green. Do you do that on purpose so I'll notice?"

He closes his eyes. "Kate. Stop." His body's gone completely rigid.

"Stop what?"

My voice is breathy as I continue my hand dance, my fingers stroking a slow perusal down his abs until I hit the waistband of his jeans. I'm very close to his bare skin and all my horny brain can focus on is finding out if it feels as good as I think it will. I go to raise his shirt a little.

Ben's arm shoots out and he lifts my hand from his waistband, gently placing it back at my side. A lungful of air shudders out of him as he steps back, holding me at arm's length like he needs to put space between us. Of course, *now* he chooses to leave room for the Lord.

"You need to get inside and drink some water." He's staring up at the ceiling as if searching for something. *Come back, eyes.*

"Don't be a spoilsport. I was just admiring the view," I grumble.

I can barely stand upright anymore—I need to get these heels off like *yesterday*—and I sag against him, resting my head against his chest. His resulting half-hug embrace envelopes me completely, and for the first time, I appreciate how ideal his size is. He's the perfect cushion, a comforting pillow of hard and soft. It's impossible to feel anything but safe and protected in his arms, surrounded on all sides by strength and masculinity. His hand goes to my lower back, tangling in my hair, and I feel his deep intake of breath under my cheek.

He turns back to the lock. In my drunken haze it looks like his hand is shaking, but it's probably just my swaying vision. My eyesight isn't exactly reliable right now.

He switches on the lights and I'm nearly blinded. I throw my elbow over my eyes. "Nooo. Too bright."

He flicks them off, then fumbles around, looking for a lamp, presumably.

"Ahh, home." I kick off my shoes and throw myself in the direction of my couch but end up whacking my head on the back of the frame instead. It makes a sickening cracking noise. *That was graceful.*

A table lamp flicks on. "Jesus, Kate, are you okay?"

Ben kneels in front of me, his expression anxious. He reaches behind me, his thumb gently skimming a path along my scalp, searching for a bump. Everywhere he strokes, my skin burns. I want more touching, more of his hand. I nudge my head into his palm like a dog looking for a nuzzle. *Real subtle, Kate.*

At my movement, he withdraws his hand, returning it to his lap—

but before he can, I reach out and grab it, holding it in front of me and inspecting it. His skin feels rough but smooth at the same time, that strange juxtaposition that only a man's hand can be. I flatten my palm against his.

"Even your hands are huge." I'm fascinated. I lace my fingers through his and note the pale baby hairs on his knuckles.

He is giving me . . . a Look. Like a mixture of hunger, apprehension, and tense restraint, and as I analyze it, I'm seized by a thought. If I yanked on his arm, he'd end up in my lap. Could I get him to kiss me? Could I kiss *him*? God knows I've thought of almost nothing else for the past week.

I dismiss the idea as quickly as it originates. If Ben ended up on top of me, I'd probably die of suffocation.

Ben breathes out slowly, disconnecting our hands and setting mine in my lap, then heads in the direction of my kitchen. I hear water running, then shut off. When he comes back, he places a glass of water in front of me. "Drink."

I do as he says, chugging huge gulps like a dehydrated camel.

"Not so fast," he warns. I slow down, taking delicate sips like the lady I am.

"Now. Do you feel like you're going to get sick?"

"No," I respond, deeply offended. "I know how to hold my alcohol."

Actually, I'm lying. I'd felt a little nauseous on the way home but chalked it up to being carried and all the jostling that came with it—but now that I'm sitting down, the queasiness hasn't eased. The thought of vomiting in front of Ben is so disturbing I promptly lose my buzz.

He eyes me dubiously, clearly unmoved by my booze-fueled bravado. "Where do you keep a bucket?"

"In my laundry area . . ." I point vaguely down the hall and flop back on the couch, closing my eyes. My head is spinning. My happy-drunk high is wearing off, reality is setting in, and it's not pretty.

He returns with the plastic bucket and sets it on the coffee table. The couch cushion depresses beside me as he sits down.

"Are you staying? You don't have to stay." *Please stay.*

"I'll stay for a while, if that's okay with you."

"That'd be nice," I murmur sleepily, not opening my eyes.

He lifts my head slightly and slides a pillow under my cheek. The last thing I remember is the feel of his fingers on my forehead, smoothing my hair back as I drift off.

★

I wake up sometime later—minutes, hours? There's no way to know—groaning as I roll onto my side. As soon as I shift my weight, I know I'm going to be sick. I bolt upright, groping for the bucket.

Ben grabs it first, thrusting it under my chin just as I am forcefully sick. I start to stand but he stops me with a hand to my arm.

"What are you doing? Don't get up."

"Bathroom," I croak.

He helps me up, walking me down the hall with one arm clasped around my waist. When we reach the bathroom, I collapse on the floor in front of the toilet.

I point shakily to the vanity drawers. "Can you . . . hair tie . . ." I rasp out as another wave of nausea hits me. I bend over the bowl, heaving, then flush as soon as humanly possible. I can't believe Ben is witnessing this.

The weird thing is, I'm both horrified and grateful that he's here. Ben's the last person I would choose to see me at my lowest—and make no mistake, it doesn't get more rock bottom than my bathroom floor. I'll need to join the Witness Protection Program after this.

On the other hand, who wants to be alone when they're sick? I've always had someone to hold my hair back—my mom, my grandma, any one of a hundred sorority sisters—and it's one of the most basic human desires, to be taken care of in times of distress.

I can't decide if I want him to leave or stay. My head pounds with the conflict. And the alcohol. And the couch-induced head injury. So basically, I'm throbbing all over. I am a scalding-hot mess.

He sets the bucket on the floor of my bathtub and I hear him rummaging around in the drawers for a rubber band. I reach my hand out for it blindly but grasp nothing but air.

I startle when I feel his hands in my hair, gently gathering it up and tying it back so the loose strands are out of my face. I say a silent but fervent prayer that I don't have puke in my hair.

"Thank you," I breathe, bracing my head on the bowl with an arm.

"You're welcome."

I brave a glance up and spot his reflection in the mirror. His face is etched with concern.

"How much did you drink, Kate?" His voice is soft, unaccusing. I'm so mortified I can barely bring myself to answer.

"A few glasses of wine, then some martinis. I don't really remember how many."

"You mixed your alcohol."

I think he's talking more to himself than to me. I don't respond.

"When you're done . . . getting sick, I'll get you some Advil."

"Okay," I whisper weakly. "Actually, you should go. I'm—you don't need to—"

"Kate, I'm not leaving." He is firm.

"You should." I slither to the floor, the cool tile a welcome pit stop for my throbbing head, and close my eyes.

Chapter 12

"Kate. Wake up, let's get you into bed."

Someone's prying me off the floor. I look around, groggy and disoriented. I'm on my bathroom floor. The room is spinning. Ben looms in my vision.

Ben?

"Come on." He's lifting me up, his voice cajoling. All at once I come to, remembering with a jolt.

I manage to brush my teeth before he guides me out of the bathroom, and what I see in the mirror nearly makes me keel over: My face is patchy and pale, my hair matted on one side, with smeared mascara-ringed eyes. I'm basically a panda. My degradation is complete.

He leads me into my bedroom and I collapse on the bed in exhaustion.

"Where are your pajamas?"

I eye him warily from my prone position. "Um, I can handle that. Can you leave the room, please?"

He gives me a look. "I wasn't going to *watch* you change. I'll go get you more water and some Advil." I mutter a thank-you as he pulls the door shut behind him.

I undress and change at warp speed, throwing my defiled work clothes in the corner of my closet and burrowing into my cool sheets. I swipe my fingers under my eyes in a fruitless attempt to make myself look more like a human and less like an endangered species. I'm saying a grateful prayer to the creator of heavenly beds when I hear a soft knock on my door.

"You can come in," I call, then tunnel deeper into my sheets. Like if I just hide, then none of this ever happened.

Ben walks in holding a glass of water in one hand and a bottle of Advil in the other. He's also holding the bucket, empty and washed out.

I groan. "You cleaned my vomit."

"It's fine." He sets the water and pills down on the nightstand and the bucket on the floor, and I watch him hesitate for a moment before taking a seat on the edge of the bed.

"It's not fine. I should probably have a roommate for times like this, huh?" I let out a self-conscious laugh.

"Fine, it was gross. But that's what friends are for."

"Friends." I roll the word around in my mouth like a marble, testing it out. "Is that what we are?"

A shadow skims over his eyes, but he says nothing. He looks resigned.

"You'll never let me forget this."

He makes a face, a little V forming between his eyebrows. I've started to recognize his expressions, and this one reads: pained.

"You didn't have to do this," he says quietly. His hand goes to my forehead again, smoothing the loose hair away from my face. It feels so soothing that a little sigh escapes and my eyelids flutter closed.

"I'm allowed to self-destruct when the last nine months of my life just went down the flippin' drain." I laugh bitterly.

"Won't even curse when you're drunk. Now that's commitment." I hear the smile in his voice and I can picture it perfectly even with my eyes closed: the upturned corners of his mouth, the amused twinkle lighting his eyes.

I reach out for his hand, curling my fingers into his palm. After a brief moment of hesitation, his fingers close around mine. I feel tears pricking at my eyelids, but I will not give in to them. I will *not* cry in front of Ben. I open them and blink furiously.

"Guess I should have listened to you weeks ago, huh? You warned me I was wasting my time. You told me I was going to fail. Shocker, I wouldn't listen."

I hate how pathetic I sound. I hate even more that I've proven him right—I'm too idealistic, I take things too personally, I'm fighting losing battles. I tense, waiting for the inevitable *I told you so* that I'm sure is on the tip of his tongue.

But it never comes. He just sits there, his fingers threaded in my hair, his thumb tracing my palm.

"*You* didn't fail. The bill failed." His voice holds an urgency, like he's desperate to communicate this to me. "It was bad timing, Kate, that's all. Maybe I knew it was a long shot. But I don't know everything."

"You knew," I insist, tears clogging my throat. "But then you told me not to give up, and I listened. You made me feel like I could *do* this. Why did you do that?" My chest burns with the need to cry, and I have to pause briefly to compose myself. "I got my hopes up, and I know better than to hope for something that's *never* going to happen."

I can hear the change in my voice, and I know I'm not talking about the bill anymore. I'm seven years old again and I'm crying myself to sleep because I miss my dad.

There's a long silence, long enough that I assume he's not going to respond—and, really, what do I expect him to say? I'm barely making sense at this point. But then, softly—so soft I barely hear it—his voice cuts through the darkness.

"I couldn't stand to be the one to put this look on your face."

It takes a second for his words to sink in, but when they do, they slam into my chest, squeeze, twist, and wring me out. It's the most intimate exchange we've ever had—no defensiveness or one-upping, no walls hiding our true feelings. Just Ben, with raw emotions and a vulnerability I've never seen from him before.

I don't know how long we sit there, my hand in his, staring at each other in silence—but the silence eventually becomes another entity entirely, something we can't ignore, like another person in the room. When he finally looks away, breaking the moment, I feel the loss acutely. It felt like he truly *saw* me. I wonder if I'll ever feel that way again.

He gives my hand a firm squeeze and moves to get up. I grip his wrist forcefully, tugging him back down.

"Are you leaving?" For all my waffling earlier, I now have clarity: I am desperate for him to stay.

Uncertainty blankets his face. "I think you'll be fine now. You'll wake up with a nasty hangover, but I'm sure you know how to handle that." He seems to regret his choice of words. "Not that I'm implying you do this all the time or anything." He closes his eyes briefly and shakes his head.

"Don't go. Please."

I'm near tears again. The thought of him leaving makes my loneliness feel overwhelming.

He hesitates. "I can stay if you want me to."

"I want you to," I practically beg. The irony isn't lost on me that I'm now pleading with Ben, my sworn enemy, to spend the night with me— but in this moment I don't care about our jobs, or our friends, or anything else that would come between us.

I just want him to keep holding my hand.

"Okay," he says. "I'll stay."

★

I wake up a couple of times during the night, my sleep marred by restless, tumultuous dreams of Rhett Butler carrying me through a burning pine forest. The first time I stir, Ben is still awake and reading something on his phone, the brightness turned way down. When he notices me watching him, he murmurs for me to go back to sleep.

He's no longer holding my hand or caressing my hair, and I long for his touch like an addict needing a fix. I've gone so long without affectionate human contact, I've forgotten how good it feels. How *necessary*. My hands literally shake with the desire to reach out and touch him, to claim his hand in mine again, but I know how unwise that decision would be. We've already blurred our battle lines so much that I have no idea how I'll face him at work on Monday.

And then I reach out and grab it anyway. If he says anything, I'll plead drunken insanity.

I tuck his big bear paw between my two palms and pull it over to me, using our hand sandwich and his substantial forearm as my pillow. In my peripheral vision I see his lips curve in a tiny smile, but I close my eyes so if there's any judgment in his expression, I won't see it.

My cheek is resting on his shirt-sweater sleeve and I nearly swoon at the softness. I need to find out the manufacturer of this bewitching garment and write them a gushing love letter. Better yet, I'll track down the supplier and secure reams of fabric to get a pillow and sheet set made. I'll wrap myself in this heavenly cocoon every night. The idea of it makes me sigh with pleasure as I drift back to sleep.

The second time I awaken, Ben is asleep. I'm groggy and my head is pounding, but even in my feeble state I recognize the rare opportunity to stare at him unobserved and resist the urge to fall back into my comfortable cloud of sleep. He's sleeping on top of my bedspread, a respectable distance from me—always the gentleman, which I'm currently finding more annoying than noble. He's kicked off his shoes and they're lying haphazardly on the floor, though he's otherwise fully dressed.

I drag greedy eyes over his profile, exploring the lines and contours of his face up close: his hair, too long and ruffled by the pillow; wide-set cheekbones; his nose with just the slightest ski-jump curve at the end; his mouth, so sharp and expressive in life, relaxed and guileless in the repose of sleep. Those spellbinding eyes—the ones that make me question everything—mercifully hidden beneath his lids. He really has a very nice face.

Nice. I almost laugh. What a ridiculous understatement.

His face is magnificent. Gorgeous, even. Under the cloak of night and darkness, I can admit what I haven't been willing to: Ben is insanely attractive—especially when he's not talking.

He has one of those angular jawlines that's a mesmerizing series of cuts and right angles you only see on movie stars. A portrait artist would beg to sketch his likeness in charcoal. His cheekbones are basically chiseled from stone. It's the Mount Rushmore of faces.

I desperately want to touch it.

My adrenaline spikes and my breathing shallows as I weigh the ramifications of him waking up and finding my hand molesting his face. It would *not* be good.

But if I can just do it softly enough . . . and if he stirs, I can snatch it away and pretend to be asleep . . .

I'm floating outside my body as I watch my hand reach out to his face. I trail my fingers lightly—ever so lightly—over his cheek, his prickly stubble rough under the pads of my fingertips. His skin is warm, and I gulp as my heart jumps into my throat.

He breathes out a small sigh and I freeze, drawing my hand back slightly. But he doesn't stir, just sort of tilts his head fractionally closer to where my palm had been. I smile, the realization warming my belly: *Maybe I'm not the only one hungry for human contact.*

I replace my fingers and continue tracing them down his jaw to his chin, then brush my knuckles up toward his ear in a lazy circuit of discovery. I run my hand up and back for about as long as I dare, then cradle his cheek in my palm, testing the shape of him, and it's as I suspected: His face fits perfectly in my hand.

I let it rest there for a moment, savoring the solid heat of him, because I know it'll never happen again. I sear the memory on my brain before reluctantly pulling my hand away, breaking our contact.

He's a peaceful sleeper, his breathing slow and deep and quiet. It's surprising—I would have expected a guy his size to snore like a bear. I'm willing to bet he gives off so much heat that if I were wrapped in him, I wouldn't need the thick electric blanket I use in the winter.

I'm such a creeper.

An uncomfortable sense of disquiet steals over me. The fact that I'm noticing—fine, *appreciating*—so much about Ben's body is not good. Not good at all.

Okay, Kate, let's recalibrate yourself here.

I look at him, trying to conjure up memories of all the rude and offensive things he's said and done to me since I met him. I command myself to dredge up the feelings of hatred and annoyance that typically accompany his presence.

I dig deep.

But they just aren't there. I can't do it—and I feel guilty for even trying when he's spent his whole night taking care of me. Consciences are the worst.

Am I really experiencing this inner turmoil all because Ben's finally shown me a modicum of kindness? Am I willing to reevaluate his entire personality based on one night of human decency? Is that all it takes to forget the weeks of abuse I've suffered at his hands?

Or have I been wrong about him this whole time?

I cringe as I recall all the nasty things I've said to him, all the ways I've belittled him since I met him. I've reduced him to a stereotype, an archetype—basically, all the types. I've called him every name in the book, both to his face and in my head. I told him he was everything I hate about this town. The memory makes me wince.

How will I go back to hating him after this?

One thing's for sure: I need to figure this out, or things are about to get really weird around the office.

I'm not sober enough for this level of introspection. I make a mental note to analyze it further when my head isn't pounding. I resettle myself under the covers and—flicking away any lingering misgivings—scoot a little closer, cuddling up to him as much as I dare with me under the covers and him above. I relax against him, matching my breaths to his long, slow inhales and exhales.

His peaceful face is the last thing I see before I drift off again.

Chapter 13

I wake up to noises in my kitchen. I live alone; why are there noises in my kitchen?

I sit up but immediately regret it when my head screams in protest. I sink back onto the pillows, heart galloping in my chest, trying to figure out what's happening.

Do I have an intruder? Or worse, did I bring someone home last night and . . . forget? I wince at the thought.

I smell coffee. *If it is an intruder, they're courteous at least.*

I glance around my room in a daze, cursing the sunlight that's filtering through my curtains and splicing into my throbbing head. My eyes zero in on a foreign object on the floor: men's shoes. I stare at them for a moment before muddled memories begin to wash over me.

Me drunk. Ben carrying me. Me vomiting. Ben sleeping *in my bed.*

The images are hazy, blurred—I can't remember much of what I said, what we talked about—but I do know Ben brought me home. The pit in my stomach all but guarantees I've said incriminating things.

And now he's in my kitchen. Making or drinking *coffee.*

My headache is threatening to shut my brain down, so I swallow the two Advil I spot on my nightstand. Maybe I can just stay in my room until he gets the hint and leaves. It seems like a viable option.

I pull the sheets over my head and hide for a full minute. Two. I can't really breathe. I'm hyperventilating. Eventually I poke my head out and hear the clinking of dishes. *Yep, he's still here.* I'm going to have to man up. Woman up. Whatever.

I creep to my door and peek out. I see nothing. I open the door a little wider, slip into the hall, and peep into the kitchen. He must hear me because he instantly turns my way.

"Morning. How are you feeling?"

He's all smiles, bright-eyed and bushy-tailed. Oh God—he's a morning person. Of course he is. By this time, he probably would have run ten miles and caught his breakfast with his bare hands.

"Oh, uh. Um. Fine." I pause. "So you actually are here. That wasn't a dream."

He chuckles as he gives me a once-over. I probably look like the Crypt Keeper. I cower farther into the hallway in shame.

"You need to eat something. Last night you said you hadn't eaten."

At just the mention of food, my stomach turns over. "Oh, I—I don't think so. Need to eat, I mean. I just. Um, need to take a shower."

I'm stuttering like a kid on her first day of kindergarten. I back away, fleeing down the hallway to the bathroom.

I lock the door behind me, turn on the shower, and crumple onto the closed toilet lid, cradling my pounding head in my hands. What am I going to do about this? How can I get him out of my apartment? I've embarrassed myself so epically, I will never leave this bathroom. It is now, literally, a panic room. I stare at my shower curtain as more of last night's memories come flooding back, this time of my vomiting and his gentle hair tying. I groan miserably.

There's a light rap on the door. "Kate?"

I jump a foot. "What!" I shout. *Dial it down, Kate.* "Um, yes?" I say, a bit more demurely.

"Are you okay?" A pause. "I can leave if you want." *Praise Jesus!*

"Oh . . . well, okay. You can leave if you want. I don't care. Whatever. I just—I need to shower." *Please, for the love of all that is holy, be gone by the time I get out.*

Another pause. "All right, well, I'll just finish making you breakfast. You don't have to eat it, but you really should get something in your stomach."

My belly growls a bit. Now I'm hungry? Why am I so all over the place? My body is a traitorous wench.

"Okay," I call. I watch the shadows from his feet retreat from the door.

I throw myself into the shower, taking an extra-long time to wash and condition my hair. I shave my legs. I let the water stream onto my head endlessly in a pointless attempt to wash away my disgrace. When I'm done, I've steamed up the bathroom so completely I can barely breathe. I wrap myself in a towel and crack open the door, listening. I don't hear anything.

I make a beeline for my bedroom and slam the door. I throw on a pair of my comfiest yoga pants and an old, soft V-neck tee, then brush my hair out slowly, wincing at the tender spot on the back of my head. Only I am talented enough to make a hangover worse by ensuring my head pounds in the front *and* back.

I feel halfway human again, my headache dulled some, thanks to the Advil. I don't look quite as horrifying, though I have dark circles under my eyes and my face is still leached of color. When I scan the floor, I notice his shoes are missing and breathe a deep sigh of relief. He must have left.

I open my door a crack and listen, hearing nothing. I'm satisfied that he's gone, so I open the door fully and walk into the kitchen. A plate has been laid out with a piece of buttered toast, scrambled eggs, and a glass of ginger ale. I bend over and inhale. It smells heavenly.

"You're looking better."

I yelp in fright, peering through the opening of my kitchenette to the living room.

Ben's sitting on my couch—which I now recall with a sinking feeling was the site of vomiting episode number one—sipping leisurely on a mug of coffee. He looks entirely too comfortable and familiar in my apartment.

I place my hand over my thumping heart and sag against the counter. "Jesus. I thought you'd left."

"Apparently."

He stands and saunters over to the breakfast bar, an amused smile lighting his face. I find it nearly impossible to maintain eye contact.

"Just wanted to make sure you were good before I head out."

"I'm good." I am *not* good. I am the opposite of good. "Thanks for . . . all this." I sweep my arm through the air, gesturing to the food, but hoping he knows I mean everything involved in the last twelve hours.

Ben sets his mug on the counter and shoves his hands in his pockets, not acknowledging my thanks. "What's with all the food in your freezer?"

Huh? Holy left field. "What are you talking about? It's a freezer."

He smiles patiently. "It looks like you're hoarding meals for the apocalypse."

I laugh, relaxing some, then cross from the kitchen into the living room so I'm standing next to him. "Those are just my leftovers. I intentionally make extra food at dinner so I don't have to buy lunch every day."

"Don't you find it annoying to cook for one person?"

"Well, yeah, but that's why I triple the recipe, so the effort pays off over multiple days."

"Huh." He scratches his chin. "Sounds like a lot of work."

"I like cooking." The next words are out of my mouth before I can stop them. "Would you want to come over for dinner sometime?"

We both simultaneously widen our eyes. *What am I doing?* Remorse must be written all over my face because the smile he gives me is guarded.

"I'll allow you to take it back."

I let out a stilted laugh, immediately feeling ridiculous. It's only dinner. What's the worst that can happen?

"No, it's fine. It's the least I can do to thank you for . . . your help." I can't even indirectly reference the events of last night. Just thinking about it makes me want to hurl myself out the window. "Plus, it'd be nice to cook for someone else for a change. Though knowing your appetite, it would probably be more like cooking for four," I tease.

"You're not wrong." He looks . . . pleased. "All right, then, I accept. I have a policy of never turning down food."

I grin. "I do know that about you."

There's an awkward silence as we appraise each other uncertainly.

"I changed a couple of your lightbulbs," he blurts out, apropos of nothing.

"You changed my *lightbulbs*?"

"They were out. I thought I'd make myself useful," he says sheepishly.

"I can't reach them. I've been meaning to call the super."

"I figured." He points to himself and shrugs. "Tall guy. *Super* handy."

I can't help my laughter. Who *is* this person? Thoughtful and considerate are absolutely not what I was expecting.

"Thanks. That was sweet of you." I reach out and brush his elbow in thanks.

He smiles, wide and unguarded this time, his eyes bright and bottomless. Seriously, how is this a real color? Against the green of his shirt, they're practically electric.

I jolt like I've been shocked by a doctor's paddles. Memories flood my brain and I'm left reeling. I remember my hand moving up his arm . . . down his chest . . . into his waistband . . .

My hand flies to my mouth. *Oh my God.* Humiliation rolls off me in toxic clouds. It's the atomic bomb of embarrassment. I am the Fat Man and the Little Boy.

"Ah, I can see you're remembering some things from last night." His mouth holds an amused smirk.

"I—I'm so sorry . . . I don't know what to say . . ."

"Don't be sorry. It's fine." He waves it away, like the fact that I sexually assaulted him is nothing.

"It's not fine. You helped me and I . . . I can't believe I would have . . ." I can't finish my thought. I'm brain-dead with embarrassment. "I'm horrified."

His smile drops.

"I didn't do— I mean, we didn't—?"

His mouth falls open, his expression shifting from surprise to anger. "No. Nothing happened. Jesus, Kate, you think I'd take advantage of a sloppy drunk? Some of us have better decision-making abilities than that."

I visibly flinch at his words, absorbing them like a physical blow. They tangibly hurt. But once I'm over the shock, fury builds in its place. Humiliation and rage churn inside me like a swirling tornado.

So I do what I know how to do. Like the reverse of a snake shedding its skin, I slip on my hating-Ben armor. Hitting back is familiar territory for us. As familiar to me as my own name.

"Thank God," I say nastily. "Or else I'd need to take another shower."

Ben stares at me for a long, loaded moment. "Really? That's how you want to play this?"

"I'm not *playing* at anything. Listen, I never *asked* you to—"

"Do you have any idea what could have happened to you last night if I hadn't shown up? Who could've *seen* you?"

Outrage spikes my blood. "What is *that* supposed to mean?"

"What if one of our colleagues had walked in and seen you like that? How do you think it would look for one of Senator Warner's top aides to get caught fall-down drunk the same week her signature legislation gets killed? What if that guy at the bar had been a reporter? Shit gets around this town. You may not care about your reputation, but I've seen people get fired for a lot less."

I'm incensed. "Are you *kidding* me? I go out drinking *one* time and suddenly I'm publicly shaming my boss? I don't know who appointed you the morality police, but I can take care of myself. Have been for years now."

"You can take care of yourself. Really." He barks a loud *ha!* and too late I realize how I've set myself up again. "Which part of last night demonstrated that you can take care of yourself? Was it when you drank enough for six people on an empty stomach? Or was it the part where you couldn't walk without falling? Or when you thought it was a good idea to flirt with slimy barflies scouting for an easy target?"

A fireball of indignation lodges in my chest. "Oh, you're so self-righteous. I forgot I was talking to Mr. Perfect. Well, you can take this caveman act and shove it. I don't need this crap in my life."

"*I'm* a caveman?" He's incredulous, anger pluming off him like smoke. "This *caveman* picked you up wasted at a bar and *carried* you home. This *caveman* held your hair back while you threw up. This *caveman* made sure no one took advantage of you."

He's practically spitting the words at me, his entire body coiled in restrained anger. He's the Hulk building into a frenzy, and at any moment there'll be an explosion of fury and ripped clothing. He's standing so close to me that I glimpse the flecks of yellow and blue in his eyes colluding to give them their otherworldly glow. He doesn't deserve those eyes.

"If I was a *caveman*, I would've taken you up on it when you threw yourself at me." He wields the proof like a sword, and it slices clean through me.

"I did *not* throw myself at you." I nearly choke on the words.

"Could've fooled me. Or I guess all friends paw each other?"

I think I'm going to be sick again. A high-pitched alarm crescendos in my brain. *Escape,* it screams. *Run.* But there's nowhere to go. I'm a deer in the headlights, an animal in the crosshairs.

He takes a step toward me and his eyes are cold, the teasing twinkle gone, wallpapered over by bitterness and contempt.

"You're reckless and irresponsible and God forbid someone calls you out on it. It's the worst kind of privilege, the way you walk around like nothing will ever happen to you. You think you're the first person to have a bill go down in flames? You think you've wasted nine months? I've been doing this for *eight years.* Grow up, Kate. Most people pick themselves up and fight harder, but you, you'd rather lash out at me and make every bad decision in the book." He shakes his head in disgust. "I knew you were stubborn, but I didn't think you were stupid."

His harsh words echo in my head like a skipping record. I take a ragged breath, trying to loosen the tight fist of hurt in my chest.

"Wow," I say, shaken. "Tell me how you really feel, Ben."

I watch the darkness drain from his eyes, his hard look replaced by one of blinking surprise. He seems a little shell-shocked, like even he is stunned by what just came out of his mouth.

"You know what, I *am* stupid," I say as I step back, silently cursing my wobbly voice. I can't let him see how much his words have hurt me.

"I'm so stupid, I actually thought we were becoming friends. But thank you for reminding me why that won't *ever* happen."

He starts to speak but I raise a hand to silence him. "You showed me who you were the first time I met you: a rude, arrogant prick. I should have believed you then. But I've got good news for you." I sidestep away from him and cross to my door. "You don't need to worry about me anymore. Thank you very much for your help last night, but no further assistance needed. I don't need to be saved, by you or anyone else. You're not my knight in shining armor, you're not my brother, you're not my bodyguard. You're not my *anything*."

I wrench the door open, the message crystal clear: *Get the hell out of my life.*

Ben stands there as several silent seconds tick by, then grabs his phone and wallet off my coffee table and brushes past me without looking back. I slam the door behind him.

Chapter 14

I'm so fired up after he leaves, I end up prowling my apartment like a caged tiger. There's enough adrenaline coursing through my system to power a tractor-trailer. I'm dropping so many mental f-bombs, someone should call a SWAT team.

I can't believe I ever thought he was considerate. I can't believe I let him in my *apartment*. How could I have been softening toward him? How could I have thought we were *friends*? The fact that I contemplated kissing him makes me physically ill.

I spend the rest of the day plotting his demise in a variety of provocative ways. Sending him anthrax-laced mail would be too painless. I imagine firing a poisonous dart across the atrium. Drowning him in the Reflecting Pool. Blinding him with the Mace that, ironically, he's given me.

I've probably been watching too much *Scandal*.

I'm not exonerating myself—I know I behaved badly—but I also know our fight wasn't all my fault. Maybe I *was* a sloppy drunk, but he didn't need to rub my nose in it. Aren't we all entitled to a bad night? In the face of my obvious mortification, he was needlessly cruel. Is that what a *friend* would do?

But by Sunday morning, with my temper cooled and the sting of his words faded, shame and regret start to eat away at me. As more of my transgressions come into focus, I'm forced to face an inconvenient truth: I'm in the wrong on this one.

I set off this chain reaction by questioning Ben's integrity—something he clearly values above all else. So what if he clapped back? Washing out my barf bucket surely earned him a snarky comment or two. He put himself out for me—*way* out—and I haven't exactly shown him the same kindness.

As I lie in bed—my pillow smelling of him in its own twisted form of psychological torture—I remember all the ways he took care of me. The concern in his eyes when he tied my hair back. His compassion when I melted down about my bill. The fact that he made me breakfast— even though he doesn't cook.

That *is* what a friend would do.

I'm the one who owes him an apology this time, but frankly, I'm too chicken to do it. Is there even a socially acceptable way to say, *I'm sorry for sexually harassing you, puking on you, then insulting you?* Not sure Emily Post covers this one. I should send him one of those inedible arrangements, those baskets of hard fruit shaped like flowers. They're terrifying and gross, but since it's food, he'd probably love it.

Instead, I decide to do . . . nothing at all, rationalizing that it's best if we make a clean break and go our separate ways. To assuage my guilt, I come up with a grab bag of excuses for absolving myself: our pseudo-friendship was always headed for a fiery end; the world is too fractured and polarized for bipartisan camaraderie; I'm better off without his mockery and mind games; after our showdown, there's no way he's interested in hearing from me anyway.

Ben and I were never meant to be friends in the first place.

★

And so begins our period of silence. I ignore Ben; he ignores me. I keep my blinds closed, and so does he. It's almost like we never met, and none of this ever happened.

Almost.

It's when I'm alone—and *only* when I'm alone—that I allow myself to wallow in my hurt feelings. I hadn't realized just how large a space I'd let Ben take up in my head, and his sudden absence makes me feel . . . I don't know, bored? Lonely? I can't quite figure it out.

I suppose our office antics provided a break from the drudgery. Since the election, life's been pretty dreary for those of us on the losing side. It's hit after hit with no end in sight. Our mail shenanigans were something silly and fun to look forward to in an otherwise depressing existence. Every opportunity to annoy Ben charged me up like a battery pack. It gave my days some zip, and honestly? He made me see our Republican opponents as human again.

Now the days are back to feeling interminable. Stress is high and I have no outlet. The excited hopefulness of the bill is gone and I'm reminded why hope is my enduring enemy. Hope. *Pah.* It's just as offensive as other four-letter words I don't allow myself to say.

I throw myself into the job, barely coming up for air, but even that doesn't work like it usually does. Stephen and Tessa know something's up, though mercifully they don't force me to discuss it, probably because they're still eating crow after the LeftField debacle. Besides, what could I even say? I'm still so upset about the bill's failure that relating the story of my drunken misbehavior is a bridge too far for me right now.

Still, I'm able to convince myself I'm doing fine until Tessa and I walk into a midweek lunch briefing and I immediately spot Ben, across the room and piling his plate with food. I'm so thrown by his presence that I freeze in the doorway—and he chooses that moment to glance up, as if he can feel me watching, feel the weight of my indecision. And somewhere in that flash of recognition, after we lock eyes but before he looks away coolly, I realize something shocking.

I *miss* him.

Or maybe it's our fledgling friendship that I miss. The constant drive to one-up him kept me sharp and engaged at work. Our mail mischief was an entertaining distraction from the daily grind. Our banter-filled runs were way more fun than exercising alone. I finally found a worthy competitor, someone I'd (grudgingly) begun to respect.

I even miss the arguing, of all things. His words from the bar replay in my head on an endless loop: *I'd rather argue with you than get along with anyone else.*

I think I have Stockholm syndrome.

I need to stop obsessing over this. To snap out of it, I force myself to list all the negative things about him: Politically undesirable. Arrogant. Bossy. Condescending. Physically intimidating. Eyes unfairly pretty.

Even the worst things make my stomach hurt.

★

Almost a week into our stalemate, I'm home making dinner, glass of wine in hand, an episode of *The Office* playing in the background. There's very little a dose of Michael Scott can't fix. When my phone dings with a text, I lean over to look at it, my hands covered in chickeny goo.

Stephen: Check out our two favorite people working overtime.

There's a video attached, and I hit PLAY with my elbow—but when I see it's Ben and Corinne, I screech and knock the phone to the floor.

Thank God there are no witnesses, because my reaction would expose me instantly. I stand there frozen, my mind racing in time with my heart. I quickly wash my shaking hands and mute Jim and Pam's playful banter and nauseating heart eyes, then pick up the phone like it's a ticking time bomb. My stomach churns as I hit PLAY.

The video's a little grainy—Stephen's clearly zoomed in some—but I could no sooner mistake Ben than Bigfoot. He's sitting in a booth, his head bent toward Corinne, a glass of wine on the table between them. She's wearing a skirted business suit and heels, her long brown hair cascading down her back. I can't see her face from this angle, but I can see Ben's perfectly—he's focused on her with rapt attention, their conversation earnest and animated. Near the end of the twelve-second video he laughs, she pokes her fork at him playfully, and then they both laugh.

This is no first date.

I wonder if Corinne is his picture-perfect future wife who ticks every box on his imaginary, magical list of attributes. I'm sure they agree on everything. I imagine they're laughing about the social safety net programs they plan to cut. They'll probably attend a gun rally after dinner. Maybe they'll stop and change into matching shirts that say PRACTICE SAFE SEX: DATE A REPUBLICAN.

I want to hate her, but even I have to admit they make a striking pair. I imagine their eventual Christmas cards: They're strolling down a Nantucket beach dressed in matching chambray, tanned and laughing at nothing as they clasp the hands of their Amazonian, athletically superior brunette children.

To torture myself, I watch the video a couple more times before forcing myself to stop.

Me: Interesting. They look good together.

Stephen: . . . You okay?

I'm on the verge of tears, actually, Stephen, thanks for asking.

Me: Just peachy.

I return to my dinner prep, smashing the garlic cloves with renewed vigor. I focus all my energy on making this meal a culinary masterpiece, but when I sit down to eat, I find I've lost my appetite.

I give in and watch the video one last time. It's as if Ben and Corinne are taunting me. Even after I banish my phone between the couch cushions, the flirtatious forking plays in my mind like one of those insufferable Instagram boomerangs. I'll stab her with that stupid fork if she doesn't vacate my thoughts.

I'm unsettled for the rest of the night—and the fact that I'm upset at all just makes me more upset. Why am I so worked up over this? Corinne all but said they were dating; none of this should be a surprise.

But I guess I feel betrayed. Why would he come to my rescue on Friday night if he had a girlfriend? Surely Corinne would never agree to him carrying me home from a bar and spending the night in my bed—not that he reciprocated any of my clumsy attempts at seduction. I recall his derision at my "pawing" him and blush anew. No wonder he was so disgusted by my behavior.

I shake my head, trying to jog myself loose from this downward spiral. Why do I care who Ben dates?

You don't, I tell myself.

But there's a nagging voice in the back of my head I'm having a *really* hard time ignoring. The voice sounds something like this:

You loved it when he carried you. You analyze how he looks at you. You dream about that shirt-sweater. Suddenly you're adding cinnamon to everything. You sneak peeks at his office window thirty-seven times a day. You miss him.

I sigh. Why does it I feel like I've lost something I never even had?

Chapter 15

It's Friday evening and I'm packing up to head home. I've just turned off my light when George, my favorite night-duty police officer, pokes his head in the main door. When he sees me exiting my office, he makes a dramatic show of checking his watch.

"Why am I not surprised you're still here?"

"Because we have this same conversation every night around this time."

He laughs as he holds the door open for me. "I know I'm old-school, but I'm going to tell you the same thing I tell my grandkids: Nothing good happens after hours. And what are you doing hanging out in a dark and deserted old building, anyway? It's Friday night. You young people should be out having fun, not burning the midnight oil. The country will still be standing on Monday." George's age and impending retirement are his favorite topics of conversation.

"Yeah, yeah, save your judgment. We can't all have the rip-roaring social life you do."

He snorts. "Rip-roaring, right. Said to the old man on the graveyard shift."

The two-way radio at his hip crackles with feedback as he walks me to the elevator. "So where's your young man tonight?"

"Great question," I joke, playing along. "If you stumble across any eligible bachelors, will you let me know?"

He looks confused. "Did you break up, then?"

"Break up?"

"With your young man."

Now *I'm* confused. "My young man?"

"You know, the big guy. Also works late?" George holds his hand above his head in the universal sign for *tall*.

"Are you talking about the guy who works across the way?" I point across the atrium. "Ben?"

"That's the one. I thought he was your boyfriend."

"My *boyfriend*? Whyever would you think that?"

"I just assumed when he asked me to keep an eye on you that—"

"Asked you to keep an *eye* on me?"

George's eyebrows shoot up. "A few days ago he asked me to check in on you when you were working late. It seemed like an innocent request." He looks puzzled. "The way he said it, I thought you and he . . ."

"No."

I steal a glance at Ben's office window. His blinds are still closed, though light shines out the edges. Of course he's there. He's always there.

"I'm sorry, I shouldn't have made that assumption. Us old men, we see what we want to see." He winks at me. "But you can never be too careful, right? Nice that you have friends looking out for you."

I force a smile. "Yes, it's very . . . *nice* of him. Thanks, George. Have a good weekend."

"You too."

He ambles off down the hall at the same time the elevator doors in front of me snap open. I stare into the empty space, feet rooted to the spot.

I can't believe it. Ben is *still* watching out for me. Even after everything that's happened.

The guilt I've managed to keep at bay comes roaring back, and this time it looms larger than my pride. There's no excuse I can hide behind now—I have to apologize. This undeserved act of kindness has forced my hand.

When the doors slide shut I'm spurred into action, advancing toward his office with a determined stride. Our standoff has gone on long enough. He apologized to me once; I should be brave enough to do the same.

When I get to his door, it's slightly ajar and the sound of his voice wafts out; he's on a phone call. I take a deep breath, swallow my pride, and knock lightly, nudging the door open a little.

When he glances over and sees it's me, he stops midpace. I point to one of his desk chairs with raised eyebrows, but instead of answering he turns away, circuiting to the window and continuing his conversation. *Very mature.* I sigh and enter, giving myself permission to snoop around his office a bit while he finishes his call.

In one corner there's a small round table with a bunch of newspapers and financial magazines littering the top. A muted TV playing the Fox Business channel rests atop a bookshelf crammed with hardbacks and three-ring binders. Framed UVA diplomas adorn the walls. As usual, stacks of paper cover every square inch of available desk space. Those piles give me hives.

I casually scan his desk, searching for proof of Corinne as Serious Girlfriend—a framed photo, a handwritten note, some ticket stubs, perhaps—but the only personal items I see are a picture of a group of guys holding up some glistening, just-caught fish, and a bobblehead of a Washington Nationals baseball player.

"He thinks going to the press will give him leverage, but he's wasting his time. He has no choice here." I have no idea what Ben's discussing, but his body language screams *irritation*.

I make a face at the conversation and move to take a seat at the desk. It's by sheer divine intervention that my eyes land on a file peeking out from underneath his laptop. The tab on it is simply marked, KATE.

I freeze midsquat. My thighs burn. I snap my eyes to Ben but his back is still to me, his line of sight trained out across the atrium. He's totally oblivious to my discovery.

Why does Ben have a file with my name on it?

I reach across his desk as stealthily as possible, determined not to rustle anything and alert him to my clandestine activity. It's the highest-stakes game of Jenga I'll ever play. I pinch the file in my fingertips and slide it out as silently as I can. I almost have it free when *wham!*

Ben's hand slams down on the file and I jump about a foot in the air. He whisks it away, depositing it in one of his desk drawers and slamming it shut with a *bang*.

The hell?

I gape at him but he goes back to ignoring me, turning away again but standing sentinel in front of the drawers like a guard at Buckingham Palace.

"I'll call over there and talk to Dean. I'm sure he's not happy with the grandstanding." A pause. "I'm not worried about it. It'll be over by tomorrow's news cycle." Another pause. "Yeah, that's fine. I agree. Thanks, Bill."

He hangs up, facing the window for an extra beat. Eventually he turns, tosses his phone on the desk, and sits, scooching in his chair. Only once he's all settled does he look at me.

"What can I do for you, Ms. Adams?" His tone is coolly professional.

Is he serious?

"Why do you have a file with my name on it?" I demand.

"Why are you here?"

"What's in that file?"

"What file?"

"Are you seriously going to pretend I didn't just see you hide it?"

He rolls his eyes and turns his attention to his computer, clicking his mouse and tapping a few keys. I stare at him, incredulous, but he goes right on ignoring me. *I guess he is.*

Remember why you're here. I take a deep breath and give the elephant in the room a backbreaking shove. "Fine, I came by to talk to you."

"About?" He frowns at his screen, clicking absently.

About how annoyed I am that I miss you. Can we go back to the way things were?

The glow from the monitor slants across his face and I find myself studying his profile, my memory summoning images of his sleeping form and my late-night hand creepage. His five-o'clock—or, technically, seven-o'clock—shadow is visible and I gulp as I remember how it felt beneath my fingertips.

Get back on track, Kate.

"Um, about . . . this standoff we have going on."

He doesn't reply, just clicks around, glaring at his screen.

"Ben."

No response.

"Benjamin. Benjy," I poke, but not even his nickname can break him.

"Kate, you came to *my* office. What is it you need to say?" He is not going to make this easy.

"I came to apologize."

He finally looks at me, reclining slightly in his chair and folding his arms. It is all power pose.

"I'm sorry about the things I said to you. I shouldn't have lashed out like that, especially after you helped me. It was clearly a result of my own embarrassment about my behavior. I wish I'd handled it differently."

I wait for him to say something, but he just sits there, stoic. His face betrays nothing.

I'm so uncomfortable, I'm practically twisting out of my skin. Nevertheless, I persist. "While I'm at it, I'll add an apology that you had to take care of a belligerent, ungrateful drunk. You didn't have to do that, and I really appreciate it."

I should probably apologize for making unwanted advances toward him, but since that went over so well the last time, I figure I'll just leave it unspoken. Besides: I'm not really sure I'm sorry. It's the most action I've seen all year.

I wait a beat for him to respond, but he stays stone-faced, still leaned back in his chair. I'm starting to feel pathetic at his lack of reaction and my continuous word vomit. I'm struck by an idea, but if this doesn't work, I'm bailing out faster than you can say *Goldman Sachs*.

"I was wrong, you were right. You're the best, I'm the worst." There! I spot it—a lip twitch. "You are good-looking, I am not attractive."

His mouth curves up in a reluctant smirk. He smothers it in a hurry, but the damage is done. I had him there.

He rubs his jaw as if to wipe away the evidence of his smile. "So, you think coming in here and quoting *Happy Gilmore* is going to fix this?"

"I don't know. Will it?"

His eyes narrow. "You forgot 'I'm stupid, you're smart.'"

"Let's not get carried away."

He squints further, considering me. With no warning, he straightens and his chair snaps upright, startling me.

"You called me a *caveman*. After I spent the night taking care of you." His eyes glitter in anger, all signs of joking gone.

I bite back my first instinct, a fiery retort. Instead, I take a deep breath and wait for my heart rate to slow. "You're not a caveman. I shouldn't have said that."

"You're damn right you shouldn't have."

"And *you* didn't need to make me feel worse," I snap. Welp, so much for restraint. "Look, I've spent the last year of my life working on this bill, and right now it all feels like a colossal waste of time. I'm embarrassed that it failed, I feel guilty that I made my boss look bad, and I'm angry at myself for getting my hopes up about one stupid thing in this town. And now I get to add to it that I humiliated myself in front of you."

His face softens a fraction. "You don't need to feel embarrassed in front of me."

"Sure I do."

There's a loaded pause. "Well, I'm sorry I made you feel worse."

It's a stiff apology, and I know why: it's because he meant every word he said during that argument. And if I'm being honest with myself, I'm more embarrassed by the truth of his words than angry at him for saying them.

I decide I'll take what I can get. "Shall we call a truce, then? Put this behind us?"

He blinks at me a couple of times, then nods slowly.

Mission accomplished. Quit while you're ahead.

"It's late, I'm gonna head out." I move to stand, then decide to extend an olive branch. "I'm grabbing some dinner on my way home. You're welcome to join me."

When he makes no move to follow me, I feel every ounce of the crushing weight of his rejection.

"What, not enough groveling for you?" I force a laugh, trying to disguise how deeply pathetic I feel.

His expression is unreadable. "Nah, I'm just not quite done here. How are you getting home?" *Of course.*

"Walking, as usual. And yes, I have my scary rape whistle and Mace,"

I say, jingling my keys at him. "Though perhaps I could ask George to escort me? Since he's been tasked with *keeping an eye on me* and all."

Ben's eyebrows jump. *Caught.*

"Yeah, I know what you've been up to. I'm surprised you haven't implanted a tracking chip behind my ear. Or maybe you did in the middle of the night and I slept through it."

"I probably could have, you were snoring so loud."

"I do *not* snore."

"You sure about that?" He smirks.

It's the first sign of the old Ben, the Ben I know. Bantering Ben. Relief washes over me like a waterfall.

"Okay, well . . . have a good weekend," I say, giving him an awkward little wave. I'm halfway out the door when I hear his voice.

"Kate. Wait."

I poke my head back in. "Yeah?"

"Run with me tomorrow."

Something in his voice makes my stomach constrict.

"Okay."

He smiles, a real one this time, nodding his approval.

I turn and flee.

Chapter 16

I tap my foot impatiently, checking my phone again.

Mom: I'm in the building . . .

Mom: I'm on the elevator . . .

The elevator doors open.
"I'm here!"
"Mom!"

I practically dive into the elevator for a hug, and we only separate when the doors start to shut on us. We're laughing and talking a mile a minute as I take her suitcase and wheel it down the hall.

My mom is visiting for the weekend, something we trade off doing every couple of months. Per our usual routine, she takes the train to Union Station, conveniently located across the street from the Hart Senate Building. She loves seeing where I work and gets a kick out of spotting the "celebrity senators" she sees on the news.

"I'm ready to go, but Stephen wants to say hi and I need to pack up my stuff," I explain as I lead her through the maze of cubicles, introducing her to some coworkers along the way. It isn't long before my small office is crowded with people, drawn by my mom's irrepressible laugh and any excuse to kick off the weekend early. I've just started shooing people out when Ben appears in the doorway.

"You know your blinds are open, right? Guess my invitation to this party got lost in the mail," he says, strolling in like he owns the place.

"Honest mistake," I say disingenuously.

Since my apology and our cautious truce, things have mostly returned to normal between Ben and me. We even ran together last weekend without resorting to blows or bloodshed. Stephen told me he's just thrilled I stopped moping.

Ben waltzes right past me, heading straight for my mother. "You must be Beverly. It's so nice to meet you in person."

My mom goggles at him. "Oh! You're Katie's running friend?"

"Something like that," he says with a wink, extending a hand to shake. She bypasses his hand and pulls him in for a hug, shooting me a wide-eyed look over his shoulder and mouthing, *Oh my God.*

Here we go.

"You're bigger than you look on the phone." She's already heroworshiping him, gazing up at him with admiring eyes.

He laughs. "And you look even younger than you do on the phone."

I jump in before she can say anything incriminating. "Please don't get her going. She loves when people mistake us for sisters and I need therapy for all the creepy 'Stacy's Mom' stuff I have to deal with."

He smirks. "So, Beverly, does the feisty attitude run in the family, or just the good looks?"

My mom whoops. "He's got your goose, Katie! Where have you been hiding this tall glass of sweet tea?"

I loudly snap up the handle on her suitcase, breaking up their little lovefest. "All right, that's enough of that. Mom, we have reservations." I shovel her toward the door.

"So what kind of trouble are you ladies getting into tonight?" Ben asks, walking ahead with my mom as I bring up the rear.

"Oh, we're just going out to dinner . . ." she starts, then pauses. When she turns to glance at me there's a gleam in her eye, and I suddenly know what's about to happen before the words have even left her mouth. "Ben, do you have plans tonight?"

And there it is.

I nearly dislocate my shoulder trying to muscle between them. "Mom, it's Friday, I'm sure he's bus—"

"I'm not busy at all, actually. I'm completely free," he interjects. "How fortuitous!"

"Then you *must* come to dinner with us, I insist. I never get to meet any of Katie's friends!"

He flashes me a shit-eating grin and I narrow my eyes, trying to conceal my mounting panic.

He shifts his gaze back to my mom. "Thanks so much for the invitation, but I couldn't impose on your mother-daughter time. I'm sure Katie wants you all to herself."

At least he gave me an out.

"You wouldn't be imposing. We have all weekend! Tell him, Katie." She looks at me expectantly as Ben presses his lips together, unable to hide his amusement.

I know my mom—she won't let this go. "Ben, we'd *love* for you to join us," I say as insincerely as possible.

He grins. "Thank you *so* much for including me, Katie Cat. Why don't I just grab my stuff and meet you downstairs?" He winks at me before loping off down the hall.

As soon as he's out of earshot, my mom clutches my arm in a death grip. "Katie, he is *gorgeous!*" Enthusiasm seeps from her every pore.

I give her some *settle down* hands. "You can stop right there. We're just friends. Actually, barely even that. More like frenemies."

"Are you *crazy*? Why?"

"Well, he's a Republican, for one."

She gasps in mock outrage. "The horror!"

"It *is* horrible. We're constantly butting heads. We don't agree on anything. He's *for* just about everything I'm *against.*"

I feel a niggling of self-doubt as soon as the words are out. I don't *really* know where Ben stands on most issues; I've just assumed he touts the party line. In a position like his, he'd have to beat the drum. *Right?*

Whatever. Transitive property.

"Oh, *pfft*. Plenty of people have fallen in love across the aisle! Look at Matalin and Carville. Arnold and Maria. Joe and Mika!"

"If you're going to make comments like this at dinner, I will disinvite him. I'll do it right now." I hold up my phone menacingly.

"Oh, lighten up. You're too uptight."

"I am *not* uptight."

"You need to live a little."

"Are you going to say YOLO next?"

"We should get YOLO tattoos!" she shouts gleefully.

Sometimes I can't tell when my mom is joking.

★

After a quick stop-off at home to drop my mom's suitcase and change clothes, Ben meets us in the lobby of my building and the three of us head to the restaurant on foot. The first thing I notice is he's changed into another green sweater—though this time it's hunter green, not the same shirt-sweater I absolutely do *not* think about when I'm lying in bed at night. He keeps pressing a hand to my back as we walk, and maybe it's because I'm already nervous—or maybe it's his woodland forest–cinnamon scent that knocks me over the head like a two-by-four—but this tiny, unexpected crumb of affection is throwing me totally off-balance.

But I quickly realize my anxiety is unfounded: Best Behavior Ben came to dinner. He regales us with tales of working on the tax plan, impersonating some of the high-maintenance personalities on the committee and lampooning their over-the-top demands. My mom hangs on his every word, and honestly, I can't blame her—on the charming Richter scale, he's running a magnitude 8.5. He's laughing at all her jokes, drawing her out with questions about her life in New York and my childhood in Tennessee, praising my job performance and commitment to Senator Warner's initiatives. He comes across as charismatic, thoughtful, and intelligent. It's like *Invasion of the Body Snatchers*.

If I didn't know any better, I'd say he's trying to impress my mom—and giving an Oscar-worthy performance, at that. I catch myself staring at him more than once, trying to make sense of this impostor in Ben's body. Where are the insults? The barbs? It's unnerving—because frankly, I'm starting to believe it too.

When the conversation hits a lull, my mom goes in for the kill. "Ben, tell me about your parents."

I nearly groan at her obviousness, but he doesn't blink. "Mom and Dad, sure. My mom is a high school English teacher, and my dad's an accountant. They met at the University of Texas and they've been married for thirty-some years now."

"And you didn't want to follow in their footsteps and go to UT?"

He hesitates. "No, I needed a change of scenery. It's a big state, but Texas started feeling very small after a while."

"I don't know anyone like that," my mom quips, dry as day-old paint. "So how did you two meet?"

This should be good. "Yes, Ben, how did we meet?" I echo, tilting my head. Let's see how Mr. Charming handles this one.

He shifts in his seat. "Well, uh, Kate and I met during the course of her work on the child care bill." He glances at me as I make a face, and then his eyes spark, as if struck by inspiration. "We really hit it off. Got along great," he lies. "And we discovered so many shared interests, didn't we, Kate? Like running, for example. Although sometimes she gets tired and needs to be carried. Oh, and we both *love* trying new restaurants. Of course, she likes bars more than I do—"

"All right, she gets it, we have things in common," I cut him off, glaring daggers. He grins back as if to say, *Checkmate.*

My mom continues her interrogation, oblivious to our power struggle. "And what brought you to Washington?"

"You don't have to respond to her third degree," I break in, frowning at her. "This isn't an interview."

He waves me off. "There were a few different factors. I've always been interested in finance—it runs in our family, I guess," he says sheepishly, "but politics was never really on my radar until I got to college. It was during the recession, and a lot of my classes were analyzing the economy, the factors that led to the housing and banking crisis. I'd seen up close how badly the recession hurt small businesses. My uncle had a construction company that didn't survive the downturn. My cousins and I all worked for him at certain points, so it made it personal, you know? His business was his life's work." He pauses to drain his glass of water. "There were so many different theories about how to fix the economy, or even how the recession could have been avoided in the first place. I guess I just got swept up in the idea that I could be part of the solution, help people like my uncle."

My mom and I are both staring at him in rapt attention. He looks from me to her and lets out a self-conscious laugh.

"Sorry, that was a really long-winded answer to your question. Anyway, that led to my first job on the Ways and Means Committee. And that's how I got to know some of Hammond's team, and he was looking for a director . . ." He trails off.

"And he poached you away," I supply.

"Sort of, I guess." He looks embarrassed.

"Can't say I blame him," my mom pipes up, eyeing me meaningfully. She's practically drooling.

I keep my face neutral, but I'm shriveling into myself. In ten minutes, my mom has learned more about Ben's passions and motivations than I have since I met him. Am I this self-absorbed? Have I never even asked him why he does this work?

"Good for you, Ben," my mom continues. "That's very noble, especially since I'm sure you could be making a lot more money elsewhere."

I look at him like he's someone new. "You never told me any of this."

"You never asked."

We stare at each other in a charged silence until my mom breaks in.

"Well, I, for one, am ready for lower taxes. Ben, how much am I going to get back?" She rubs her hands together like a greedy Scrooge.

"*Mother!*"

"What? I've never understood how we became the party of higher taxes. No thanks. Unsubscribe."

A laugh bubbles out of me. "*Unsubscribe?* What are you, sixteen?"

"No, I just look it," she says, tossing her hair and preening. "Oh!" She snaps her fingers. "Speaking of being young, how are your sisters? Didn't Alexis just have a birthday?"

Ben looks puzzled. "You have sisters? I thought you said you were an only child."

Now it's my turn to squirm. "I *was* an only child until recently. Besides, what you actually asked was if I had an older brother, and I don't." My voice is a little testy.

My mom's giving me a look. "You haven't told Ben about your sisters? Why not?"

"It hasn't come up."

I keep my voice light, but inside I'm fuming. Why should I have to broadcast my family history to everyone I meet? If I want to keep the details to myself, that's my prerogative. Britney Spears backs me up.

My mom frowns in disapproval. I beam back a silent message of my own: *Drop it.* Ben looks from her to me, caught in the middle and clearly lost.

Silence descends on the table. I'm suddenly keenly aware of every noise in the restaurant: the clinking of water glasses, the crash of silverware in the kitchen, the buzz of background conversation. I feel a foreign weight on my leg and glance down.

Ben's hand is on my knee.

I look up at him and his eyes silently communicate: *Are you okay?*

Oh no. No way am I going to allow him to give me that *injured bird* expression he's so good at.

I push my chair out abruptly, dislodging his hand. "I'm going to the restroom," I announce, then take off without looking at either of them.

I hide out in the ladies' room, taking a few minutes to collect myself. I should be used to my mom's thoughtless disclosures by now; she's done this my whole life. She's never cared who knows what—maybe because she never really had a choice—and she's never understood why I feel differently. It was one of the things I was happiest to leave behind in Tennessee, everyone knowing everything about me. Now people know what I *want* them to know—except when my mom feels the need to blurt things out, apparently.

On the way back to the table, I see the two of them conferring intently, heads bent together as if they're discussing something sensitive. I quicken my pace, but when my mom sees me coming she sits back, her mouth set in a firm line. Ben won't meet my eyes either. *What now?*

"What'd I miss?" I ask as I take my seat, looking from one to the other.

"Honey, are you walking home alone at night?"

I nearly get whiplash snapping my head toward Ben. He at least has the grace to look guilty.

"Seriously? This is what I get for bringing you? You *tattled* on me?"

He opens his mouth to answer but my mom gets there first. "Don't blame him. He said he tries to walk you but you're very stubborn. You should be thanking him!"

Oh, Ben is going to live to regret this. Or *not* live to regret this. "I am a grown woman, and I *don't* need a babysitter."

"But you're putting yourself at such unnecessary risk, Katie. Don't you know how dangerous this city is?"

"Yes, I hear about it every chance this guy gets. Who may never live to say it again." I violently spear the last of my chicken.

"Well, Ben, *I* appreciate you letting me know how irresponsible she's being."

I throw my fork down. "What is this, the Bev and Ben tag team? You're both being absurd! Plenty of people walk around this city every day. I don't appreciate being treated like I'm helpless." I glare at both of them. "Are we done here?"

Ben opens his mouth but this time *I* cut him off. "That was rhetorical for you. I *know* you're done here."

I give him the cold shoulder on our walk back to my building, rolling my eyes as he and my mom say their goodbyes. She fawns all over him, thanking him for picking up the check and gushing about what a good influence he is on me. If I hadn't just had such a delicious dinner, I would throw up. When she makes a comment about staying in touch, I get between them.

"All right, that's enough."

"It was great to meet you, Beverly. Maybe we'll get to do it again sometime."

He gives her a preemptive hug this time, which she returns with gusto. When he steps toward me I watch him hesitate, as if assessing the degree of grievous bodily injury he'll sustain if he tries to touch me. He must decide it's worth the risk because he leans in, wrapping me in a hug too.

"Bye, Katie Cat. Thanks for a lovely evening." He doesn't even sound sarcastic.

I glare at him sourly as he pulls away, which only seems to amuse him. He squeezes my shoulder and waves before strolling across the street. *And what is with all this touching?*

As soon as he rounds the corner, my mom drops the smile and turns on me. She's like Jekyll and Hyde. "Okay, *what* are you thinking?"

"What do you mean, what am *I* thinking? You threw me under the bus back there!"

"Threw you under the *bus*? I just assumed you would have told him about your family by now."

I huff and throw open the door of my building. "Right, because that's the first thing I tell my *work colleagues*. Maybe I should add it as a line item on my résumé: 'Special talents: I'm a prom souvenir'? 'I have daddy issues'?" I stalk across the lobby and aggressively stab the elevator button.

"Do you make eyes at all your 'work colleagues'?" she asks with exaggerated air quotes.

"That's called glaring." The doors open and I sweep her inside.

"What are you, blind? The way he was looking at you!" She swoons, falling back against the elevator wall. "To be looked at like that again . . ."

"Oh please, Mom, men look at you that way all the time. And I do see how he looks at me. With total contempt."

"Oh, *right*." When the elevator dings she floats down the hallway, carried away by her own false fairy tale. "I feel so much better knowing you have a man like that looking out for you."

"Mom, *stop*. I don't feel that way about him." *I don't think.*

"Don't even try to tell me you're not interested in him, it's written all over your face. You two are the most obvious fakers on the planet. You always were a terrible liar. That's one of the things I love about you, honey, you're so pure of heart." She stops at the door while I fumble for my keys.

"Mom, try to hear me. Okay?"

She raises an eyebrow indulgently.

"Ben and I are not dating. We will not *be* dating."

"And why not? Give me your best excuses." She crosses her arms.

"For starters, I'm pretty sure he has a girlfriend."

"Oh, hogwash. Fiddle-faddle."

I laugh in spite of myself. "It's not hogwash! Listen to yourself." I unlock the door and immediately kick off my heels. *Yesss. Sayonara, shoes.*

She jerks her thumb over her shoulder. "That guy? The one I just watched stare at you for two hours? The one who chose to spend his Friday night with you and your *mother*? He does not have a girlfriend."

"I'm telling you, he's seeing someone." I fill her in on Corinne and she sighs heavily.

"Well, if he is seeing this other woman, just make him forget about her." She flicks her wrist like this should be simple, like I'm Venus or Cleopatra or something.

"You're acting like he's confessed his undying love for me and I've turned him down, but let me be clear: he has never once displayed romantic interest in me." *I don't think.*

"Maybe you're not giving him an opportunity. He probably thinks if he's honest with you, you'll bite his head off. You're very intimidating." She flops onto the couch and kicks her feet up on my coffee table.

"He's had opportunity," I shoot back before I can censor myself. No way am I telling her about my night of drunken debauchery.

"I think you're trying to force your brain to overpower your heart. He may not be who you saw yourself with on paper, but you can't help who you fall in love with. The heart wants what it wants," she trills. She's a poet now.

"Stop saying I'm in love with him! You barely know him. He could be a serial killer."

"Serial killers typically aren't worried about getting you home safely."

I exhale in frustration. "We need a subject change."

When I walk past the couch, she tugs me down next to her, forcing me into a hug. I give in to her embrace and take a deep inhale of her peach-scented shampoo, letting the familiar scent wash over me.

"I just want you to be happy," she murmurs into my hair. "You seemed . . . all lit up with him. It's been a long time since I saw you like that. And what are you so afraid of? He seems sweet and supportive and protective. I hardly think that's someone who's going to hurt you." She pulls back, nodding decisively. "I'm rooting for him. I'm Team Ben."

"I think what you meant was, you're Team Kate. You know, your *only daughter*? And why are you so desperate to pair me off, anyway? I don't need a man to be happy."

"Of course you don't *need* a man. You've always been enough, all on your own. But we're not meant to go through life alone."

"Says the woman who never married even though many have tried."

She tsks. "I wasn't alone. I had you. And don't use me as an excuse to hide."

"Hide?"

"You're scared of your feelings for this guy. You forget that I know you. Your excuses may work on other people, but they won't work on me."

I shake my head and don't answer her.

She smiles, patting me on the leg. "Just promise me one thing."

"What's that?" I ask warily.

"If he works up the nerve to tell you how he feels, don't shut him down. Get out of your own way for once." She doesn't wait for a response. "Now, let's talk about this walking-home-alone business. It's about the stupidest stunt you've ever pulled."

I blow out a breath. "Jesus, Mom, not you too. I am *so* tired of getting shit for this."

She recoils like I've slapped her. "I hope you don't talk that way in front of Ben. It's so unbecoming. No man wants a potty mouth, sweetie."

Chapter 17

I don't think I can be friends with Ben anymore.

After my mom left on Sunday night, the anxiety I'd been keeping at bay started creeping over me like rising floodwaters. Between the awkward family feud he witnessed and my mom's blunt analysis of our relationship, I hardly know how to behave around him anymore. It's as though with dinner, we've crossed some invisible red line.

I'd be lying if I said I looked at Ben as just another friend. I actually lay in bed on Friday night re-creating all the ways and places he touched me: back graze, knee grab, bear hug, shoulder squeeze. It's a new dance move: the Mack-arena. My body's a color-coded Ben heat map at this point.

But another part of me is desperate to starve this attraction, bury it so deep you'd need an excavator and a miracle to find it. Ben and I are opponents; rivals in every sense of the word. There's no world in which a nonplatonic relationship between us would end in anything but mutual destruction.

I wake up Monday with fresh resolve. This is lust, plain and simple. It's his fault for carrying me home and awakening antiquated cavewoman urges I didn't even know I had. As an evolved, feminist woman, I cannot allow these primal instincts to prevail.

But my newfound willpower lasts about as long as my commute. When I get back from a Monday all-hands and sift through the mail stack on my desk, a flyer catches my eye—and all my plans to avoid Ben fly right out the window. *It's perfect.* I nearly cackle with evil glee.

I crane my neck to see if he's in his office. Sure enough, he's on the phone, pacing a hole in the carpet. I watch him for a minute, admiring one of my favorite looks on him: jacket off, sleeves rolled up. Business Casual Ben. He stops with his back to me, but his arms must be crossed because even from here I can see the shirt fabric stretched taut across his shoulders. I let my gaze drift down, eyes lingering on his tight—

Absolutely not. I shake myself. Where was I going with this? Right— the flyer.

I wait until he's returned to his desk, then shoot him a text.

Me: I have BIG news.

Ben: Do tell.

Me: I have to show you.

Ben: How cryptic. Tell me about it over lunch?

I glance out the window and find him watching me, head tilted as if in challenge.

Challenge accepted.

★

Since Ben's coming from a meeting, we agree to meet at the downstairs Dirksen Servery. I get there first and snag us a table, and as I'm unzipping my cooler I feel a tap on my shoulder. I turn and see John Conrad.

I greet him with a hug. "You're back! How was it?"

As Senator Maxwell's chief of staff, John frequently travels with him around Maryland to attend to state business, and he'd been gone all last week during the recess.

"It was good, but there's a ton to catch up on, as always. I'm spent."

You wouldn't know it to look at him—he's as eager and energetic as ever, his perfectly coiffed hair glossy as an oil slick. I smooth my own mane self-consciously.

"Thanks for sending me those briefing notes, by the way. I was actually wondering if you wanted to grab a drink some night this week? Catch me up properly?"

"Of course! Just name the day."

"Great." He beams, gesturing to the empty seat across from me. "Want some company? I was just grabbing something before our two o'clock. Can I get you anything?"

"She's all taken care of."

Ben shoulders between us, claiming the empty seat and setting down a tray piled with a veritable mountain of food. From where I'm standing I see a sandwich, a container of yogurt, a banana *and* an apple, a massive chocolate chip cookie, and two water bottles. He slides one over to me and starts unwrapping his sandwich, ignoring John entirely.

"John, do you know Ben Mackenzie?" I blurt, trying to compensate for Ben's rudeness.

John flashes Ben his practiced politician's smile and holds out a hand. "I think we've met before. At Riordan's retirement lunch last year?"

Ben's eyes flick to me. "Sounds about right." He shakes John's proffered hand and I watch John wince a little.

"You were at that lunch too?" I say to Ben in surprise. "Huh, so was I."

"I'm pretty sure the entire district was at that lunch." His eyes land on John's lapel pin and he snorts under his breath. He picks up his sandwich and takes a massive bite, effectively eliminating his ability to converse.

I narrow my eyes at him. Whatever happened to *I don't choose my friends based on party affiliation?*

John's gaze slides back to me, his signature smile a little strained. "I'll see you at two, then?"

"Absolutely."

I inject as much warmth into my voice as possible in an attempt to defuse this weird tension. He nods at me, shooting Ben a dark look as he heads off to join the lunch line.

I sink into my chair and level a glare at Ben. "What was *that* all about?"

He frowns, wiping his mouth with a napkin. "What was *what* all about?"

"Are you PMSing or something? You were so rude to him."

"I don't have time to make small talk with every Tom, Dick, and Harry who wants to stand over you and drool."

"He wasn't *drooling*," I hiss, glancing anxiously toward the line. I think John's pretending not to watch us. "He's my colleague. Kind of like how *you're* my colleague?"

He makes a face. "He's such a politician." He says *politician* like others might say *Satan*.

"Um, hello? We work for politicians."

"We might work for them, but that doesn't mean I'd want to *date* one."

Whoa. "Who said anything about dating him? He's my *coworker*."

"Pretty sure I just heard you agree to go out with him."

"That's to catch up on *work*. He's been out of town." I don't know why I feel the need to justify this. "Anyway, moving on."

"So what's your big news?" he asks, munching on his apple now.

I thought you'd never ask. "I know what you're doing for our bet!"

"You actually going to follow through this time?" he taunts, and I make a face.

Over the past couple of weeks, I've tossed out a number of potential bets designed to make any dyed-in-the-wool conservative squirm: an immigration rally, an LGBTQ+ Pride parade, a climate change seminar. The only problem is, every time I propose something, Ben agrees readily, even acting *excited* about going. Maybe he's bluffing, but since the reaction I'm going for is more *extreme pain* than *enthusiasm*, I keep demurring at the last second. Even more vexing is that he's playing coy about his plans for me, saying only that "he'll know when he's hit on it" and "you can't rush genius." *Eye roll.*

"Well, don't keep me in suspense. What will I be doing?"

I pluck the flyer from my purse and slap it down on the table. "Oscar Vega is holding a fundraiser, and we're going."

His food shoveling pauses momentarily. "Representative Vega? The socialist?"

"The Democratic Socialist, yes."

He resumes chewing, keeping his face carefully blank. "No problem, Princess. I can make it through a fundraiser, especially if there's free food involved."

"It's really more of a seminar. It's not plated. But I think you'll enjoy the keynote." I point to a spot midway down the page.

He reads it aloud. "How Taxing the Rich Can Pay for Universal Healthcare." He looks up at me. "Seriously?"

"I know, doesn't it sound fascinating?"

He pushes the flyer back toward me. "You know I can't be seen at an event like this."

I feign ignorance. "Whyever not?"

"As an architect of the tax plan, I can't attend an event *attacking* the tax plan."

"'As an architect of the tax plan'? Do you even hear yourself? You sound like one of those celebrities who says, 'Don't you know who I am?' while they're getting arrested."

He crosses his arms. "I'd prefer not to get fired over a *bet*."

"Hey, this whole thing was *your* idea. But if you'd like to forfeit, just say the word." I smile with all my teeth.

His eyes narrow, and we stay locked in a silent standoff until he exhales, shaking his head. "Fine, I'll figure something out. But if you expect me to sit there and listen to some quack disregard *centuries* of evidence as to why a socialist system doesn't work, then I'm cashing in my dinner invitation."

"What dinner invitation?"

"You promised me a home-cooked meal." There's a glint in his eye. "And I'm collecting."

I feel my face flame. He's breaking the cardinal rule.

As if by tacit agreement, neither of us ever mentions my night of drunk and disorderly conduct. I don't know if it's out of respect for me or if he's just as disturbed by that whole fiasco as I am—maybe both— but we avoid the subject like Stephen avoids carbs. It's like the Voldemort of events: the Night That Must Not Be Named.

"Fine. If you're a good boy during the event, I will make you dinner as a reward."

His lips twitch. "Deal. I have one request."

"What's that?"

"Will you cook at my place? Instead of yours?" The casual way he asks makes my stomach drop to my knees. I must look thrown because he leans toward me, lowering his voice. "I have an ulterior motive."

"What's that?"

When he grins, he's like a kid with a shiny new toy. "If you cook at my place, I'll get to keep the leftovers."

Chapter 18

L imes, huh? Those must be for margaritas."

I roll my eyes but don't comment.

"Mm, jalapeño. That must be for the queso. You are making queso, right?"

"Stop it."

Ben and I are at the store, shopping for our dinner. That's right, it's D-Day. Dinner Day. I haven't told him what I'm making and he's currently trying to pester me into spilling the details—in between griping about the event we just attended.

"I can't help it, I'm starving. You didn't tell me that guy was going to drone on for *two hours*. And at dinnertime!" The real crime, apparently.

"You're lucky I'm making you dinner at all after the heckling you did."

He raises a finger in dispute. "I did not *heckle*. I merely asked a simple question about his numbers not adding up. He should have been prepared for it."

"You heckled," I reiterate, selecting an onion as he trails behind the cart. "I thought your head was going to explode. You were sighing so much, I'm surprised you didn't pass out."

"If he said 'wealth redistribution' *one* more time . . ." he says, then shakes his head. "The important thing is, I've proven how open-minded I am. Good luck beating me now."

"It's hard to beat you without a task," I remind him.

"Be careful what you wish for, Katie Cat, especially after that nonsense I just suffered through." He furrows his brow. "Why are you picking out grapefruit? Is that for tomorrow's breakfast?"

I sigh loudly. "You need a task." I tear off the bottom of my list and hand it to him. "Go next door to the liquor store and get the things on that list."

"Your wish is my command." He starts to leave before turning back, leaning on the cart with an elbow. "Now, don't try to check out before I get back. I'm paying for this."

"You're darn right you're paying for this. What do you think, I'm cooking *and* buying?"

He's chuckling as I shoo him away, and I finish gathering the rest of the items on my list without his meddlesome snooping.

I'm playing it cool, but I'm pretty anxious about this dinner. There's been a noticeable shift in our dynamic over the last couple of weeks, a simmering undercurrent of tension that coats every one of our interactions like pollen in springtime. I see or hear from Ben every day, whether it's a spontaneous drop-by, a lunch, a text, or more recently, when he seems to magically finish up work the same time I do so he can walk me home. I tell myself I'm letting him because it'll get my mom off my back, but I'm not sure who I'm trying to fool. Those walks are the best part of my day.

Another thing that's changed? The amount of flirtatious physical contact between us has skyrocketed. Every one of his hugs, hands on the back, and playful hair ruffles triggers deep theoretical analysis when I'm lying in bed at night. I'm sure a casual observer wouldn't bat an eyelash at our low-level PDA, but compared to how we behaved before? We may as well be publicly fornicating on the steps of the White House.

Stephen's taken to calling us "friends without benefits," and it's excruciatingly accurate. It's bizarre, this romantic purgatory I've found myself stranded in. I've never had a guy best friend before (a straight one, anyway); is this what it's like? Constant flirting with no hope of it leading anywhere? If so, I'd like to unsubscribe. Delete my account. I'm so sexually frustrated, I could scream.

By the time he gets back from the liquor store, I'm ready to check out. He insists on carrying all the bags, so I load him up like a pack mule. Between his massive workbag, the liquor bags, and the grocery bags, I'm thanking God he can bench-press twice my body weight.

His building really *is* close to mine—like catty-corner close. When I realize, I widen my eyes and whisper, *"Stalker,"* but he only laughs.

Ben's phone starts ringing as he's shouldering into the apartment. Since my hands are free, I pluck it out of his pants pocket, trying to ignore their dangerous proximity to his crotch.

"You have a FaceTime call from *Mom*," I report, unable to suppress my grin. "How sweet that you're FaceTiming now, too."

He groans. "I did it once and created a monster. Just let it ring through." He heads in the direction of what I assume is his kitchen.

"Sure thing," I tell him, then press ACCEPT. This should be fun.

"Hi, Mrs. Mackenzie? This is Ben's friend Kate. He has his hands full, but he wanted to make *sure* he didn't miss your call."

Ben's head swivels one hundred eighty degrees. He's Linda Blair in *The Exorcist*. His look of abject distress has already made this little gamble worth it. *It's payback time, buddy.*

The woman on the screen has shoulder-length brown hair the same shade as Ben's, round cheeks, and a friendly smile that's familiar. "Oh! Kate, it's so nice to meet you! I've heard so much about you. And please, call me Susan," she chatters in a lilting Texas twang. Her eyes are lit with excitement as she takes me in, her effusive hopefulness radiating through the screen like sunshine. She may even be more transparent than my own mother.

Moms. I guess once you're single past a certain age, they're all the same.

"You have? Well, isn't that just so sweet of him?" I say, playing up my southern accent. I keep an eye on Ben's agitated form in the kitchen as he frantically tries to free himself from his plastic web. "I'd just *love* to hear what he's told you."

He's across the room and snatching the phone out of my hand before the words are even out. "Never mind that, Mom." He shoots me a dirty look.

You don't screen moms, I mouth to him, then call out, "Nice to meet you, Susan! Hopefully we'll talk again soon."

I'm snickering as I head into his kitchen and busy myself unloading and organizing the dinner ingredients. He has basic cooking utensils, but it's pretty sparse. I open drawers and find one dedicated entirely to takeout menus and another full of assorted tools. Apparently Ben is really into pliers, because he has like six pairs. If I have jewelry that needs fixing, I'll know just where to go.

His mom's voice drifts over from the living room. "Oh, Ben, she's lovely. She's as pretty as you said."

I freeze.

"Mother," he says sharply.

I pretend to focus on meal prep as he crosses the living room and disappears into a room off the hallway. I try to activate my superhearing but can't catch anything beyond a few hushed murmurs. In fact, imagining Ben in his bedroom makes my pulse go haywire. I wonder if I'll get to see it. It seems only fair, since he's seen mine—and, you know, slept in my bed.

I take stock of the situation. Ben's mom said she's "heard so much" about me. I'd chalked that up to your standard southern small talk, but now that I know he told her I'm *pretty*? That's kind of a big deal, right? Should I acknowledge that I heard it? Is there even a way to bring it up without sounding like I'm fishing for compliments? I'm thinking no. Guess I'll just pretend I didn't hear it. No point in making things awkward. Or awkwarder.

I belatedly look around, taking in his apartment for the first time. It's slightly larger than mine and newer, though very bachelor pad–ish in décor—brown leather couches, lots of heavy wooden furniture, a giant flat-screen mounted on the wall. It could use a woman's touch, the overall effect a little dark. If I lived here I'd pick a lighter paint color, hang some art, add some plants. Every home needs something green and alive—like Ben himself, I guess you could say.

If I lived here? Settle down, Kate.

I think I was expecting something more like his office, with towering piles of paper and detritus everywhere, but it's surprisingly neat. Everything has a place, and everything in its place. *Darn.* He'd be so much less appealing if he were a hoarder or something. I vow to unearth more of his flaws. I should check his cable history; it can tell you a lot about a person. My eyes snake down the hallway like a burglar casing the joint. Maybe I can find some closets to rummage through.

I'm demurely cutting peppers when he emerges from his room, smiling tightly. I remind myself not to make things weird.

I last about three seconds. "So, what have you told your mom about me?" I can't help myself. I'm the worst.

He exhales. "I just told her about dinner with your mom, that's all. Don't go getting any ideas."

He crosses to the fridge and pulls out a couple of water bottles, handing one to me. It's one of the things I've noticed about him, his innate good manners. He doesn't say *Water's in the fridge, help yourself*; he goes and gets me one, always without being asked. I don't think he even realizes he's doing it, which is probably the sexiest part.

I've got this virile man-god standing in front of me, and his *manners* are what turn me on. Go figure.

"What ideas would I get, *Benjy*?"

That you think about me too? That you can't help but talk about me to other people? That you're in love with me?

Whoa. Where did that last one come from? *SETTLE DOWN, KATE.*

He huffs and walks out to his TV, crouching down to open a media cabinet. "See, this is why I said to let the call ring through. You of all people know how moms are, always trying to pair us off. I don't need her thinking we're halfway down the aisle or something," he mutters. A second later, music fills the air. A second earlier and I wouldn't have heard it.

I freeze, knife poised above the jalapeño, as a painful ache unfurls inside my chest. I think the dismissive tone he used hurts even more than his words. He may as well have said, *What a crazy idea, you and me.*

This is ridiculous. It was an offhanded comment, nothing more. Of course we aren't halfway down the aisle; we're not even dating. I have no right to care about this.

Then why are your hands shaking?

I set the knife down very deliberately. "Can you point me to your restroom?"

"Sure, it's just down the hall." He's walked back into the kitchen now but stops when he sees the look on my face. "You okay?"

"Yep," I say brightly, struggling to keep my voice steady. "I just need"—*you*—"uh, the bathroom."

I don't wait for a response, brushing past him as I flee down the hallway. Maybe I can blame the onion.

Ten seconds later I'm in his bathroom and staring at my reflection in the mirror, gulping lungfuls of air and willing myself not to cry.

This is not good. I'm in real trouble here.

How did I get here? And by *here*, I'm not talking about Ben's bathroom, which is irresistibly scented with his pine forest cologne or body wash or whatever the hell this intoxicating smell is that's driving me slowly insane. With each breath I suck in, he tunnels a little deeper into my chest. I should have picked a different place to hyperventilate.

How did I go from hating Ben with the fiery passion of a thousand suns to being reduced nearly to tears by his casual dismissal of our relationship? Should I have seen this coming? If I rewind time, could I pinpoint the second, the moment, the interaction that changed everything?

Somewhere along the line, I stopped despising him and started dreaming about him. Hoping he'd touch me, argue with me, notice me.

Want me.

How can I be falling for someone who's so obviously wrong for me? I'm smarter than this. Ben and I together would be a disaster. We're oil and water. Hamilton and Burr. Kanye and Taylor Swift. We don't mix.

What am I supposed to do now? I'm *cooking* for him, for crying out loud. Like I'm his girlfriend or something. And what's the deal with Corinne, anyway? Is he dating her or not? And if he is, does she know Ben's inviting other women to his apartment at night?

I take a deep breath and let it out slowly. I need to come up with a plan of attack. I can't let on that I've just had an existential crisis in his bathroom. I'm good with lists. I'm even better at crossing things off. So here's what I come up with:

Step 1: Leave the bathroom.
Step 2: Act normal.
Step 3: Analyze this later, when I'm not cowering in Ben's erotically spiced bathroom.

It's a solid plan. I think I can manage it. But before I can leave, I have to do one thing.

I stand and cross to his medicine cabinet. I'm a woman on a mission and not even my freshly minted crush-shame can stop me. I open the door and spot it immediately: cologne. And it's in a green bottle, of course. What other color would it be? My whole world is painted green these days.

When I uncap it and take a big whiff, the thunderbolt of attraction that rips through me is so intense, I have to grip the vanity. And that's when it hits me:

I am totally infatuated with Ben Mackenzie.

Chapter 19

Sugar or salt rim?"

"Salt, definitely."

I've successfully executed the first two steps of my three-step plan, and Ben hasn't appeared to notice my jumpier-than-usual behavior, thank God. I drag his glass through the salt and pour in the freshly made margarita, then present it to him like a winning lottery ticket. He takes a sip and his eyes widen.

"What did you put in here? Crack?"

"Sorry, can't tell you. It's my special recipe."

He surveys the various citrus carcasses and cocktail artifacts strewn about the countertop. "I guess I'll have to use my powers of deduction."

I laugh. "No, I mean I can't tell you because I make it a little differently every time. It's mostly the fresh-squeezed fruit. Margaritas taste so much better if you don't use mix."

"Evidently." He scans the ingredients I have laid out. "So how can I help?" He starts unbuttoning his shirt cuffs, then glances down at his suit pants. "Maybe I should change."

"Oh, no you don't. If I don't get to wear comfy clothes, then neither do you, sir."

I'm proud of how steady I keep my voice, like the thought of him shedding clothing doesn't put me at risk of a cardiac event.

"I can't even take off my tie?"

I let out a loud sigh, like this is an outrageous request. "Fine. You may remove your tie." *I'm so generous.* "But for every item you take off, I get to take one off, too." What am I even *saying*?

He reels back. "Seriously? I'll take them all off, then."

"Never mind. I . . . misspoke." *Backpedal, backpedal.*

"Can I pick the item?"

"*No!* Just forget I said anything."

Ben narrows his eyes, very deliberately moving his hands to his neck. Keeping his eyes locked on mine, he loosens his tie, pulls it over his head, and throws it on the counter.

It's so erotic, I can barely stand up straight.

I arch an eyebrow and place my hands at the neck of my blouse. His eyes flare.

"Just kidding." I kick off my leopard-print heels and cackle. I'm quite a seductress.

He unbuttons his top couple of shirt buttons, not breaking my gaze. He's calling my bluff. Well. If he thinks I'm backing down, he's in for a surprise.

I unbutton the top button of my blouse. He untucks his shirt. I untuck mine. He slides off his watch, and off come my earrings. We're contestants on *Strip Chef,* the hottest new show on the Food Network.

When he puts his hand on his belt, I hold my hands up in surrender. "All right, I give. I have nothing else to take off."

"I could suggest something, if you need ideas." The oven beeps then, and it's not the only thing that's preheated.

Ben is giving me a very . . . unplatonic look. For the first time, a bloom of hope swells inside me, like a heart-shaped balloon inflating in my chest. *Ben and me together . . . could it actually work? Is he wondering the same thing?* I know I'm not imagining this tension saturating the air between us. There's no way he's seriously dating Corinne if he's playing strip . . . er, cooking with me in his kitchen.

Unless . . .

What if Ben *is* dating Corinne—and bringing me back here because he brings *lots* of women home to his apartment? What if I'm just one of many? What if *I'm* the other woman? I may have feelings for Ben, but there are lines I won't cross. I'm not a woman who screws over other women. And I'm certainly not lining up to be another notch on his bedpost.

I take a step back. Then another.

Confusion clouds his expression. "What's the matter?"

I swivel toward the counter, obscuring my face as best I can. "Nothing."

This is getting ridiculous. I should just ask him—*Are you dating Corinne?* Find out once and for all. But something's stopping me, a combination of pride and fear and doubt that has me paralyzed with indecision. What if I'm totally misreading him? What if he's just messing with me again, like he did on our run? What if I lay my cards out on the table and he rejects me—or worse, gives me the *just friends* speech? I'll never recover from the shame.

"Did I cross the line? I was just kidding around."

See? It was a joke, Kate.

I force a smile. "You're fine. I'm just hungry." *So hungry for you, you have no idea.* "Let's focus on dinner."

I start bustling around the kitchen, keeping my back to him as I talk. "I should warn you, the cleanup on this meal is steep. We're probably going to use every pot and pan you have." I open his lower cabinets and they're practically empty. "Which apparently won't be too hard." I drag out his two lonely pans and set them on the stove.

"I'll clean, so don't worry about that."

He rolls up his sleeves and I have to avert my eyes. It's such a routine male gesture, but the way my body reacts you'd think he was doing a striptease.

When he holds up his hands and says, "Okay, put me to work," I nearly break into hysterical laughter. The kind of work I want him to do would make a hooker blush.

I set him up chopping the onion instead while I quickly assemble the queso and get it in the oven. Working side by side in his kitchen is a challenge—it's a small space, and since he's not a small guy, I find myself constantly brushing against him. Every graze of his shirt-clad arm sears me like a drop of hot oil. I need to simmer down. I need to bite down on a strip of leather and scream.

"Do I get to find out what we're having yet?" His voice pulls me out of my stupor.

"Sure. Pulled chicken and pulled pork tacos." I laugh when his face lights up. "You look like a kid on Christmas morning."

"I *feel* like a kid on Christmas morning."

"Flattery will get you everywhere."

"But will it get me another home-cooked meal?" He arches a brow.

"How about you let me finish this one first?"

"Ugh, fine." He puts his knife down. "Done. What's next?"

My phone dings, but I can't check it because my hands are covered in meat product. "Can you see who's texting me?"

He cranes his neck. "Mom: *Don't forget it's your grandmother's birthday tomorrow.*"

"Ooh, good reminder." I wash my hands so I can text her back.

"Do you think it says something about us that the only people who call us are our moms?" Ben muses.

"Says something about *you*, maybe." I finish my text and toss the phone down. "My mom says hi. And she's sending you heart-eyes emojis." I make a retching noise and shudder.

"Please tell Bev I said hi. In fact . . ."

He wipes his hands on a towel, then grabs my phone, fingers flying. I don't even want to know what the two of them are talking about.

Okay, I do. I'll check later.

"So you're into cougars, then?" I ask innocently as I set some garlic and avocados on the cutting board for him.

"Ha. No, I just needed to taunt her about Words with Friends. I've beaten her three times in a row."

I stare at him. "Did I just hallucinate, or did you say you're playing Words with Friends with my *mother*?"

"Uh, *yeah*," he says in a Valley girl voice, like I should know this.

"I cannot even. I have lost my ability to even."

He smirks and starts peeling the garlic, as if the revelation that he's been in contact with my mother warrants no further explanation. I beg to differ.

"So your grandparents are still alive, then?"

"Yep. Actually, all four are still alive."

His eyebrows jump in surprise and I could kick myself. Great, I've piqued his interest.

"Wow, really? You're lucky."

"Yep."

I load both pans of meat into the oven and set the timer. When I turn back, he's watching me.

"What'd I say?"

God, he's like a bomb-sniffing dog. "Nothing."

"You are the *worst* liar. Absolutely no poker face."

My heart rate ticks up but I keep my face neutral. I'm not in the mood for this conversation tonight. I think I know something that'll distract him.

"Queso's ready!"

I pull it from the oven and set it up on his countertop alongside some chips I've poured into a bowl. "Now remember, if you fill up on queso, you won't be hungry for the tacos."

He gives me a look.

"I'm sorry, I forgot who I was talking to. Queso away."

He loads up a chip and one-bites it, then moans. "How do you do it?"

"I know, I'm good at everything. It's my cross to bear."

We banter back and forth until the oven dings, then I shoo him out of the kitchen so I can build the tacos. This is my favorite part: It's all in the presentation, and since I'm usually only cooking for one, I don't have a reason to make it pretty. I take my time sprinkling the cotija cheese and drizzling the chipotle mayo, adding a wedge of lime and painstakingly arranging the avocado, setting up his plate as artfully as if we were at a restaurant. When it's finally ready, he ushers me to a dining table he's diligently set with place mats and cloth napkins. *Cloth napkins.* What single man owns table linens? Is he *trying* to make me swoon?

When he takes his first bite, his eyes widen, then close.

"What do you think? Good?"

He holds up a finger, chewing. When he swallows, he locks eyes with me. "I think . . . will you marry me?"

I've just taken a sip of my drink and I immediately start choking, margarita spraying everywhere.

"Jesus, I'm sorry. I was just kidding. Are you okay?" He's out of his chair instantly, crossing to my side of the table and thumping me on the back.

"Yes, yes," I splutter, grabbing for my water glass and gulping some down. "I'm okay." I cough a few times. "Funny guy."

"For what it's worth, I wasn't really kidding," he says as he returns to his chair. "Maybe we can work something out. Your cooking skills in exchange for a twenty-four/seven security detail."

"You can be my muscle."

"I'm telling you, it's a solid trade."

We lapse into silence for a bit as we eat—or rather, I eat while Ben shovels. He powers down three tacos in the time it takes me to get through one. So much for those leftovers.

When he finally comes up for air, he clears his throat. "Okay. Twenty questions."

"That sounds like a bad idea."

"Come on, I'll keep it aboveboard."

"Fine. But we alternate the question asking. And we both have to answer each question," I add as an afterthought. He's not going to slip any *gotcha* questions in on me.

"Deal. Okay, I'll start." He thinks for a second. "Have you ever pictured me naked?"

I drop my fork and it clatters onto my plate.

"That was a joke. Just warming you up." His eyes are twinkling. "Let's see. Favorite food."

I blink a couple of times, still recovering. "Um, that's easy. Da—"

"Dark chocolate," he answers before I can get the words out.

I pause. "How'd you know that?"

"I pay attention." He winks. "My favorite food is what I'm currently eating. And I need a reload. Your turn." He stands and heads for the kitchen.

"What do you *really* think of the president?"

"No comment," he calls out. When he gets back to the table, he pauses. "No work questions."

"Fine." Probably for the best. "If I looked at your cable history, what would I find?"

"Fox Business, ESPN, reruns of *The Office*."

Of course he says *The Office*. I wonder if we're watching the same episodes from our apartments every night. The thought makes my heart smile.

"What about you?"

"Too many to count." He needs to ask the next question before I blurt out that we're *Office* soul mates. I'm one margarita away from asking him to be the Jim to my Pam. "Your turn."

He grins. "Least favorite thing about me."

"I can only pick one? Your party affiliation," I say, holding my nose. "How about me?"

"Don't have one."

I guffaw. "Nice try."

"What? I'm trying to earn more dinners here." He drains the last of his margarita and holds it up in a *cheers* gesture. "This was really good."

"Thanks." I pick up my own glass and swirl it around. "What's in the file with my name on it?"

He freezes, and I have to stifle my laugh. I don't think he thought this game through.

"Papers," he finally answers.

"*Papers?* Seriously?"

"Best I can do." He leans in, voice lowered. "I'm afraid you don't have high enough security clearance."

"Nice try. And your shifty behavior's just making me more curious, by the way." He shrugs, unrepentant. "Fine, since you ducked that question, I get another one. Where do you see yourself in ten years?"

He rocks back in his chair, patting his abdomen. "Let's see. Forty." He widens his eyes in a faux-panicked expression. "Hopefully married with some kids, *not* working in government anymore."

I smile at the thought of Ben as a dad. He'll be an amazing father—I know it with a rare, soul-deep certainty. The realization startles me. Are these the thoughts lurking in my subconscious?

He's giving me a funny look. I've been quiet too long.

"You want to get out of politics?" I ask quickly, latching onto the second part of his statement. The idea of Ben not working down the hall is . . . strangely depressing.

He nods. "How about you?"

I think for a minute. "Thirty-seven. Hopefully still doing similar work, but getting paid a lot more. Maybe married, maybe kids. I don't like to put that pressure on myself."

His eyes search my face with interest until my skin heats. "Your turn," I note pointedly.

"What was the fight with your mom about?"

This time, I'm the one who freezes. "Pass."

"Come on, I think I've shown serious restraint not asking you about this."

"Is that what this little game was about? Trying to sneak this one in?" I grab my water and guzzle the whole glass.

"No. But your reaction just makes me more curious."

I make a face.

"If you want, you can ask me something about my family first," he offers.

"Oh please, what would I need to ask you? You have 'nuclear family' written all over you."

I should've known he wouldn't let this go. When a week passed without it coming up, I assumed he was doing the gentlemanly thing and pretending that whole scene never happened. Guess there's only so much chivalry he's got in the tank and the table linens tapped him out.

"Just tell me, what am I missing?"

I blow out a breath. "Fine. So my parents were high school sweethearts and they had a very romantic time at prom apparently, because my mom ended up pregnant with me. They got a lifetime souvenir out of a high school dance. My dad went off to college and we stayed back." There. That's it in a nutshell. Hopefully, conversation over.

Unlike me, Ben has an excellent poker face. His expression doesn't waver during my confession. He doesn't even crack a smile at my *prom souvenir* line, and that one's usually a crowd-pleaser.

"So what happened when he came back from college?" *Argh.*

I squirm in my seat. "He didn't really *come back*, per se. I didn't see him a whole lot growing up. Like a few times a year, maybe, when he would come home from college on breaks, and then after . . . he just wasn't ready to be a parent. Until I was twelve, at least."

"Until you were *twelve*? What happened when you were twelve?"

"He decided he wanted to be a dad. Funny how that happens. He turned thirty and realized, 'Oh wait'"—I slap my forehead—"'I have a kid!'"

Ben's eyes sharpen and I immediately regret my sarcasm. I sound bitter, and that's a dead giveaway I'm more affected by this than I'm letting on. After nearly thirty years I've learned: *deflect, play it off, light jokes, wrap it up.* It's the surest way to avoid being pitied.

"So when he did start coming around more, what happened?" He's like a dog with a bone.

"Well, I was twelve—it wasn't like he could just swoop in and pick up where he left off. Anyway, it didn't last long because he ended up moving to North Carolina for his job shortly after that." I trail my finger through the condensation on my water glass.

"What's he like?"

I sigh. "Why do you want to know all this? It's so . . . untoward."

"I want to know you."

The look on his face is so kind, words start spilling out before I can stop them.

"My dad is . . . well, he's funny and smart. Everyone who meets him likes him. My mom tells me he was very popular in high school. He was an athlete. The running, I get that from him. He played basketball in college. I used to watch him on TV."

I feel a lump in my throat and pause for a second to shove it back down into my stomach where it belongs.

"My nose is my dad's, and my stumpy thumbs. He's more serious while my mom is flighty. As you saw." I smile halfheartedly. "I was a teenager when I realized my personality is actually more like my dad's than my mom's, and I was so angry about that at the time. I didn't want to be anything like him. Can't fight nature, I guess."

I pause for breath. The whole time I've been rambling, Ben's expression has stayed inscrutable. God only knows what he's thinking.

"Hmm," he says, reaching for his water. *Helpful.*

"*Hmm?* What does *hmm* mean? I'm out on a limb here, telling you all this."

He shakes his head, swallowing. "Sorry, I'm just trying to wrap my mind around it. You and your mom must have been such an adorable pair. I can't imagine how any man could walk away from that."

His words hit me like a punch to the gut. Emotion squeezes my throat.

"What's your relationship like with him now?"

I feel like I'm in a therapy session. "It's . . . fine, I guess. I don't know. We'll never be close in the way my mom and I are, but it's not acrimonious, at least. It's important to me that I know my sisters, so I'll always make the effort."

"It must be hard to watch him with his new family."

I can only give him a small nod. I don't trust my voice right now.

"I can't pretend to understand what it must have been like for you, but I think it's pretty incredible you were able to forgive him enough to have a relationship at all." He gives me a small, sympathetic smile, oblivious to my near meltdown. "Now. Why did you think you couldn't tell me this?"

"Oh . . ." I look down and swallow. Then swallow again. Darn this lump. "It's not you. I just don't like talking about it, to anyone. People make judgments."

He opens his mouth and I rush to intercept him. "I'm not saying *you* would. It's just when you say *teenage pregnancy* people automatically assume you grew up in a trailer park, that sort of thing. I prefer not to let it define me."

He looks thoughtful. "I think it might define you in other ways."

"What do you mean?"

He smiles gently. "Might this be why you do the work you do?"

"Oh. Yes, maybe in part. Kids in single-parent households deserve as much help as we can give them. Parents too. But it's more than that."

"What is it about, then? For you?"

I think about how to articulate the persistent ache in my soul. "It's just that people don't realize all the ways coming from a broken home affects kids. It's a lot of subconscious stuff I bet you've never even thought about. Like . . ." I trail off. "I feel silly saying some of this out loud."

"Nothing you've said has sounded silly."

Something about his quiet encouragement makes me want to open up in a way I almost never do.

"Well, for example, I used to dream about going on a family road trip like my friend Jess's family would do every summer. She would complain about it, of course, whining about how she hated being in the car that long and how annoying her siblings were. But all I could think about was how desperately I wanted to go on a road trip like that with my mom and dad and imaginary siblings. I used to hope and wish and pray so hard for it." I look down at my plate. "But hoping doesn't make things happen."

Awareness dawns on his face. "Ahh."

"What is *ahh*?" I say, exasperated. I definitely don't know his noises.

"*Ahh*, now I understand a comment you made . . . before." From his sheepish look, I know he means the Night That Must Not Be Named. "When you said you knew better than to hope for things that aren't going to happen. I . . . wasn't sure what you were referring to."

I open my mouth, then close it. I'm feeling the strangest compulsion to keep talking, to say things I've never said aloud. What I was once desperate to keep from him, I'm now desperate to divulge.

What is happening to me?

"What is it?"

He's watching me so closely, and with so much concern, I have to look away.

"Tell me."

It's his voice, so steady and authoritative, that pushes me over the cliff.

"I used to think my dad would come back. I had this whole fantasy scenario in my head where he would finish college and come home and say he did it all for us. And then when that didn't happen, I thought once he made some money, he'd come back and *then* we'd be a family."

I'm zoning out as I talk and suddenly I'm seven years old again, a lonely kid crying in her bed, wishing her daddy would come in and kiss her good night. Behaving like a perfect angel at school because surely if she's polite and obedient, he'll want to come back. Wishing on every set of birthday candles for her dad to come home. Praying at church, harder than any kid should ever be praying, for God to just send her dad back.

When I come to, I realize I'm crying. I brush the tears away with the back of my hand.

"I even picked North Carolina for college because I thought living closer to him would . . . Actually, I don't know what I thought it would do. Isn't that pathetic?" I laugh bitterly. "Anyway, spoiler alert: He didn't come back. He married Melanie ten years ago and started poppin' out some babies. My new siblings. So, do-over! New family. Looks like he got the one he wanted this time."

When I brave a glance at Ben, he looks so startled that I'm instantly mortified. I've said way too much. He had no idea his questions would rip the Band-Aid off a decades-old wound.

"I'm sorry. I didn't mean that. I love my little sisters. I don't know . . ."

"You don't need to apologize," he assures me.

"No, I shouldn't be complaining. I sound ungrateful and, really, I'm not. God knows my mom could have made a different choice. And I had two sets of grandparents helping. I had authority figures coming out of my ears! There are so many people who have it worse than I did."

He looks almost angry. "Would you stop trying to brush this off? Of *course* you can complain. Everyone deserves two parents."

It could be the way he says it, so matter-of-fact and sure, or maybe it's that he's giving me permission to do something I never do. Whatever the reason, the floodgates open and I break down completely. And these aren't dainty lady tears. This is ugly crying.

When he sees my face crumple, his eyes widen in that panicked look all men get when any female within a ten-foot radius is crying. He springs from his chair and kneels beside me, pulling me into a hug.

And I let him.

He strokes my hair while I bury my face in his shoulder and fall apart. He doesn't say a word. He doesn't *shush* me or tell me it's going to be okay; he doesn't offer advice like men are so wont to do. He just lets me cry. He's just *there*.

When I start to wind down, embarrassment taking the place of heartache, he pulls back, giving me a tentative smile. He passes me my napkin, and when I pull it away from my face, it's streaked with mascara.

"I'm ruining your napkin," I say between shuddery breaths. "And it's so nice that you have them. I'm sorry."

"I can wash it."

"And I made a mess of your shirt."

"Fuck the shirt."

I laugh in spite of myself, then swipe under my eyes again, likely in vain. I am not a pretty crier. I don't need a mirror to tell me I look awful, all red and blotchy.

"Aren't you so glad you asked that question? Hot Mess Express over here," I say, trying to make light of yet another cringe-worthy break-down Ben's witnessed.

"Honestly? I *am* glad I asked because it explains a lot about you. But I'm sorry I upset you."

I wave away his apology. How can I tell him I'm *glad* he pushed me? It's been a long time since I've talked to anyone about my dad—years, maybe—and it's cathartic. All this time I've been keeping things from Ben, I never would have guessed he was the one I should have confided in all along.

He goes quiet and I register just how close we are, his face level with mine, his hand resting protectively on the small of my back. I can't help but think how easy it would be to lean forward and kiss him.

I don't think he's thinking the same thing, though. His face radiates concern, and here it comes: his patented *injured bird* expression. Nothing like a little snot to kill the vibe.

"Well, your friend Jess was right."

Not what I was expecting.

"What do you mean?" I pull back a little, needing to put some space between us.

"You didn't miss much with the road trips."

I let out a laugh-sob through my sniffling. When he pats my back a final time and stands, I feel his absence acutely.

"I'm serious. Family road trips are the worst. All we did was fight. My parents wanted to murder us. And I would get carsick. I ate a lot back then, too, so you can imagine." He grimaces as he retakes his seat. "It wasn't pretty."

I'm laughing even harder now. "Your poor mother."

"She's a saint," he agrees.

"She seems very sweet."

"She liked you."

"She could tell that from the whole two minutes we chatted, huh?" I force a smile.

"That, and maybe a few other things I've told her." He winks.

When he starts eating again he focuses studiously on his plate, and I know he's giving me space to collect myself. When I've recovered some, I break the silence.

"Ben?"

"Hmm?"

"Thank you."

"For making you cry? Anytime. Bringing women to tears is one of my many talents." He huffs on his fingertips and polishes them against his chest.

I'm laughing again. "I know what you're doing."

"Do you now?"

I nod.

"Is it working?"

I don't even have to think about it. "Yes."

Chapter 20

This must be what hell feels like.

More specifically, the volcanic pit of sexual frustration in which I'm currently burning alive.

Last night when Ben took me home—the one-minute walk next door apparently deemed too dangerous for me to navigate on my own— I'd somehow convinced myself he was going to kiss me good night. I psyched myself up for it and everything. I was minty fresh. I was ready.

But he just squeezed my hand and told me he'd see me tomorrow.

I wallowed in crushing disappointment on the lonely elevator ride up to my apartment. Then I chased that disappointment with hours of tossing and turning. Does Ben not feel the sexual tension between us? Is he that oblivious?

Or worse—is it completely one-sided?

I'm on system overload here. It's saturating my bloodstream. Clogging my lungs. Steaming from my pores. "Friends without benefits" is all fun and games until you're lying awake, heartsick and horny.

If only I were the type who could be friends *with* benefits. I never could engage in meaningless hookups, even in college; it's just not my style. It's a shame, too, because I bet I could get him to bite. He'd suggested it himself, hadn't he? *Scratching the itch,* he'd called it.

"Hate sex isn't my style."

"It's not mine either, but for you I'd make an exception."

Ben's clearly my exception, too. A mouthwatering exception to all my carefully crafted rules. A handsome devil in a well-tailored suit, holding out a big, juicy apple.

Is it such a bad thing to want something that isn't good for you? Can't I just allow myself this one little indulgence? It's like eating that extra piece of dark chocolate. Staying up an extra hour to finish your book. Skipping your morning spin class to go to brunch instead.

Ben could be my extra piece of chocolate.

The thought plagues me as I dress for work the next morning. I need to quash these cravings, but it's easier said than done. Ben's dominating my thoughts like the president dominates the news cycle.

It's impossible to focus on work with my mind this scrambled. In a bit of Monday morning quarterbacking, I want to kick myself for retreating in his kitchen last night. Why couldn't I have just swallowed my pride and asked him if he's available?

A lightbulb blazes on and I jerk upright in my desk chair. *Duh, Kate!* It's time to do something I should've done a long time ago.

I peek across the atrium; his office is dark. Even so, I creep toward my window like a criminal and slap my blinds shut, like he's going to appear out of thin air and scold me. I grab my laptop and pull up Facebook, mentally calculating just how long it's been since I logged on. This past election murdered any desire I had to ever go on Facebook again, but this is an extenuating circumstance. A Benmergency.

Relationships leave a digital footprint. It's a truth as undeniable as death and taxes. If Ben is dating Corinne—or anyone else, for that matter—Facebook will prove more historically valuable than the National Archives.

I type his name into the search bar. There are plenty of results for Ben Mackenzies, but the second listing is the one I'm looking for: there's his smiling picture and underneath it, *Washington, DC.* We have six mutual friends. I click on it, pulse racing.

The gods are smiling on me—his page is public, though I quickly realize it's because he's rarely, if ever, posted on it. *Crap.* Most of the entries on his timeline are random photos he's been tagged in, which I soon realize is a blessing in disguise—I'm able to get an unfiltered look at his history this way.

My breath catches when I see the most recent post: Ben in a tux (gasp!) in a group picture from one of the inaugural balls (groan). He's beaming, the pride and elation on his face practically glowing out of the picture. I stare at it until my eyes blur, recalling how depressed I was that night. I scroll on with a heavy heart.

I surf past shots of Ben in a tropical location, nattily dressed in a linen suit as part of a groom's party; Ben at an outdoor concert, looking happily sunburnt in Wayfarer sunglasses. I gorge myself on information, reading every comment and noting each like, poring over his Friends list like the stalker I am. I don't learn much I don't already know—Ben likes to tailgate, Ben goes on annual fishing trips with a group of outdoorsy, sweaty-hot men. There are women in some of the photos, but I can't tell if he's actually *with* any of them. I'd guess not, based on the absence of any cheek-to-cheek, coupley posed shots. More importantly: no Corinne.

I scroll and scroll, then scroll some more. Before I know it I'm four years back, so deep in his profile I'm terrified of inadvertently hitting the LIKE button. I start to sweat, focusing on my mouse movements with rabid precision. I'm Tom Cruise in *Mission Impossible*, contorting my body to avoid the laser labyrinth, and one wrong move will trip the alarm bells. I imagine Ben receiving notifications in triplicate on his watch, phone, and laptop that scream: *Kate Adams liked your photo from 2013. And in case you weren't aware, she's stalking you!*

There's a knock on my door and I stifle a scream.

"Yes?" I call out, clicking frantically to X out my screen. Just my luck, it would be Ben in one of his unannounced drop-ins.

The door clicks open and Stephen pokes his head in. *Thank God.* My breath rushes out in a gale-force *whoosh*. He takes one look at my paranoia-laced posture and narrows his eyes.

"Am I interrupting something?"

"No! Not at all."

"Whatever you're doing—and I don't want to know—just remember, there are eyes everywhere." He points to the ceiling and mouths, *Big Brother.*

I roll my eyes. "Did you need something?"

"Obviously." He shuts the door behind him and takes the chair across from me, crossing his legs primly. "I need to hear about your date last night, of course."

"It was *not* a date. And it went . . . fine. Kinda." If you can call me crying on Ben's shoulder *fine*. I'd classify that somewhere between *terrible* and *call your therapist.*

"A *fine, kinda* non-date. Sounds fun." He emits a loud snoring noise.

"What do you expect me to say?"

"That passion finally overtook you and you got busy on his floor."

"Not this time. Sorry to disappoint."

"So next time, then? I'm counting on you to let me know what's underneath those Ralph Lauren suits."

In an unexpected twist, Ben and Stephen have become friends, a development that seems to make zero and perfect sense at the same time. I suppose I shouldn't be surprised—both of them could make friends with a tree—but after their inauspicious beginning, I was caught off guard one day when I spotted them in the midst of an animated discussion in line at the servery. When I asked Stephen about it later, all he'd say was they'd "buried the hatchet."

"You probably stand a better chance of finding out what's underneath those suits than I do."

"Are you telling me that you went over to his apartment, cooked him dinner—which I assume included alcohol—and *still* nothing happened?"

"There was a moment . . ." I trail off. "But I just don't think it's like that between us."

Saying the words aloud breaks my heart a little, because of course what I mean is, it's not like that for *him*. I am currently shipwrecked on Infatuation Island, population: one.

"Oh, please. The sexual tension between you two is giving *me* blue balls! I can only imagine how a guy with that much testosterone is holding up."

Talking about this so openly is having a strange effect on me. My fragile emotions, already simmering below the surface, are threatening to boil over. I swivel my chair to face the window and take a couple of cleansing breaths.

"What's wrong?"

I don't answer. I *can't* answer.

There's a pregnant pause. "Oh my God."

"There's no *oh my God* necessary, okay? I'm just tired." My voice, thick with unshed tears, betrays the lie.

"How did I miss this? You're smitten! You're a smitten kitten!"

"Stephen, *stop*. And lower your voice." I glance uneasily at my closed blinds, as if Ben might be huddled there, listening.

"You love him! You want to have all his babies! Honey, I don't blame you. It's a natural instinct in the presence of so much raw masculinity. Your ovaries are probably exploding anytime he's around. Frankly, I'm surprised you haven't gotten pregnant from the looks he gives you."

The laugh that bubbles out of me is laced with hysteria. "I need you to take it from a ten to a three. Please? I'm hanging on by a thread here."

He studies me as I rub my eyes. Even after an ocean's worth of eye drops, they're still raw from last night's cryfest.

"When did this happen? Why didn't you tell me?"

"Why do you *think*? You and Tessa have been all over me about this! And please don't say anything to her, okay? I don't need her judgment on top of everything else."

"Okay, first of all, I *never* told you not to date this guy. If you like him, you should date him. It shouldn't matter what I or Tessa or anyone else thinks."

"You know how it would go over around here."

He's unfazed. "So people will gossip for a while. Who cares? You're not really going to let that stop you, are you?"

"It's not just about what other people will think," I admit. "It's about what *I* think."

He sighs. "You can't get past it."

"I can't!"

He props his elbows on my desk, regarding me seriously. "Why not?"

"*Why not?* Because we're polar opposites! Because our belief systems are totally incompatible. Because . . . that!" I fling my arm in the direction of my muted TV, where Senator Hammond is currently being interviewed. "He's defending gun rights right now, Stephen. *Gun rights*. And I'll give you one guess as to who wrote those talking points."

"That's his job," Stephen says gently. "You know as well as I do that the job doesn't define you."

"So you would date a Republican, then?"

He pauses. "That depends. Does he look like Ben?"

I throw up my hands. "You're not helping! I need you to tell me how to move on from this . . . *crush* I seem to have developed."

"Well, you've come to the wrong place, because I am *way* too invested in hooking you guys up." He claps his hands gleefully. "Project! Okay, first things first. Are you sending him any signals that you're interested? Meaningful glances, lingering touches, risqué comments? Anything?"

I shoot him a frosty glare.

"That's not your idea of a suggestive glance, is it? No wonder nothing's happened."

"What do you expect me to do? Pass him a note in study hall that says, *Do you like me, check yes or no*? Drape myself across his desk and say, 'Take me'?"

He purses his lips. "Either of those would probably work."

I groan and bury my face in my hands.

He snaps his fingers. "Wait, why don't I drop some hints? I can be your middleman. Your wingman. Your fixer!"

"You clearly have no idea what a fixer does, Olivia Pope. And don't you dare."

His eyes spark with mischief. "You could do something to *make* him notice. Something not even *he* could miss."

I hold up a hand. "I know where you're going with this, and you can stop right there. I'm not going commando or braless. No accidental nudity. No nip slips." I know how Stephen's twisted mind works, and I need to cover every base. "Besides, if anything is going to happen here—and I'm not saying it will—he has to make the first move. I can't be the one to put myself out there this time. Not with him."

I heave myself out of my chair and cross to the window to peek out the blinds. Ben's office still sits dark and empty and I'm irrationally disappointed.

As hard as it is to admit it, I think it's time Stephen and I acknowledged the uncomfortable truth we've both been dancing around:

Ben Mackenzie is just not that into me.

★

I hear his voice before I see him, laughing with Stephen just outside my office. My stomach's twisting before Ben even pokes his head in the door.

"Lunch? I've got thirty minutes." He raises his eyebrows expectantly.

"Lost my appetite." I nod at the TV.

Right on cue, Senator Hammond's voice pierces the air between us: *"This isn't commonsense gun reform. This legislation infringes on the Second Amendment rights of law-abiding gun owners, and that's why it got defeated today."* The same sound bite they've been running all morning.

"Universal background checks go too far, huh?"

Ben's face stays carefully blank.

"You think Senator Hammond would be interested in cosponsoring a bill adding guns to school supply lists? Looks like kids will need 'em."

"I can see you're looking to bait me into an argument and normally I'd be all over that, but you'll have to take a rain check. The clock is ticking on my lunch and I'm starving."

I tilt my head. "How hungry are you, would you say?" I ask, reaching for my cooler.

His face lights up. "Did you bring me something?"

I pull out a Tupperware that holds one of the two wraps I made this morning and slide it across the desk. He pumps a fist in the air and shuts the door, then folds himself into one of my desk chairs.

"You're an angel." He opens the lid and takes a deep inhale, breathing in the bouquet like a sandwich sommelier. "Were you not even going to tell me about this? What if I hadn't come over here?"

"I figured your homing beacon would guide you this way sooner or later."

He smirks, nodding at the TV screen. "Mind if I shut that off? You know I can't stomach CNN while I'm eating."

"Sure. You're already eating my food, why don't you commandeer my TV too? Anything else I can get for you? A cold beverage, perhaps?"

"If you have one, that'd be great." He winks as he gets up.

I ogle his backside as he leans over to switch off the TV. If I had loose change handy, I'd toss some at him and watch it bounce off. When he turns back around, I run a quick audit. Today he has on a silvery-green tie with a pattern of tiny diamonds all over it. His shirt is neatly tucked into navy suit pants, his brown leather belt right at my eye level, though I refuse to let my gaze stray south of the equator. His sleeves are haphazardly rolled to his elbows, a heavy-looking watch hugging his left wrist, and all I can think is: *Forearms. Hair.* His casual handsomeness makes my stomach hurt.

I need to quit noticing everything about him. Maybe if I pinch myself every time I do, I can train myself to stop, like one of Pavlov's dogs. Or I could try electroshock therapy. Hypnosis.

I want to squeeze my eyes shut and crawl under my desk, but I force a smile instead and watch him eat. He's like a human vacuum cleaner, devouring everything in his path.

I prop my chin on my hand. "So do you really believe all that stuff?"

"You're referring to . . . ?"

I nod toward the TV.

"Ah." He finishes chewing, then swallows. "Passing that bill wasn't going to change anything and you know it."

"So I guess we shouldn't try."

He takes another bite, not answering.

"How does it feel to be on the wrong side of history?"

"Upholding the Constitution feels great, actually, thanks for asking." I roll my eyes.

"Look, you really don't want to debate me on the Second Amendment. I will nail you to the wall." *Sweet baby Jesus.*

My mind immediately goes to A Bad Place. I'm in Christian Grey's red room of pain and Ben's got me in wall restraints. He smiles seductively as he skims down my torso with a riding crop.

When he speaks again, I nearly seize out of my skin. "You've been warned."

"Right, because 'assault weapons for everyone' was what our forefathers had in mind when they wrote about a well-regulated militia."

"You were *there*? Please tell me about your conversation with the framers of our Constitution." Ben is feisty today.

"So you think anyone should be able to order a gun on the internet, no questions asked?"

"Not *no* questions asked." He hoovers his last bite, then eyes my untouched wrap like a stalking predator.

"Don't even think about it."

As he smirks, a disturbing realization settles in my gut. I'm about to ask a question I don't want the answer to.

"Do *you* own a gun?" *Please say no.*

He blinks at me. "Of course I do. I'm from Texas, Kate."

I taste acid. I want to rail at him. I want to howl in frustration. I want to erase the last ten minutes of my memory, *Men in Black* style.

"What?" he asks. Guess my crappy poker face is betraying me again.

"That's just . . . *so* disappointing." Understatement of the century. I feel like throwing up.

"Why?" He looks genuinely interested. "I shouldn't be allowed to defend myself? Exercise my American right to own a firearm?"

"You should do whatever you want, Ben."

I'm suddenly drained, my desire for debate dead and buried. As if I needed another reminder of why we'll never work.

"You're the one who picked this fight. Defend your position."

"I'm too tired." *And heartsick.*

He squints at me as if not quite believing I'm giving up. "This isn't small-town Texas or Tennessee. We live in a dangerous city with an incredibly high murder rate. I consider it a matter of safety to own a gun."

"How about leaving things to the police? You know, people adequately trained to use firearms?"

"I *am* adequately trained to use a firearm, and I'll protect what's mine. I won't apologize for it."

"*'I'll protect what's mine'*? Listen to yourself! This isn't caveman times."

At my use of the forbidden word *caveman*, his eyes narrow to slits.

"Calm down, crazy eyes. I didn't call *you* a caveman. I was simply referring to caveman *times*, where men used to go out and hunt and gather their dinner. They also protected their little women with clubs. I thought we'd moved past that mindset in the twenty-first century, but I guess not."

He scowls at me. We've slipped back into our old personas: foe versus foe, enemy combatants once more. It's helpful, really; a reminder I obviously needed. We've been getting entirely too close lately, our battle lines so blurred I'd almost forgotten how things *really* stand between us.

Like clouds parting in a stormy sky, his face clears and a diabolical smile spreads across his face. I can only describe it as the type of fiendish grin Wile E. Coyote sports after he's hatched yet another plan to catch the Road Runner.

"*What?*" I snap.

"I know what you're doing for our bet."

An avalanche of dread tumbles over me. "Whatever you're about to say, the answer is no."

"You're coming with me to the gun range, and you're going to learn how to shoot."

I vault out of my chair. "Absolutely not!"

He stands too. He can never let me have a height advantage, even for a minute. "You're going. And you'll see it's different than you think."

"Nope. Definitely not going."

He peers at me like I'm a puzzle he can't decipher, then makes a noise like *huh*. "You're scared. I didn't think you were scared of anything."

"You're damn right I'm scared! I'm scared of bungee jumping and skydiving too, if you're keeping track."

"There's no reason to be scared. I'll be right there the whole time and I know what I'm doing. I've been handling guns since I was a kid."

"Oh, that makes me feel *much* better."

"Kate, do you honestly think I'd let anything happen to you?"

We stare across the desk at each other in charged silence. Looking into his eyes like this makes my brain fuzzy. He has a very unfair advantage, this one.

"No," I finally concede.

He crosses his arms. "Look, I've seen what can happen to someone when their guard is down. You *never* want to find yourself in that position. You have a responsibility to keep yourself safe, and if you won't do it for you, then do it for me."

I blink, startled by the sudden change in his voice, the sharp vehemence I hear there. I study the rigid set to his shoulders and the taut, tense line of his jaw.

"Why is this so important to you?"

A shadow passes over his features, his expression darkening, before his eyes shutter and he looks away. "I have my reasons."

It's the clearest sign yet there's more to his overprotectiveness than meets the eye—something I've long suspected—but if I'm ever going to find out what he's hiding, I need to do this his way.

I exhale. "Fine. I will uphold my end of this bet and go to the range with you. But I don't like it," I add, retaking my seat at the desk.

He grins in triumph, showing off his perfect white teeth. "Excellent. When can you go?" Like we're negotiating dinner plans.

"I don't know. I'm very busy and important." I violently jerk my mouse to wake my computer.

"Kate . . ."

"What? You don't know my schedule. It's . . . packed."

"Packed with what? TV shows?"

I glower at him. "I have a speech to write. I'm working on it right now."

An ad starts blaring on the random webpage I'm on, exposing my bald-faced lie. I frantically click to mute it, but it's too late.

His mouth curves into a smirk. "Tonight, then?"

"No. Over the weekend or something."

"Saturday, then." His chin lifts in defiance, and I can't help but admire his jawline in profile. I hate myself.

"I didn't say *this* weekend."

"Kate . . ."

"Fine, Saturday."

"Good." He taps his watch and heads for the door. "This will be a very eye-opening experience for you. I can't wait."

"I can. I can wait forever, in fact."

He stops halfway out and turns, gripping the jamb on either side and leaning back in. *Muscles. Flexing.* I grab a rubber band off my desk and snap it against my wrist. Definitely not painful enough.

"If you're a good girl and go with a positive attitude, I'll treat you to dinner after."

My heart does a stutter-step. "You actually owe me two meals now."

He snaps his fingers. "That reminds me."

"What?"

The smile he throws me is blinding. "Thanks for lunch."

Chapter 21

Saturday afternoon finds me standing in front of my closet, puzzling over something I never thought I would: appropriate gun-shooting attire. When I texted Ben for guidance, he told me to wear something comfortable that covered most of my skin—a rather alarming directive I don't want to think too much about. I eventually settle on a pair of jeans, flat brown leather boots, and a cashmere V-neck sweater in a shade of blue that matches my eyes. I keep my hair loose and wavy and my makeup light, taking pains not to overdo it, but I can't help it—I want to look good for him.

I want him to *notice* me.

When I'm done, I eye myself critically in the mirror. Not bad. This sweater is on just the right side of tight, the V deep enough to hint without screaming, *Here are my boobs!* I look put together, but not like I'm trying too hard.

Not like you're secretly pining for him, you mean?

I wonder with simultaneous hope and trepidation if he'll wear something green tonight. The guy has more green in his wardrobe than a leprechaun. Green sweaters, ties—I even noticed green socks one day. I think he's doing it on purpose to embarrass me.

I get my answer before I even walk through the glass doors of his building: he's wearing the Sweater.

More precisely, it's the same green shirt-sweater he'd been wearing on the Night That Must Not Be Named. The sweater that clings to every muscle of his upper body like a second skin. The sweater I want to wrap myself in and huff until I'm high. It's the sweater of all my Ben fantasies.

I take a deep breath as I walk in and wave casually, doing a passable job of pretending my stomach isn't tied in knots. He gives me a once-over and visibly swallows. He looks . . . uneasy. So maybe he does notice what I wear—and likes it? The coil in my stomach loosens a bit.

"I told you to cover your skin."

Or maybe not.

I look down at my outfit, confused. Was he expecting a nun's habit? "I did."

"No, you didn't. There's going to be flying brass from the shells. It could land in your . . . shirt." He points vaguely to my chest area. I think he was going to say *cleavage*. He is all flustered.

"Oh." I hadn't known that. "I brought a jacket," I offer, holding it up.

His shoulders relax. "That should work." He pauses for a beat, eyeing me. "You look . . . nice."

"Just nice, huh? Not striking?" I wink at him. *Okay, I'm fishing.*

His face goes a bit frozen. "You always look striking," he says, glancing away before I can react. Maybe I'm not the only one having wayward thoughts tonight.

"Do my ears deceive me, or did you actually just compliment me?" I feel his forehead with the back of my hand. "Are you ill?"

He snags my wrist. "I have definitely complimented you before."

I pretend to think about it. "Hmm. Nope, I think I would remember if the world had ended." If he had complimented me, I would have dissected it and rerun it in my head a billion times. Infinity times. A googolplex times.

He frowns. "No compliments. Guess I'll have to rectify that."

He stands there for a long moment, squinting like he's running through a myriad of possibilities and rejecting them one by one. After ten seconds of silence, I shoot him a dirty look.

"What? I'm thinking," he says, laughing.

"Don't hurt yourself."

I start to move away but he catches my hand, a ghost of a smile curving his lips. When he speaks, his voice is an octave lower.

"Kate, you look *strikingly* beautiful tonight. Even more distractingly beautiful than you look every day at work."

I suck in a breath. I was expecting something like, *Kate, you are exceptionally talented at annoying the hell out of me.* Not a *real* compliment. The combination of his nearness, the handholding, and his velvety chocolate sex voice nearly liquefies me into a puddle on the floor. A blush crawls up my neck.

He looks amused. "Wow. This flustered from one measly little compliment? You're really opening up a can of worms here." He tugs me toward the elevator, not releasing my hand.

I press a palm to my neck, embarrassed. My skin is so hot, my clothes are incinerating.

"Come on. You know you're beautiful." He says it a little shyly, and I feel like the Grinch—my heart grows three sizes. "You leave a trail of men in your wake wherever you go."

My laugh is strangled. "That is such a lie."

"You just don't notice."

His barrage of flattery has me so off-balance, I'm running a beat behind on our normal banter tempo. "Well . . . thanks."

It's an entirely inadequate response. He deserves a reciprocal compliment, but when I consider telling him I think he's the sexiest man alive, *People* magazine be damned, I can't make my lips form the words.

"You're welcome."

His smile burns through my chest like a brand. I smile back, feeling timid and hopeful and nervous and . . . happy.

At some point as we stand there staring at each other, the air palpably changes, a crackling electricity whipping between us like static. My pulse intensifies as his eyes search my face, finally landing on my lips.

He looks like he's going to kiss me. Or maybe—he *wants* to?

My heart pounds as I mentally prepare for it—*this is it*—and I can't seem to access the air in my lungs and I hope I don't pass out, when a woman with a stroller wrestles open the front door of his building, huffing and puffing and making a ruckus. He drops my hand and rushes over to hold the door open, exchanging pleasantries as she struggles into the lobby.

My brain is absolutely screaming. Goddamn Ben and his chivalrous manners! I want to yell obscenities at this woman and her awful, cherubic-looking baby. Doesn't she realize what she's interrupted?

I hear Stephen's voice echoing in my head—*make a move*—and now I'm listening. I frantically try to concoct a plan that's obvious but not blatant. Unmistakable but subtle.

I realize these things are oxymorons.

Ben lopes back over and hits the DOWN button. We're standing shoulder to shoulder and the missed opportunity is soul crushing. Can he feel it too?

"You okay there?" he asks, nudging me.

My expression must be murderous. I need to calm down. No sense in frightening small children.

"Sure, fine."

I'm unconvincing. I'm desperate to get our moment back. I need to do something—*anything.* I fake-smile at him and let my eyes rove down his body. My brain zeroes in on the shirt-sweater. It's definitely a sweater. I think.

"I recognize this," I murmur, reaching out to pinch his sleeve. I can't help myself—I have to touch it. It's calling to me with its siren song.

He throws me a quick smile as a faint shade of pink blooms up the back of his neck, coloring the tips of his ears. His body language is suspicious and I puzzle over it until it dawns on me.

Wait—did he wear this sweater on *purpose*? So I'd be reminded of the night when, by his own characterization, I'd thrown myself at him? *Pawed* him, as he put it? Is this a signal or am I reading too much into it?

"So." He clears his throat, breaking into my reverie. "We're just heading down to the parking garage to grab my car. The range I like is in Maryland, but it's a short drive."

"You have a car?"

"Yeah. Though I don't get to use it all that much." The elevator dings and he ushers me in, pressing the button for the basement and leaning against the opposite wall. As far away from me as he can get.

"What kind of car is it?"

"You'll see."

"I bet it's a gas guzzler and terrible for the environment."

He rolls his eyes. Guess the moment is truly broken now.

When the elevator thuds to a stop, he leads me out with a hand on my back. "I'm just over here," he says, nodding to the right, and I follow a step behind him until he stops in front of a sporty dark blue SUV.

"I'm clairvoyant," I poke as he pulls open the passenger door for me to climb in.

I'm immediately enveloped by the Ben-scent of his car, the masculine tang of leather seats commingled with his signature cinnamon. It must be some sort of mints—Altoids?—and as he crosses around to the driver's side, I inhale so hard I probably sprain my sinuses. Can you orgasm from a scent? Because I'm dangerously close.

His car is pristine, lending credence to what he said about not using it much. There's no trash lying around, no empty containers of food, and no clutter, just a jacket laid across the back seat and an old parking stub in one of his cup holders.

"They say the car you drive says a lot about you," I comment as he reverses out of the space.

"So what does my car say about me?"

That you're a neat freak who smells orgasmic.

"That you're a sensible father of three who coaches youth soccer."

He laughs. "More like I'm six-four and need leg room."

I snoop in his center console and discover a sleeve of CDs that I immediately pluck out, seizing the opportunity to mock his taste in music. I am not disappointed.

"Fall Out Boy!" I hoot. "Ja Rule!" He tries to grab it but I hold it out of reach. "Creed! Oh, this is too good."

"Those were from high school, okay? I haven't bought a CD in years."

He maneuvers us up and out of the parking garage, turning out onto Eighth Street. It's barely five o'clock and we still have some light left, but the sky is starting to turn.

I hold up another one. "The *Jonas Brothers*?"

"It helped with the ladies."

"You should burn some of these. Honestly, I'm embarrassed for you."

"Like I wouldn't find a One Direction CD in your car."

"I wasn't into One Direction," I sniff. "I prefer the smooth vocal stylings of *NSYNC."

He snorts. "Same difference."

"Are you a Backstreet Boys fan, then? Is that where this animosity is coming from?"

He shakes his head sadly. "You're hopeless."

"Oh look, you've redeemed yourself." I select Tim McGraw's *Greatest Hits* album and pop it into the CD slot.

"You know, I have music on my phone we can listen to," he says, holding it up. "Cars have these fancy things called Bluetooth these days."

"Nope, we're going old-school now." I skip forward until I find "Just to See You Smile" and immediately start singing along. "This is one of my favorites," I tell him, semi-apologetically. Been in the car two minutes and I'm already playing radio commando.

"One of?"

"Well, they're all my favorites."

"Tim fan, huh?"

"I'm more than a fan."

Ben gestures to the radio. "Do you two need some time alone?"

That cracks me up, and I'm relaxing for the first time tonight. I spot his wallet in the cup holder and rifle through it like a pickpocket, pulling out his license.

"Ugh, you actually have a decent license photo. I can't even find anything to make fun of." I hold it up to his face to compare. "Shorter hair, though."

He grimaces. "I know. I need a haircut, but I keep putting it off. I have no time."

"I could cut it for you."

"You know how to cut hair?"

"No. But how hard could it be?" I flash him my winningest smile.

"Oh sure, like I'm going to let you near me with a pair of scissors."

"Says the man who's about to put a gun in my hands."

He pauses. "Touché."

The reminder of our final destination subdues me a bit, and he must notice because he steers us toward neutral topics for the remainder of our drive. We chat easily, and when our surroundings eventually turn rural, stretches of farmland and sheared cornstalks lining the road, we compete to see who can spot more cows and horses, getting progressively punchier until we're giggling like a couple of four-year-olds.

Eventually he slows and turns into a wide, dirt-covered driveway. A large brick and glass-front building stretches out before us, a sign announcing RIGHT ON TARGET TACTICAL glowing beneath the roofline. The range is the only structure around, fronting a wide-open field. A handful of cars scatter the lot. I might be imagining the storm cloud of doom looming over the building.

As soon as he parks, I hop out before he can open my door. I'm ready to get this over with.

"Hold up a minute."

I turn as Ben walks to his trunk and pops the lift gate, pulling out a nondescript black bag.

"Oh God. Is that it? Your gun?"

He smiles like I'm funny. "Yes. These are my guns."

"*Guns?* As in plural? More than one?"

"Yes, I own more than one gun." He slams the lift gate closed, locking the car with a *beep.* "Three, to be exact."

"*Three?* Why do you need three guns?"

"I don't *need* three guns. I wanted three guns, so now I own three guns." He prods me toward the door.

"You've had them in your car this whole time?"

I'm panicking. I take in my surroundings, belatedly realizing the dangerous situation I've placed myself in. I've traveled off the grid to an unknown location with my sworn enemy and his *three* guns. What if I've been a long con, and Ben's taken me to a secluded field in Maryland to finally off me? I should text Stephen my coordinates.

I've probably been watching too much *House of Cards.*

Ben's talking, blissfully unaware that I'm picturing him in a perp lineup. "I normally keep them in my apartment, but I put them in the car earlier. I had a feeling if you saw me carrying them, you'd run screaming."

It's disturbing how well he knows me. "You feel correct."

He smirks and raises an eyebrow as if to say, *See?*

I let him guide me through the door, then take a guarded look around my prison for the next hour. At first glance, the room looks like a typical retail store—albeit for the firearm obsessed. Shirts with gun graphics and slogans like SUNDAY GUN DAY and KEEP CALM AND PACK HEAT are hanging on clustered clothing racks. Displays of trucker hats and aviator sunglasses flank a long, wide countertop.

What is *not* typical are the rows upon rows of menacing-looking assault rifles, shotguns, and handguns crisscrossing the walls.

I stop dead in my tracks. *Nope.* I can't do this. I shuffle backward, inching toward the door.

When he glances over his shoulder and sees I'm moving in the wrong direction, he pivots, walks back, and stops in front of me. "Kate."

"So, here's the thing. I thought I could do this, but it looks like I can't. You can go in there and shoot it up, that's cool. I'll just wait for you in the car. I'll have Tim to keep me company, so we're good. Seriously, I think I'm going to be sick if I stand here a minute longer. And that's no big deal, I guess, since you've already seen me do that, but it's actually pretty embarrassing for me and I don't—"

He puts his hands on my shoulders and turns me a little, crowding my field of vision. "Kate, look at me."

I drag my eyes from the wall of weaponry to his face. My feet itch to run out to the car. Or maybe all the way home.

"You are not going to be shooting those guns. Don't even look at them."

I plead silently with my eyes: *Please don't make me do this.*

"You're only going to shoot my guns. They're much smaller and totally manageable for you. I know how to use them, and I'm going to teach you." His voice is calm and steady. "There's no reason to be nervous."

I let out a brittle laugh. "Nervous doesn't begin to describe what I'm feeling. Terrified, maybe. Disturbed. Sickened."

"You'll be fine. I promise."

I close my eyes and take a deep breath in through my nose and let it out through my mouth. Then another. He waits patiently, and when I open my eyes he raises his eyebrows in question. When I give him a small nod, he takes my hand firmly in his and leads me up to the counter.

"Ben, how you doing, man?" A tall guy in a baseball cap leans over the counter, doing that shaking-hands, slap-on-the-back routine guys do. Of course they're on a first-name basis. How often does Ben come here? He probably has a frequent shooter card.

"Hey, Rick, I'm great. How are you?"

"Good, man, I'm good." His eyes flick to me. "And who's this?"

"I've got a newbie here. She needs some eyes and ears." Ben glances at me and squeezes my hand. "And could you give us a lane that's away from other people? If you can."

"Sure, I'll put you at the end." He nods at me. "She gonna be all right? She doesn't look so good." Gun Range Rick is very astute.

"She's a little nervous, but she'll be all right." The glance Ben shoots me is laced with pride. "She's tougher than she looks."

Well. That puffs me up some. *Time to woman up, Kate.*

"*She* can answer for herself, thank you." I throw my shoulders back, cracking my neck like a prizefighter. "And I'm fine. Point me to this eye and ear protection." I see Ben hide a smile out of the corner of my eye.

Rick fits me with a flesh-colored over-the-ear headset that looks like noise-canceling headphones, only uglier. The clear goggles I'm supposed to wear cover more than half my face and aren't very comfortable but, according to Ben, are totally necessary.

I strike a pose. "How do I look?"

He smirks, an amused twinkle in his eyes. "Like Ballistic Barbie."

Rick gives us a couple of papers to initial and when I make a crack about signing my life away, he eyes Ben warily. Humor is wasted on Rick, apparently.

I follow Ben through a door and into a small room that appears to operate as a sort of soundproof antechamber. Once we're inside, Ben shuts the door behind me, and just as I'm registering how close we are in this tiny, enclosed space, he opens another door directly in front of us and I'm bombarded by a cacophony of terrifying noises, sights, and smells.

If I was scared before, this sends me into overdrive. The sound of rapid gunfire assaults my senses and I'm jolting in fright every time I hear a blast, which is about every two seconds. If they're this loud and terrifying with the headphones on, I shudder to think how quickly I'd go deaf if I took them off. The stench of gunpowder—the same sulfuric smell I'd previously associated with fireworks—singes my nostrils. *Thanks for ruining Fourth of July for me, Ben.* Spent shell casings litter the floor, and my boots kick a path through them as Ben leads us down the row.

How in the fresh hell did I get here?

I abandon all pretense of bravery and glue myself to his back, clutching his sweater like a frightened kid at a haunted house. He steers us down an alley that's lined by partitioned stalls on our right and a long bench to our left. There are plenty of other people here, mostly men who look exactly as I'd imagined: law enforcement types with buzzed heads, stocky guys in muscle tees. I see a couple of women, including an elderly grandmother type with a shock of white hair, and I'm intrigued by her in spite of myself. They all ignore us as we walk by.

Ben stops at lane twenty, the last cubby as Rick's promised, and sets his case down on the bench. He unzips it and pulls out a gun that's not much bigger than the palm of my hand. I feel an acute sense of dread.

"This is a revolver. It's the smallest gun I own. It actually folds in half, so it's a good choice if you wanted to carry a concealed weapon. It would fit in your pocket or your purse. It's the right type of gun for a woman who foolishly insists on walking home alone at night."

I roll my eyes. "Concealed . . . do you carry a concealed weapon?"

"Not generally, no. There aren't a lot of places you can carry in DC due to federal building restrictions. But in Texas . . ." He trails off.

"What about Texas?"

"People bring guns to church."

I blanch. "Have you ever had a gun on you without me knowing it?"

"No. Though God knows I've needed one." He winks, then holds the revolver out to me. "Enough stalling. Take it, get a feel for it. It's not loaded."

I don't reach for it. "Or maybe not? How about I just watch you for a while? I think that might be better." More visually appealing for me, at least.

"Kate, are we feeling a little . . . *gun shy*?"

I groan. "Did you google *gun puns* or something?"

"I may have been gunning to use a few."

I pause. "How many more do you have in your arsenal?"

He throws his head back and laughs. "You're loosening up. This is good."

"Hardly."

He grabs my hand and holds it out, palm up. "Kate, take the gun." And here I am, holding a gun for the first time.

It's surprisingly light, closely resembling a child's toy, making me even more concerned about the perverse world we live in where kids play with realistic-looking toy guns. I turn it over in my hand and curl my finger into the trigger, testing the catch and release. It looks like a gun Bonnie Parker would slide back into her garter post-heist.

"How do you load the bullets?"

I practically have to shout the question. The cracks of surrounding gunfire coupled with the noise-canceling headphones make it nearly impossible to communicate. As it is, I have to stand about an inch away from him and read his lips when he speaks to me. Not helping my anxiety: having to stare intently at Ben's *mouth*.

He reaches into his case and pulls out a box of bullets, shaking a few into his hand. "You load them one at a time into the cylinder here. This is the hammer. You have to pull it back before you can shoot." He toggles it back and forth to demonstrate. "Remember, you should only be pointing the gun at the target, or it should be down on the counter with the safety on. Always keep the safety on. You don't want it to go off accidentally." He hands the revolver back to me. "Now, let's run through your posture and get the feel of shooting."

He crosses behind me and then his hands are on my hips, nudging my leg over to widen my stance, positioning me at just the right angle.

Christ on a cracker. I hadn't even considered this. Are his hands going to be all over me for the next hour? My poker face is going to get a serious workout.

"Since you're right-handed you're going to hold it like this." He demonstrates, grabbing my arms and clasping them in front of me, placing my right index finger into the trigger and curling his fingers around my left hand to show me how to brace the butt of the gun. Then he moves behind me again and stretches his arms around mine, holding me in position. Every inch of his body is wrapped around mine.

Welp, I was wrong before—*this* is what hell feels like. Lady parts on fire, surrounded on all sides by a man I'd like nothing more than to roll in sugar and eat for dessert. A bead of sweat forms between my breasts and slides down my belly. This sweater was a mistake of epic proportions.

I will myself to calm down; I'm shaking and I don't want the gun to slip out of my hands. "What happens if I accidentally drop the gun?"

"It could go off."

"*What?!*" I nearly drop it right then.

"Calm down. You're not going to drop it." He looks entirely unconcerned.

"You don't know that."

When I hear his voice next, he's speaking into my right ear from behind. I jolt at his proximity.

"Now practice shooting it. Since it's not loaded you won't feel a recoil. When you shoot for real, there will be a kickback. That'll be the scariest part for you. I can't really explain how that feels until you experience it for yourself."

He finally steps away and I let out an unsteady breath, then set my feet in the stance he's instructed and look to him in question. When he nods his approval, I slide my gaze back to the target, close my eyes, and squeeze the trigger.

"Not bad. You should probably keep your eyes open, though." He's laughing. "How did it feel?"

"Like I'm Olivia Benson on *Law & Order*."

He laughs again and I relax another inch. Making Ben laugh is like a drug. I crave the sound, each hit feeding my habit.

His mouth still twisted in a smile, he picks up the bullets and loads them into the chamber. "All right. Now we're going to try that with ammunition."

"Oh no. No, no, no. I'm not ready for that yet. You need to go first."

He opens his mouth to protest, then closes it, considering. "Okay. If that'll make you feel more comfortable."

He moves to his bag and pulls out another gun, this one a little bigger. I step closer to inspect it.

"What is this gun? How is it different?"

He smirks. "Getting interested now, are we?"

I make a face, but the truth is I *am* interested now. I'm naturally curious—a lifelong learner—and my inner nerd demands to know everything there is to know about something. I realize with sudden clarity that I want to impress Ben. Sure, I didn't want to do this, but now that I'm here I have a new goal: dazzle him with my sniper-level marksmanship.

Ben takes my place at the counter and lines up his shot. It's strange to see him in this mode: so serious and authoritative and un-Ben-like. He looks as comfortable with a gun in his hands as he does discussing exemptions and withholdings.

"Do you see how I'm holding this? Firmly, with both hands, but don't choke the trigger. A light touch is all you need."

Choke the trigger. Light touch. Good God, must everything he says sound so sexual?

He motions for me to come closer. "Feel how I'm gripping it. You can close one eye or keep both eyes open, whatever feels more natural for you."

Great idea. I'll just drape myself over him and close my eyes. That won't be problematic.

I eye him doubtfully but step closer and mimic his stance. I press myself against his right side, laying my arm over his to simulate his grip. I'm locked into his body like a puzzle piece, my front to his back, closer than a shadow. I pray he can't feel my heart hammering through our flimsy cotton layers. When he looks back at me in question I nod like I've got it, but spoiler alert: All I've got is a raging case of Ben-lust.

Once I move away he fires a couple of rounds, the bullets hitting the target right in the outlined chest box. I jerk-jump like a dancing mario-nette after each one. He sets the gun down on the counter calmly and turns to face me.

"Okay. Your turn."

My anxiety ratchets up as we switch places. I stare the little revolver down like it's my evil adversary. I'm just about to pick it up when I feel Ben's hand squeeze my shoulder and I nearly leap out of my skin. I spin around, exasperated, and he's holding out my jacket. *Oh.*

I turn and he helps me shrug it on, but when I go to zip it up, my hands are trembling so much, I can't line up the zipper. After a couple of tries, he stills my hands and zips me up himself. He fusses over the col-lar, untucking my hair from the back, his fingertips repeatedly brushing against the sensitive skin of my neck. Everywhere he touches me, I burn. I'd shatter a thermometer if it got close. He may as well be *undressing* me for how my body is reacting.

Before I register what's happening, he leans in and presses a soft kiss to my temple.

You've got this, he mouths, his breath whispering across my cheek. His hand is still on my neck and I. Am. Deceased.

"Remember, you'll only be nervous at first. In a minute, you're going to tell me how easy this is."

"Yeah, right," I say, my voice shaky.

He kissed me. It may have been the most chaste kiss in history, but it was a kiss.

He turns me so I'm facing the target again. I pick up the gun and glance at Ben, and he nods encouragingly.

Let's get this over with.

When I squeeze the trigger, time slows down. My whole body tenses and the split second it takes to fire feels like an hour. When the gun finally discharges, it's so loud and the kickback so powerful that I gasp. I look at Ben, shell-shocked and dazed.

"You did it! How'd it feel?" He's grinning, pride palpable on his face.

I just blink at him, wide-eyed.

"Go again. Do the rest."

On autopilot, I comply, squeezing one eye shut and firing the remaining bullets in the cylinder. *Well, that wasn't so bad.*

He reels in the paper target and inspects it. "You hit the target three times. That's great."

I peer over his shoulder. "I missed the body entirely!"

"Nah, you grazed the shoulder there," he says, pointing. "That'll cause some bleeding."

I hold up a hand. "Don't need the color commentary, thanks."

He smirks. "Again?"

"Sure."

He reloads me, and I do it again. I focus on the outlined chest area—the one he hit perfectly with both his test shots—and I quickly determine that my shots are going high and wide and adjust my aim accordingly. I do better this round, actually landing two inside the box.

"Do you want to try one of the other guns? They're automatics, not revolvers."

I appreciate that he's letting me decide. "If you think I can handle it, then . . . okay. Sure."

He moves to his case, smiling to himself as he rummages through it.

"What's with the cat-that-ate-the-canary grin?"

It falls a little. "Nothing."

I set the revolver down on the counter. "Spill, or I stop."

"Fine, I just already feel better, seeing you do this. It's like you're safer."

It's such an odd statement. "Why are you so obsessed with my safety?"

"*Someone* has to be."

A classic nonanswer. I change tacks. "How did you learn so much about guns?"

"Where I'm from boys go hunting starting pretty young, so I don't really remember a time when I didn't know how to shoot. But I got more into it when I was about seventeen." A muscle tightens in his jaw.

"Why?"

"None of your business, Katie Cat. Now, focus, and let's see if your aim improves with this one."

He passes me the now-loaded gun, and I set up my shot, aiming for the head this time. *When in Rome . . .*

The blast of this gun is louder and stronger, and I'm knocked back by the recoil. I see now why he wanted my skin covered. The shell casings—or flying brass, as he'd called it—eject up and out, and I flinch when one hurtles toward me.

"Wait, I see what's happening now. When you close your eye, your arms are moving. Let me show you."

He circles behind me, wrapping his arms around my shoulders and holding the gun out in front of me.

"Look along the sight line. Do you see it? Your feet should be about hip width apart." He nudges my foot over a bit with his. "And you're a little stiff."

I wiggle my hips from side to side to loosen up, inadvertently brushing against him in the process, and that's when I feel it:

His erection, hard as a tent pole and pressing into my backside.

I freeze, eyes pancake-wide, glancing back at him before I can stop myself. He springs away from me like he's been scalded.

"You—it—you're ready to shoot now. Your form looks good," he stammers; then his face goes white. He pivots abruptly and moves to the bench, effectively obscuring his front from view.

I stare at his back for a second, unsure what to do. I'm not about to shoot this gun without him standing next to me. He appears to be shuffling things around in his case with no sense of purpose. I want to laugh, but I take pity on him and turn back around.

I'll just give him a minute.

Chapter 22

So why do you go to a gun range in Maryland? Surely there are closer ones in the city."

We stopped for dinner at an Italian place halfway back to DC, though what had seemed like a good idea at the time—we were both starving and inhaled our meals—is now making me pause. Our cozy corner table, replete with white tablecloth, candlelight, and Frank Sinatra crooning seductively in the background, is only encouraging my romantic fantasies. It's easy to imagine we're on a date.

"It has a tactical setup outdoors. Moving targets, real-life obstacles, the whole nine. I'll have to take you back when the weather's better." I don't miss his sly grin.

"Nice try. I'm a one-and-done."

"I saw the look in your eye. You were enjoying yourself. Admit it."

I enjoyed his hands on me, that much is true.

"I admit nothing. And on Monday, I go back to campaigning for gun control. Don't think you've turned me," I warn as I sip my wine.

"Oh, I'll turn you. It's just a matter of time."

The cocksure way he says it makes me pause. Is Ben trying to *convert* me? Is that his goal here?

"I *cannot* be turned," I say firmly.

"We'll see. You know, you took to it really quickly. I bet you'd dominate in a self-defense class. I'd do it with you, if you wanted."

"Self-*defense* class? Ben, *stop.* You're so overprotective. I feel sorry for your future wife."

I regret the words as soon as they're out. I wish I could cram them back down my throat. He tenses and straightens, avoiding eye contact as he fiddles with the candle in the center of the table. I may as well have poured a bucket of ice over our heads.

I push my wineglass away. "It's time for you to tell me what this overprotectiveness is really about. Every time I ask, you deflect and evade."

"Deflect and evade, huh? You've been watching too much CNN."

I fold my hands in front of me, pinning him under my gaze. His smirk falls away when he realizes he's not getting out of this without talking. He sips his beer, staring at a point somewhere over my right shoulder. I'm about to snap my fingers in his face and shout *Benjy!* when he clears his throat and speaks so softly, I have to lean forward to hear him.

"When my sister was in college, she was date-raped at a fraternity party."

I gasp and recoil, my hand flying to my mouth. I was *not* expecting that.

"Oh God, I'm so sorry. You don't have to—"

He waves me off. "No, you're right, I can be a little nuts about things and I've taken it out on you, so . . ." He trails off, shrugging as if to say, *It is what it is.* "It's a story I'm sure you've heard before. She liked the guy, they were drinking, he didn't stop at *no.*"

The raw pain in his voice clenches my heart.

"Shelby didn't tell us right away, but she ended up coming home a couple months later. She was a mess. My parents made her report it, but there wasn't anything the police could do at that point. It wasn't like there was any proof." His voice is flat.

"Ben, I'm so sorry. I can't even imagine what it must have been like for your sister. For your whole family."

"I was a senior in high school at the time. I was so filled with rage. I wasn't there to protect her and there was nothing we could do about it. Just completely fucking helpless. I wanted to murder the guy. Still do." His mouth tightens. "Anyway, that's when I got more into guns." He flicks his eyes toward mine, then away.

An icy fear grips my insides. "Did you . . . confront him?" Images flicker across my mind like some bad revenge movie. By the look on his face, I wouldn't be surprised if Ben tells me he killed the guy and buried him in the backyard.

"No. I was enraged—I'm *still* enraged—but I knew it wouldn't change anything. Not that I don't picture his face on that target. Shooting was more about channeling my anger. I needed an outlet, to feel like I was taking control back."

"I get it."

"It was a rough time for my family. He got off scot-free while Shelby walked around like a zombie for two years." He white-knuckles his beer.

"I don't know what to say." I can't believe I forced him into telling me this. I am the world's worst person.

"There's really nothing *to* say. There are a lot of bad guys out there."

Realization dawns. "This must be why you get that look on your face every time I mention my sorority."

"I've never been much for drinking." He nods toward the half-full pilsner glass he's been nursing.

Memories fall into place like dominos. His agitation over my walking home alone. The insistence that I carry a weapon. Showing up at the bar that night—and his visceral anger at the "slimy barfly" who was circling me. His anger at *me* for dismissing his concerns. It all makes a sad sort of sense now. What I'd thought was overprotectiveness and chauvinism was actually fear; scar tissue from a deep wound. The righteous indignation I've spent weeks indulging evaporates in a puff of smoke.

I'm not used to seeing him like this. The Ben I know is a rock, a bulletproof tower of strength and fortitude. Resilience is his currency. In contrast, the man in front of me seems to have shrunk. His shoulders sag as if they can't bear the weight of this memory. His eyes are empty, devoid of their usual playfulness and spark. I wonder how often—or even *if*—he talks about this, with anyone.

I'm not sure what to say to comfort him, so I reach out and take his hand, brushing my thumb over his knuckles. He gives me a tight smile that's more of a grimace, then wraps his big hand around mine and squeezes. I don't let go.

He clears his throat and shakes his head, as if jogging himself loose from his melancholy. "Anyway, I'm not some seventeen-year-old kid anymore. And I won't let something like that happen again to—well, I just won't let it happen again."

I'm certain he'd been about to say *someone I care about*. I wish he'd just let himself say it.

"Now you know why I get so pissed when you blow me off."

My response is instant. "I won't blow you off anymore."

His eyebrows arch in surprise. "Thank you," he says sincerely, squeezing my hand again.

"Thanks for trusting me enough to tell me all this."

He nods in acknowledgment, then exhales a long, slow breath, like he's exorcising a ghost. I watch his shoulders relax, a calmness spreading over him. Is my acquiescence the reason for this lightness? Is it possible

I hold this much power over him? If so, it's a relief—I feel like he holds so much power over *me* that it's like a balancing of the scales.

I cough, trying to dislodge the ball of emotion clogging my throat. "So how is your sister doing now?"

His face lights up. "She's great, actually. It took her a couple years to get right, but she eventually transferred schools and finished her degree. She works in finance also, for an investment bank in New York. And she married a great guy. He worships the ground she walks on." He smiles. "As he should."

"That's fantastic. And wow, so many math brains in your family. Quite a group of supernerds," I tease.

"You should hear us when we get together. You'd be bored to tears."

I chuckle at the thought of them talking animatedly over the dinner table about . . . numbers. "You guys sound really close."

He flashes his signature boyish grin, and it's a sure sign the heaviness has passed. "We are. It was just the two of us growing up, so we sort of had to be. Oh, and she just told me—I'm going to be an uncle." He beams with pride.

"Wow, congratulations! Something tells me Uncle Ben will be a *big* spoiler."

"Oh, it'll be obscene. I'm thrilled for her. So are my parents, obviously. First grandchild and all." He tips his head back to drain his water. "It should get my mom off my back for a while."

I smile wryly. "I know the feeling."

"She keeps asking about you, you know," he says casually, crunching some ice in his teeth.

"Oh yeah? And what do you tell her?"

He eyes me over the rim of his glass. "Honestly? I have no idea what to tell her."

Alarm bells start ringing in my head. That was a warning shot, and I can tell by the way he's holding eye contact he wants to see how I'll respond. Will I run with it or punt?

But before I can decide, he beats me to it. "You ever wonder what might've happened if our first meeting had gone differently?"

My eyes widen, but he just sits there, all casual nonchalance, his expression impassive. He's cool as a cucumber. Meanwhile, I'm trying to prevent every thought from playing out on my face like some melodramatic street mime.

He's looking at me expectantly—I'm not off the hook this time. He wants to hear me say it.

"Sure, sometimes. I think it's only natural." When he looks at me blankly, I clarify. "You know, the whole *When Harry Met Sally* thing."

"I've never seen it."

"*What?* I thought that movie was a rite of passage."

He sits back. "Enlighten me."

"The basic premise is that men and women can't ever really be friends, if you . . . uh, find the other person attractive. Because . . . well, for obvious reasons." I flush.

"I see."

A heavy silence settles between us. *Awkward, party of two.*

"So, you're saying we can't be friends, then."

I arch an eyebrow.

"Since you're so attracted to me."

I snort. "How did I know that was coming?"

"It's okay, you can admit it. I won't make things weird." His sly grin liquefies my insides.

"*Stohhhp.*"

"Seriously? I tell you you're strikingly beautiful and I can't even get a *Ben, you're not entirely hideous?*"

"Ben, you're not entirely hideous."

He slants me a look.

"If you need your ego stroked, why not go ask Corinne?" I blurt before I can stop myself. *Guess I'm doing this.*

His brow furrows. "Corinne?"

"Yeah, you know, tall, brunette." *Frigid as a freezer.* "Aren't you two dating?"

He stares at me blankly. "Why would you think *that*?"

Because she told me so.

"She . . . alluded to it," I reply haltingly. "And I've seen you two together. And Stephen saw you out to dinner one night."

He looks taken aback.

"It makes sense; you two have a lot in common," I rush to add, lest I seem like some stalker who's been tracking his every move. *May he never find out about that video.*

He nods slowly, lips pursed like he's thinking it over. "Have you ever gone out to eat with a male colleague after work? Say, John Conrad, perhaps?"

I pause. "Perhaps, but—"

"And are you dating him?" His eyes hold a sharp intensity.

"I see what you're getting at, but John's not running around telling people we're together."

"Well, whatever she told you is false," he says, looking annoyed. "I'm not dating Corinne."

"I think you and I might have different definitions of what *dating* means," I say bluntly.

He cocks a brow. "I'm going to pretend you didn't just imply I'm some sort of male slut. I'm not *dating* her, romantically or otherwise."

He's monitoring my expression closely, so I keep my mask of indifference firmly in place. But inside? I'm soaring. Pure, unadulterated joy surges through my veins. I want to stand and do a cheer. I want to run a marathon. I want to cannonball into his lap and nest there.

He tilts his head. "Would it bother you if it *had* been a date?"

Oh, sugar. That question sends me crashing back down to earth. If I was taking a lie detector test, now is when the sensors would start jumping. He may as well have his thumbs on my wrists.

"Who you date is none of my business." *I'm such a cowardly lion.*

"That's not an answer."

I shrug, but my face burns, exposing my lie. We're dancing around this so expertly, we could be pairs figure skaters.

"Is it really such a hard question? Here, let me model it for you."

"I don't think—"

"You might ask me, *Ben, would it bother you if I was out on a date with someone? And then I would respond, Why yes, Kate, that would bother me a whole hell of a lot.*"

My jaw drops. My heart starts performing an elaborate tap dance in my chest.

He calmly lifts his beer to his lips and sips. "See? Not so hard."

"What are you doing?" I whisper.

"Something I should've done a long time ago."

He sets his beer down and exhales a long, slow breath, and it's the sound of surrender. The sigh of someone at the end of their rapidly fraying rope. When he looks back up at me his eyes are emerald green fire, glowing brighter than I've ever seen them. *Kryptonite eyes.* I watch, transfixed, as they gradually darken, the pupils dilating right in front of me.

There's no mistaking this look. He wants me. I may as well be naked.

"Kate." The smile he gives me is somehow both calm and nervous. "Do you think about me even half as much as I think about you?"

I freeze. The world stops. If this were a TV show, there'd be a record scratch.

"I—I guess to answer that I'd need to know how much you're think-ing about me," I stammer.

His eyes are locked on mine. "All the time. When I'm with you, when I'm without you. Since the day we met I've thought of almost nothing else. I *pretend* I don't. That's the killer, you know. The pretending. Pretending I don't have feelings for you, pretending that being friends is enough. I've gotten really good at pretending. But goddamn, I'm so tired of it, Kate. Every minute I'm with you that I don't tell you feels like one step closer to insanity."

He reaches out and winds a lock of hair that's fallen over my shoul-der around his finger, like he can't help himself, like he doesn't even know he's doing it. Like he's tethering himself to me.

"I thought if I told you, I'd scare you off, or ruin whatever this is. And it's good, what we have now. But it's not what I want, and I can't keep pretending."

His voice holds a deep resolve. His expression is so honest and de-termined and sweet, I wish I had my phone handy so I could snap a picture. I'd make it my wallpaper and stare at it all day. I would, but it's like someone's pressed pause on me and I'm stuck in a freeze-frame. My hand is pressed to my mouth, where it's been ever since the words *pre-tending I don't have feelings for you* fell out of his mouth.

"I kept thinking if I gave you enough time you'd come around and . . . I don't know, want to ruin things too? Sometimes I think you do, but other times . . ." He squints at me, shaking his head. "I don't know. I've been driving myself crazy trying to figure out the right way to do this, but what I finally realized is, if you find someone who makes you happy, don't you have a responsibility to tell them? Just say it out loud and go for it?"

I haven't taken a solid breath since he started talking and I'm slowly dying. Or maybe it's his words that are making me light-headed. I'm teetering on the ledge of a high cliff, toes over the edge, trying to decide if I'll fly or die if I jump. My heart is in my throat. His heart is in his eyes. Before he's even finished speaking, I'm frantically trying to imprint the most beautiful words anyone's ever said to me on my memory.

I lean into his hand, the one that's been fussing with my hair, and his palm automatically opens to cradle my cheek. His face is just inches from mine.

I take a deep breath and leap.

"Of course I think about you, Ben. I think about you so much, it's making me crazy. Where can I sign up for the ruining of things?"

About fifty different emotions kaleidoscope across his face in the span of a few seconds. Surprise. Relief. Joy. *Desire.* He slides his hand to the back of my neck and pulls me in until we're nose to nose. His eyes search my face.

"Kiss me already," I breathe, and his lips are on mine before I even get the words out.

When our mouths touch it's more than a kiss; it's a caress. Soft. Warm. Testing. Tasting. When I sigh into his mouth he presses closer, grunting softly and giving my lower lip a gentle bite. I squeak in pleasure and he sweeps his tongue against mine.

Somewhere in the deep recesses of my brain, I know there are people surrounding us, whispered conversations and prying eyes, but I register none of it. He's my spinning center axis. My body has only one frequency and it's tuned to the man in front of me. I only know Ben's lips. Ben's hands. He tilts my head gently, angling my face to possess my mouth a different way, and I reach up and tangle my fingers in his hair. It's seconds. It's hours.

When he pulls away, he rests his brow against mine and the breath that shudders out of him is heavy and rasping. His hand drops to the table and it's shaking.

Eventually he lifts his head and scans over my shoulder, not meeting my eyes.

"Ben?"

He nods at someone in acknowledgment, raising his hand in the air and making a scribbling motion.

Check, please.

Chapter 23

The next few minutes are a blur.

Ben tows me through the restaurant.

We race across the parking lot.

We're up against his car.

Ben is frenzied, eyes wild. His hands touch me everywhere: face, hair, back, butt. His kisses are desperate, like I'm air and he's drowning. His body surrounds mine like a cocoon. I grip his arms and nearly swoon at the muscles I can't even fit in my hands. I'm overcome by sensations: hard body, soft sweater, warm lips, jaw stubbled like fine-grit sandpaper.

In all the times I imagined this, my only thoughts were of him. How he would feel. Taste. The scent of his skin. The weight of his hands on me. What I didn't account for was *my* hunger, my need. Now that it's laid bare, it's almost violent.

I'm lunging, pouncing, frantically trying to climb him. He's so tall, and without my extra heel height I'm not getting the access to him I'm craving. My hands scrabble against his shoulders until he grabs me under my thighs and hoists me up. I lock my legs around his waist and cling to him like a spider monkey. I wrap my arms around his neck and devour his mouth. I want to consume him.

It's a searing heat: hands grasping, tongues tasting, bodies gorging. We're animals freed from our cages. I'm starving and greedy and can't be satisfied. I can barely breathe, but I won't stop to fill my lungs. It's like if our mouths separate, even for a second, this moment might slip away and never have happened. Through our kisses, we're saying everything we haven't been able to: *What took you so long?* and *Finally* and *I'm desperate for you* and *Please don't stop. Never, ever stop.*

"Kate." His voice is gravelly. "You're . . . this is . . . we need to . . ."

He can't finish a thought because I won't surrender his lips long enough for him to speak full sentences. My brain pounds a relentless drumbeat: *more-more-more.* More of his mouth. More touching. More *Ben.*

He pulls away slightly and brushes my hair out of my face, a smile playing on his mouth like he's privy to a juicy secret. He cradles my cheekbone, giving me a series of gentle tasting bites on my top lip, then bottom. His other hand is gripping my ass, dangerously close to the apex of my thighs, and I tighten my legs around him, needy hips grinding against firm abs. His hard length presses up against my bottom.

"Kate," he exhales softly, and it sounds like a prayer.

He's still kissing me as his hand skims down my neck to my shoulder, bounding south in a leisurely exploration. His fingers trail down my side, steal across my rib cage. When he grazes the underside of my breast, my back arches and I briefly lose myself. I start to slide and his arm tightens around me, holding me up. I'm basically parked on top of his arousal now and every nerve ending between my legs is on fire.

"I need to get you . . . somewhere else," he pants between broken breaths. "Somewhere that's not here. Somewhere with walls."

"Home?"

I've taken an interest in his ear now and I nibble at his lobe, kissing and sucking along the hinge of his jaw. I've never given a hickey before, but there's a first time for everything. I want to mark him, stake my claim on this rugged, uncharted territory. He looks at me and if he realizes I'm considering branding him, he gives no sign. He swallows heavily and I watch the movement of his throat up close. I want to taste every inch of his skin.

"Home," he murmurs in agreement, and the single word sends a frisson of anticipation to my core. "But to do that, we're going to have to get in the car."

"Not yet," I whine and snuggle deeper into his neck. His husky laugh in my ear is nearly my undoing. Out of nowhere my brain flashes to the two of us in bed, tangled in sheets, the teasing musical notes of Ben's laughter trapped and echoing in my sternum. The scene is so vivid I wonder if I've just had my first psychic vision.

"I think we're about thirty seconds from indecent exposure. Or a lewd act. Or something." He scrubs a hand over his face, clearly torn, and the combination of his tortured expression, mussed hair, and ravenous eyes has me nearly catatonic with lust.

I bury my face in his neck and inhale. Then inhale again. God, he smells glorious. I could get high off him. He chuckles and goose bumps scatter my skin. This husky laugh is my new happy place.

"Are you smelling me again?"

"Yep. Sorry not sorry."

When he laughs again, I duck my head and press an ear to his chest. The deep rumbling vibrates through my body clear down to my toes, permeating every nook and cranny. I feel it in my elbow. I feel it in my spine.

He tips my chin up to kiss me again and I cannot. Get. Enough. I'm so lost in him that I barely notice he's opened the passenger door until he's lowering me onto the seat. I see what he did there. *Sneaky Benjy.* I reluctantly release him from my octopus tentacles but when he reaches for my seatbelt, I grab his face and pull him deeper into the car. He accepts my ambush with a smile against my lips, but when I try to deepen the kiss he pulls away with a tut. The gentle tenderness in his eyes softens the blow.

"Katie." He's looking at me like I'm a priceless treasure. "I've waited a long time for this. I'm not going to have you in the back of my car."

I sigh and let go, keeping my paws off him long enough for him to buckle me in. When he's done he gives me a light peck as if to say, *Good girl*. It's so sweetly protective that it takes all my willpower not to barrel-roll over the console and burrow into his lap.

I'm pretty sure Ben breaks land-speed records driving us home. We can't keep our hands off each other, which is alarming considering he's pushing eighty. His palm skims up and down my thigh, squeezing every so often in an unconscious gesture of possession. *Mine*. Like he's confirming I'm real. For my part, I'm running my fingernails up and down his forearm, alternately scratching, then smoothing down the hairs. I can't believe I finally get to touch him this way.

I start giggling. "What would you have done if I'd said I just wasn't that into you? This would have been one awkward car ride home."

"I'm very persuasive." He curses under his breath and cuts around a car driving too slowly—and by too slowly, I mean they're doing the speed limit.

"Can't argue with you there. Your speech back there was very sweet."

"Sweet?" He looks offended. "I assume you mean manly. Very masculine and sexy."

"It'll be sexy if you admit you practiced it."

"I'll never tell." He winks. "How'd I do?"

"It worked, obviously. Although you probably could have just quit after you said my dating would bother you a hell of a lot."

"I overshot it, then? Damn."

"I'm not complaining."

His thumb is tracing lazy circles on my thigh, and it's so distracting I can barely focus on our conversation. I reach my hand out to massage his neck and he shifts a little closer to me, hum-growling in pleasure. "Please do not stop doing that."

I love that he thinks this massage is for him and not just an excuse to touch him.

His playful expression fades to seriousness. "Tell me something. How long ago should I have done this?"

Headlights from a passing car flash across the windshield, briefly illuminating his face, and I glimpse the sincerity in his expression. He's interested in this answer.

"The night at your apartment was a turning point. But if I'm being honest, there was a lot going on before that. I was . . . sad when we stopped talking. I missed you."

Considering how long it took to admit that to myself, I'm proud of how freely I tell him. His speech must have been a truth serum.

He glances at me, a surprised—and slightly cocky—grin on his face.

"That's not supposed to make you happy. I was a miserable human. Stephen wanted to kill me. Besides, I could ask you the same question. What took you so long?"

His jaw drops. "What *took* me so long? Kate, tell me you're kidding."

"Do I *look* like I'm kidding? You drove me half-crazy with wondering! I couldn't figure you out!"

"I will crash this car. You're the *queen* of mixed signals. I was constantly testing the waters and you either slammed the door in my face or ran away. Every time I thought we were making headway you'd make some comment like, *I could never be with a green-eyed, fiscally conservative giant.* What was I supposed to think?"

He exits the highway and when we slow at a stoplight he turns to face me, frustration plain on his face. He's really worked up about this. Over his shoulder I see the Capitol Building, looming and stately and vaguely threatening. It's a reminder of everything at stake for us, and my stomach twists with unease. Have we really considered how complicated things are about to get? I swing my gaze back to Ben, shelving my misgivings for the moment.

"I can see how you'd be confused," I concede, "but I was confused too. Maybe next time you should speak up instead of trying to *test* me."

"Or maybe *you* could have just asked me if I was dating someone."

"Uh, no."

"*No?*"

"No. I do not chase guys. I don't make the first move. That's *your* job."

"Says the feminist!" He claps a hand to his forehead.

"You can still be a feminist and believe in the traditional rules of courtship, okay? I don't need to lead in every aspect of my life. That's the entire point of feminism, anyway, that I can do or be anything I want. And I want to be pursued."

"You are a contradiction wrapped in an enigma, Kate Adams." He shakes his head, muttering to himself. "*'Not a romantic. Wants to be chased.'* I'll show you a first move."

"Is that a threat or a promise?"

The next time we stop, he looks over and he's wearing his bedroom eyes again. Dark and dangerous. He leans over the center console and kisses me like he's trying to tell me something, and while I'm not sure what the message is, I'm sure enjoying the delivery. We make out like teenagers until the blast of a car horn jolts us back to the present.

Finally, we're at his building. We stumble to the elevator bank, latched onto each other like the world will end if we let go. He pins me to the wall, one hand cradling my face while the other snakes under my sweater, his fingers stroking up and down the bare skin of my back. It feels so good I'm practically purring. I bury my face in his neck, sucking in indulgent lungfuls of his addictive scent. I will buy cinnamon Altoids at my earliest possible convenience. I start laughing when I remember our earlier elevator ride, which now feels like it took place in another lifetime.

"I was about to kill that woman and her damn stroller."

He draws back, eyes heavy-lidded. "You were giving me all these looks."

"*Me?* You were giving *me* the looks!"

We're laughing as we fall into his apartment. We kick off our shoes like toddlers at a bounce house and come back together in a tangle of limbs. I've just started to wonder where we'll wind up—couch? bed?—when he pulls back slightly and squeezes my hand. He looks unsure.

"I want you to know, I don't have any expectations. Obviously. It's not like I knew we'd end up here tonight." He's so earnest I could eat him.

"*No* expectations? Gosh, now I feel like a perv. I had all sorts of ideas . . ."

He smiles, but there's an edge to it. "You know what I mean. I just want you to feel comfortable with . . . I mean, I'll do whatever you . . ." He pinches the bridge of his nose. "Jesus. This came out a lot smoother in my head."

"I'm not sure I've seen you this nervous before. Heck, I'm not sure I've *ever* seen you nervous."

He glances down at our linked hands and hesitates. The air between us thrums with tension.

"When you've been thinking about something—*someone*—this long, you don't want anything to screw it up. You're calling the shots here. You need to tell me what you want."

"You'll make me heady with power," I warn, faux threatening, but the emotion squeezing my throat makes my voice shake.

I'm the nervous one now as I identify the look in his eyes. I don't want to focus on what it means, so I raise one of our linked hands and place it on my chest, just above my breast, and give him my naughtiest *come hither* look. He takes the hint.

He wraps his arms around me and lifts me clear off my feet. God, the fact that he can just pick me up like I weigh nothing is such a turn-on. I'm about to tell him I want to ride him like a bike when he starts to walk us toward the couch, and I can't help myself.

"Wait." I press a hand to his chest, feet dangling.

"What's the matter?" Concern brackets his eyes.

"I'm just not sure we should do this . . . without some background music. Maybe some Nickelback? Or a little Fall Out Boy?"

He closes his eyes and blows out a breath. "Kate, I swear to God. I will put you over my knee."

"So that's the kind of thing you're into? I was going to ask."

We laugh against each other's mouths; then we're kissing again and he's walking and we hit the couch and collapse in a jumbled heap.

I can't talk anymore because: the kissing. It's old-fashioned making out, the kind where my lips will be swollen in the morning, face chafed from Ben's stubble, and I don't even mind. In fact, I *hope* he marks me. I'll wear my face abrasion as a badge of honor.

He explores me with his mouth, an achingly slow and thorough study. With each press of his lips I sense that he's learning what I like, teasing out what makes me respond and rewarding me with more. He goes slow, then fast. Deep, searching kisses that steal my breath, then light, affectionate nips and pecks that leave me begging for more. He's peeling me back, layer by layer. He's under my skin.

His fingers stroke my face, lace into my hair, cradle the back of my neck. His tongue dances with mine, in and out, warm and wet. When his mouth moves down my neck I shiver, gooseflesh pebbling my skin. He kisses it away.

At one point I pull back and study his face. It's perfection. Symmetrical and chiseled. Pupils savagely dilated. I run the pads of my thumbs over his cheekbones, trace the smile lines at the corners of his mouth, tweak his chin. I groom the mussed hair at his temples.

"What are you doing?" His smile is amused.

"Looking at you. I've always wanted to just stare at you, and now I can."

He seems to like that answer, his kisses taking on a new intensity. It's unexpectedly emotional, this closeness with him. The teasing, the laughter, his eyes on me hooded and soft, almost reverent. He makes me feel coveted and cherished. Each touch denotes another wall torn down, bulldozed to rubble.

After a while we both seem to need more, our hands straying beyond the boundaries of our clothing. I roll on top of him and slide my hands under his sweater, and—*yes!*—I'm finally getting my greedy pincers on his abs, which are every bit as washboardy as I imagined. I nudge his sweater *up, up, up* until he pulls it over his head and *oh my God*.

He's all muscles and skin, gloriously tan skin and hard abs everywhere. I'm momentarily blinded by the sight. I don't know where to focus my eyes first. I reach out and lay my hands on his biceps, taking pleasure in the curved, heavy muscles filling my palms. *Firm muscles, soft skin.* I slide my hands to his stomach, flatten them and push. Everything about him is rock-solid and sculpted to perfection. I let out a choking noise and blink in odd, irregular bursts. He laughs, abs flexing on each deep rumble, and I nearly pass out.

"Jesus, Mary, and Joseph," I murmur.

"Nah, it's just me."

"Funny guy."

He smirks, cocky and pleased. "Hey, now. If my shirt is coming off, then so is yours."

I don't need to be asked twice; my skin is a thousand degrees. Still, I feel a little shy as I lift my sweater over my head and drop it to the floor. I'm wearing a silky camisole underneath and when I reach for that next, he stills my hands and does it himself. His sharp intake of breath feels like it was snatched straight from my lungs.

I'd chosen a pale blue lace bra to match my sweater—one of my rules for simplifying life: match my underthings to my outfit—and he looks fiercely worshipful of my choice. I send up a prayer of thanks to whatever divine power compelled me to bury all my utilitarian beige bras in the bottom of my drawer after my night of drunken debauchery.

He sits there and stares, appreciating me. His eyes move over my body like he's memorizing every curving inch of me. He stares until I'm so self-conscious I want to cover myself, but I resist. His hand moves up as if in a trance, then stops about an inch from my skin.

"Yes?" he breathes.

"You can if I can."

When his fingers touch my skin his eyes briefly close, as if the sight and feel of me put together is too much. His other hand moves to my right breast, and his eyes look drugged as he runs his index finger lightly along the top edge of my bra, back and forth, featherlight. When he dips his fingers inside, I gasp and arch against him.

He coils an arm around me and sits us up, our chests pressed together. Skin on skin at last. I'm straddling his lap, knees bent and bracing him on either side. I grab the back of the couch and my arms cage him in.

"Got you right where I want you." I'm so turned on, I'm practically slurring.

He slides me forward until the heavy jut of his erection presses against my groin.

"No, *now* you're where I want you."

I shiver and moan and attack him with renewed energy. I kiss down his throat, across his shoulder, along his pectoral. He doesn't want to let me—he keeps trying to pull me upright—but I persevere. I wiggle my butt in his lap, grinding against him. If his ragged breathing is any indicator, I might be killing him.

"It's my turn," he says on a groan, his voice hoarse.

I try to respectfully decline but he ignores me, using his superior strength—not really fair—to drag me back up. He repositions me on his lap, gripping my hips while he places a series of wet, swirling kisses on the swell of my breasts. When his eyes flick up to mine, I nearly slither off his lap. It's the single most erotic experience of my life—and I'm still half-clothed.

He migrates across my chest with agonizing slowness, focusing first on one breast, then on the other, giving each equal time. I'm about to commend his commitment to fairness—if I can form words—when he slips a finger underneath my bra strap. I suck in a breath. He toys with the lace, pinching the elastic between his fingers, gliding his hand up and down the strap. He can see the effect he's having on me; I'm coming undone. He smiles and lingers at my shoulder, teasing me. *Torturing* me. Finally he slides it off, leaving it dangling over my arm, and presses a soft kiss to my collarbone.

His other hand's been resting on my ass, and he slides it into my jeans between the denim and my underwear and squeezes. I buck against him, his hardness and our combined friction nearly driving me to madness. I want more. I *need* more.

I'm burning up, our bodies heated and glazed with sweat. These jeans are restricting my movement and I need them *off*. I'm simultaneously fumbling with my zipper and wondering how we can teleport to his bedroom when the sudden blare of loud voices jars me out of my lust fog and I nearly fall off his lap. Ben's TV has somehow switched on, and the brash male host of this particular news show is currently shouting down his female guest.

"The current welfare system incentivizes people not to work. The president has every right to make changes and it's long overdue."

"I know that's a favorite talking point of conservatives, Spencer, but the president can't just unilaterally decide to cut the welfare budget by half. That's a radical move that will leave the most vulnerable Americans out of options. We're talking single parents, low-income families, the disabled. There are forty million people on food assistance programs. These aren't just numbers. These are kids who won't be able to eat."

"Shit," Ben mutters, fumbling in the couch cushions to find the remote.

"Enacting basic work requirements to get welfare benefits isn't a radical *idea. Having to pass a drug test isn't a* radical *idea. I'd like to remind you that Democrats are the ones who said, 'Welfare should be a second chance, not a way of life.' The point here is to separate the needy from the greedy. These people have been freeloading for—"*

The screen goes black midsentence and the room lapses into silence. My heart is racing, as much from lust as from fright, but now there's something else: foreboding.

"Sorry about that," Ben murmurs, sliding me back onto his lap. I feel vaguely out of body as he replaces his mouth on my neck, and I squeeze my eyes shut, trying to lose myself again in the feel of his lips on my skin.

You're hooking up with the enemy.

The thought materializes unbidden and I nearly gasp. My eyes pop open and I glance at Ben, but his face is buried in my cleavage. He's pulled my other bra strap down and in about two seconds, it will be off altogether. I start to panic, unpleasant thoughts and questions ricocheting in my head, so loud I can't ignore them.

Nothing's changed here. He's still for everything you're against.

How exactly will this relationship work? What will you talk about over dinner? Certainly not about what you did all day.

He wants to turn you. That's what tonight's been all about.

Just because your bodies are compatible doesn't mean this is a good idea.

Ben hums against my chest and all I can think is, *I just want my piece of chocolate. Please, just let me have my mother-fudging piece of chocolate!*

His fingers dip into my waistband.

This is never going to work.

I pull back, pressing a hand to his chest. "Wait. I'm sorry. Time out." I climb off him and curl into a ball beside him, hugging my knees.

"What's wrong?"

I brave a glance at him. It's a mistake. He is *glorious*. An Adonis. Skin flushed. Lurid, raging bedroom eyes. Hair a hot mess, ruffled and wild and sexy as hell. Even sitting, the most universally unflattering position for all mortals, his abs stay flat and firm with nary a belly roll in sight. Am I seriously pumping the brakes on this? I've officially lost my marbles.

I bury my face in my hands. "I have no idea how to verbalize what's going through my head. It's going to come out all wrong."

He reaches out and clasps my hand. "Hey. Just tell me."

When I meet his eyes, my throat constricts. He's so beautiful I could cry. He's impossible to resist when he looks at me this way: eyes nurturing and kind, even in the face of my bizarre behavioral whiplash.

"I'm freaking out, okay? You were an idea before. A figment of my horny, hyperactive imagination. Now, you're . . . look at you! You're rip-pling everywhere!" I motion to his abs like they're holding me hostage. Which they kind of are. "This is a problem, okay? We work together. Actually, no, it's worse. We work *against* each other. We're professional enemies. We barely even get along most of the time. How on earth are we supposed to navigate this?"

He blinks. "So you're telling me while we were just doing all that, you were thinking about *work*?"

"Ben!" I'm nearly hysterical.

"All right, calm down, just trying to lighten the mood. I like teasing you almost as much as I like kissing you." He grimaces, shifting again on the couch. "Almost."

"I'm sorry. I feel really bad about . . ." I gesture uselessly.

"Stop apologizing. I told you I had no expectations and I meant it. I just . . . need to not be looking at you for a minute." He grabs my cami-sole from the floor and passes it over. "Put this on."

I obey, then nudge him. "What do you think of when you're trying to calm down? Hammond naked?"

"Jesus Christ, Kate. *No.*" He laughs softly and grinds the heels of his hands into his eye sockets.

I reach out and brush his arm, and a powerful wave of desire threat-ens to pull me under. "I don't want you to think I don't want to. I do want to. Like, a lot. I'm just . . ."

"You're not ready. I get it."

He puts his arm around me, pulling me close, and kisses my temple. It's such a casual, affectionate gesture, and simultaneously devoid of any expectation, that I mentally exhale. *He doesn't hate you.* I wrap my arms around his middle and press my cheek to his chest. Maybe if we stay right here, nothing will touch us.

"There's no rush. This is a lot for one night. I pressed my luck even bringing you back here. I can't seem to help myself when it comes to you."

I smile and look up at him with lusty eyes. He hugs me tighter and when I snuggle into the crook of his armpit, I have to talk myself out of sniffing him. I'm a heathen.

"All right, let's deal with this. You're concerned about . . . work implications." I detect a note of skepticism in his tone, like he doesn't believe me.

"You're not the only one who's been thinking about this for a long time, okay? But I can't just ignore how complicated it's going to be. I refuse to wear Ben blinders. Reality is right outside that door. It's the exact reason I fought this for so long."

"I think you're overreacting."

"Ben, we *work* together. It's an issue."

"We really don't. We're not in the same office. I'm not your superior. We're not even on the same side."

"Aha! And therein lies the bigger problem."

His eyes narrow. "I don't care who you work for."

I press my lips together and don't say a word.

"But you do." He exhales, shaking his head. He's pissed. "Really, Kate? *Still* with this?"

"It matters. Stop pretending it doesn't."

"Why does it matter?"

"You think this won't come between us? Our jobs are literally to obstruct each other's progress. We'll spend all day bad-mouthing each other, shooting poison darts, then what? Come home and eat dinner?"

"You're being dramatic."

"I'm being *realistic*. What happens when I have to publicly denounce the tax plan? No hard feelings?"

He scowls. "Are you done listing all the ways this isn't gonna work?"

"Don't do that. Don't make me the bad guy. I'm trying to tell you I'm worried. Sticking your head in the sand isn't going to help us figure this out."

He blows out a breath. "Fine, so there are some minefields to navigate. We'll handle them."

"We'll *handle* them? That's it?"

"What do you mean, *that's it*? You just laid this on me two minutes ago." He squeezes my knee. "Look, I don't have all the answers. Yet. I just know we can figure this out, if we want to make it work. And I *want* to make this work."

"So do I," I whisper.

He brushes some hair out of my face, trailing a finger down my neck, and I nearly stop breathing. "I can separate work from personal. Can you?"

"Honestly? I don't know. I can try." I pause. "Along those same lines, I think we should keep this to ourselves. At least until we figure out what *this* is."

His finger ceases its movement. He leans back, giving me a *looong* look. "Why?"

"Because of all the reasons we just talked about! We work together. It's frowned upon. I don't want to be the subject of speculation. I don't need people wondering where my loyalties lie. People who've made this mistake before have watched their careers implode. Take your pick! We have a lot to figure out and we hardly need other people getting involved."

"This isn't a mistake." His voice is flat.

"You know that's not what I meant."

He regards me silently and I squirm inside my skin.

"Come on, you just said it yourself. Separate work from personal."

"That wasn't what *I* meant."

He sits back on the couch, putting even more distance between us. A muscle ticks in his jaw and even though I know he's not happy with me, it takes all my self-restraint not to press my lips to it and kiss the tension away.

"So what, we'll be in a secret relationship? I'm not supposed to look at you or talk to you?"

"No," I say calmly, resisting being drawn into a fight. "We can do what we did before. Talk. Eat lunch. Invent reasons to drop by each other's offices. Pretend not to watch each other through the window."

The corners of his mouth turn up briefly.

"Oh look, I got a smile."

He rolls his eyes at me, and this time I do lean forward and kiss him. His hand automatically cups my cheek and I can feel when he relaxes, the taut muscles of his upper body loosening beneath my fingertips.

Eventually I pull back an inch and make eye contact. "Are we okay?"

"We're okay."

"And we're agreed about . . . ?"

He exhales. "Fine, we can keep this under wraps for now. Only because one day we'll look back and laugh about all this hand-wringing you did."

My eyes widen. It's the closest we've come to talking about Long-Term What Does This Mean. My stomach's twisting as I sidestep.

"I'm pretty sure only grandmas use the term *hand-wringing*."

He smiles but his eyes dim a little, and I know it's because I ignored his comment. I also know he's going to give me a pass.

He pats my knee and stands, pulling me to my feet, but instead of dropping my hands he loops them around his lower back. When I step into his hug, his arms wrap around my shoulder blades, pressing me to his chest. Still bare. Still divine. I feel the pressure of a kiss to the top of my head and try to commit this moment to memory. Everyone should experience a hug like this.

"We're going to be fine," he murmurs in my ear.

"We're such a mess." My words are muffled by his magnificent chest.

"A beautiful mess." He tips my head up and kisses me, gentle and sweet. "Come on, I'll take you home."

I grab my sweater off the floor and hand him his undershirt reluctantly, beating back a wail of despair when he pulls it over his head. When I finish pulling on my boots, I stand and lean into him again. His eyes are soft as he embraces me, and my heart swells.

"Let's leave in, like, five more minutes," I propose, gazing up at him with some bedroom eyes of my own.

"Don't tempt me." He gives my butt a warning squeeze. "Let's go, Goldilocks."

"Wait, one thing." I grab his sweater before he can put it back on. "I'm taking this. I'm . . . cold."

He shakes his head, amused. "And you call me a stalker."

Chapter 24

There's a bouquet of blush-colored peonies on my desk when I get to work on Monday.

I squint at them, confused. It's not my birthday. No work victories to celebrate. *Who would send me flowers?*

Ben. It has to be. A teasing nod to my drunken flower rant. *Very funny.* They're beautiful, I'll give him that. Peonies are my favorite. *Who has he been talking to?* I shake my head as I lean forward to smell them, and that's when I figure it out.

They're fake. Incredibly realistic-looking, but definitely fake.

I howl in amusement. There's a small white envelope peeking out from underneath the vase and I extract the note with shaking fingers.

> *Hassle-free. Require no work or effort. Will never stink and will live forever. Also:* ~~nice striking~~ *beautiful, like you.*

I beam at his note like a lovesick teenager, then scurry to my window and peer across the fishbowl. Ben's at his desk, eyes glued to his computer screen. I start to wave, then feel like a moron when he doesn't look up. I grab my phone instead and hit CALL.

I watch him look at his phone, then glance out the window. I wave, and he breaks into such a massive, genuine grin, I want to slingshot myself across the atrium.

He answers as he rises out of his chair and heads to the window. "Hey, you."

God, he has a sexy phone voice. It's deep and throaty and totally obscene.

"Hey, yourself. So, flowers, huh?"

"I took a chance," he says, and I can both see and hear the smile in his voice. "All part of those traditional rules of courtship you so politely requested. You like them?"

"I love them. They're perfect. Thank you." *You get me like no one else does.*

He blinks in surprise. I think he was expecting sarcasm. "So, good surprise, then? That's a relief. Could've gone either way."

I laugh and feel a flush sweep up my neck. I can see the fire in his eyes from fifty yards away. It's a weird thing, watching someone while you talk to them on the phone. Like the strangest form of foreplay.

"I'm not even going to ask how you found out I like peonies."

He smiles. "I have my ways. Let me take you to lunch today."

He looks at me expectantly and I take a moment to appreciate the view. He has one arm drawn tight across his chest, making his biceps appear even more ginormous than usual. His legs are planted in a stance that should be displayed in the dictionary under *swagger*. He looks mouthwatering.

"I wish I could, but I have a lunch meeting. Dinner?"

"Of course I have a dinner meeting."

"Tomorrow?"

"Can't wait that long."

"Flatterer." I squint at him and tap my finger against my lips.

"Don't do that."

"Do what?"

"Touch yourself. It feels like forever since I touched you."

A full-body shiver ripples through me. "It's been two days."

"Well, it feels like two *years*."

He's standing stock-still, eyes locked on me. I'm so close to the window my breath is fogging up the glass.

We are *so* going to get caught.

He lifts his chin. "Meet me at the south elevators."

"Right *now*?"

"Right now."

We have an entirely nonverbal conversation in the span of about five seconds. I turn and rush out.

"Where are you headed?" Stephen calls as I dash past him.

"Oh, just . . . to Cups! I'm grabbing a coffee, I'll be right back."

"Great, can you get me one? I'm dying for a—"

"Text it to me!"

I practically sprint down the hallway until I reach the elevator bank. No Ben. I turn in a circle, confused. The elevators are closer to his office than mine. How could I have beaten him?

A door opens behind me and I spin around. Ben pulls me into the women's room, locking the door behind me. I start to protest but he cuts me off.

"I scouted it out, we're good." And then his mouth is on mine.

We fall against the door, letting out matching sighs of relief. The next couple of minutes are a soundtrack of panting breaths, sliding lips, fingernails clawing against fabric. I slip my arms underneath his suit jacket and fill my hands with the solid flexing muscles of his back. This is my new favorite place, right here.

I splay my hand against his chest and feel it rise and fall. "You know, this is exactly what we said we weren't going to do."

"I lied."

A laugh bubbles out of me as we swap happy smiles. We're a couple of grinning fools. I tuck my head into the cradle of his collarbone. He smells like crisp linen and Ben. I breathe in and it feels like the first real breath I've taken in two days.

"Honestly, I worried you'd take one look at me and regret everything that happened this weekend. And based on how you freaked out on me, it's not farfetched." There's insecurity in his eyes and I hate that I've put it there.

"Well, I *don't* regret it. Although I have been regretting certain other things . . ." I gaze up at him with my best *wanton seductress* look.

"And those would be?" His eyes are looking a little pornographic themselves.

"Not getting to see more of what you're hiding under these perfectly pressed suits." I trace a meandering path up his chest with my fingertips and tug on his tie. He's vibrating with tension. "How long until someone knocks on this door?"

"I'm surprised it hasn't happened already. Sorry, it was all I could come up with on short notice."

"Pity. We should probably go before we get caught."

"Probably."

I fist my hands in his shirt instead and drag him closer. I feel him hard and heavy against me and I could scream for wanting him. A war's being waged on his face, an epic battle between desire and restraint. The Battle of the Bulge versus Boy Scout Ben.

"Keep looking at me like that and you'll be taking a sick day."

"Will you just loosen your tie like I always watch you do? *Please?* It's my favorite part of the day." I barely recognize the sound of my own voice. It's hoarse and husky as a porn star with strep throat.

He closes his eyes and takes a deep breath. "Okay, so this has officially become a problem. If I'm not going to see you tonight, when will I?"

"Well, you haven't exactly taken me on a real date yet."

"And what do you call the shooting range? That was some of my best work."

"My mom always told me to find a guy who would treat me like gold. I'm not sure I would describe firearm instruction as *like gold*."

"You've obviously been dating the wrong guys."

I smack him.

"I'm kidding. I wouldn't dream of disappointing Beverly." He takes my hands in his. "Kate, are you free to go out with me tomorrow evening on a *real* date?"

"I believe I am."

"Good. Then it's a date."

"Good."

We grin at each other, two teenagers playing hooky. I fuss with his tie, which has gone askew from my groping. Oh, who am I kidding? I'll find any excuse to touch him. I'm seventeen again and want to make out by the lockers—or, you know, up against the door of Hart's seventh-floor women's restroom.

"I don't want to go back," I whisper against his mouth.

His eyes flame. "You want to meet here again this afternoon?"

We make another bathroom date for three o'clock.

★

When I get back to the office, Stephen raises his hands in question. "Where's my coffee?"

"Oh, um . . . the line was too long. I'll go back later."

He shoots me a funny look as I retreat to my office and shut the door. I'm overheating again, so I strip off my jacket and fan myself with a file folder—then glance out the window.

Ben's watching me and wearing a big smile.

Chapter 25

Monday passes in a flurry of texts, mostly silly, unimportant things that make me giggle: screenshots of our step counts to taunt each other; an update about a lingering smell in one of the Dirksen committee rooms; Ben's observations of the shameless nose picker in the office two windows below mine; a story about a new intern in his office who quit after just two hours of answering the phones. It's all the normal, mundane parts of the day that are only interesting to others who are living it, and it's ridiculously fun to have someone to share it with.

I'm also discovering how thoughtful he is. On his way back from meetings, he texts to see if he can grab me coffee or food. He makes me promise not to stay late since he can't walk me home tonight. He congratulates me on some positive press Carol received for a bill she's co-sponsoring. It's wonderful. Also, weird. The evolution of our relationship is so improbable, I feel like I should buy a lottery ticket.

On Tuesday we're both out of the office for large chunks of the day, which means no steamy bathroom trysts. Sad trombone. By the time I meet him in the lobby at six o'clock, I'm so eager to see him I'm ready to jump out of my skin. We're not two minutes away from our building before he nudges me, dropping his mouth to my ear.

"Are we out of jail? Is the coast clear?"

I make a dramatic show of looking around. "I think so," I whisper back.

He leans over and kisses me, like it's the most natural thing in the world to do, like he's done it a million times before. It's short and sweet, the equivalent of a welcome-home kiss from a significant other—nothing like what I know he's capable of—yet something about its inherent possessiveness makes me weak in the knees.

He takes my hand in his, interlacing our fingers. "Any ideas on where we're going?"

The only hint he's given me was a cryptic text I received late last night asking me if I had cowboy boots, to which I'd flippantly responded:

Me: What kind of Tennessee girl do you think I am? Of course I own cowboy boots.

"A country concert? Some sort of live music?" I guess like this is the first I've considered it and didn't spend my day obsessively googling which bands are in town.

"Hmm," he says mysteriously. "I guess you'll find out."

"Should I wear my cowboy hat, too?"

His eyes light up. "Yes, absolutely. Thank you for thinking of that."

I'm laughing as he drops me off at my building.

"I'll be back to collect you in fifteen minutes. Don't be late."

He gives me another kiss before he leaves, only this time he adds a little butt squeeze, and I'm floating on air.

I get ready as fast as I can, taking my hair down and refreshing my makeup, but I'm stymied when I try to figure out what to wear. First, I throw on my standard country concert ensemble: jeans, denim jacket, cowboy boots and hat, but when I look in the mirror it resembles a denim-on-denim fashion crime not seen since the likes of Justin and Britney circa 2001. I could wear a dress—I'd love to look a bit more girly since all he ever sees me in is work attire—but I'm afraid I'll freeze to death in the still-brisk April air. I decide to text him.

Me: Will we be inside or outside?

Ben: Inside. And no more hints.

It's the only nudge I need, and I quickly replace my jeans with a flirty white sundress I haven't worn in forever. When I pair it with the jacket, boots, and hat, I think I look pretty darn cute.

I'm fidgety with excitement and nerves by the time he walks into the lobby. When he spots me his stride falters, and he closes his eyes and gives his head a firm shake before coming the rest of the way. *I'm so glad I wore the dress.*

"You're gorgeous," he says simply once he's standing in front of me. He leans over and kisses me lightly, his hand automatically finding mine at my side. There's nervous energy in his kiss, same as mine.

"So, better than *nice*, then?" I tease when he pulls back.

"Nice, striking, beautiful, and gorgeous. And any other words you want to throw in there." It's his low, scratchy voice, and he's looking at me like I'm something new.

"We're matching too." I finger the collar of his white button-down. "No green this time?"

"Gotta keep you on your toes. Besides, some stalker's been stealing my clothes." He grabs my hand and tows me toward the door. "Come on. We're gonna be late."

He leads me a little ways back up the street in the same direction we just came from work. The looks we're getting from passersby are priceless, both of us bedecked in cowboy boots and cowboy hats like a couple of country bumpkins. We're as out of place on the streets of DC as ballerinas at a monster truck rally.

After we squeeze past a guy who gives me a leering once-over, Ben scowls and tucks me under his arm. "You'd think these morons would know better than to look at you when I'm standing right here."

I can't resist teasing him. "God forbid they *look* at me. What are they thinking?" I bump my hip against his.

"Not funny," he mutters. "You don't know what I deal with."

"Well, can you blame them? I'm a redneck woman."

"You're a country cutie, is what you are."

"I'm Backwoods Barbie."

"You're a hot little hillbilly."

We're laughing as he stops abruptly in front of a glass door, and when he opens it for me, I know just where we are: It's a dance studio, one I pass every day walking to and from work. I gawk at him. We're going *dancing*?

He laughs when he sees the shock on my face. "I knew you'd never guess this. I've passed this place a million times but never had a reason to go in. They have group classes a few times a week apparently, and they pick a different style of dance each time, like the tango or swing or whatever. When I called and they said they were doing country-western this week, I thought it was almost *too* perfect." He grins his boyish grin. "Surprised?"

Stunned, more like. "I never would have guessed," I say, my voice a little unsteady with emotion. I can't believe he came up with a date this charming on only a day's notice. It seems I'm destined to be surprised by this man over and over again.

We take a look around, the interior much larger than it appears from the street. Floor-to-ceiling mirrors surround us on three sides and a parquet wooden dance floor spans the center of the room. Additional private rooms line a back hallway. A woman who must be the owner or instructor waves in greeting and heads toward us as Ben takes charge.

"Hi, you must be Clara? I spoke with you on the phone. I'm Ben, and this is Kate."

She's a sixty-something woman, her hair in a tight gray bun, and she moves gracefully as she shakes our hands. Yep—definitely the instructor. I watch her take Ben in, sizing him up, and I want to laugh. She probably doesn't get many giants in here looking to square dance.

She turns to me, smiling warmly. "Wonderful. So are you looking to learn how to dance for a special occasion? A wedding, perhaps?"

I laugh nervously. "Oh no. This is just for fun."

"She's being shy," Ben breaks in. "We actually *are* considering a modern take on a line dance for our wedding. Thought it'd be fun to get all of our guests out there, shake things up a little. Isn't that right, honey?"

I slow-blink at him, the smile frozen on my face.

"She's a bit nervous, all those eyes on her, you know," he says to Clara in a confidential tone. "I thought taking this class might boost her confidence."

I will *kill* him.

Clara beams, totally under his spell. This must be a new record—he's charmed her in under ten seconds. "That's just lovely! This is a great way to overcome stage fright. If you have any questions as you go along, just ask," she says, patting my arm. "And if you schedule a private lesson, we could put together a routine specific to your wedding song." She raises an eyebrow at Ben, totally bypassing me, the inept half of this duo. I take offense on behalf of shy brides everywhere.

She flashes me an encouraging smile before going to greet another couple. As soon as she's a safe distance away, I seize his hat and attack him with it. "You are dead to me."

He shushes me and makes an unsuccessful grab for his hat. "Don't let Clara hear that or she'll think our engagement is on the rocks."

A few more couples trickle in, about ten of us in total, before Clara starts the class. "Country-western dancing is all about having fun. It's informal, the music upbeat and traditional Americana. It won't be as complicated as some of the dances we've learned in recent weeks." Ben shoots me a wide-eyed look, like we're already in trouble and behind on the syllabus, and I have to stifle an unladylike snort. "If any of you have ever been to a honky-tonk before, you'll probably recognize some of the dances we'll be doing tonight. The Texas two-step, the western prome-nade, and some line dancing.

"I applaud those of you who wore the traditional clothing tonight," she continues, eyeing us approvingly. "Many of the dances incorporate heel and toe taps, so that will be an advantage for those of you wearing boots."

"She loves us," he whispers to me.

"She loves *you*," I whisper back.

Clara takes the class through the paces for the two-step, offering us pointers as we practice with our partners. After a few minutes, she an-nounces it's time to try it with music. She glides to the stereo and a mo-ment later I hear the opening strains of Tim McGraw's "Just to See You Smile."

I gasp and clutch Ben's arm. "Can you believe they're playing this so—"

The words aren't even out when I catch the look on his face: mouth open and eyes wide in a phony display of surprise. Understanding slams into me.

"You *planned* this?"

"Guilty."

I gape at him in disbelief as he laughs, clearly delighted by my re-action.

"You look like you're having an aneurism."

He loops my left arm around his neck and grasps my right hand in his, pulling me close so we're in position and ready to start.

"You're very pleased with yourself," I manage.

"Guilty again."

"So is this what dating you will be like?" I ask, shy all of a sudden.

"Like what?"

"Oh, you know. Full of romantic crap like this."

He barks a laugh as we start shuffling our feet. "I have a theory," he says, dropping his mouth to my ear so I can hear him over the music. "You say you're not a romantic, but I think that's just because no one's ever done it right."

I'm overcome by a foreign emotion at his words, happiness and fear colliding in my chest. It's like the final piece of myself I've been holding back breaks loose, dropping into the sea like a melting iceberg. I burrow into his shoulder, not wanting him to see the wild spectrum of emotions parading across my face. He seems to recognize that I'm having a moment, and to his credit he doesn't tease me about it, just holds me tighter as we whirl around the room.

After the two-step, Clara teaches us the Cotton-Eye Joe line dance, a traditional square dance, and finally a promenade to end the class. Ben proves to be a great dancer, prompting me to wonder if there's anything he *isn't* good at. He spins and dips me, even when the dances don't call for it; steals kisses whenever Clara's back is turned; twirls me all over the dance floor, placing proprietary hands on my back, sides, and neck. It can't be a coincidence that both dates we've been on have required him to put his hands all over me. We don't stop laughing for the full hour, and by the end my cheeks hurt from smiling. I like to think our good humor rubs off on the other participants; at any rate, we only get a couple of warning looks from Clara when we get a little rambunctious with our boot slaps.

When the class is over, we stumble into the night air, sweaty and crowing about our stellar moves. We're both starving so we duck into the first restaurant we see, a fifties-style diner a few doors down. It's the kind of place with an eighteen-page menu, but we still order burgers, fries, and ridiculously large milkshakes and eat like teenagers during a growth spurt. There isn't a lull in the conversation for two hours. It's just a guy and a girl on a first date—the best first date in the history of first dates.

It's nearly ten when the waitstaff starts giving us the evil eye and we drag ourselves out of the diner. Ben carries our nested hats at his side and claims my hand, as he's been doing all night. I can't believe how normal it feels. I start to wonder what will happen next—am I going to end up back at his place again? Is he coming to mine? How far am I willing to go? My heartbeat ratchets up at the uncertainty.

"So, where are we headed?" Subtle, I am not.

Ben tightens his grip on my hand. There's a long pause.

"Home," he finally answers.

"*Whose* home?"

He eyes me sideways. "Yours."

"Okay—"

"To drop you off."

I stop walking abruptly, forcing him to a stop. "What do you mean? You're not coming up?"

"I don't put out on the first date."

If he's looking for a cheap laugh, he's not getting it from me. "You weren't this bashful on Saturday night."

He blows out a breath. "I just didn't want to bring this up tonight, especially since we did such a good job avoiding sensitive topics." He grimaces slightly and looks away, and I know whatever he's about to say, I'm not going to like it. "You said you didn't want anyone at work to find out about this. I take it that's still the case?"

Why does this feel like a trick question? My Spidey senses are tingling.

"Yeees . . ." I answer slowly. What does that have to do with him coming up? Does he think Senator Warner's hiding in my apartment?

He looks me straight in the eye. "Well, I don't want to date you in secret."

I drop his hand. "Excuse me?"

"The sneaking around, the hiding. It's not how I want to do this."

My heart's beating so loud, I swear I can hear it. "You know I'm not ready to put this out there."

"I do know, which is why I'm trying to come up with a solution we can both live with."

"So your big solution is to stop *touching* me?"

He takes a deep breath. "Kate, how would you feel if I said I wanted to date you, but only under the cover of darkness or behind closed doors?"

"That is a *total* misrepresentation of my reasons for wanting to keep this private."

"Maybe it is, maybe it isn't."

I stare at him. "I'm not *ashamed* to be dating you."

"Okay," he says, after a pause.

He doesn't believe me.

"Ben. I'm not."

"I said, *okay*." He's getting testy.

"But you still don't want to come up."

"Of course I *want* to come up."

"But you're not going to." I cross my arms over my chest. They're a shield, an attempt to shore up my heart, which is cracking clean in half. "So sometime between yesterday's bathroom rendezvous and now you had a crisis of conscience?"

He slants me a look. "You're proving my point. I hardly think a bathroom stall should be what we're striving for."

"So you don't want me in a bathroom stall, or your car, or my apartment. You do not want me here or there. You do not want me anywhere."

It's the wrong reaction—flippant and petty when I know he's just as frustrated as I am—but he's keeping himself from me and it's not fair. It's like he's spent the whole night making me fall in love with him only to rip the rug out from under me. I'm so tired of him being just beyond my reach, I could cry.

"You know I want you," he says quietly. "I want you more than I've ever wanted anything. I want you so much that I'm willing to put what I want aside to give you time to wrap your mind around this."

"So that's it, then? You've made this decision and I don't even get a say."

"I suppose you're the only one who's allowed to pump the breaks?"

I narrow my eyes. "Maybe I need more time with you to *wrap my mind around this*, ever think of that?"

"All right, let's play that out. I come up, right now. You and I both know what will happen. And then what, you ignore me tomorrow? I'm supposed to ignore you? Pretend it never happened?" He shakes his head. "No. I'm not built that way. You're asking for something I can't give."

I turn away, needing to block out his wounded expression and the reality of our situation. The worst part is, I know he's right. I've been so consumed by my feelings for him that I haven't considered how we'll navigate all the complicated situations we're bound to find ourselves in. My shoulders sag with the realization. *Another obstacle.*

He's watching me as I process this. "The more time we spend together, the more I'm feeling. More invested, more protective, more . . . *everything*. I can't just turn it off depending on where we are and who's in the room. I'd do just about anything you ask, but I can't do that."

I take a tentative step toward him, propelled forward by the honesty and vulnerability in his words. He wastes no time pulling me in, crushing me in a hug. I clutch the back of his shirt like a lifeline.

"I'm sorry," I whisper into his chest. "I shouldn't have reacted like that. I know you're just trying to do the right thing. I don't know what's wrong with me. You should probably run the other direction."

"Nah, I've got too much time invested."

"You must have the patience of a saint."

His chuckle rumbles beneath my cheek. "I wouldn't go that far, but I've waited this long for you to see what was right in front of you. I can wait longer."

His words knock the wind out of me.

"Sometimes you say things . . ." I shake my head, overcome.

He smiles and tilts my face up, just looking at me, drinking me in. I'm doing the same. I'm lost in his eyes. I'm as pathetic as an eighties song.

"If you're about to tell me that kissing is on your forbidden list, I will murder you in your sleep."

"Now you're just talking crazy." He kisses me in proof.

When he pulls away, I want to weep. "Remind me again why you're saying no to this?"

"I just think if we take certain things off the table—"

"Off the *table*?"

"—for the *time being*, we'll be able to focus on addressing your concerns more quickly. And the sooner that happens, the sooner you can admit I was right all along, and we can pick up where we left off." He presses a hand to my back, nudging me forward.

"Where did I go wrong? It was all that *like gold* talk, wasn't it? I put the fear in you."

"It did make me think."

"Ugh, *no* more thinking. You're entirely too sensible and evolved. Where can I find the Ben from Saturday night? The devil-may-care, rip-my-clothes-off-and-damn-the-consequences Ben?"

"He's under firm orders to stand down until further notice." He tucks me tight against his side as we cross the street.

"You must be into torture."

"You want to talk about torture? Let's talk about this naughty cowgirl getup you've been prancing around in all night."

"*Prancing?*" I start giggling.

"For a guy from Texas, it may as well be a French maid's costume."

I'm dragging my feet as he leads me into my building by the hand.

"Come on now, I'm walking you to your door. And spoiler alert, you're getting a goodnight kiss."

I can't let it go. "So what exactly is it you need me to do at work? Put out a press release announcing we're dating? Let you throw me up against the window and have your way with me?"

He grimaces and adjusts his pants. "We need to not be hiding in bathrooms, to start." He prods me into the elevator and pushes the button for my floor.

"So I just need to be comfortable enough to tell people. That's it?"

"That's it. See? Easy." He brushes his thumb across my knuckles and just that minor amount of friction leaves me quivering with want.

"Stephen knows!" I shout triumphantly.

"And I'm sure you swore him to secrecy." Drat, he's got me again.

I can't believe he's denying me—denying *himself*—especially when I can see how much he wants this. The evidence is visible from across the elevator. Apparently, I've found the only incorruptible man in DC. *Lucky me.*

The elevator dings and he tugs me out. I follow at a snail's pace, the condemned headed to the gallows. When we reach my door, he grabs me by the jacket lapels and pulls me close. The way he's looking at me reduces me to a consistency similar to the milkshakes we just consumed.

"What time do you leave for work in the morning?" It's his husky voice, the one that makes me forget my own name. I want to close my eyes and let it wash over me. I want him to tell me a bedtime story.

"Eight forty-five. Why?"

His eyes shine down at me like two brilliant stars. "Because I'm going to walk you, silly."

He kisses me slowly, his hands migrating up my jacket to cradle my face. It's soft and light, lovely and unhurried, like he's tasting me and committing me to memory. He's going slow, making it last, leaving an impression. If he's not going to stay, he's going to make damn sure I know what I'm missing.

When he pulls away, I'm gasping and overcome. I wonder if you can die from unfulfilled lust.

"If you come in, we don't have to do anything. We can just talk!" I plead, clutching his shirt in a death grip.

"Oh sure. We're very good at 'just talking' when we're alone together." He replaces my hat on my head and smiles.

"Your moral uprightness is getting annoying," I grumble.

"Nah, you love it. You want me even more now."

"I knew it! This is all just a ploy. You're into long, drawn-out foreplay."

"Maybe you'll find out someday."

"I bet I could break you."

"I bet you could too. Please don't try. I'm a good guy, not a priest."

I feel it so strongly then, standing there and grinning up at him, my heart nearly beating out of my chest. *I'm in love with you.* It's on the tip of my tongue. It's tripping out of my mouth. I want to breathe it into him. Tattoo it on my forehead. Shout it through a megaphone so loud his hair blows back.

But how can I say *I love you* in one breath and deny him the acknowledgment of our relationship in the next? It would be wrong and unfair to him. I say something else instead.

"It's weird. I already miss you, even though you're standing right here."

He looks at me so sharply, I wonder if I've said something wrong.

"If you only knew how many times I've had the exact same thought."

He kisses me again and this time there's a fierceness to it, a violent longing in his touch that wasn't there before. He turns me so I'm pressed up against the door, and there's no doubt we're playing with fire here— but if he thinks I'm going to stop him, he's got another think coming.

When he finally does break it off, I whimper my displeasure. A small smile teases his lips as he plays with my jacket collar.

"So what do you think? Was this a good enough first date?"

I don't answer him. I just wrap my arms around his neck and lose myself in him for as long as he'll let me.

Chapter 26

Over the next couple of weeks, Ben and I establish a routine of sorts. He picks me up in the morning (often with wet hair from a predawn workout and shower, which sends my mind down all sorts of filthy rabbit holes), and we walk to work together. Occasionally our schedules align enough for us to grab lunch, but as the tax vote draws nearer, Ben is so busy that his spontaneous drop-ins mostly become a thing of the past. More often than not, I don't see him again—beyond some hungry looks through the window—until the end of the day, when we meet in the lobby for our walk home.

As agreed, we play things down at work, and though Ben doesn't seem to care in the least who finds out about us, I sure do—not that anyone seems to notice or care what we're up to. Part of me wonders if it's because my colleagues don't believe I'd ever date the opposition. For the first time, I wonder what that says about me.

Our nights are spent at home, low-key and coupley and extraordinary in their ordinariness. Ben repealed his own mandate and reinstated apartment privileges once he realized its fatal flaw: no home-cooked meals. Instead, we came up with a list of ground rules:

1. Bedrooms are off-limits.
2. Clothes must stay on.
3. Alcoholic beverages: limited to one.

This last rule was self-imposed—any more than one glass of wine combined with his intense sexual force field and I seem to magically forget rule number two.

Our rules don't stop me from messing with him every chance I get. I trade my comfy, oversize loungewear for something skimpier and tighter. I leave my birth control out where he can see it. I ask him for a backrub one night, then channel my inner Meg Ryan and moan suggestively until he catches on and nearly tickles me to death in retaliation.

Post-dinnertime—otherwise known as Make Out on the Couch Time—is far and away my favorite part of the day. Despite our fleshly restrictions, we manage to push our PG-13 hookups as far as physically possible without actually crossing the line. While our clothes technically stay on, it's a murky distinction at best.

"Kate," he says between kisses one night, and I can tell by his ragged groan-sigh that he's breaking. "You're killing me. I want you so much. Please tell me you're getting closer. *Please.*"

I'm a little stunned; he never acknowledges the toll the waiting is taking on him. He brushes me off whenever I bring it up, reiterating that there's no rush, he'd never pressure me, that we have all the time in the world. The desperate longing in his voice tells a different story.

The thing is, I *am* getting closer. Not that I'm necessarily ready for him to sweep everything off a committee room table and kiss me senseless (his preferred method of taking things public—he's kidding . . . I think), but I *am* growing more comfortable with the idea of Ben and Kate: The Real Deal. Out and proud—if only to move us out of this sexless limbo that will surely lead to some sort of premature death from carnal combustion.

But it isn't *all* roses. The personal-professional tension I predicted rears its ugly head daily in the form of avoided topics, awkward silences, and the unspoken agreement not to press each other for details of our workday. It's as though we both know that to dig too deep is to shake the delicate foundation of our relationship in ways we're not yet strong enough to withstand. To wit: When our bosses fall on opposite sides of a big vote, we tiptoe around the topic like we're dodging land mines. When a controversial Supreme Court justice confirmation is all anyone can talk about, we stick to lighter subjects like our weekend plans, even as the issue looms larger than an elephant in the room.

While avoiding conflict is clearly the right decision for us—and ethically necessary, as well—I find myself becoming resentful. Resentful that our relationship isn't normal and easy like Tessa and Luke's, resentful of the circumstances that have forced us into our respective corners, resentful of the things I don't know—*can't* know—about him. It's as though there's a velvet-roped VIP area of his life I'll never gain access to, a private place inside him housing his professional ambitions that I'll never know intimately. In my darker moments, I wonder how we'll ever move forward if we can't share our highs and lows, expose the deepest parts of ourselves without fear or favor.

It's a delicate balance, one that fills me with hope and anxiety in equal amounts. Case in point: One night we're making dinner in his kitchen when Ben's phone starts blowing up. I don't *mean* to snoop, but since it's sitting right there on the counter, I can't help but see the texts stacking up on his screen like Tetris blocks.

Marcus: Did you see that email?

Marcus: Shit, you may actually have pulled this off.

Bill: Are you free? I just got off the phone with Hank.

Corinne: Wow, man of the hour! When can you meet up tomorrow?

The last one turns my stomach. *Corinne knows more about my boyfriend than I do.* Before I can ask him what's going on, his phone rings.

"Hey, Bill," he answers, then slides his eyes to me. "Uh, yeah, I can talk. Hang on."

He squeezes my hip as he passes behind me, then disappears into his room and shuts the door.

And I can't even ask him why.

As I stare at the closed door, I reflect on how many times a day I wish I could tell him something—celebrate an achievement, commiserate over a setback, or even just speak freely, without restraint—and the painful realization each time I remember I can't.

When he finally emerges, he looks deep in thought.

"That sounded important," I say, keeping my voice light. "Did something happen?"

Here's your opening, Ben. Share your success with me.

"Just some work stuff." He crosses behind me and opens the refrigerator, burying his head inside. As if something will have magically appeared since the last time he checked.

And once again, I get nothing. "Hiding in your room isn't suspicious at all," I say pointedly, trying to mask my hurt with a joke.

He comes up behind me, caging me against the counter with his arms and nuzzling my neck—and I soften, just like I always do. "Sounds like someone missed me."

And that's another thing. When he doesn't want to answer a question, he's evasive to the point of frustration, redirecting the conversation by making a joke or distracting me. He'll barely debate me on *any* issue, even those that have nothing to do with our jobs. He used to dish it out with no hesitation, no remorse, and no holds barred. Now he might lob a couple of easy volleys my way, then change the subject before I get too ramped up. This, of course, just makes me more determined to provoke him.

It comes to a head one night while we're curled up on my couch. I'm flipping channels mindlessly while he's reading some thick economics book that looks like my idea of personal hell. When I land on CNN, a panel of talking heads are discussing the tax bill—or perhaps more accurately, slamming and dismantling it point by point. I casually set the remote on the arm of the couch and train my eyes on the TV, like I'm riveted by the onscreen discussion. I know he won't be able to help himself.

I'm so right.

"Do you mind?"

I feign innocence. "I'm sorry, is this bothering you?"

He lowers his book. "I can read at home, you know."

"It's not like they're saying anything that isn't true. The tax breaks do disproportionately favor the wealthy."

I swallow down a fit of nervous giggles. I basically just lobbed a smoking grenade. My arms itch to duck and cover.

"You're too smart to regurgitate superficial talking points like that. Educate yourself before trying to poke me."

"I *have* educated myself. I'm dating you, aren't I?"

He tilts me a look. "These tax breaks benefit *everyone*. There'll be more money in people's paychecks, which means more disposable income, which just rallies the economy further." He pulls my legs onto his lap and starts massaging my thigh. "Maybe you should read this book when I'm finished."

I refuse to be sidetracked. "If that were true, shouldn't those living under the median income get much larger breaks? And why make individual tax cuts temporary while the ones for corporations are permanent?"

He sighs and picks his book back up. "If you don't believe me, why don't you ask Marcus? Maybe you'll listen to him."

"I don't *want* to ask Marcus! I want to hear what *you* have to say. Since when are you afraid to argue with me?"

"*Afraid?* Please," he scoffs.

"You're avoiding any disagreement. Deny it."

He pauses. "I prefer to leave work at work."

"Says the person reading the *work* book."

"It's *pleasure* reading."

"So, what, you're just never going to debate me again? That's not how a real relationship would work between us and you know it."

"Newsflash, we're in a real relationship," he says calmly, turning a page.

I kick my heel against the couch. "You know what I mean! You can't walk on eggshells around me. You can't be afraid to rock the boat."

"When I'm confident we're seaworthy, I'll rock your boat all night long, darlin'. Now, why don't you turn on one of your shows and scratch my neck?" he says, guiding my hand to the nape of his neck.

"Scratch your own neck," I say irritably, yanking my hand back.

"So I have to be asleep, then?"

I blink at him, momentarily confused, until my brain connects the dots and I let out a strangled gasp. *"No."*

He mimics me with a theatrical intake of breath. "Yes."

"You were awake that *whole time*?" I grab a throw pillow and start beating him with it.

Laughter gusts out of him as he ducks my blows. "You think I could sleep with you rubbing up on me all night long?"

"I can't believe you let me embarrass myself like that!"

"What should I have done, popped my eyes open and said, 'Gotcha'? I couldn't tell you *because* I didn't want to embarrass you. I had to let it run its course." He wrestles away the pillow and chucks it across the room. "Frankly, I'm shocked it took you that long to succumb to my raw sexual magnetism."

I groan. "I can't even look you in the eye. I'm changing my name and moving to another state." He chuckles. "And don't think I didn't just see what you did there."

He raises his eyebrows innocently.

"Distracted me from our argument. It won't work."

He flashes a rakish grin. "If I wanted to distract you, I'd just do this . . ."

He tosses his book on the coffee table and climbs over me, silencing any further arguments with his lips.

Well, alrighty, then.

★

The day it all comes crashing down starts out like any other.

We walk to work and ride up in the elevator together, something we've avoided doing too much of so as not to raise eyebrows among our colleagues. It's a testament to how comfortable I've gotten with the idea of us that lately, I can't be bothered to check who might be watching. I'm too busy looking at him.

Since we're the only two in the elevator, Ben leans over and gives me a goodbye kiss before the doors slide open. When he tells me to have a good day, I can almost imagine it could be like this every day, if I could calm down enough to let it. He's become as integral to my morning routine as my coffee: a tall vanilla latte with a shot of Ben's delicious lips and a hit of whipped cream.

Around lunchtime there's a short rap on my door, and before I get a chance to respond Stephen barges in.

"I just got a call from someone at Senator Hammond's office wanting to set up a meeting between him and Carol."

"What's it about?"

"They wouldn't say. I wonder if it involves the illicit fraternization of their staffers." His eyebrows shoot sky-high.

"Stephen! Don't even joke about that," I hiss as I hurry to shut the door behind him. "They have way more important things to worry about than us." *Don't they?*

"I thought you'd want to know."

The concerned look on his face is freaking me out. "Do you think I need to say something to Carol?"

Before he can answer there's another knock on the door and I jump about a foot in the air. I'm suddenly terrified it'll be Ben, here to blow our cover.

It's not.

"John! This is a surprise."

I plaster on a smile, trying to hide how deflated I feel. Of course, now I wish it had been Ben. I've officially lost it.

John beams back at me, totally misreading the vibe in the room. "Are you busy? Mind some company for lunch?" He holds up a plastic bag and my stomach sinks further.

"Uh, no, I'm not too busy. Come on in."

Stephen makes a face behind John's back and leaves. I motion to a chair and when my gaze sweeps over the window, I pause. If Ben's in his office, he'll see John in here—and judging by their previous interaction, I don't have to wonder how he'll feel about it.

Then I scold myself. John's a work colleague, nothing more. If Ben has an issue with that, he'll have to get over it. Besides, it's not like he's avoiding contact with certain icy, leggy brunettes I don't particularly care for. The fact that I started cracking my knuckles when I saw them walking together the other day is neither here nor there.

John and I chat about several of our shared projects as we eat, and before long he's filling me in on some behind-the-scenes drama I'm thrilled not to be a part of. I'm only half listening when he says something that makes my ears prick up.

"I assume you heard the latest tax drama?"

"Tax drama?"

"You won't believe it. They're doing away with the two-hundred-fifty-dollar deduction teachers can claim for school supplies. Or trying to, anyway."

"*What?* Where did you hear that?"

"Where did I *not* hear it, you mean? It's all over the news."

"It is?"

I grab my phone to search for it and quickly scan the first article that pops up. I'm dumbstruck. How could Ben support something like this? His own *mother* is a schoolteacher!

"Whoever came up with this bright idea should be named and shamed," John sniffs. "But then again, they all go along with it like the power-hungry pricks they are. I mean, how dumb are these people? They'd have to know this would result in horrible press. It's like they *want* to give us ammunition."

A protective instinct roars to life inside me like a lion. I could leap across this desk and tear John's eyes out.

"There has to be more to the story," I insist. "Maybe they're replacing the deduction with something else? The tax cuts are supposed to *help* the middle class." *Or so Ben claims.*

"Yeah, right. The cuts only benefit large corporations and the one percent. Who cares if the little guy gets screwed as long as rich guys get their loopholes? That's their MO and it'll never change."

I clench my jaw shut before the words *superficial talking points* can spill out.

"Anyway." John uncrosses and recrosses his legs, his polished leather shoes catching the light. They probably cost more than mine. "I actually had an ulterior motive for stopping by. Besides your charming company, of course."

"Oh yeah?" I say, playing dumb. I pray what's coming isn't what I think it is.

"Are you going to the event next Saturday at the Willard?"

The event he's referring to is the White House Correspondents' Dinner, or what's commonly referred to in DC as Nerd Prom. Every April, celebrities descend on the city for a night of presidential roasting and pretend politics while our bosses gleefully rub elbows with Hollywood's elite. Post-dinner, the deep pockets behind a conglomeration of cable news networks are throwing an after-party at the Willard InterContinental Hotel. Senator Warner and her entire staff were invited, as well as every other senator and political bigwig in Washington.

"I'll be there. Our whole office will, I think."

He beams. "I was hoping so. I'd love to take you."

Son of a biscuit.

"Oh, John—thanks, that's so sweet of you, it's just that I'm going to be working, Carol's given me a list of people to talk to that's as long as my arm—"

He holds up a hand. "That's all right, I get it. I'll have a ton of schmoozing to do too, so it's probably not the best setting for a first date.

I just couldn't pass up the opportunity." He smiles, eyes bright and hopeful, like he hasn't just been rejected.

As soon as I hear the words *first date*, my stomach constricts. *Tell him you're seeing someone. Now's your chance. Do right by Ben.* My conscience begs me.

Instead I say, "Well, I'm sure I'll see you there."

In my silence, I feel like I've betrayed Ben. I'm Judas. No, I'm Peter, and I've just denied Jesus three times. I can practically hear the cock's crows.

"For sure. Save me a dance," he says, then winks.

I summon up my fake smile so I don't have to answer.

He gathers up his trash, giving me a little wave as he departs. The first thing I do once he's gone is look across the atrium.

Ben's blinds are closed.

Chapter 27

On our walk home that night, Ben is silent.

"Everything okay?" If he's pissed about John, he's going to have to come out and say it.

"Bad day."

"Anything I can help with?"

"No."

"You want to talk about it?"

"No."

Oh-kay. Bad Mood Ben. This is a new one.

We continue our solitary march for a few blocks. He hasn't taken my hand like he usually does and it's crazy how much that's killing me.

"Any thoughts on dinner? Do I need to break out the big guns and make queso?"

He grunts in response.

"Wow, no reaction to the gun pun *or* the queso?"

We stop at a crosswalk and I watch him as we wait for the light to turn. When he finally makes eye contact, I get a tight-lipped smile that doesn't reach his eyes.

"I'm sorry you had a bad day."

He nods, still saying nothing.

"I'd like to help."

"You can't help," he snaps. "I can't talk to you about it and you know that, so quit asking."

Whoa. I blink and take a step back.

"Actually, I didn't know that. I wasn't even sure the reason you're upset was work related."

"What else would it be?"

He stares me down, eyes glittering. I'm a long way past being intimidated by him, but I haven't seen this look on his face since I called him a caveman. It's not a memory I'm eager to relive.

"I thought it might have to do with the reason you closed your blinds today." *There.* Gauntlet thrown.

"I closed my blinds so I wouldn't have to watch my girlfriend eat a cozy lunch with a guy who wants to get into her pants." My face must do something funny because he bites out, "I'm sorry, I meant my *secret* girlfriend."

I'm so taken aback by his vitriol, it takes me a moment to work up a response.

"Wow. So as a reminder, John is my *colleague*, nothing more, and I work with him a lot, so you better make your peace with it now." I flush as I recall his date invitation and my subsequent sin of omission. Definitely not sharing that tidbit just now. "And I guess *you're* the only one who's allowed to feel jealous? Because you don't see me interrogating you about the time you spend with Corinne, the woman who *heavily* implied you two were dating. But I'm just expected to ignore all that, right?"

He opens his mouth to respond but I cut him off.

"You know what, don't answer that. I don't think this has anything to do with John. This has to do with your bill imploding. Or maybe you feel guilty about stealing money out of schoolteachers' pockets. As you should, by the way. I'd love to know what your mother thinks about this." The light finally changes to WALK and I take off, forcing him to jog to catch up with me.

"Is this the *help* you were offering me a minute ago?" he calls as I rush ahead. "Please, pile on. Tell me more about what a shitty job I'm doing and what a heartless monster I am. I didn't get enough of that today."

I take a deep breath before answering. "Look, I'm trying to give you the benefit of the doubt here, but you don't get to take your bad day out on me. I'm not your punching bag."

"Ha! That's funny. You've *never* given me the benefit of the doubt."

"I *did* give you the benefit of the doubt today. I even went so far as to make excuses for you. Though I have no idea why."

I barrel down the sidewalk, weaving my way through slow walkers and phone talkers. Ben's keeping up, though it's not quite as easy for someone his size. He's knocking people over like bowling pins.

"Did you really defend me?" he asks, muscling past a tourist who's staring at his map app in muddled confusion.

"Well, not *you* so much as your precious tax plan."

"God forbid you admit to knowing me."

"You know, we agreed this is how we would handle this," I say without slowing.

"No, *you* agreed. It's your rules, all the time. I'm just along for the ride."

"*My* rules? You're the one holding back from *me*! Don't stand here and tell me *I'm* the one calling the shots."

I stop in the middle of the sidewalk and we start drawing attention from passersby, my raised voice as conspicuous as his clipped, angry one. He glances over my shoulder at the busy street and grimaces, hauling me away from the curb and over to the brick facade of a nearby storefront. It says something that—even as furious as I am—I don't want him to drop my hand.

He lowers his voice further, probably hoping I'll follow suit. "It's not the same thing."

"How is it not the same?"

"I'm doing this to protect both of us. You're trying to hide me."

"I'm not trying to *hide* you! When are you going to *get* that?"

He shakes his head like he doesn't believe me. "You need to want me the same way I want you."

"I *do* want you! How many times do I have to say it?"

"No. I want all of you. Not just a part. Not a fraction. The whole thing."

"You have the whole thing! I'm standing right in front of you!"

He's struggling to keep his composure. "*No.* I am painfully aware of what I don't have, and I won't settle for less. I'm not going to be your dirty little secret, Kate. You don't get to fuck me behind closed doors, then pretend you don't know me in the morning."

My jaw drops, the air rushing from my lungs. I try to suck in a breath but can't. It's like there's a hole in my chest where my heart and lungs once were. I pivot and sprint away, tears blurring my vision.

He catches up easily, grabbing my elbow. "Wait."

"Don't! Leave me alone. I can get home on my own."

"I'm not going to leave you alone. I'm sorry, I shouldn't have said that. It was over the line."

"You think?" I wrench my arm away. "Because I'm pretty sure you just called me a whore."

"You know that's not what I meant. I'm all fucked up today. Please, can you just *wait*?"

He shoulders in front of me, blocking my escape. When I hesitate, he steers me into a nearby alleyway, stationing himself between me and the street. He starts to reach up like he's going to touch me, then thinks better of it, dropping his hand back down to his side.

"Kate, I'm just . . . frustrated. I'm running in circles trying to give you what you need, but I have no idea what that is anymore. I'm not even sure *you* know."

"I need time! And for you to stop pressuring me!"

"Is that really it? Truly? Because if it is, I can give you that. I'll give you all the time in the world. But it doesn't feel that way sometimes. It feels like you're trying to get me out of your system."

"That's ridiculous."

"You've been one foot in and one foot out since the very beginning. Don't try to deny it."

"You think I'm not *in* this just because I'm not Mr. Happy-Go-Lucky? Because I don't know that everything's going to work out fine? I'm sorry I'm worried about all the ways our differences could end up biting us in the ass!"

"Fine, please list all the horrible scenarios that are just waiting to befall us. I'll wait." He crosses his arms over his chest.

"All right, I will. What will our Friday nights look like? You dragging me to the gun range? Me dragging you to a women's rally? How fun does that sound, Mr. Rose-Colored Glasses?"

"Sounds fine to me," he fires back. "I'm happy to do the things you like, though I'd never force you to do anything you didn't want to. And I'm sure you wouldn't force me, either. We could also just go to dinner and a movie like normal people."

Of course he has some stupid levelheaded comeback.

"What about work? It's already coming between us. We could get fired. We'll make everyone around us uncomfortable. Not to mention how much drama it'll cause, today being a prime example."

"You think we're going to have these jobs our whole lives? In a few years we'll both be doing other things."

"Don't be absurd, we're not quitting our jobs," I scoff.

"I could get another job in five minutes. I don't care about the job, Kate. The job is not my life."

"What happens when we have kids?"

He blinks once. Twice. I've shocked him. "Kids?"

"I teach them one thing, then you turn around and teach them the opposite. How will that work? We'd be setting them up for an identity crisis, not to mention a lifetime of pitting us against each other."

His mouth opens, then closes. "Well, I can't say I've given this one a ton of thought, but off the top of my head, we could present all sides to an issue and let them form their own views?"

His reasonable response is the last straw.

"That's ridiculous!" I explode. "Everyone knows the whole point of having children is to indoctrinate them!"

He shakes his head, amusement warring with frustration on his face. "See, this? This is why."

"This is why, *what*? Stop speaking in code!"

"You want to know why I don't want to debate you? Because you're looking for an excuse to run, and I'm not gonna give it to you."

"I'm not looking to *run*."

"You are. You're scared. You're *petrified*."

"I'm not *scared*. Stop psychoanalyzing me."

I shove past him and haul ass down the sidewalk. Well, now I am running. *Damn*. Didn't time that very well.

"This is real and you know it." His voice chases my back. "It's long haul and that terrifies you."

"It's so long haul that we can't go one day without having some explosive, relationship-ending fight." I speed up as my building rises in the distance, glowing bright and resplendent as an Olympic finish line.

"You just talked about our kids!"

"I was proving a point!"

"You're planning our future and you can't even admit it. You're so scared you can barely see straight. You think I don't see it in your eyes? I've been looking at you for months, Kate. I've memorized your every expression. I know you better than you know yourself."

I spin around abruptly and he plows into me, knocking us both off-balance.

"This is the relationship you want, then? Fighting all the time? Here's your opposites attract, in the flesh." I throw out my arms.

"We're hardly opposites. Our political views may be different, but we're compatible in all the ways that matter." He growls, exasperated. "I can't believe you don't see this by now. You have so many blind spots."

"See *what*?"

"We have the same values. The same approach to life. The same sense of humor. We even have the same *jobs*. We just have different ways of solving problems. And isn't that what life's all about? Learning from each other? Appreciating that another person can teach us something?"

He takes a step toward me and catches my hand. How does he do that? Go from angry to sweet in a matter of seconds?

"I'm not looking for someone who agrees with everything I say. I want someone who will call me on my bullshit. I want surprise in my life. Someone who will drive me to take more risks. Someone who *challenges* me." His mouth hitches up. "And boy, are you a fucking challenge."

At his words, I freeze completely solid. I can't pretend I don't hear what he's really saying.

Ben's in love with me.

He loves me so much, he's convinced himself that I'm the woman for him. No matter how badly I've treated him or how many times I screw up, he'll always be right here, ready to forgive my every transgression. Even if it's to his own detriment. Even though he deserves better.

It's *me* he sees through rose-colored glasses.

"What is it? You look like you've seen a ghost."

I feel sick. "I think . . . I need some time."

"I already told you, I'll give you time."

"No, I mean . . ." It's taking every ounce of resolve not to dissolve into a puddle at his feet. "It's not right, what I've asked you to do. What was I thinking, forcing you to keep this a secret? Who *does* that?"

His eyebrows knit in confusion. "Did I miss a turn somewhere?"

"Any woman would be proud to be with you. You're *perfect*. You deserve to be shown off. You deserve the best woman, one who's going to put your needs first. Look at you—you're the one who had a crappy day and you're standing here comforting *me!*"

He raises a hand like he's trying to calm a skittish animal. "I was being a dick. You were right, I was taking my shit out on you. Things at work went off the rails today. I wish I could explain—"

"Stop apologizing to me! Don't you see? I'm the one who should be apologizing to *you* for wasting your time!"

"*Wasting* my time?" The edge in his voice is razor sharp.

"You deserve a girlfriend who's clearheaded and supportive and appreciates how wonderful you are. Not one who's selfish and damaged and confused. Who makes your life *harder.*"

"Kate, you're none of those things. And you make my life better, not harder." He lifts a hand to my face but I jerk back.

"I've done nothing but put you through the wringer since the day you met me."

"Where are you getting all this nonsense?" He furrows his brow. "When did you last eat?"

"I'm serious! I can't hold you back anymore. I couldn't live with myself."

He sighs. "And what exactly is it you're holding me back from?"

"Your perfect woman! What if she's out there and you're too busy looking at me to see her? I'm so far from your perfect match, Ben."

I wish I didn't believe it. It's hard enough to say the words out loud, but knowing they're true nearly kills me. I'm not what he needs. He deserves so much better than the scraps I've been feeding him. I'm the one who's not good enough for *him*.

"So let me just make sure I've got this. You know better than I do what I want. *Who* I want. And there's some *other* perfect woman out there for me, and I should let you go because I'm missing out on her right this very minute."

"I know you think I'm crazy, but I . . . I just . . ."

"You just *what*?"

I stall, gathering my nerve. I hate myself for what I'm about to do, but deep down, I know he won't let this go—won't let *me* go—unless I burn us to the ground.

"I don't feel the same way you do."

The words tumble out in a breathless rush. I flick my eyes to his face, then quickly away. If I look into his eyes, I won't be able to go through with this.

"We're not a good match. Not long-term, anyway. I'm attracted to you, I won't deny that, but I think our chemistry's been distracting us from the bigger picture."

"The bigger picture." His voice is flat.

"We're not right for each other."

I cough to cover the sob that nearly escapes. Every part of me wants to grab him and hang on for dear life. Instead, I force myself to keep going.

"This isn't going anywhere, and the longer we pretend it is, the harder it's going to be when it eventually ends. I think it's . . . better for both of us if we do it now."

I can barely get the words out. I stare down at the sidewalk, battling back the tears stinging my eyes.

"I don't believe you."

He knows your expressions. You need to sell it.

I force myself to meet his eyes. What I see in them breaks every piece of my heart: layers of hurt, love, and denial so intense that the tears I've been keeping at bay spill over before I can stop them.

"You don't *want* to believe me, but you know it's the truth. Our differences are going to come between us eventually. And I think . . . what you said before about wanting to get you out of my system . . ." I close my eyes as I brush away tears. *God, please forgive me.* "You were right."

His lips are pressed together so hard, they're practically white. He's pissed as hell. "I was right."

"Yes."

No. I'm a filthy liar who doesn't deserve you.

"You want to walk away from this."

There's a kind of disbelieving wonder in his tone. I can't bring myself to respond. It's one more lie than I'm capable of.

He expels a loud breath. "Fine. You win, Kate."

"I *win?*"

His jaw is clenched so hard, it looks painful. "You want to push me away, I can't stop you. I can't *force* you to be with me. And I'm done trying."

He stares at me, eyes cold and hard. The look on his face is one I've never seen before. *Hatred.*

"You know something, maybe you're right. Maybe we *aren't* a good match. I don't live my life wondering what's lurking behind every corner, waiting for the sky to fall. When something special comes along, something *good*, I grab onto it with both hands. You're fine to let it pass you by."

He turns away, staring into the street as cars speed past, and I use the moment of respite to rein in my emotions.

When he speaks next, his voice is impersonal as a stranger's. "It's cold out. I'll drop you at home."

"You don't have to. You can go ahead of me."

He glares at me. *"Walk."*

I don't dare argue with him. Besides, the quicker I get home, the quicker I can fall apart.

We cover the last couple of blocks wordlessly, Ben following several feet behind me like an executioner. When we arrive at my building, he pulls open the door and I force him to look at me.

"I'm so sorry. I never meant—"

He holds up a hand, silencing me. "Just so you know, I still don't believe you. You're as bad a liar as you've ever been. I don't know why you're doing this, but I do know one thing—I can't carry you over the finish line. You need to meet me in the middle, Kate. I thought we could get there together, but I see now it's something you need to come to on your own." His eyes soften a touch. "But we sure got close for a minute there, didn't we?"

I watch him walk away, not moving from the doorway until he disappears around the corner.

He never turns around.

Chapter 28

On Friday I do something I never do. I call in sick.

Even if I wanted to, I can hardly go into the office looking like the puffy-eyed zombie I currently resemble. Truth be told, I wonder how I'll ever go to work again. The idea of glimpsing Ben through the window— or worse, casually running into him, forced into awkward hellos and stilted conversation—seems like such cruel and unusual punishment that I wonder if I should spend the day updating my résumé instead of crying in bed. As a compromise I decide to embrace my forced vacation and stay in pajamas all day. I will not positively contribute to society, nor will I put makeup on. That'll show the patriarchy.

I mope and watch soaps. I order Seamless and carb it up. Stephen calls to check on me but talking to him just reminds me of work and Ben so I rush off the phone. I stumble upon *My Best Friend's Wedding* on TV and bawl. I listen to "On My Own" three times in a row before deciding that's too tragic, even for me.

I do everything in my power to avoid thinking of Ben, but he's taken up permanent residence in my head and refuses to be evicted. When I curl up on my couch, I'm bombarded by memories of our nightly cuddling. My kitchen seems huge and empty without his considerable bulk to navigate around. I can't watch my favorite news shows without hearing his voice poke holes in their narrative. He's even ruined Tim McGraw for me, which is about as heinous a crime as I can imagine.

Over the course of the weekend, the kernel of doubt I felt when I threw myself on the sword metastasizes to boulder-size uncertainty. Could I have tried harder? Was I too quick to give up on us? Now that I think about it, Ben was the one bright spot in the otherwise colorless existence I've built for myself. What if I just threw away the best thing in my life?

I shake myself. *Stop this. Stop second-guessing.* I pushed him away for the right reasons. I'm saving him from himself. He wouldn't be happy with me long-term, even if he thinks he would. It won't take him any time at all to find someone else. He'll meet some lovely, boring girl next door who'll worship the ground he walks on and thank God every day he looked at her twice with those heart-stopping green eyes.

The thought nearly makes me regurgitate my Seamless.

I want someone who challenges me.

You make my life better, not harder.

I'd rather argue with you than get along with anyone else.

Throughout the next week, my boulder of doubt becomes an asteroid. I wake up each morning hoping the pain will have faded, but the vise around my heart only seems to tighten. Stephen tries to get me to open up, but I feel even more protective of the relationship now that memories are all I have left. I haven't run into Ben, though it's by design—I've stayed holed up in my office as much as possible, blinds closed. I know my limits. If I run into him and he seems fine, it'll send me into a tailspin I'm not sure I'll recover from.

By the end of the week, I'm barely functioning. I'm exhausted from fighting back tears and so groggy from tossing and turning, I can barely carry on a conversation. The pit in my stomach has made it impossible to eat and I'm about as energetic as a rag doll.

"Knock-knock."

I glance up to see Tessa striding through my door, a manila envelope in her hands.

"Hey, lady," I greet her, then cringe at the lifeless tone of my voice. *Nobody likes a Debbie Downer.*

"I was clearing off my desk and found this mixed in with a stack of my files. Don't ask me how I ended up with it." She hands it to me and keeps talking. "So a few of us are heading over to Hamilton's for drinks, if you want to . . ."

Her voice fades away as I recognize Ben's all-caps scrawl across the front of the envelope, and my heart leaps. Did he send me mail?

"How long have you had this?" I cut her off, my voice tingeing on desperate. "Do you know when it got delivered?"

She frowns. "I'm not sure. A week ago, maybe? Could have been two? That pile has been sitting on my desk for ages." She pauses at the look on my face. "Crap, was it important?"

I take a deep breath, donning the *everything's fine, nothing to see here* mask I've been sporting all week. "No, don't worry about it. Uh, I can't make it tonight."

She eyes me with concern. "You sure? You look like you could use a night out."

I almost laugh. I haven't breathed a word about Ben to Tessa, but she has no idea how badly I wish I could just go out and forget about him.

I force a smile. "I'm sure. Next time."

She narrows her eyes, unconvinced. "Okay, but next time I won't take no for an answer. I'm dragging you by the hair whether you like it or not."

After she leaves, I stare down at the envelope on my desk, my heart beating a million miles an hour. I splay my shaking fingers over the letters of my name, as if I can touch him through the pen strokes slashed onto paper.

I muster up every ounce of courage I possess and open the envelope. When I slide out the contents, my heart nearly stops.

It's the Kate file.

An involuntary sob escapes as I flip it open. Stacked inside are a bunch of computer printouts, each a few pages long and stapled. A note is paper-clipped to the top.

Kate,

When you told me you'd never date a Republican, I knew the day would come when I'd need to make my case. So I started building one.

I know you have concerns, but for now, I have enough confidence for the both of us.

Ben

Tears blur my eyes as I unclip the note and see the headline on the top printout: RELATIONSHIP SURVIVAL TIPS FROM POLITICAL OPPOSITES. I leaf through the rest: POLITICS CAN MAKE STRANGE BEDFELLOWS. HOW MIXED POLITICAL MARRIAGES SURVIVE ELECTION SEASON. HERE'S WHY YOU SHOULD DATE A REPUBLICAN, EVEN IF YOU'RE A DEMOCRAT. (The one that makes me laugh out loud? REPUBLICANS ARE HAVING MORE SEX THAN DEMOCRATS, SURVEY FINDS.) There are ten or fifteen articles in total, including profiles of several prominent power couples with opposing political views: the unlikely marriage between a conservative strategist and a liberal news commentator; a former first lady who quietly donated to progressive organizations while her Republican husband was in office; the conservative media mogul who married an activist movie starlet.

I spend the next half hour devouring everything in the file. The articles delve into the psychology behind "politically mixed" relationships, citing communication, common ground, and mutual respect as the keys to making it work, but it's Ben's handwritten notes scribbled in the margins that take my emotional state from precarious to downright unstable.

On avoiding getting into unwinnable arguments, he's written: *Now you know why I don't want to debate you.*

On not judging each other's character for a difference of opinion: *I respect your opinions, even if they're not mine.*

On healthy debate being good for your sex life: *Desperate to find out.* That one's double underlined.

I check the date of his note and want to weep—it was sent a week and a half ago, the day after I gave him a hard time about his refusal to engage. Before our fight. *Before I ruined everything.*

I flash back to the moment in his office when I first discovered this file, so long before he confessed his feelings, and my breathing goes shallow. The thought of Ben researching ways to make our relationship work—before there was even a relationship to speak of—makes my heart shatter into a thousand tiny shards of glass.

I set the last article aside with shaking hands, my chest feeling like it's been hollowed out. I glance across the atrium and when I see Ben's office is dark and deserted, regret and raw panic begin to claw at my throat.

I gather the file and my things in a rush, somehow managing to stave off my Category 5 meltdown until I burst through the door of my apartment. I head straight for my fridge and liberate a bottle of wine, then end up staring at it on my kitchen counter while memories of all the times Ben's saved me from myself wash over me. He would hate that I'm self-destructing like this.

Finally, I cave and call my mom. The story pours out of me in fits and starts, through wracking sobs and gasping hiccups. When I finish, I'm met with silence.

"Well, what do you think?" I release a shuddery breath. "You think I'm a complete idiot, I'm sure. *I* think so."

"No, I think you're wonderful."

I laugh sardonically. "I'm clearly not wonderful."

I abandon the wine and move to the couch, flopping down and hugging a pillow to my chest—then throw it to the floor because in yet another indignity, it smells like him. "What are you thinking over there? I need earplugs for your silent judgment."

"I'm thinking Ben's got your number. Which, I might add, I knew after one minute of watching you two together."

"Would you like a medal?" I mutter.

She sighs. "Katie, you've waited your whole life for a man to show up for you, and what do you do when he does? You run the other direction! It doesn't take a psychology degree to see what's going on here, sweetie."

"But can a relationship even work with such different belief systems? I mean, sure, we like each other *now*, but once the newness wears off and we don't agree on any big issues, then what? I'm terrified of getting invested in something that's just going to crash and burn."

"You're so focused on protecting yourself from future disappointments, you can't see what's right in front of you! Look, do you respect Ben?"

"Of course I do. He's brilliant and compassionate and kind, and that's why I can't understand how he can support the things his party is doing!"

"Do *you* agree with every position our party takes? I know I don't. Life isn't so black-and-white, Katie. It's messy and gray and complicated. Ben isn't just one thing, and neither are you. Wouldn't you rather be with someone who complements you? Someone who isn't afraid to go toe-to-

toe with you? Stop focusing on what could go wrong and start focusing on what's *right*. Or left." She pauses. "Get it? That was a political joke."

"I got it."

"The point is, you can disagree with someone and still love them. They're not mutually exclusive."

When I don't respond, her voice softens. "I know you have this mental checklist with all these boxes just waiting to be ticked. Follow this roadmap, end up with the perfect life." She laughs ruefully. "But maybe leave yourself open to some of life's surprises. They turn out pretty great sometimes."

I'm the one who goes quiet this time as a fresh round of tears forms. And just when I thought my tear ducts had dried up.

"Mom, you don't get it. He's so perfect. He's always saying and doing just the right thing while I make mistake after mistake. How can I ever live up to that?"

"And *he's* the one with rose-colored glasses? He's a *man*, Katie, he's not perfect. You just think he is because you're in love with him."

Silence stretches the line.

"You're not denying it. That's a step forward, at least."

I take a deep breath. "I do love him."

It's the first time I've said it out loud, and it's like a fog lifts. *I'm in love with Ben.* Of course I am. Why did it take me so long?

"Then you need to tell him," she says gently. "He deserves to know. When will you see him next?"

"I don't know, never. I'm never leaving my apartment again."

"*Katie . . .*"

I sigh. "We're all supposed to be going to this big fancy reception tomorrow night. I was going to bail on it."

"Ooh, it'll be like a movie! You can meet him at the ball!" Great, I've unleashed Hopeless Romantic Bev.

"It's not a ball." I think that over. "Okay, it's kind of a ball."

"So get yourself all dolled up, get your hair blown out, wear a dress that'll knock his socks off, then stroll in there looking like a million bucks. He'll forget the whole thing ever happened."

"But what will I *say*?" I wail.

"Just tell him you were on your period. He won't ask any follow-up questions."

"Mom!"

She hums. "How about . . . you complete me. Or, we go together like peas and carrots. No, wait, I've got it. I'm just a girl, standing in front of a boy, asking him to love her!"

"Mom! I cannot use movie lines."

She heaves a sigh. "Fine, just tell him you're sorry, you're an idiot, you'll make it up to him forever if he'll let you."

She pauses.

"And then tell him I said hi."

Chapter 29

I do as she says.

I apply a set of those amoeba-shaped de-puffing eye patches before bed, then another set in the morning. I make an appointment for a blow-out, and for once, I instruct the stylist to go as big as she wants. Let's give the Texas boy some Texas hair.

In a stroke of divine intervention, I actually have the perfect gown already hanging in my closet, having purchased it a couple of years ago with the hope I'd find a worthy occasion. It's navy and floor-length, with a plunging V-neck that's mirrored in the back. It hugs my body like a second skin, as flattering and timeless as anything I've ever owned. It's too revealing for a typical work event, but for a night of hobnobbing with the Hollywood glitterati? It's just right.

I don't have much nice jewelry to speak of, but I add my grand-mother's cross necklace for luck and a pair of small diamond earrings that were a graduation gift from my mom, and I'm ready. Stephen and I had planned to go together, and when he arrives to pick me up, he gasps.

"You let your hair out to play," he exclaims tearfully, clasping his hands to his heart like a proud dad.

I laugh, relaxing a little. No matter what happens with Ben, I've already won the night. Stephen's approval means more than a thousand straight men's.

As we pull up to the Willard, I feel a surge of nerves and adrenaline. Between my mom's, Stephen's, and my own pep talks, I'm ready to race up these hotel steps like Rocky.

The hotel is a mob scene. Wall-to-wall photographers and reporters with blinding lights and video cameras pack a red carpet rolled out at the entrance. I have to physically drag Stephen away from the step and repeat. Once we're inside, we're shepherded through the lobby with a horde of other revelers and funneled into a sprawling ballroom. Tuxedoed servers mill about passing hors d'oeuvres while a ten-piece band loudly covers pop hits from decades past.

Every time I turn around, I run into someone I know: fellow staffers, members, lobbyists. Stephen and I manage to link up with a group of our coworkers and check in before deciding to circuit the room and get the lay of the land. Only a couple of minutes have gone by before he clutches my arm in a death grip and whispers hoarsely, *"Bradley Cooper!"* and suddenly, I'm alone. I look around, wondering how I'll even find Ben in this bedlam, when the crowd parts and there he is.

In a tux. Dashing and devastating. He's James Bond, but I'm the one who's shaken. His broad shoulders can barely be contained within the confines of his jacket, making every man in the vicinity look puny and undersize in comparison. He's like a Disney prince on steroids. Sexy with a whiff of danger. Prince Charming meets Gaston.

But it's not quite the fairy tale I envisioned because when I look closer, I see he's with Corinne.

They're deep in conversation, his head bent close to hear her over the music. Of course she looks stunning, even taller than usual in sky-high heels and with bloodred lips I can see from across the room. A toned, tanned leg peeks out from a high slit in her black gown, and she's looking at him like he hung the moon.

At that exact moment, he turns and catches me staring. He starts, like he wasn't expecting to see me and doesn't know how to feel about it. He must read the dismay on my face because he casts a guilty look at Corinne. I lift a hand in a halfhearted greeting, then weigh my threshold for humiliation. If I sprint out of here, how much worse would it make things, really?

Before I can decide, he leans over and whispers something in her ear, then heads toward me, fighting his way through the crowd. I dimly register the sour look on Corinne's face before the crowd swallows her up and I don't see anyone but Ben anymore. I notice he's gotten a haircut and feel a pang of self-doubt. *While you were home crying, he's been going about his day, business as usual.* Not a good sign.

I smile nervously as he stops in front of me.

"Hey." He leans over to kiss my cheek and my stomach does a somersault. "You look beautiful." He hasn't taken his eyes off my face.

"Thanks, so do you. Guess you finally found time for that haircut." I reach up and brush my fingers through his hair before I remember: *He's not yours.*

"What do you think? Not too short?" He palms his nape self-consciously.

He looks mature and polished, not like the ruffled teddy bear I'm used to. I can't decide which Ben I prefer. Both are exceptional to look at.

"No, not too short," I manage, swallowing the lump in my throat. "So how's Cor*inne*?" I can't help my inflection when I say her name. It just . . . naturally does that.

His mouth twitches. "Probably pissed that I left her back there."

"Oh." I realize I'm not being very nice, so I add, "Shoot."

"Your concern for her is heartwarming," he says dryly, then glances behind him. "Well, I should probably get back to my date."

"Your *what*?!"

"Wow, you have *completely* lost your sense of humor." He grabs my wrist as if to take my pulse, then checks his watch. "Time of death: eight thirty-seven p.m."

I shake off his hand, then immediately wish I hadn't. "I'm glad one of us is having a good time with this," I mutter.

He sobers. "I'm *not* having a good time. Just trying to bring back your smile." There's concern in his eyes. "How have you been doing? Since . . ."

I've already decided: There will only be honesty going forward. As pathetic as the truth might make me look, I'll never lie to him again.

"Not great." *Understatement of the century.* "Pretty miserable, actually." I feel a pricking at the back of my eyelids. *Do not cry.*

"I gathered as much."

"How? You haven't checked on me." I hear the accusation in my voice and wince. "Sorry, forget I said that."

His eyes flick over me uneasily, like I'm a ticking time bomb. "Of course I checked on you." He starts to say something else, then thinks better of it.

I should have known. "So Stephen's been your mole this whole time. I knew it."

He half smiles. "I have a vast network of spies."

He shoves his hands in his pockets, like he doesn't quite know what to do with them. I'm having the same problem. I'm desperate to touch him but can't, and since my dress doesn't have pockets, I have no escape hatch. We stand there awkwardly, neither of us able to achieve the proper ratio of body language to words for small talk.

What are you waiting for, Kate?

"Listen, do you think we could talk?" I blurt.

He eyes me warily, as if gauging whether I'll make a scene if he says no. "Uh, sure. Just as soon as I finish everything I need to do here."

My stomach sinks. I want to resolve this *now*. My grand gesture is burning a hole in my nonexistent pocket. "What do you mean?"

"I have a bunch of people I need to talk to tonight. Speaking of which, I need to get back to it. Why don't I plan on—"

"Mackenzie, there you are!" A voice booms behind me and I jolt. A partially balding man in spectacles sidles up and claps Ben on the back, and I nearly growl in frustration. I'm so hopped-up on adrenaline, I could rip this guy's head off.

As if he can feel my ire, the man turns to me. "Sorry to interrupt. I'm Bill Laughlin. And you are?" He gives me an overly friendly look, his eyes flicking down my chest and back up.

Ben subtly shifts between us, partially blocking me with his body. "Kate, Bill is Senator Hammond's chief of staff. My boss." His eyes bore into mine, and I receive his silent message loud and clear: *Be discreet.* "Bill, this is a colleague and friend of mine, Kate Adams. She's one of Carol Warner's staffers," he explains, and I detect a note of warning in his tone.

Colleague. Friend. The words slice through me like a knife, stem to stern. So this is what it feels like to be publicly forsworn. It's unexpectedly devastating.

I do my best to disguise my distress and reach out a hand. "Nice to meet you, Bill. You guys look busy, so I'll leave you to it."

I start to edge away and Ben brushes my hand. "I'll find you later?"

"Sure."

Well, that didn't quite go according to plan, but he didn't slam the door in my face, at least. I decide to take it as a victory. All part of my new optimistic mindset, visualizing positive outcomes. *Thanks, Mom.*

I take a page out of Ben's book and spend the next hour glad-handing my way around the room. Though making small talk isn't my favorite part of the job, I find that swapping stories of celebrity encounters provides the perfect icebreaker for every member and staffer I need to touch base with tonight. After all, who doesn't want to brag that they just stood behind George Clooney getting a drink or heard Tina Fey tell a dirty joke?

But no matter where I travel in the room, I can't seem to stop tracking Ben like a tagged shark. Every cell in my body is attuned to him, no matter how hard I try to concentrate on the person standing in front of me. Eventually, I quit trying, grab a water, and head for a table where Stephen, Tessa, Luke, John, and some of our other friends have congregated.

"Hey, guys," I say, slipping my heels off briefly and groaning in relief. "What am I missing over here?"

"Oh, not much, just talking about how nauseating it is to watch the never-ending victory laps our Republican friends insist on taking," Tessa says.

"They have no shame," Luke agrees.

"Midterms, guys, midterms," John reminds everyone, tireless cheerleader that he is.

I'm barely able to suppress my eye roll, suddenly so *tired* of this endless disparagement and petty hostility. In fact, I'm tired of everything: my friends, this job, the judgment and vilification that go along with it. Tired even of my own prejudices. Is this what I've sounded like these past few years? Is this what I sound like to *Ben*?

"Aren't you guys *sick* of this?" I say suddenly, and a bunch of heads swivel toward me. "It feels like all we ever talk about. All we ever *think* about. So they're doing things differently than we would. Does that really make them the *enemy*?"

There's a beat of silence as they eye each other. "Kate, honey, I think you need a drink," Tessa says, holding out her glass. "Here, have some of my champagne."

"I don't need a drink. I just need to feel like I'm not part of some adult version of *Mean Girls*," I mutter.

Right then I notice Marcus approaching our table and, ignoring the nonplussed looks on my friends' faces, step forward to greet him. He surprises me by wrapping me in a tight hug.

"How are you?" he asks in a low voice when he pulls back. "I was hoping I'd run into you tonight."

"I'm okay," I answer hesitantly. While I never asked Ben outright if he'd told Marcus about us, it's obvious from the sympathetic way he's looking at me that he knows *something*. I hang on to him for an extra beat, feeling closer to him than to any of my so-called friends back at that table.

"Just okay, huh? Sounds like someone else I know." At my uneasy expression, he pats my arm. "Don't worry, I know how to be discreet. And you don't have to talk about it. I just wanted to lend an ear if you need one."

"Thank you," I say, touched by his kindness. "It's been . . . a rough week."

"It's been a rough week for those of us who have to work with grumpy, miserable assholes, too."

That gets a laugh out of me. "What about you? No date tonight?" I ask, anxious to change the subject.

He shrugs. "I have a few irons in the fire."

"A *few*? How many ladies do you string along at one time?"

He grabs his chest in mock offense. "String *along*? Ouch."

"Hey, no judgment. Some of us can't even manage one." I sip my water and avoid his eyes.

He studies me for a moment. "Listen, he hasn't told me much about what's going on between you two, but for whatever it's worth, you won't find better than him. He's who I'd pick for my sisters."

I swallow the lump in my throat. "I know I won't. It's just . . . complicated. I've made a mess of things."

"Then uncomplicate it," he says, matter-of-fact.

"I'm trying," I say, voice wobbling. I'm too emotionally raw for this conversation.

Marcus clams up, clearly recognizing a volatile female psyche when he sees one. "Let me get you a refill. What are you drinking?"

"Water," I respond, a little hoarsely. *Do not lose it in the middle of this ballroom.*

"Hope you're not driving tonight." He winks and squeezes my elbow before moving away. "Be right back."

I'm furiously blinking back tears when Tessa materializes at my side.

"First you go all scorched earth on us back there, then I have to watch you flirt with *another* guy from Hammond's office? Maybe I should've signed you up for *Right*Field instead."

It's the last straw.

"Tessa, *stop it*," I snap. "He saw that I'm down and tried to console me. I hardly think that deserves your scorn."

She finally notices the unshed tears in my eyes and goes alert. "You're down? Why are you down?"

I take a deep breath. "I broke up with someone."

"You've been dating someone? Who?"

"Ben Mackenzie." At her look of shock, I add defiantly, "Yep, *that* Ben."

I can feel the eyeballs of everyone at the table on my back and I don't even care. Suddenly, I want to shout this from the rooftops.

"You've been dating *Ben*? Since when?"

"Since a while," I answer, before turning to address the blatant eavesdroppers at the table. John looks scandalized, while Stephen's wearing a shit-eating grin. "And he's *wonderful*. The most amazing man I've ever met, actually. And I kept it a secret so I wouldn't have to deal with y'all's judgment." I'm so fired up, I can't even remember to suppress my southern accent. "But you know what? I don't care anymore."

I grab the glass of champagne out of Tessa's hand and knock it back in one deep swallow, then slam it down on the table. "And I'm going to fix this."

Stephen whoops.

I scan the crowd for Ben, finding him deep in conversation with a group of men I've never seen before. I march over and tap him on the shoulder.

"Hey," he says, reflexively pressing a hand to my back, then dropping it once he realizes. My expression must be alarming because his eyebrows knit together. "Everything okay?" he asks in a low voice.

"Everything's fine. I just wanted to dance with you."

His companions glance at one another, then at me, quickly excusing themselves.

He turns toward me, quirking a brow. "You want to *dance*?"

"What, you're suddenly shy?"

He shoots me a bemused look but takes my outstretched hand, letting me lead him out onto the dance floor. When I find us a space that's not too crowded, he places a hand at my waist and clasps my other hand out to the side, a yawning football field between us.

"There are eyes everywhere," he murmurs.

His tone is teasing, but I know it masks a real hurt. There's a wall between us now that didn't exist before, and it's all my fault. That I've dimmed the light in his eyes feels like a worse crime.

I drop his hand and twine my arms around his neck, pulling him to me until our bodies are touching. He raises an eyebrow but follows my lead, clasping his hands on my lower back and pressing me closer. I melt into him, molding to his contours like a strawberry dipped in chocolate. I try to memorize the feel of him in my arms in case it doesn't last beyond this song.

"This event reminds me of the inaugural ball," he muses.

"I wouldn't know. I was too busy rocking myself in the fetal position."

"I'll have to fix that for the next one."

I don't know whether to laugh or cry at all his statement implies.

He scans the crowd. "What do you think, should we break out the two-step? That would really get this party started."

"Mm, I don't think I could stand the attention. I'm a wallflower bride, remember."

He nods off the dance floor, where my friends are doing a poor job of pretending not to gawk at us. "Your not-so-secret admirer is watching us."

I sigh. "You know I'm not interested in John."

His face grows serious. "I do know."

"If you know, then why did you give me such a hard time about him?" I ask, exasperated.

"Because I'm a jealous asshole."

My heart leaps. *This is a good sign.*

"Besides, even if I wasn't sure, your coma face makes it very obvious."

"My *coma* face?"

"When you talk to him, you're asleep with your eyes open. I've seen you do it loads of times."

"I don't do that!" I protest, indignant.

"You *absolutely* do that."

"I've never done it with you!"

"Not with *me*," he says, like the very idea offends him to his core. "To people who bore you."

I consider that. "One thing we're not is boring."

"Ain't that the truth." As if to prove his point, he spins me out in dramatic fashion, then reels me back in. The song's already starting to wind down and my pulse picks up.

It's time. Enough stalling, Kate.

"Hey, Ben?"

"Hey, Kate?"

"I'm so sorry for the things I said. I didn't mean any of it. I can never begin to express how much I regret it."

His dancing slows, his lips parting in surprise.

"You were right, I was scared. So, *so* scared of my feelings for you. And I thought I was doing the right thing for you, finally, after doing so many wrong things, but then I realized I did the worst thing of all by pushing you away. It was the biggest mistake of my life, and if nothing else, if you can't forgive me, I want you to know that."

Our swaying has stopped entirely now, and he's staring at me like I'm speaking in tongues.

"I think you're such an amazing person. Like, the best person. And sometimes I feel like I can't live up to that, but I know it's just the fear talking." I swallow, pulse pounding in my ears. "I've let so many things get in the way of us, and I've hurt you and I'm ashamed and I want to fix it because there's *nothing* worth losing you.

"I know I have no right to ask you for anything, and I wouldn't blame you a bit for wanting off this crazy train, but . . . do you think you could forgive me anyway? And forget I ever said any of those things? And . . . take me back?"

He hasn't moved in a full minute. I'm pretty sure if I poked him, he'd tip over. I decide to take advantage of his solidified state and rise up on my toes to kiss him, but he turns his head at the last second.

"People are watching," he says roughly. He looks shaken.

"That's the idea."

"You don't want to do this," he says, glancing around. "You won't be able to walk this back, Kate. You're going to regret it tomorrow."

"I'm *not* going to regret this. What I regret is the way I've handled things until now. If I could go back, I would do so many things differently. I had you so wrong from the very beginning. I wanted to make you out to be something you weren't, but you're perfect how you are. Perfect for *me*. And I just . . . I couldn't see . . ." I stop, getting choked up.

He looks alarmed. "Let's just go home and talk. You don't need to do this here."

"No, I *do* need to do this here." I clutch his jacket with renewed urgency. "Or else you won't believe me."

Awareness dawns on his face. "Of *course* I'll believe you. You don't have to make a spectacle of it. I was just kidding about that."

"Damn it, Ben, I came here tonight to make a fool of myself over you, and I'm not leaving until I do!"

A slow smile stretches across his face. "A fool of yourself, huh?"

"Yes. Now, please just let me do this for you."

Amusement lights his eyes. "All right. Let's see what you've got."

"First, this."

I throw my arms around his neck and kiss him, pouring every ounce of love and apology and emotion into it possible. This time he embraces it—embraces *me*—lifting me off my feet like he did in his apartment that fateful night. It's only been a week, but dear God how I've missed this. I lose myself in him, lamenting that I can't ravage his shorter hair as easily. I want to mess him up, unbutton his shirt, rip off his bow tie. I'd wrap my legs around his waist if my tight dress would allow it.

He eventually pulls back an inch, his eyes shining. "I think you've made your point. Can we go home now?"

"No! I'm not done yet. That was only part one."

He carefully lowers me down and sets me on my feet. "How many parts are there?"

"Just two."

He's full-on grinning now. "All right, what's part two?"

I take a deep breath and look up into his eyes. The eyes that hold everything: joy and mischief and strength. Eyes that own my heart and our future. Eyes bright with love.

Here goes nothing.

"I'm in love with you."

Chapter 30

You're in love with me."

"Crazy in love."

"*Crazy* in love."

"Like so in love I can't think straight. Or sleep. Or eat."

He purses his lips. "That sounds serious."

"It is."

"Huh. Interesting." I can't read his expression *at all*. It's the perfect poker face.

I stare at him. "Aren't you going to say anything?" *Back??*

"Oh, were you looking for a response?"

"Benjy . . ."

"Oh, all right." He clasps my hands in his, looking at me seriously. "It's about fucking time."

Not what I was expecting.

"What?" I sputter.

"Do you have any idea how long I've been waiting for you to figure this out? Good Lord, Kate, I thought we'd be old and gray by the time you caught up with me." He prods me off the dance floor as I stumble over my feet.

"I'm sorry, caught *up*?"

"I've only been in love with you since the day we met. As if that wasn't obvious by the way I've been trailing after you like a lost puppy dog." He nods at someone who's trying to get his attention but keeps ushering me forward.

"Since the day we *met*? That was never obvious."

"Pretty sure it was." He looks around. "Where's your purse?"

"My *purse*?" I can't seem to do much besides echo him.

"It's right here!"

Stephen materializes out of nowhere and shoves it at me, then laces his fingers under his chin. He's the personification of the heart-eyes emoji. "Just tell me, so I can be the first to know. You worked it out? You're together now?"

"We're together. And I'm taking her home, is that all right?"

Stephen looks at me, eyes saucer-wide. "Of course! I'm so thrilled for you both. That sounds like I'm congratulating you on your engage-ment or something, but you know what I mean." He glances from me to Ben. "Wait, you're not *engaged*, are you?"

"Good night, Stephen," we say in unison.

★

After an Uber ride that lasts a short eternity, we're back at Ben's apart-ment and I'm in his arms before he can kick the door shut.

Ben's kissing me like a man possessed. He's got one arm around my waist while his other hand roams all over my body. His hips tilt into mine as he presses me against the door, legs planted on either side of me, staking their claim. He's all around me and everywhere at once.

I've never been so turned on.

"Bedroom, please take me to your bedroom," I beg him.

He smiles against my mouth, then drops down and scoops me into his arms. As he walks us through his darkened apartment, I bury my face in his neck and breathe him in like an asthmatic.

"You know, I'm pretty sure I fell in love with you the night you carried me home."

"Was that before you told me carrying you was antifeminist or . . . ?" He turns us sideways to enter his room and my heel knocks against the doorframe.

"I changed my mind. Carry me everywhere from now on."

He's chuckling as he sets me down on the edge of his bed. When he flicks on the nightstand lamp, my heart skips a beat.

He's standing over me, eyes dark and hungry, though still soft somehow, and a little awed, like he can't believe I'm here. He's never looked more beautiful. A wave of desire engulfs me and I leap to my feet, scrambling to push his jacket off his shoulders. I'm desperate to touch him, freed from the handcuffs of our rules. I reach toward his neck and my fingers shake with anticipation.

"I finally get to take off your tie. I've been dreaming of this."

"Your fantasies are pretty PG," he teases, his hands flexing on my hips.

"Not all of them," I warn as I pull one of the ends free.

I let out a tiny delighted gasp as it unravels, the silk tails hanging loose and open around his neck. I grab them and savagely yank him to me for another kiss. The tie drops forgotten to the floor as my fingers work feverishly to unbutton his shirt. When the last one pops free, I try to tug it off but it snags on his wrists. I growl in frustration.

"Hang on, sweetheart. Cuff links." He looks amused as he fumbles with a sleeve.

"Did you just call me *sweetheart*?"

"Maybe." He eyes me as he works the first one loose and drops it into my hand. "Is that antifeminist too?"

"No, I loved it. Say it again."

He smirks. "I think you're more of a romantic than I am."

"Hmm, that didn't sound like *sweetheart*."

A smile teases his lips as he takes the link from me and sets them on his dresser; then I yelp when he grabs me by the waist and hauls me against him. His shirt's still on, flapping open, and I slide my fingers under the crisp cotton, laying my palms on his bare chest. His heart beats a wild rhythm under my hand.

He brings his lips to my ear. "*Sweetheart,*" he murmurs. He presses a string of featherlight kisses down the side of my neck to the hollow of my throat. "*Honey.*" He nips and pecks up the other side until his breath tickles the shell of my ear. "My little . . . *pumpernickel.*"

I can't help laughing, though my nipples are standing at attention. "God, we're disgusting. And you're distracting me," I admonish. I grab him by the placket of his shirt and peel it off, sucking in a breath.

It's like I'm seeing him for the first time. He's a mirage in the desert. All cuts and angles and hard lines, every segment of his body chiseled and perfectly defined. He's a ride I need to hold on to with both hands. His chest is the most expansive surface area I've ever seen. I want to drape myself across it sixteen different ways.

"What's the matter?" he asks when he sees I'm overcome. My breaths are coming out in little huff-pants.

"You. You're my new personal trainer. How do your shoulders even get this big?"

"All the cow tipping, probably. Though I have a few ideas on how to build your stamina . . ."

"Mmm, me too."

I resume my exploration, running my hands down the bare skin of his torso. It's warm, like every place I've ever touched him. I slide lower, fingers splayed out toward his obliques, and squeeze. His sharp intake of breath cracks open my chest.

He brings a hand up to cradle the back of my neck and threads his fingers through my hair. "I've thought so much about your hair. What it would feel like . . ." He brings a handful to his face and does some inhaling of his own, then lets it sift through his fingers like sand.

A tremor shudders through me and I grip his arms to steady myself. His muscles are hard, but his skin is smooth as silk. How can someone be so hard and so soft? What will it feel like to have all this skin on mine?

I smooth my hands down his biceps and triceps, tracing a raised vein from his elbow to his wrist, then vault my hands back to his stomach, trailing my fingertips through the light smattering of hair gathered near his waistband. The hair that leads to the promised land.

He reaches for me. "My turn now."

I don't argue. My lips curve in a tiny smile as I remember my surprise and I do a quarter turn, lifting my arms above my head. "The zip's right here," I volunteer, peeking up at him from beneath my lashes.

His breathing audibly shallows as he reaches for the zipper at my side, pausing first to sweep my hair over my shoulder. He kisses the nape of my neck and his hot breath ghosts over my spine. A frisson of electricity crackles through me at the realization that I'm *finally* going to be nude in front of Ben.

He lowers the zipper carefully, taking pains not to snag my skin. His thumb grazes my flesh all the way down, leaving goose bumps in its wake. I work the straps off my shoulders, letting the dress fall to the floor and puddle at my feet. I step out of it and stand before him, fully naked save for my emerald green lace panties and heels.

The sound he makes is a garbled grunt, like *unf*. He stares at me, lips parted, eyes feasting on every curve of my body like a man starving. I take a step toward him before he stops me.

"I want to look at you."

It's a little like being on display at a museum, the way his eyes devour me like a priceless work of art. No one's ever looked at me the way he does. I've never been particularly brazen, modest in locker rooms and reserved in past relationships, but with Ben I'm like a new person, a woman in every sense of the word. I feel completely uninhibited for the first time in my life. I *want* him to see every inch of me.

A small eternity passes before he steps forward and tugs me to him by the hips, his large hands spanning my entire waist. In my heels I line up almost perfectly against his groin, and the rock-hard erection that's tenting his pants strains against my pelvis, heavy and demanding. He slips a finger inside the elastic of my skimpy underwear and my knees quiver.

"You wore these for me." His voice sounds strained, like he's running short of air.

"I did. And it's not as easy as you might think to source green underthings. I had to search for these. For a minute there I worried you'd never get to see them."

"And what a sacrilege that would have been." He runs his finger along the lace edge. "Rather presumptuous of you to assume I'd be seeing them tonight. Guess I'm a sure thing."

"You're the *opposite* of a sure thing. But I figured I'd take a page out of your Boy Scout handbook and be prepared."

The contrast of his huge, strong hands against my bare skin and the delicate lace makes the pulsing heat between my legs throb harder. It's coarse versus soft, masculine against feminine, the juxtaposition of male to female at its most primal. He rubs a thumb against the gossamer-thin threads and exhales like he's in pain. This tiny wisp of fabric cost way more than it should, though I'd pay it three times over for the look on his face.

His fingers skim around to my backside, grabbing dual handfuls of flesh and lightly squeezing. He groans, his forehead falling to mine.

"I've been thinking about this for so long. Too long. It's . . ." He shakes his head, unable to continue.

"I know."

His eyes have gone a bit feral. The pupils are so dilated I can barely see any green, yet they hold a bright gleam, like a wild animal in the moonlight.

"Is this when you go full caveman on me?"

His eyes glow brighter. "No, this is when I savor you."

He tugs me over to the bed and sits on the edge, facing me. I slip my heels off, immediately losing a few inches of height, and when I take his outstretched hand, he pulls me in between his legs.

And then he takes my breast in his mouth.

Now I'm the one who's groaning, eyelids fluttering closed, knees turning to jelly. I grip his shoulders and hang on for dear life. He licks and suckles and teases, first one breast, then the other, while his hands knead my ass. I arch into him, wanting to get closer, *be* closer, the minuscule amount of distance between us still too much. He hums against my sternum and it vibrates straight to my core. It's an onslaught of sensations: his tongue on my nipple, the soft, wet sucking sounds, his hot skin pressed to mine, his pine-cinnamon-soap scent, intoxicating and so very *Ben*. My body's so taut with want, I can barely stay upright.

I'm so focused on not slithering to the floor that I barely notice his hand has moved until he slips a finger inside me.

I surge against him, my body tightening around him even as my knees buckle beneath me. He grabs me before I can fall, winding his free arm around my waist.

"I've got you."

"I'll come," I warn him desperately. "I'll come right here, I swear to God."

"I believe I'd like to see that."

"I would *not* like to see that. Please, Ben, not yet. I want you inside me the first time. I've been waiting so long . . ."

He smiles mildly against my ribs, his finger continuing its languid rhythm of swirling and stroking. "I am inside you."

"Please please please," I beg, even as my hips start rocking against his hand. I throw my head back and moan.

"Please . . . keep going?"

My answer is another keening moan.

"I love seeing you like this. Coming apart for me and I've barely lifted a finger."

I'm dangerously close to doing just that. I try to wriggle out of his grasp but he tsks and adds a second finger. I groan and shudder and clench around him, and his fingers swirl faster. I'm dissolving into his hand.

"I know you didn't wear these panties so I'd go easy on you."

"You're not playing fair," I gasp out. "Your pants aren't even off." I grope blindly for his belt.

"Wait." He moves to catch my hands, letting go of me in the process, and I collapse onto his lap.

"*You* wait. You think you're the only one who gets to tease?" I pin my knees on either side of his thighs and struggle to free my hands from his grasp. I'm frantic with lust.

"Hang on, babe. Just . . . let me."

He lifts me off his lap, setting me next to him on the bed, then stands and starts unbuckling his belt. *No fair, I wanted to do that.* I'm leaned forward on the literal edge of my seat as he slips his pants down his muscled thighs and off, and then he's naked down to his charcoal-hued boxers. The already impressive bulge looks even more promising.

I'm nearly levitating with anticipation. He smiles, keeping his eyes trained on me as he pulls down his boxers and springs free, and

He.

Is.

Massive.

I blink a few times. It's still there. Miles longer and inches thicker than I've ever seen.

"You still with me?"

I gape at him.

"You've got your aneurism face on again."

I finally recover my voice. "Holy fuck."

"*This* is what it takes for you to curse?" He smirks as he kicks off his boxers and takes a step toward me, looming even larger.

I reach out and take him in my hand, testing his heavy weight, grazing my fingers over his length. He's hard but smooth, the skin here as soft and satiny as the rest of him. He fills my hand and then some. He fills *two* hands. I stroke lightly up and down his shaft and he groans, pressing deeper into my hand.

He's magnificent. He's a god among men. This specimen of physical perfection is at my mercy, sheathed in the palm of my hand. If I wasn't sure before, I'm now certain—I'm about to have the most earth-shattering sex of my life. I need him inside me. I need him so badly I'm trembling with it.

"I can't believe you waited until *now* to spring this on me. Literally. Pun intended."

"I thought about sending you some dick pics in the interoffice mail, but I wasn't sure how it would go over."

"You could've slipped some into the Kate file. Just saying."

He's laughing against my mouth, and I don't think I'll ever tire of this feeling, this drive to meet his wit and intelligence with my own. It's one of my favorite things about him. About *us*.

I pull him back onto the bed, then climb over him so I'm straddling his lap again, knees pressed to the mattress on either side. His arousal presses hard and insistent against me, but for the moment, I ignore it; there's something I need to say. I cup his neck and stare into his eyes. My heart is exploding with love for this man.

"I never thanked you for putting my needs above your own." He tries to speak but I won't let him. "No, I gave you a hard time instead of appreciating what you were doing for me. You knew what I needed even when I didn't, and I love you for making sure we did this right. Thank you for waiting for me."

His eyes are soft on mine as he smooths some hair away from my face. "You never need to thank me for doing what's right for you. But how about from now on, we leave all that in the past—the fights, the bets, the regrets—and start over with a clean slate. It's just you and me, on the same team from now on."

I lunge forward and kiss him in answer, and one kiss turns into ten, and we begin a slow slide into the abyss. We kiss each other like we're dying and this is our last moment on earth. Like we're all each other needs or will ever want. And for me at least, it's true.

Minutes slip by, or maybe it's an hour, our bodies moving against each other, skin heated and damp, our breath bottoming out until we're panting. I'm so lost in him I can't tell where he ends and I begin. I'm giving him everything, pouring myself into him, and he accepts it all with reverent gratitude, his adoration revealed in every kiss, every sigh, every stroke. He's straining so hard against my entrance that with one strong thrust he could be inside me. The suspense is wrecking my sanity.

"Ben," I gasp out. "I need you. Make love to me."

The next thirty seconds are a jumble of limbs and linens and resettling. Ben lays me back against the pillows, sheets crisp and cool against my skin, then takes me in his arms, picking up where we left off. We touch and taste, nip and grope and pet, rolling around and laughing when we get tangled in the sheets. We fondle and tease until a fine sheen of sweat mists our skin. He slips a hand between my thighs and finally, *finally* peels my panties down my legs. I snake a hand between our bodies and stroke him until he's groaning.

Eventually he rolls over me, rising onto his elbows and caging me in with sturdy arms. When he looks at me, it's like he's staring straight into my soul.

"I love you, Kate." His voice is hoarse with emotion. "You're everything to me."

The look on his face is so raw, so passionate and penetrating, my breath catches.

"I love you too," I whisper.

When he pushes into me, just the tiniest bit, I gasp. He stops instantly.

"Are you okay?"

"Yes. Yes." I can barely speak. "Can't . . . form words."

That earns me a smile, and he rewards me by pressing in a little more. My eyes roll back in my head. *"Oh my Goooooood."*

"Still good?"

I babble a string of indecipherable mumblings mixed with his name. My brain is fuzzy and things are nonsensical. The earth is flat; the moon is made of Swiss cheese.

He laces our fingers together above my head. "Stay with me."

"I'm with you," I slur. My voice sounds very far away.

It's incredible, this fullness. It's intense and moving, an overpowering sense of submission I've never experienced before. He's filled me so completely I'm already worried about how empty I'll feel when he's gone. I let out a moan-sob because I know with sudden clarity: This is the moment where my life splits into Before and After. I'll never be the same.

"Is it too much?"

I nod, a tear slipping from the corner of my eye, trailing across my cheek. *I love you too much.*

"We can slow down," he says, already starting to withdraw.

"No!" I hook my legs around his waist and lock them at the ankles, pinning him to me. "I mean, it feels perfect. Don't stop."

"You're *crying.*"

"Because I'm happy."

He hesitates, searching my face for signs that I'm lying. His eyes are carnal and unfocused, but also cautious, like he's warring between what we both want and what he thinks I need.

I grab his face and kiss him, reassuring him the only way I know how that I'm fine, that I'm ready, that I love him. I can feel the exact moment when any resistance he's holding on to slips away, and he kisses my tears away and kisses love into me as he buries his entire length inside me.

I cry out, digging my nails into his shoulders as my body acclimates to him. Even with my head thrown back I still feel his eyes on my face, watching me, studying my reactions. He pulls one of my legs up and hugs my thigh as he rocks into me, slow and deliberate. A strong push forward, a light slide back. It's like a dance. It's what I imagine heaven is like.

The term *making love* has always felt flowery to me, too cloyingly romantic, but it's the only way I can describe what's happening between us, this soul exchange, the overwhelming sense of *rightness.* We've entered a sexual stratosphere beyond anything I knew existed, though comparing Ben to anyone else feels like a crime against humanity. He's Da Vinci in a world of finger-painters.

I start to feel guilty; he has me so out of my mind with need, I'm barely contributing. I'm loose-legged and insentient, completely lost to the euphoria of his rolling thrusts. I'm also knocking on the door of an orgasm and we're barely a minute into this. I beseech my body to wait, but it's like trying to stop a speeding train.

"Ben," I warn on a broken breath, "I can't . . . I'm going to—"

He chooses that moment to take my nipple in his mouth again and my mind goes entirely blank. I buck against him and scream his name, coming apart in his hands. Where he fills me throbs as waves of pleasure roll through my body. He holds me through my shuddering, the tremors going on and on, and I clutch his arms and whimper soft cries in his ear as he kisses me back to earth.

As I slowly come down, embarrassment sets in. "I'm sorry I didn't last longer," I whisper into his neck.

He draws back, jaw dropped. "Are you *apologizing* for coming underneath me while screaming my name? If you only knew how many times I've dreamt of that . . ."

"In your dreams did I last longer than a minute?" I joke, self-conscious.

He silences me with a nip to my lips. "My imagination didn't even come close. You have no idea what a turn-on it is for me to see you lose control like that. See what I can do to you. And don't you dare hold back, ever. I will take it as a personal affront."

I laugh and cling to his neck. "It must have been the months of foreplay . . ."

He runs a thumb over my bottom lip and I try to bite it. "Or it's just me."

"Probably just you," I concede.

"It's just you for me too. Only you," he murmurs. "Always you." He grazes the tip of his nose against mine. "I bet I can give you a round two."

I start to laugh before I realize: If anyone could give me multiple orgasms, it's Ben and his magic penis. *Here's to trying.*

"I'll take that bet, only because it's one we'll both end up winning."

He rocks into me before I've even finished speaking, and I let out a load moan.

"See? Halfway there already."

"Tell me more about these dreams," I croak, resetting my legs around his backside.

He laughs huskily. *Oh God, his husky laugh.* "They start and end just like this."

He increases his pace, sliding an arm under my back and lifting me partway off the bed, driving deeper inside me, if that's even possible. I know he's thinking about my comfort because there's no punishing pounding, just a sweet intimacy, soft strokes and gentle caresses, lovely whispered words of admiration and kindness. He tells me I'm perfect, I'm beautiful, how amazing I feel, how long he's been dreaming of me. How much he loves me. I respond with sweet nothings of my own, between sighs of pleasure and increasingly desperate recitations of his name.

Making love to Ben is everything and nothing like I thought it would be. I anticipated the physicality of it, his dominance versus my delicateness, but it's the emotion in his eyes and tenderness in his words I didn't see coming. His body overpowers mine in every possible way, but I know I can bring him to his knees with the brush of my hand, the scent of my skin, the press of my lips.

After a while I realize he's holding himself back. I'm desperate to see him lose control, watch his eyes go dark and wild with need.

"Stop holding back," I implore him. "Let go and take what you need from me."

"Kate," he sighs in time to his rolling thrusts. "Kate." My name on his lips is an oath, a prayer.

I love his voice right now, wrecked and broken and desperate for release. He's barely hanging on. I get a taste of how he must have felt watching me come: heady with power and possession. I revel in all his sex mannerisms I'm discovering tonight: the unconscious lip bite when he's concentrating; the vein pulsing beneath his eye; his tangy sweat scent I can't get enough of. I want to lick his entire body.

I attempt to, starting with his chest, but he must not be able to endure it because he drags me back up, capturing my mouth with his and kissing me with an aching intensity that drives me nearly to madness. When he pulls away, my chest feels empty, like he's stolen out my heart, my breath, and my soul in one fell swoop.

"Are you close? I can't hold off much longer." His eyes are glassy.

"Don't worry about me. I want to see you lose control. I want to make you feel as good as you made me feel."

"I can't feel any better. Trust me."

"Challenge accepted."

"That wasn't—"

I redouble my efforts, clenching around him, grinding my hips, grabbing fistfuls of his hair. I bring him to the brink and in the process, I bring myself there, too.

"Oh God," I gasp when I realize, and I see his eyes spark with satisfaction that he's going to win this bet after all.

We both break at precisely the same moment. I shatter a second time and scream his name while he drives into me in two mighty thrusts so powerful, I'm backed up to the headboard. I run my hands over his face, across his shoulders, and down his arms as his breathing slows and evens out. I'm belatedly worried he'll collapse on top of me but he rolls us to the side, keeping his arms locked around me.

"Fuck," he says, still panting. "That was . . ."

"The best sex anyone's ever had? Should be written about in history books?"

He laughs and kisses my shoulder. "I was going to say worth the wait, but that works too. Are you okay? I wasn't too . . ."

"Ben. Do I look okay?" I stare into his eyes.

"You look . . ." He shakes his head, not finishing his sentence.

"I look what? Striking? Nice?"

He laughs into my neck, deep and rumbly.

I keep trying. "Satisfied? Doubly pleasured?"

His arms tighten around me.

"Mine."

Chapter 31

I blink my eyes open to light slanting through cracks in the blinds, and it takes me a second to figure out where I am.

In Ben's apartment. In Ben's *bed*.

I briefly wonder if last night was a dream before I turn my head and see him sprawled out on his stomach, spectacularly nude. That ass is definitely not a dream.

He's got an arm flung over me and it's heavy and warm. I scan the room; it's like a clothing tornado blew through here. My dress is draped over an upholstered chair in the corner, my nude heels shoved haphazardly underneath, while Ben's shirt hangs off a tall bookcase that's crammed full, spines jammed in every which way. The rest of his clothes litter the floor from doorway to bed, charting our sexual progress like a naughty treasure map. Across from the bed is a tallboy chest of drawers, his cuff links and my hastily removed jewelry resting on top. A framed black-and-white portrait of a midwestern landscape is mounted above the tufted leather headboard. This is a grown-up's room.

I tuck the gray linen bedspread around me and stretch like a cat. I feel like I do after a day at the beach: skin heated and tingling, hair wild, relaxed and content in a soul-deep way. I'm also parched and in desperate need of some water. I try to wriggle out from underneath him but his arm tightens.

"Where are you going?" His voice is extra-deep and roughened by sleep.

I lean over and kiss him on the cheek. "I need water."

"I'll get it."

After thirty seconds go by with no sign of life, I poke him. "I can do it."

"Just give me a minute." He yawns and flips onto his back, and it's a *gooood* morning indeed.

"I thought you were the morning person of the two of us," I tease. He stretches and I try hard not to stare.

Scratch that, I'm totally staring.

"Not today." He palms my butt cheek and groans, then rolls out of bed, lumbering over to his nightstand. He starts rummaging in his drawer and I leer at him like a deviant, letting out a wolf whistle.

"Hot damn."

He tosses a drowsy grin over his shoulder. I watch the muscles of his upper back bunch as he pulls on a fresh pair of boxers and swipes at his bedhead. Sleepy Ben may even be hotter than Tux Ben.

"How many calories do you think we burned last night?" I call as he pads into the kitchen. "As my trainer, you need to make sure I'm hitting my goals."

"Which time?" he calls back. He definitely sounds smug.

My cheeks burn at the memory. I fell asleep almost instantly last night, wrapped in his arms, my head pillowed on his very comfortable biceps. At some point during the night I woke facing away from him, and when I snuggled against him, my back to his front in a "big spoon, little spoon," I couldn't resist stroking his thigh—which led to Ben kissing my neck and fondling my breasts, which led to me stroking *him* until I climbed on top of him and slowly sank down, riding him as moonlight shone in the window and danced across the shadows of his face. We barely spoke this time, wordlessly taking everything each other had to give, our bodies saying everything we needed to say.

His lips are curved in a smirk as he reenters the room and I accept the water bottle he hands me gratefully. "Speaking of calories, I'm starving," I add.

"Me too. What are you making?" He grins.

"Do you even have any food here?"

He grimaces sheepishly.

"*Seriously?*" He shrugs and I groan. "Fine, let's go to my place. I need clothes anyway."

"You do *not* need clothes." He drops back onto the bed and pinches my butt.

"I most certainly *do* need clothes. I refuse to put on a gown and do the walk of shame across the street. Can I steal something of yours?" I'm already up and rifling through his drawers.

"This should be amusing," he says, lying back against the pillows and lacing his fingers behind his head.

I pull out a worn navy T-shirt with VIRGINIA emblazoned across the chest. It's cozy and well-loved, no doubt softened by hundreds of trips through the wash. I pull it over my head and it falls nearly to my knees. Why does it always look sexy in the movies when a woman puts on a man's shirt, but I look like I'm wearing a tent? "It's just a tad big."

He doesn't seem to mind. "This is like my every college fantasy come true."

"*This* is your fantasy?" I hold out my arms, swimming in the tee. "So much for all the lingerie I had planned."

"Uh, forget I said that."

I help myself to some pants with a drawstring, then glance over at him. "Can you get dressed already? Move it along."

"Hangry Kate's a little scary." He finally rolls out of bed.

"Guess I'm going to have to wear heels with this ensemble." I slip them on and look in the mirror. "This is quite a getup."

I force him to carry my dress and purse across the street so I'm not the only one who looks ridiculous. Of course it just makes him seem chivalrous.

Once we've made ourselves eggs, toast, and coffee and are lounging comfortably on my couch, we compare notes on the week we spent apart. I fill him in on the misplaced Kate file and we laugh about the shocked expressions on our friends' faces after our exhibitionist dance floor display.

"Speaking of which, now that it's out there we should probably talk about how we'll address this at work," I say, already steeling myself for being the subject of the office gossip mill for the foreseeable future. "I guess the first thing to do is disclose the relationship to our bosses."

"Yeah, I already did that," he says around a bite of toast.

"You did *what*?"

He finishes chewing and swallows. "I disclosed the relationship to Bill."

I sit up. "Bill your boss? As in the one I met last night?"

"The very same."

"But you acted like you didn't want him to know about us!"

He looks at me strangely. "No, I didn't."

"Yes, you *did*. You gave me a very pointed look when you introduced us."

"That look was for *your* sake. I was trying to clue you in that he was my boss and if you didn't want him to know anything, not to let on. That was before you mauled me on the dance floor, of course." He smirks.

I'm not following. "So wait, what does 'disclose the relationship' mean? Does he know about us or not?"

"Ah, sorry. Yes, I told him, but I didn't mention your name."

"When did you do this? Last night?"

"No, it was . . . a while back." He's being evasive.

I narrow my eyes at him. "What aren't you telling me?"

He hesitates. "I sat down with him the morning after you made me dinner."

I scroll through my mental timeline. "The morning after . . . but that was before—"

"Before anything happened between us, I know. It was preemptive." His mouth twitches. "I was . . . optimistic."

"Presumptuous."

"I prefer glass half-full. I wanted to get my ducks in a row, make sure I wouldn't be jeopardizing our jobs. The good news is, since we don't work together directly, we're mostly fine. We're supposed to avoid one-on-one collaboration and we can't discuss any confidential information."

"Why wouldn't you *tell* me this?"

"I wasn't about to share that I told my *boss* about us after you flipped out and demanded we keep it a secret from everyone at work."

I snap my fingers. "That reminds me. Do you know anything about a secret meeting between Warner and Hammond? For a second I was worried it might be about us."

"I can see you're going to be good at the 'not sharing confidential information' part," he notes dryly, taking a sip of his coffee.

"You *do* know what it's about! Of course you do. If there's a secret out there, you're keeping it."

He exhales and sets his mug down. "I could get fired for talking to you about this, but I think you'll find out soon, so fuck it. There's a small but vocal minority who thinks they can strong-arm everyone into getting their way on a few provisions of the tax plan. We've been trying to work with them, but because our margin for passage is so slim they've become less and less reasonable."

"They're holding it hostage."

"Exactly. The teacher credit debacle is one example. When that got leaked, it really lit a fire under Hammond, so we're trying something a little different. We thought if we could get a few of the more moderate Democrats on board, then the problem goes away."

"What makes you think you can convince Carol?"

He smiles. "One of the ideas floated was to triple the child care credit."

"*Triple* it?" I nearly drop my plate.

"It'd be a way for Warner to salvage some success from your bill, reframe the narrative a little. Not to mention, her numbers would get a bump for supporting the tax breaks. She could be part of the victory lap. It's a win-win. That's how we're framing it, anyway."

"If Carol flips and throws her support behind the tax bill, that will be a *big* deal."

"That's what we're counting on. We think where she goes, others will follow." He takes my hand and starts playing with my fingers, and awareness dawns.

"Wait, was this *your* idea?"

"I can't take all the credit, but I campaigned hard for Hammond to go this direction, yes. I was inspired by a certain ball-busting blonde . . ."

I can hardly process all these developments. "So you've been working on all of this behind the scenes and didn't tell me."

"I *wanted* to tell you. Desperately." He brings my wrist to his lips and kisses it.

"But you couldn't. I get it. However, I'm a bit concerned about what a convincing liar you are. It's a serious boyfriend red flag."

"To clarify, I never actually *lied*." He drops his head to my shoulder, pressing kisses along my collarbone.

"A sin of omission is still a sin. Any other secrets you're keeping? Now's your chance to come clean."

"Hmm, let's see." He tilts his head like he's considering it.

"I was kidding."

He purses his lips, eyeing me thoughtfully.

"You can't possibly be hiding anything else."

His expression shifts, the look in his eyes distinctly guilty, and my insides tense up. "Okay, now you're making me nervous."

He chuckles as he takes my hand again, his other arm wrapped around my legs on his lap. "So you know how I've never told you the number one criteria for my ideal woman?"

I stare at him like he's just asked me to explain nuclear fission.

"Just go with me on this."

"Um, okay?"

"I never could figure out a way to tell you this without it coming off wrong, but here goes." He shifts in his seat, clearly uncomfortable. "My future wife needed to give me the same feeling I got when I met . . . someone else a while back."

My face heats. Is he seriously talking to me about another *woman*?

His eyes take on a faraway look. "About six months before you showed up in my office, I was at an event and saw this woman across the room. I was immediately captivated by her. It was like a lightning bolt. There was just something about her . . . she stopped me in my tracks. I knew I had to meet her, so I wrangled an introduction somehow."

He's staring off into space, and I'm simultaneously desperate and terrified to find out where he's going with this. I hardly want to be compared to some dream woman he's built up in his mind. I try to remove my legs from his lap, but his arm tightens, holding me in place.

He looks back at me and smiles tightly. "But when I told her what I do and who I worked for, she looked *right* through me. I mean, she beelined outta there." He lets out an angry-sounding grunt. "I was . . . I don't know, pissed. Disappointed." He takes a deep breath, shaking his head like he's shaking off the memory.

"So imagine my surprise when I looked up one day and saw that same woman working in the office across from mine."

I'm so engrossed in his story that I didn't see the obvious twist coming.

"Wait, *what*?!" Now I do swing my legs off his lap and sit up. "You're saying the woman you met . . . was *me*?"

He continues like I haven't spoken. "I started watching her. It became sort of a thing for me. What's she up to today? Can I figure out what she's working on from here? Do I know the person she's meeting with? Who's the guy who's always in her office? What insane footwear does she have on today?" He smiles to himself. "No matter how difficult my day was, I could always look over at her and just . . . feel better. Even if it was only for a minute." His eyes catch and hold mine. "You were the most beautiful distraction."

"Ben," I breathe.

He holds up a hand like he's not done. "Imagine my surprise *again* months later when I saw her name show up in my email asking for a meeting." He laces our fingers together. "It was my second chance to make a first impression."

A sunburst of emotion flares in my chest. "If that was how you felt, then why were you so mean to me?"

He grimaces. "It wasn't exactly planned. From the email you'd sent, it wasn't obvious if you remembered meeting me or not, and in my mind I think I just expected you to recognize me." He swallows. "And then you didn't."

"Ben, I'm so sor—"

He cuts me off. "I was agitated that I'd kept you waiting, and then you immediately introduced yourself like you'd never seen me before. Keep in mind, at that point I knew you eat dark chocolate when you're stressed and I could tell exactly how you felt about something based on which smile you used."

The tears I've been keeping at bay spill over, and he squeezes my hand.

"I treated you like shit because my ego was bruised. It was irrational and stupid and wrong of me. And I'm so sorry for that, Kate. I thought your bill was smart and important, and I wish I'd told you that."

A sob escapes and the tears are really flowing now, streaking my face like raindrops. He brushes them away with his thumbs.

"But something good came out of all that stupidity. The more I poked you—and poked and poked—the more pissed you got, and it was like a lightbulb went on. If I just kept poking, then there was no way you could forget me this time."

I close my eyes, overcome. I can't believe . . . this whole time . . .

"I realize this was the worst, most juvenile courtship strategy I could've come up with, okay? But once I started, I couldn't walk it back." He grins guiltily. "And in my defense, it did work. Kind of."

"I can't believe you," I laugh-sob, swiping at my eyes.

"As soon as you left, I regretted it. I knew I had to apologize, so I went to your office that night to do just that, and . . . well, you know the rest."

"Backwoods Ben," I murmur. "I do know the rest."

I climb onto his lap and hug his neck as hard as I can. I wish I could climb inside him. His arms tighten around me and we stay that way for a long time.

When I finally pull back, I stare into his eyes. "I'm so sorry, Ben. I'm sorry I didn't recognize how special you were the second I met you. I'm sorry I didn't remember you. I'm especially sorry I wasted all these months not knowing you." I take his face in my hands. "How could I have ever *not* seen you, when now you're all I see?"

He exhales, and now *he* looks shaken.

"Please forgive me."

He makes a strangled noise in his throat and crushes me to him.

"I'll take that as a yes," I say into his neck.

When he laughs, I feel it clear down to my toes. Eventually his lips find mine, and we're kissing and he's picking me up and walking us back to my bedroom.

I pull back, breathless. "That's the end of your surprises, right?"

"Ask me again tomorrow." He lays me back against the pillows.

"Next thing you'll tell me Ben's not your real name."

"It's Benjy, actually." He drags his shirt over his head.

"You're secretly a Russian spy. You were planted here to sabotage our financial system."

"One thing I will never be is a Communist." He kicks off his jeans and crawls over me, nipping at my thigh as he tugs my pants down my legs. "We should form our own party. The no underpants party."

I giggle as he attempts to remove my panties with his teeth.

"A party of two. I'm in."

Epilogue

Ben

It's been nearly a year since Kate and I made things official, and professionally, it's been a year of victories—for both of us.

In December, the tax bill officially passed the House and Senate, and was signed into law by the president a few days before Christmas. Thanks to the increase to the child care credit, Senator Warner and a number of like-minded Democrats did cross the aisle, making it the first major bipartisan legislation passed by this administration.

The day the bill passed is among the most memorable of my life. Post-vote, we attended the first of many victory parties we'd enjoy over the following weeks, and when we got home later that night, tipsy from too many champagne toasts, Kate took me to bed and congratulated me.

And congratulated me.

And congratulated me.

Months later and I'm still thinking about that night.

Kate rebounded from the disappointment of her child care bill with a high-profile project: a resolution reforming the way sexual assault allegations are handled on the Hill. The updated Congressional

Accountability Act changed the system for reporting employees' claims of sexual harassment, established an office to advocate for employees during the adjudication process, and required lawmakers to reimburse taxpayers for any workplace settlements. Spearheaded by Senator Warner and cosponsored by a record forty-three senators—including Senator Hammond—it marked our second shared victory. The resolution passed by voice vote a mere four months after it was introduced, a near record for the slow-moving gears of Congress. I think I was happier for Kate's success than I was for my own.

I'm still working for Senator Hammond, though I've started putting out feelers to move into the private sector. Delivering on tax reform is as good as it will ever get in my government career, and supporting Kate on the sexual harassment legislation fulfilled a personal mission of mine to enact change in my sister's name. I've known for a while that I'm ready to move on, though working down the hall from Kate has certainly been a motivating factor to stay. Ultimately, I'm ready to make more money. If all goes according to plan, I'll have a family to support soon.

If it's been a year of professional triumphs, then personally? I'm living my damn dream.

When I first laid eyes on Kate at Senator Riordan's retirement luncheon a year and a half ago, I was completely knocked for six. I've never had such an instant, visceral reaction to someone. While I'm sure many would chalk it up to simple attraction—Kate's easily the most beautiful woman in any room—it was something else, something deeper, like I'd known her before and would again. When she smiled and shook my hand, I was done for.

You'd think I'd have been angry after she'd dismissed me so summarily—and maybe I was, at first—but I couldn't seem to fight her gravitational pull. I'd watch her in her office and marvel. She's a fidgeter, unable to sit still, always tucking a knee beneath her, crossing and uncrossing her legs, kicking her feet up on a chair. I'd spot her at her desk twisted up like a pretzel and tie myself into knots.

And, God, those legs. They taunted me, day in and day out.

When her name popped up in my inbox, I half expected the email to say, *I see you watching me, you perv!* (I would have deserved it.) Her meeting request was one I'd typically kick over to an assistant, though I practically tripped over myself accepting, even picking a late-afternoon timeslot in the misguided hope things would go so well I'd be able to say, *Why don't we continue this over dinner?*

Boy, did that not go as planned.

Poking and provoking her was enjoyable, I'll admit it. But the night Kate opened up about her father was a turning point for me. By then, I'd started to wonder if I was wasting my time, if pursuing her was an exercise in futility. That night gave me total clarity: Kate didn't need an antagonist, a man to frustrate and foil her. She needed a stable, steady presence, a constant in a world of variables. Someone who'd stick around and love her no matter the circumstances.

I just had to prove I was that man.

It's an approach that's served me well over the past year. Despite our rocky start, our relationship has been surprisingly drama-free. We rarely fight anymore, but when we do, we get to have wild makeup sex afterward. Sometimes I think she picks fights with me just so we can make up—not that I'm complaining.

We still push each other's buttons, but it's collaborative, not combative. We spend our days riling each other up and our nights making love. Sometimes we barely make it past the front door. I've never been so turned on by every facet of a person, as obsessed with her brain as I am with her body.

It's a combination of these sentiments that have led me to where I am today: standing on the steps of the Lincoln Memorial with a diamond ring burning a hole in my pocket, gazing at Kate while she gazes out on the Reflecting Pool.

She catches me watching her and narrows her eyes. "Uh-oh."

"What's 'uh-oh'?"

"Whenever you look at me like that, you're coming up with some brutal physical challenge for me."

I *have* been known to do this.

"You're looking extra shifty, so I'm gonna go ahead and use my preemptive veto."

"I'm not—" I laugh and shake my head. "Kate."

"What?" She sounds suspicious.

"Do you remember the first time we ran together? And at the end, I sort of . . . came on to you?"

She breaks into a smile. "How could I forget?" She steps toward me and loops her arms around my waist.

"I know you thought I did that to prove a point about your signing up for Donkey Date. And maybe that was part of it, but there was more to it than that."

Her brow furrows.

"You'd just introduced me to your mom as your *running buddy*." I spit the words out like they taste bad. "I panicked. I couldn't let you friend-zone me."

She starts laughing, covering her mouth with a hand.

"I wanted to tell you how I felt about you, but it was too soon. You weren't ready to hear it. So I promised myself that one day we'd come back here and I'd tell you what I wanted to that day."

She's shaking her head. "You've been holding this in for a *year*? Why am I not surprised?"

"I've been saving this story for the right time."

"Why is now the right time?" she asks, right on cue.

I squeeze her hands once before releasing them, then drop to one knee. She gasps, her hand flying to her mouth. It's the mother of all aneurism faces.

"Kate, I've wanted to marry you since the moment I met you. As usual, I've been waiting for you to catch up with me."

She laugh-sobs as the first tears start to spill down her cheeks.

"I've been thinking about all the things I wanted to say to you. How much I love you. What an amazing, kind, generous, brilliant woman you are. How you've made this past year the best of my life. How you own me, body and soul. That I'll do everything in my power to take care of you and make you happy." I grin up at her. "It's been a year and I'd still rather argue with you than get along with anyone else."

She's crying harder now. I hope these tears are a good sign.

"I want you to marry me. Please be my wife."

I've barely gotten the words out before she lunges at me, throwing her arms around my neck with such force that we fall backward and end up on the ground in a tangled heap. I laugh as she attacks my face with kisses.

"Should I take that as a yes?"

"Yes! Yes"—*kiss*—"yes"—*kiss*—"yes, yes, yes, yes, yes."

I pluck the ring from the box and slide it onto her shaking finger. She stares at it like she can't believe what she's seeing.

"Oh my God," she whispers. "I get to marry you."

So this is what it feels like to get everything you've ever wanted.

"You mean you get to argue with me for the rest of our lives."

She smiles at me. "Promise?"

Author's Note

When the idea for *Meet You in the Middle* came to me in 2017, it was after the wildest election of our lifetimes. You couldn't go five minutes without seeing a breathless headline proclaiming the death of bipartisanship: couples breaking up (or even divorcing) over election results; estrangement from family and friends; new dating apps designed exclusively for members of each political party. Most people took the division in stride, accepting it as par for the course post-2016. My thought? *This would make a great romance novel.*

And so I began to write what I hoped would be a funny, emotional, and timely story about a couple who falls in love despite the (massive) personal and professional odds stacked against them. I was committed to keeping the book as politically neutral as possible, as I wanted readers on both sides of the aisle to feel comfortable letting their guard down and losing themselves in Kate and Ben's love story. I hoped to find that sweet spot where readers could laugh at our protagonists' antics while laughing at themselves too—an ambitious goal when some don't believe bipartisan relationships like this can (or even *should*) exist in today's polarized world.

Clearly, I disagree—and so do the scores of people who've sought me out to share personal stories of the successful "politically mixed" relationships in their own lives, proving to me that we're all much more committed to finding common ground than the loudest voices in media would have us believe.

If you think some of the issues and legislation discussed in the book sound familiar, it's because they're all based on real-life counterparts. Ben's tax plan is the Tax Cuts and Jobs Act passed in late 2017; Kate's child care bill is the Child Care for Working Families Act, originally proposed in 2017 and reintroduced in 2019; the Congressional Accountability Act of 1995 Reform Act to update sexual harassment protocols passed in early 2018. Much of Kate and Ben's more amusing hate mail and the contents of Ben's "Kate" file were also influenced by articles I found during research.

Writing Kate and Ben's story has inspired me in so many ways: to lead with love and curiosity, to focus on what unites us instead of divides us, to approach differences of opinion with an attitude of learning rather than of "schooling." I hope you're similarly inspired—to see the person beyond the label, to embrace those that challenge you, maybe even to take a chance on someone you otherwise wouldn't. If you do, I'd love to hear about it.

Acknowledgments

I have many people to thank for the labor of love you're holding in your hands.

To Kate Seaver and the entire Berkley team: You've made my first publishing experience an absolute dream every step of the way. Thank you for being such passionate champions of this story from day one and for going above and beyond to get the book into readers' hands. The Berkley Romance team is the best in the business, and I feel so incredibly lucky to get to work with such a talented, dedicated group of people.

To Kim Lionetti: Your title might be "agent," but I think a better one might be "fairy godmother," because you appear out of thin air to make dreams come true! Thank you for taking a chance on me, for your unwavering belief in this story, your genius revision suggestions, and of course, the perfect title.

To Erika Robuck: You were the first person I told I was secretly writing this book, and your early, emphatic support (from a *real* author, no less!) was instrumental in giving me the courage to go after this big, daunting dream. Thank you for your generosity of time and friendship, for your thoughtful critiques, for shepherding me through the writing, querying, and publishing process with endless amounts of advice, and for not letting me hit "Publish" as soon as I wrote "The End."

To Kate, Kir, and Kim, my best friends and brilliant betas: It's not an exaggeration to say that without your constant cheerleading and demands for the next chapter, I may not have finished this book. Words are inadequate to describe how grateful I am for your decades of friendship. Thank you for indulging my absurd amount of texts and calls demanding your opinions on word choices, character arcs, and plot points (and never letting on just how annoying I'm sure it was). Everyone should be so lucky as to have friends like you in their corner.

Mom and Dad, you always taught me that I could do anything and encouraged me to follow my dreams—and because of you, I have. Thank you for instilling my love of reading, fostering my creativity, and bankrolling my childhood book habit. Dad, special thanks for the pages of handwritten notes detailing the finer points of firearm usage and safety, as well as for pretending you never read chapter 30.

Kristen, thanks for giving me the candid, pull-no-punches feedback I can always count on from you. I owe my love of romance novels to you and your hand-me-downs. John, thank you for redlining every last thing I ask you to, as well as helping me craft some of the better jokes that made it in. Erin, Danielle, and Dee, thank you for reading early drafts and responding with such enthusiasm. Your support and excitement have been such a gift.

Bree, thank you for patiently answering all my questions about life as a Senate staffer. Jeff, thank you for the behind-the-scenes tour of the Capitol Building. Any artistic license I took with the realities of the political process was for story purposes, and the mistakes are mine alone.

To Patrick: The night I met you I said, "I've met the man I'm going to marry." Fifteen years later, you're still the best decision I've ever made. No matter what outlandish ambition I have, your response is always the same: "Do it! You'd be amazing at that." That kind of blind, irrational faith in me is just one of the many things I love about you. Thank you for our four children; for managing said children when I needed the space, time, and absolute silence to write; for patiently, endlessly discussing the story with me; and for encouraging me to pursue this dream when we had no reason to believe anything would come of it. Any swoonworthy hero I ever write could never come close to you.

Meet You
*in the
M*iddle

DEVON DANIELS

Questions for Discussion

1. When we first meet Kate, she is closed to the idea of dating her political opposite, but by the end of the book, she realizes that she's found her match in Ben. What factors or events do you think were most influential in changing her mind?

2. Kate's behavior could be perceived as contradictory: she's strong-willed and decisive in her professional life but doesn't want to make the first move in her romantic relationships. Do you think you can be a feminist and still subscribe to old-fashioned ideals of courtship? Why or why not?

3. While Kate's mom, Beverly, is a vital figure in her life—even influencing her choice of profession—Kate's complicated feelings about being the product of an unplanned teen pregnancy follow her into adulthood. How did Kate's upbringing and relationship with her mother help shape her beliefs? Why do you think Beverly urged Kate to give Ben a chance when she herself never married? How important do you think Beverly's advice was in Kate's decision to open her heart to Ben?

4. How do you think Kate's strained relationship with her father affected her ability to trust and open up to Ben? When Kate finally did share the story of her upbringing with Ben, how did his reaction help move their relationship forward?

5. Ben told Kate that "I'd rather argue with you than get along with anyone else." Do you think opposites-attract relationships are more or less likely to succeed than relationships between people who are similar? Why or why not?

6. Ben demonstrated his feelings for Kate with a variety of romantic gestures, patiently prodding her along the path toward acceptance of their differences. What do you think was the tipping point for Kate in letting her guard down with Ben?

7. Kate makes statements like, "I'd never date a Republican." In the wake of the 2016 election, a large percentage of dating app users began filtering out prospective mates who don't share their political views. Do you think such behavior is sensible or shortsighted? What long-term effects do you think it could have?

8. Ben challenged Kate to see the person beyond the label, believing that having different approaches to solving problems is something to celebrate. Did reading Kate and Ben's story cause you to reevaluate how you interact with others about politics?

9. Do you think a bipartisan relationship like Kate and Ben's can be successful in today's hyperpartisan political climate? Can you think of any examples of successful bipartisan relationships in your own life? Would you encourage a friend to pursue a relationship with their political opposite? What do you think are the challenges and benefits of a relationship in a couple with disparate political views?

Photo by Pete Albert

Devon Daniels is a born-and-bred California girl whose own love story found her transplanted to the Maryland shores of the Chesapeake Bay. She's a graduate of the University of Southern California and in her past life worked in marketing, product design, and music. When she's not writing, you'll find her clinging to her sanity as mom, chef, chauffeur, and referee to four children, or sneaking off with her husband for date nights in Washington, DC. *Meet You in the Middle* is her first novel.

CONNECT ONLINE

DevonDanielsAuthor.com

🐦 DevonDaniels_

📷 DevonDanielsAuthor

📘 DevonDanielsAuthor

Ready to find
your next great read?

Let us help.

Visit prh.com/nextread